BY THE SAME AUTHOR

FICTION:

Red Carpet Collection
Birkenhead Novelettes
River Of Life
Grandpee and Coleman, Bed-time Stories

NON—FICTION:

My Journey to India
Russia and the Silk Road
My Journey to Africa
South America Exploration
South America Enchantment
My Journey North From Antarctica
South East Asia

POETRY:

The Colors of Life
Songs of Honour
The Best Poems and Poets of 2005
The International Who's Who in Poetry

THE PORTRAITS

robert f. edwards

Order this book online at www.trafford.com
or email orders@trafford.com

Most Trafford titles are also available at major online book retailers.

Note for Librarians: A cataloguing record for this book is available from Library
and Archives Canada at www.collections.canada.ca/amicus/index-e.html.

Printed in the United States of America.

ISBN: 978-1-4907-2629-8 (sc)

All illustrations, cover design and photography by Robert F. Edwards.

Trafford rev. 02/15/2014

 www.trafford.com

North America & international
toll-free: 1 888 232 4444 (USA & Canada)
fax: 812 355 4082

CONTENTS

TRIBUTE

—⚬⚬⚬—

HOWARDS JAMES

I WOULD LIKE TO dedicate this book to Howard James, my great-grandfather who was born in Cornwall, England and lived his life as a successful land-owner. He was the four cousins to the Royal House of England. During his life, he married an aristocratic who was directly related to the King of Spain. They were blessed with one son and three daughters. In Cornwall, they were known as the House of James, for he was well represented in the district as a leader. He had considerable mansions and lands along the border of Wales.

It was well known in the district that when a bishop or a high-ranking member of the church came to the area, they would stay at the House of James rather than the accommodations that were available at the Abbey or rectory. It should be noted here that the James were known for their generosity, with great banquets and the seamstresses that were on duty constantly making garments for the family for each season.

His son died at an early age in his 20's. His two daughters married within the station of the aristocrats they were. His youngest daughter Ada, my grandmother, moved to Edmonton, Alberta, Canada.

I'm proud of this limited knowledge I have of my great-grandfather and his accomplishments while he was on this earth.

R.F.E. 2014

FORETHOUGHT

———ΩΩ———

THIS BOOK IS DIFFERENT than any other book the writer has written, for it is both fiction and nonfiction.

The nonfiction is about how and when the paintings were painted. The time was on June 12, 1998 when both paintings were done in Odessa, Ukraine. As this book goes into detail on how the portraits were done and by whom, there is no need to go on about it here.

The painting of the writer's likeness is over the mantelpiece while the other one is looking over his desk. The cover image illustrates one of these paintings.

In the fall of the year 2006, the writer came up with the story of 'The Portraits'. He started to write the story on February 8, 2007 when he was on another of his journeys. This time his adventure was to the Polynesian Islands and Philippines. The writer hoped and did get to the Island of Samoa where he was able to visit the estate of Robert Louis Stevenson. Robert Louis Stevenson was, and still is, one of the writer's favored authors. The writer was thinking of one of Robert Louis Stevenson's works known as Doctor Jekyll and Mister Hyde when he got the idea of The Portraits.

Now, to add to this part of the nonfiction is when the writer spent the days at the estate of Robert Louis Stevenson and to his amazement, there were two portraits of Robert Louis Stevenson in the main part of the house. He saw a painting of happiness in one and the other one was a back-ground of stormy times as Robert Louis Stevenson looked out from it. At first, the writer could not believe his eyes; two portraits of Robert Louis Stevenson and what this novel is all about. If he had not had the plot and outline beforehand, he himself would have thought this was the setting.

Nonetheless, one and all can see for themselves this is not the case. This could not have been a better setting to add to the story-line soon to be known as 'The Portraits'.

Now comes the fiction part of this novel which is made up of short stories or events throughout the book. The stories unfold as the writer comes to think of each and every moment of change from one side of life to the other. Another interesting part is the different times in which the stories take place and the locations. This book is one of a kind and so are the stories within its cover. No two events are close to being the same. Therefore, on this note; read on, or put the book back for someone else to read.

It is not who wrote about it,

It is who thought about it.

To each and every one of you, thanks for the time you have spent reading this forethought.

Written February 8, 2007

THE PORTRAITS

He looked at the clock beside his bed. Yes! It was still early; in fact, it was over an hour before he would have to get up. He presently couldn't sleep any more, for it was to be too big a day in his life to stay in bed any longer. Therefore without waking his wife, he got up, had a shower and then went back into the bedroom where his clothes for this exceptionally unique day lay waiting. Oh yes! He thought his best pin-stripe suit and white shirt. His blue tie with the tie pin and cuff links to match were there. The best black shoes he owned were waiting on the floor with their black socks. With all the finishing touches being added, he looked into the mirror. There was no doubt in his mind he was wearing the best he had and he looked it.

As he went downstairs, Doctor Sebastian once more thought of what was ahead of him today. And what a day it was going to be; first to meet Lord Cole Maximilian Edwards III in person was a wonderment in itself. Some say it is over twenty years ago that anyone from outside his staff had seen or talked to him. To think Doctor Sebastian and the museum were going to receive such an honor was over-whelming to him, even now. As he got a cup of coffee, he then sat down at the table to think over each last detail which had to been done. His mind went back to what he was going to receive on behalf of the museum. He had been the chief curator at the Ottawa National Museum for the last ten years and had been there for over, my goodness, forty years. Yes, one may say a lifetime and now what a great moment, what a great gift to receive on behalf of the museum. He was trying his best to remain calm. However, even after the second cup of coffee and now with his good wife up to support him, he couldn't think of anything else, as the time moved forward ever so slowly. Today, yes, today he was going to see the original works of the writer of 'The Portraits'.

At last, the clock gave way, and the time moved on. It would be less than half an hour before the limousine would come to take him to the mansion to meet His Lordship. He was trying his best to talk about anything else to his wife. It was impossible to think of anything, other than what was ahead. At last, the limousine came and the chauffeur knocked on the front door. Doctor Sebastian's time had come at last to leave. His good wife gave him a kiss on the cheek and reassured him all would go well.

As Doctor Sebastian opened the front door for the chauffeur, both men greeted each other. With this being completed, the chauffeur returned to the limousine and opened the door of the Rolls Royce as the good Doctor got in the back. It would be the better part of an hour before they would reach the mansion. Subsequently, now Doctor Sebastian sat back trying to look out the window and concentrate on what he was seeing. At times it was working along the way of the road traveled; however, other times his mind returned to what lie ahead. 'Oh, Dear God, please let me do the right things,' kept coming back, over and over again. At last, the chauffeur informed him they would be arriving within the next few minutes.

With this information, the limousine turned off the main road, and then started its way up the long winding road towards the mansion. Doctor Sebastian had little time for any more thoughts before the mansion came into view. It was as elegant as any of the pictures he had seen before. The surroundings of the mansion were set in such a tranquil landscape in which the famous British gardener, Capability Brown, would have put his stamp of approval on this. Once the sleek Rolls Royce entered the circular driveway, a doorman appeared. Both the chauffeur and the doorman opened the door almost spontaneously for Doctor Sebastian to exit the vehicle.

"This way please, Sir," the doorman requested, and then added, "would you be so kind as to follow me?" With this, he no sooner entered into the massive hallway where the butler relieved the doorman with a greeting to Doctor Sebastian.

"We are expecting you, Sir. Would you be good enough to sit in the parlor while I make your announcement?"

Within moments, he was escorted into a large room which royalty would have wished to have in their residence. The works of art were well-recognized even by an amateur, let alone a professional such as himself. The artists ranged from the Masters to the Contemporaries, to say nothing of the Impressionists. The only thing which was lacking, and it absolutely had no purpose in the surroundings, was Modern art. The antiquities were anything from Ming vases to priceless articles of furniture which he recognized as periods from the French Baroque to the Chippendales. It was like entering a private museum in itself.

As he sat in one of the most elegant French provincial chairs, he could feel the perspiration trickling down the inner part of his shirt. He removed his glasses and took out a silk handkerchief; then quickly dabbed his face hoping that the perspiration was only within his shirt, and not prevailing on his face. Wrong. Small beads of perspiration dampened the silk fiber. He quickly folded it back and replaced it where he had acquired it from, now back in his inward pocket of his suit. He had no sooner done this when the butler returned.

"His Lordship will see you now, Sir."

"Thank you," answered Dr. Sebastian.

"Please follow me," was the request from the butler.

With this, Doctor Sebastian got up and started to follow, as the butler continually walked the familiar area which he was in. Down the long corridors and onward into a larger, more like amphitheater, they continued. After sharply turning they entered the West Wing. The doors were large with the ceilings, of course, accommodated their enormous height as the good Doctor felt dwarfed in the presence of the huge hallway.

The butler knocked on the doors with mammoth French oak casing. There was a low, creaking groan as the door released its lock and allowed them to enter.

The butler bowed and said, "Your Lordship, I wish to announce Doctor Sebastian."

At this moment the doctor came forward. Once again, the butler bowed low and exited the room.

The room was totally unique; quite breath-taking at first. Though Doctor Sebastian tried to focus on the man sitting behind the enormous desk, his eyes couldn't help but focus as well on the backdrop. The huge window which prevailed behind the man was an exquisite work of stained glass, and was showering down the morning sun in such a sparkle of diffused colors which it gave the presence of His Lordship as a mystical figure.

The desk and the window were counter-sunk into the room as if it was some giant alcove. The room was not exceptionally large by other rooms in the estate. It was designed in such a way to be somewhat eerie and yet spellbinding. The room was rather rectangular on the east to west part. However to the south, with its enormous stained glass window, and now the small but distinct corridor which Doctor Sebastian was standing in, gave it all of the appearance of a cross. The artifacts were far too numerous for his eyes to even flutter through them.

"Please," was the shrill voice which came from His Lordship. "Please sit," again as His lordship motioned his hand forward to a chair. The hand was as frail as the voice.

His name was Cole Maximilian Edwards III. He was well into his ninety-fifth year and his extremely frail appearance from the shoulders up gave him the appearance of being ageless.

Then Doctor Sebastian made his way across the room towards the mammoth desk where the small figure sat elevated as if on a throne. Doctor Sebastian's parched mouth managed to say, "Thank you."

As he sat down across from His Lordship he added, "It is a great honor, Your Lordship, to be in your presence."

The face which received the compliment was expressionless. It was almost translucent. The eyes had shaded into shadows of darkness behind the thick glasses which prevailed on the face. His skin was smooth and colorless even in these years; it had not withered like others, but was smooth and fragile. It fitted only too well to the shrill voice which had welcomed him only moments before.

His Lordship was dressed in a suit which was immaculately tailored. His hands rested together as his elbows supported them on the desk which lay in front of him.

Doctor Sebastian took another deep breath. His mind whirled as if trying to seek out what the next words would be either from his host or himself. Cole Maximilian Edwards III was eccentric, to say the least and definitely reclusive for a good many years now. Doctor Sebastian was probably one of the few people, other than His Lordship's special personnel, who had ever even seen His Lordship in the last twenty to twenty-five years.

It was His Lordship who first broke the silence.

"I've invited you here today to share something that I have treasured all my life. As one can see, my life is nearing completion. It is time for me to share what I've treasured on my own. I've chosen you, Doctor, and your institution to receive the gift that I am about to release."

Doctor Sebastian managed somehow to realize that His Lordship had taken a breath and waited for a response. What seemed to be almost an eternity, nonetheless, it was in a matter of seconds in reality, Doctor Sebastian replied.

"The honor is all mine, Sir. I'm sorry, Your Lordship."

It was the first time in their meeting in which His Lordship's thin slithered lips parted and there was a small warm glow of a smile.

"Slip of the tongue, you might say," His Lordship replied. He then added, "Please be at ease, for what I'm going to say to you is important for all of us."

Doctor Sebastian's face turned red. He knew he was blushing profusely. He put his lips close together, pulling his moustache over his lower lip. After this somehow, he managed to give some form of a smile.

"Thank you, Your Lordship."

"Well now, as you and the world have known, many of the most remarkable novels and non-fiction have been written by my grandfather. I have no care or desire to know in how many languages; let alone how many volumes have been distributed throughout the world. However, today I am going to share with you some of the most intricate parts of what transpired to my grandfather to create the works known to only the family. The novels have brought enjoyment and pleasure to so many readers; nonetheless, these works do not contain what is in his last book written and is here. They were more short stories and adventures than the reality of what my grandfather experienced. Grandfather only let the world know of these works, not the real works of 'The Portraits'. Today, you will be the first one outside the family to see and read the full adventures of what really took place, here in this room with my grandfather and why.

It started so very long ago, about the middle of the last century. Grandfather was one of those types of people which, I guess for a better word, was a traveler. He enjoyed the world. He often referred to himself as 'a citizen of the global community' and in many ways it was the right description. For though I personally have known many men and women who have traveled in many parts of this planet, I have never known anyone as well-versed or as creative and diversified as my Grandfather. Whether it was deserts or mountains or oceans, to say nothing of continents, he put his footprints on all these places.

Nonetheless, this is about a particular place and a particular time in his life. A moment which changed his life and altered it until his last breath was taken. It was a time in the history of the world when what was known as the Soviet Union was in decline or, in probability, collapsing. Chairman Gorbachev had been replaced by a man called Yeltsin. In fact, his name was Boris Yeltsin. It was a part of the collapse of a system and the reversal of many of the things which the Communist Party had changed and were reversing themselves back. The city of Leningrad had been returned to its proper name of St. Petersburg. The vast lands of Siberia had not even grasped the loss of the Czar, let alone the replacement of Stalin's Communist rule, and not too much later were Gorbachev's words like *perestroika* and *glasnost*.

However, my Grandfather had been one of the first foreigners to travel here alone. As an individual, to experience the strange changes throughout this vast collectiveness, a land known as the Soviet Union; it was in the city of Odessa in the Ukraine which this moment I am going to share with you transpired.

Now, with the collapse of what was the Soviet Union; there had been vast economic hardships throughout the countries which were under its domain. Many of the intellectuals, including the professors and doctors of the universities, no longer had jobs or positions. Some still showed up and went through the motions of lectures with the academic parts while others were forced to be almost beggars trying to survive the transition.

It was on one of these moments in this period of history when my Grandfather was in the city of Odessa. It was also on one of his, what he would call 'journeys' that he stayed across from one of the large parks in Odessa. This was where artists who had once been teachers and professors of the art of painting in the universities were now freelance artists. This was the time when they would do painting on any type of fabric or material which would work as a canvas for their works of art. Hoping against hope, they could attract someone who was known as the new catch phrase 'the New Russian', better known as the mafia, to purchase a portrait for egotism or for whatever other reason. For a commission of their talents, a small remuneration would be paid, and as a result they could keep body and soul intact.

After the better part of the week of examining the different artists which congregated each day, as pigeons would in the park, hoping for some benevolent person to fulfill their needs of survival, he chose an artist. She was of extraordinary qualities. She, too, had her doctor's degree from the University of St. Petersburg. She had studied throughout the Soviet Union and, I may add, she was in her own right more than an artist, more than a professor. She was a gifted person.

My Grandfather chose her to do his portrait. Yes, it was in the open air. Yes, it was in pastels. And, as he sat there, in the park, as the locals wandered through hoping to find some exceptional value or bargain, her skillful fingers and her magical hands, with the aid of a brush, started his portrait. However, as he sat motionless, she etched her skills upon the canvas; there was another painter, a man riddled by disease festering from an incurable kind, with open wounds that left a good portion of his face missing and part of his throat which was covered with bandages and rags. He darted in and out of his hiding place with his ghastly condition, as his fingers and his hands painted and dabbled upon his material with the paints available to him to do his portrait of my Grandfather.

My Grandfather witnessed the movement and instinctively thought, in the past few minutes, maybe this man was painting him also, however gave little or no thought, for there were so many painters around hoping they would be one of the chosen ones for someone to have a portrait done by them.

As the hours passed, finally the work was being completed. It was a masterpiece. My Grandfather related to me personally, while still sitting, a German couple stood in awe as this gifted person worked her canvas with her brush. With each stroke, she produced a replica of beauty and distinction of my Grandfather. The German gentleman smiled and said, 'Jaw! gut!'

At long last, my Grandfather viewed the portrait; it was not only a likeness of him, it was a sheer image of the qualities which he possessed, the youthfulness of his age, though he was well in his fifties, the clarity of his character and the quality of what he believed in. She had not only captured his face, she had captured the qualities of his soul.

He was well pleased and paid her accordingly the fee which they had agreed upon.

As he was ready to depart with his new-found treasure, she called him back and she asked, "Sir, would you buy my friend's painting from him?"

My Grandfather told me that when he saw the painting done by this deformed person who looked like a leper who was at the last stages of life, he was horrified. The painting was diabolical. It reflected the harshness and the cruelty of a side of my Grandfather that he had never seen in himself or in his reflection. It was immediately coarse and cruel-looking; it was almost the dark side of his soul.

At first, he declined quickly and without hesitation, and then replied, "I'm sorry. I have no use for such a painting."

However, the woman was persistent. This disfigured creature hid himself once more behind the tree. Nevertheless, the painting was held by the woman.

"You don't have to give him much. He is starving. We all are starving."

"If it's charity you want, I'll spare him enough for a meal," my Grandfather replied.

"No, Sir, he is not a beggar. He is an artist and his days are numbered. He is dying. Please make him an offer to give him dignity," was her request.

Once more, my Grandfather said he looked at the painting. There was the likeness of his face . . . Yes, there was no doubt, in some way this was a portrait of him . . . . yes, there was no doubt. It was a resemblance of his face. It was what this individual, this creature that was infested with disease had captured. The lines crossed down his forehead with the intention of penetrating towards the bridge of his nose, the squaring of his jaw and the thickness of his neck were of a dark and foreboding appearance. Nevertheless, it was the eyes. Yes, this man who had little left of life had captured the dark side of my Grandfather's soul.

Finally, my Grandfather agreed to purchase the painting at a modest sum. At this point, with the two portraits, he returned to his hotel and started to prepare for the continuation of his journey across Russia and what would be known as the book 'The Journey of Russia and the Silk Roads'.

He secured both portraits in small containers to facilitate them; in tube-like fashion as he made his way across the vastness of the journey that he took. Once he returned to Canada, he shared all the things he had brought back as well as the portraits. Immediately his wife and his daughter acknowledged the quality and the sheer artistry captured in the beautiful portrait by the woman. His wife was aghast at the other painting and questioned why he would even think in a dark moment, of purchasing or keeping such a painting. After he explained the situation, she still did not share his benevolence or his kindness.

In the course of time, the beautiful portrait received an elegant frame to facilitate its purpose, while the other one reluctantly received an adequate frame for its protection. The beautiful painting hung majestically over the mantelpiece. Friends and strangers admired the artistic qualities of the painter and the realistic capture of my Grandfather. The other painting was in an obscure room.

As the days followed the weeks and the weeks followed the months, my Grandfather almost forgot about the incident and the time. However, exactly to the day, exactly to the hour of the day when the portraits were done, the first encounter happened.

It happened without warning, without any thought on my Grandfather's behalf. He had spent another day of business and the transactions with the intention of day-to-day living. He had a normal co-existence with the world around him. Nonetheless, then it happened, without warning.

He was sitting comfortably in his study, listening to some classical music as the fire danced its way in the hearth while the beautiful portrait looked down upon the surroundings. Then, without warning he was no longer there. There he was; his mind, his body, his soul, his life in another time, another place."

His Lordship looked at Doctor Sebastian's face as he stopped; almost as if he had totally exhausted the information.

Once more he looked at Doctor Sebastian who now was almost in a hypnotic trance. Doctor Sebastian was speechless. He wanted to say something. He wanted His Lordship to continue. However in some way, he felt frozen.

What seemed to be a long pause for both gentlemen, His Lordship gave a nod, as though he was exhausted and said, "It is time for some refreshments. Please join me in a more comfortable position in the parlor."

He rang a bell or buzzer underneath the desk. Within moments the butler entered.

"Please prepare some refreshments in the parlor for both of us. I prefer my usual," was his comment.

"Doctor, what is your pleasure?"

The doctor then looked bewildered, but managed to recapture his composure and replied, "Um, the same as you, Your Lordship."

"Ah, you like malted whiskey, neat?"

"With a glass of water on the side?" the butler added.

"Yes" came the reply from Doctor Sebastian.

Doctor Sebastian knew as soon as he said that, he had made a mistake. Nonetheless, he had already given his decision.

"It would be most rewarding for me. Thank you," once more was the comment from Doctor Sebastian.

The butler then asked the doctor to follow him into the parlor and His Lordship remained behind the massive desk.

What seemed to be an unacceptable length of time, His Lordship was aided and assisted in walking to the parlor. His form looked even more fragile than when he had been sitting behind the desk. The small tufts of a fringe of hair, which once had been abundant, looked like a tonsure with the intention of working its way into a halo around his face. Doctor Sebastian, for the first time, realized how fragile and small His Lordship was.

They sat across from each other, sipping the malted whiskey.

"Ah, yes, nothing like a little stimulant," said His Lordship as he looked at Doctor Sebastian.

"Yes, it is good." Doctor Sebastian answered.

His Lordship seemed to be muttering more to himself.

"I suppose it is time, after our refreshments, for you to see what I'm prepared to give to your institution."

Doctor Sebastian nodded.

"I would be grateful, whenever it is convenient or desirable for you, Your Lordship, for my time and the institution are completely at your disposal. All we wish is to share and will always be grateful for whatever you give us to display and to cherish for the Canadian people."

"Ah, yes, yes, yes," His Lordship muttered. "Yes, my Grandfather. Oh, my Grandfather," he repeated. "What an experience. What a total experience my Grandfather's life was. Remarkable! Yes, totally incredible."

Doctor Sebastian did not even know whether it really was him; His Lordship was talking to, or to probably himself. Doctor Sebastian did not know whether to answer or even acknowledge, consequently he sat like a mummified replica of himself.

His Lordship once more sipped the malted whiskey and felt the warm glow with the purpose to warm his tired aging body. On the contraire, while sipping the malted whiskey Doctor Sebastian did not only feel the warm glow, but the effects of alcohol on an empty stomach. He felt the first wave of ooziness. He knew as a result, he was perspiring. He could feel the dampness around the rims of his glasses as if they were steaming up by the temperature in which his blood had started to reach. However, he was not going to give in, even though his hands were feeling the dampness and perspiration. He held the glass extra tightly as it seemed to slip and slide in his clammy wet hands.

It appeared that His Lordship was in no rush to continue. Without even a warning, the fragile hand reached for a cord and pulled it. Once again the butler appeared.

"Would you be good enough to show Doctor Sebastian into the large hall in the East Wing, please? Afterwards, have my aide assist me. I think it would be easier to explain what lies ahead there."

The butler looked at Doctor Sebastian and replied, "As you please, Your Lordship. Please follow me, Doctor," as the butler turned and look at Doctor Sebastian.

He bowed deeply to His Lordship. Moreover, spontaneously Doctor Sebastian followed the bow. Then they both turned and left the fragile figure to wait for his aides.

Doctor Sebastian followed the butler from the West Wing into the main part of the mansion, where they entered into another large elegant room which were dining facilities set for him and His Lordship. It had been chosen in one of the alcoves of this large massive room to be more intimate rather than the table which could easily have sat fifty couples without them being elbow-to-elbow.

Doctor Sebastian felt dwarfed by the sheer magnitude and size. Nevertheless, what continually raced through his mind were the artifacts and the elegant taste with the aim to go from one generation to another, always adding to this immense wealth surrounding him.

Shortly thereafter, His Lordship was wheeled in by two aides and positioned before the small alcove dining facilities. The luncheon was astounding. If one could imagine an unlimited variety, then they would just possibly succeed their imagination to what lay before them. The portions were small. The service was impeccable. These servants were raised and trained to serve people of the highest caliber of wealth.

Doctor Sebastian was grateful, in more ways than one; his stomach would receive something more than liquids. Maybe, just maybe, the growling would stop in his stomach. Maybe the sharp pains in which pierced through his internal organs would ease. His breathing had now started to become more normal.

His Lordship seemed to be transposed into another sphere of thought. Undeniably, Doctor Sebastian was not going to interrupt. After the lunch was concluded, His Lordship seemed to come out of the trance with the meager amount of nourishment he had taken on, and then said, "I am now ready to explain the purpose of your visit and my contribution to the museum."

Once again he rang and instantly the butler was by his side.

"Can you show Doctor Sebastian to the East Wing and my Grandfather's study?"

"As you wish, Your Lordship," came the reply.

With this, once again the butler escorted Doctor Sebastian out of the presence of His Lordship. As they walked into the East Wing, Doctor Sebastian noticed instantly something different from the West Wing. Though equally as elegant, it had almost a musty smell, as if it had been closed and only penetrated by the presence of the staff when absolutely necessary.

At the extreme far end of the wing was the study, overlooking one of the most beautiful landscapes one could imagine. This was the office of his Lordship's late grandfather. It didn't have the uniqueness or the ambience of His Lordship office. It was rather conservative, one might say. As the butler motioned to choose one of the sofas of pure leather with horsehair stuffing for his seating arrangements, Doctor Sebastian chose the large comfortable chair and settled immediately into a resting position in which it gave comfort to not only his dorsal but his limbs as well.

Once again the butler excused himself and informed him, "His Lordship will be here shortly."

It was those few moments, far less than half an hour that had been given to him, in order to have Doctor Sebastian start to peruse from his position in the chair the surroundings. At first, it was dominated by a huge hearth and, of course, the portrait of pure elegance and innocence and artistic ability.

At the extreme opposite end was another hearth and what Doctor Sebastian assumed was the other portrait, draped in a rich velveteen drapery, hiding behind it, whatever figuration or piece of art that prevailed. His imagination leaped forward thinking it must be the other portrait.

The rest of the room was a replica of the man himself, his great travels throughout the world and his moments of impulsive buying; of anything from a blow dart, to some elegant rugs from Turkey. It was endless; from an ostrich egg that had been carved intricately into a work of art; to vials containing the sands of the Great Sahara. And on and on it went. It was like looking at a collection or a collage of the world itself.

Doctor Sebastian was almost prepared to get up and start examining these famous artifacts more closely when the great doors of the study opened. Then once again the aides assisted His Lordship into the room. Once he was positioned in an adequate chair facing Doctor Sebastian's choice of chairs, the frail figure almost shrunk, if it was possible, in the presence of the room. At once there was almost a reverse situation. Doctor Sebastian actually felt more comfortable and his facial expressions were more relaxed than His Lordship's.

In that high-pitched, almost screeching voice, His Lordship said, "We're here. This was my Grandfather's study."

He looked around as if he was almost expecting the spirit of his Grandfather to materialize and instruct him to say and what not to do.

Doctor Sebastian actually looked somewhat puzzled but did not say anything.

Once again, His Lordship took command of the situation.

"It is important that you have sufficient time to see the portrait I described, which my Grandfather had commissioned by the gifted artist on that day in mention." He refused somehow to bring the date forward.

Incredibly, then he moved his hand, as fragile it was, to the other side of the room where the adjacent hearth was. Once again he rang and his aides instantly appeared. Rather than say anything, he motioned for them with scarcely a flicker of his fingers to pull back the drapes on the concealed object behind the drapes. One of the aides left his side and performed the duty.

His Lordship refused to look in that direction. Nonetheless, Doctor Sebastian did. And there it was—the other portrait.

It was everything His Lordship had said it was, and even more. It had an eerie feeling which it presented to the person who looked upon it. It was not as grotesque as Doctor Sebastian's first imagination. Nevertheless, it was equally as spell-binding and commanding as anything in which he could have imagined.

Doctor Sebastian moved his eyes back to the other mantelpiece and the beautiful portrait of a handsome man. Doctor Sebastian could not bring himself to return to the diabolical portrait. Instead he turned his attention to His Lordship.

His Lordship's shrill voice penetrated the air.

"Now you have seen what my Grandfather had written about in his great novel."

There was a long pause of silence, like the waiting of the clap of thunder after the lightning had broken the skies. As the seconds ticked away, it became a most uncomfortable moment in Doctor's Sebastian's mind, his hands gripping the armrests and, without realizing, squeezing deeply into the leather. He waited, but his eyes could not return to the diabolical portrait. For that matter, he could not look in the direction of the other portrait; instead he looked into the eyes of His Lordship.

Then His Lordship said to his aides, "Bring the books, please."

With this, the one aid went over to a selective part of the library and brought volume after volume of intricate leather-bound books, labeled with the finest of engravings.

"These are the original volumes of my Grandfather's compositions of his journeys. In one of these volumes is the reference, as I have mentioned today, of where these portraits were painted and by whom."

His Lordship motioned once more with a weak fragile gesture. As the book of 'The Portraits' came into view, he was almost reluctant to ask for it. The aide immediately went and got the book. It was the same size and volume as the others. It was a work of art like all the others. Nonetheless, it was bound in calf's leather of the finest Moroccan leather which could be obtained and dyed in a special purple Egyptian dye that was as rare as the Pyramids themselves. It was the only book, out of all the volumes with the purpose of being on display, which was concealed not only by its outward sleeve that was removed by one of the assistants but, once it was exposed, there was a binding with a gold lock around it.

His Lordship seemed to grow paler, if that was possible, from his already transparent skin. Then his eyes seemed to fade, as if he wished to be somewhere else.

The face with thick glasses looked into the eyes of Doctor Sebastian and said, "This is the original book. This is the original manuscript. These are the original records of my Grandfather's book, 'The Portraits'."

Doctor Sebastian couldn't help but be overwhelmed by what was taking place in his presence, right before his eyes.

His Lordship bowed his head almost in reverence. In a low voice which was barely heard by the human ear, he said to his assistant by his side, "Open it."

With this, one of the assistants went to a secret compartment in the panel of the beautiful oak-laden desk and returned with a key. He opened the lock. There before his eyes, and the eyes of anyone else in the room, the pages lay waiting to be personally witnessed by Doctor Sebastian. The book of 'The Portraits' now open was still in the hands of one of the assistants. His Lordship nodded once more in that direction and demanded his assistant to hand the book over to Doctor Sebastian.

Doctor Sebastian put the book firmly on his lap. He dared not hold it completely. It was much heavier than he ever thought possible, even with the enriched leather and intricate art work that prevailed over it. It felt like a huge tablet of stone. He opened the cover and there was the majestic art work of the pages encouraging him to proceed. He prayed with everything which was holy in his life, that his fingers would not leave a print, a stain, a drop of moisture from his presence on the pages which followed.

After the first two or three pages, His Lordship interrupted.

"I would prefer if you would read these pages in your own time and without my presence accountable. I am weary now and I really must rest. I wish you to spend as much time here as you want. When you are ready to leave, please ring and the butler will aid and assist you to make arrangements for the chauffeur to take you back to your home. In the days that follow, I will ask you to return without my presence being required, and come to the study to read this book; nevertheless please, in no other place than here."

They departed. Doctor Sebastian was alone. Alone in the room of the late Grandfather of His Lordship with the original volume 'The Portrait', surrounded by a lifetime of adventures by the man who wrote it.

THE MONK

—⁓—

THIS BOOK IS A *diary of what has transpired to me on the anniversary of the paintings of my likeness. It happened, as I will try my best to explain, first of all to myself and then with the aid and assistance of my beloved wife, we will try to put it in a form of records for others, if it be the will of God, to share.*

I had enjoyed a normal day in my life. Returning to my study, I sat and enjoyed a fine mellow wine as the fire crackled and danced its merriment to the backdrop of Beethoven. I was at peace with myself and my surroundings. I casually glanced over to the hearth and then quickly moved my eyes up towards the portrait of my favored artist. Instantly, I remembered nothing until the next morning.

I was told though, the servants knocked vigorously on the door, and I refused to acknowledge the request. After numerous times, they abandoned the idea, believing I wished not to be disturbed. Nonetheless, this was the first encounter of the anniversary of the day that these paintings took possession of my life.

I looked down at the valley far below from my cell window in the monastery. I had reached my 38th anniversary in this year of my Lord's existence of my life. My thoughts were drifting back to my youth, my childhood. I cared only for the moment that prevailed in my thoughts of hence long, long ago.

My mind drifted to the time when my Father brought me to the monastery. I believe I was maybe five, a little older, I could have been. It was so long ago.

I was the youngest of his sons which numbered in four. Beyond this, I was the weakest. I guess one might say I was not good for physical labor and I would have to find another means for God to let me live throughout my life.

Therefore my Father made his way, with me in hand, up the long, arduous, treacherous trail to the monastery far, far above. It looked to me like it was the castle of God, our Father, high in the clouds. It was huge. But then, all things are bigger when one is small and one is a child.

I remember my Father talking to one of the monks and the man in the robe taking my hand. I remember trying to hold back those tears, as my Father bid me farewell.

The years which followed were as one would expect for a novice in the Benedictine Order of this monastery. Most of my days were spent in prayer, or doing meager tasks always guided by a firm hand and a strong voice. I learned at an early age how to sing the Gregorian chant and what God had lacked in my physical strength he gave in my voice. I had the voice of a nightingale. I could reach those notes with the aid of the monk who instructed us and he would smile as if he had found the perfect pitch to eternal life. It became part of my contribution to the cloister. As my years followed and my life became more fulfilling both to myself and to those of my fellow monks, I belonged to God and the Benedictine Order. My years in single digit vanished and my novitiate was almost completed.

I had not only a God-given voice to reach the beautiful notes of the chant and prayer to Almighty God but also was quite gifted in learning to read and write. I was well respected, not only by the others monks and novices, but by the elder monks, and most of all by the monks who were learned.

It was a communal living. We all had duties with the purpose we were assigned to. It was God's will. And the will of God shall prevail in this monastery.

I believe somewhere around my thirteenth, maybe my fourteenth, year of life; it is hard to say, my God-given voice changed. The notes that were like the pure sound of life from heaven now cracked and deepened as if the Earth itself had broken apart.

It was one of the few times in which I have ever been in the presence alone with the Abbot. I remember it well. He placed his hands upon my shoulder and I had to look up into his face.

He said to me, in the softest of tones, "Manhood is upon you and the God-given voice of the child will no longer be a part of your life, if we do not help you. You have a choice to fulfill the needs and desires of the flesh or you can fulfill the destiny and fulfillment of the gifts of God."

I did not understand. What was the Abbot saying, so I can stay here with him and the other monks, I had to give up being a man but how could I, a child do this? The dear Abbot could see in my face that I did not know what he was asking of me.

He then said, "You must give up your manly parts to keep what God has blessed you with, and such a purpose is your voice."

I nodded.

"My life was given to me by God. I will always serve him. And I wish never to leave the monastery for this is the only home I know and the shelter on this Earth."

The days that followed were horrifying. Not only my body still wears the scars, my mind still feels the agony.

Oh, it brings such pain to my thoughts. I must rest them for a moment. I must go back and look at the valley below. Ah, the peace, the peace of finding this beautiful moment with the purpose I can look out unto the world through this window of my cell. My peace I give to you.

To facilitate God's wishes, the Order caused me to lose my private parts, my manhood, to keep my God-given voice. Even today, in my thirty-eighth year, I still can reach those high notes which gave me the gift and the privilege of serving God.

Tsk. Ah, yes, I am a monk of the Benedictine Order. I am not only still in the choir, but now I am the choir leader. I have known no other life and I seek none other than these walls with the purpose to protect me from the sins of man and the world in which I gaze upon through this window.

It is a peace one can only experience when one knows no other. Ah, my beautiful thoughts. What a wonderful life. Oh, God, Thank You! My Eternal Father!

Hark! Who knocks at this door of mine, who interrupts my thoughts? It's not time for Vespers.

Thus, I open the latch and look out to see a fellow monk's face.

"Dear Brother, I disturb your peace. However, it is the Abbot who requests your time, not mine. Please, the Abbot awaits your presence."

As my fellow monk left my presence, I once more returned to the window and look out to the Garden of Eden as it looked to me.

I could not think why the good Abbot would wish to see me. Yes, it was troubling to me, for in all my years I had only been called to the Abbot's quarters very rarely. It was not that I had any kind of fear or even concern. In the past, I was seldom called to be in the presence of the Abbot of the monastery, in all my years here. Each time, nevertheless, I was always given another task to learn or do. 'Oh! What could this good Abbot wish of this poor monk?' now came to mind as I left the window and made my way to the door of my cell.

The last Abbot, some twenty years or so ago, had asked me to go to the sanctum to learn under Brother Felix how to read and write. It took the patience of the good brother and the other monks many years; however, now I am one of them. I too, do some of the scribes' works of the translations in the great books of the library and the sanctum.

I guess it was three times and now this will be the fourth. Ah, what awaits me? What could I possibly be asked in which I am not already doing?

Upon entering the Abbot's cell, I was greeted with a smile and a gesture of friendliness accompanied with a sincere welcome.

"Sit, Brother Monk."

As I sat and received his blessing, the Abbot said to me, "Brother Monk, we have taken the vows of chastity, poverty and obedience. Moreover you have, for the better part of your life, followed these vows within the confines of this monastery. Today I ask you to go on another quest for our knowledge and your experience. This is going to be an act of obedience first, and maybe the others will follow. Nevertheless, the request in which I ask of you is to go outside this monastery and explore the knowledge which I am about to relate to you."

"I have been informed, as we know; our countries of France and England have been at war for many years. Also, things have gone badly for us French. On the other hand there seems to be a change—a young woman. Her name is Joan in the district of Arc who has rallied our spirits, reconfirmed our convictions of lands and blocked many victories over our enemy. She has claimed that her success has been guided and preordained by Almighty God and from the spirit of the Holy Ghost."

"A short time ago, I have received word in which she is now being tried as a heretic by the English. I wish you to go and witness the trial."

"There are two reasons wherein I request this from you, Brother Monk. Number one, you are a knowledgeable and extremely gifted man. You have the educational abilities and intellectual qualities to transcribe what you have seen and heard or witnessed in the records of this monastery. Second, you are still a child, not only in the eyes of God, but quite possibly in the eyes of man. The records show that you were a child when you came to the monastery and this will expose you to the other parts of the world of man with the intention of giving you knowledge of what other things exists. You have the innocence of a child. Let it be known the innocence of a child will enter the kingdom of heaven, nonetheless a grown man must learn about man's ways from his fellow beings."

"This is a two-fold request. One, with the purpose of you gaining the knowledge and the information with the intention of sharing it with all of us now and in the future by you recording it. The second one is to see if you, a child of innocence, will continue to hold what you already own of your innocence."

I could not help but be speechless. For over thirty years I had never ventured other than through this monastery and its grounds. To leave it would to me almost, in my mind, like leaving my mother's womb to enter out into the world. Although when one takes a vow and asks God to be the witness, one has no other choice but to accept the request.

After the shock left my mind as well as the reflection from my face, I looked up to the Abbot's face, into his eyes and said, "When do I begin?"

Once more, the Abbot smiled.

"Tomorrow after Mass "was the reply. "We will provide you with three days of food and a few sovereigns for your aid while you are there and for your return to the monastery."

With this once more, I acknowledged what has been said. The Abbot gave his blessing. After I received his blessing, I left his quarters.

I returned to my cell and once more looked out the window to the valley below. Somehow it had changed. It no longer drew me with wonderment and a longing to see what was beyond. It was like the unknown and I was leaving the Garden of Paradise, hoping that my soul would survive.

Consequently the next day after Mass, I received a loaf of bread, a slice of cheese and a wine gourd-pouch with the directions in which way to go to the city that awaited my presence.

After walking for most of the day and eating exceptionally sparsely, a little of bread and a small morsel of cheese, I started to find my way towards a small hamlet. As I approached one of the buildings, I asked if there was any shelter where I could stay for the night. The rough and unkempt proprietor of the dwelling sneered with a toothless smile then said, "The stable is the best I can give with fresh hay, if you are unwilling to pay."

"Ah, I will be grateful for anything in which I receive from you and God," I replied.

Once more the innkeeper sneered, and said "Let salvation be yours."

Hence, with this he took me to the back shed and threw fresh hay on already a saturated pile of straw with manure. After saying my prayers, I retired for the night.

It was a sleepless night. I turned and tossed and hoped I would overcome my fears, only with the morning dawn breaking to my total discomfort and horror. I had not only thrashed through the night turning and tossing; I was now covered with the manure of the animals that lived within the shelter. My habit was covered with their dung and I reeked of the smells of excretion. I quickly gathered my sack of supplies and waved goodbye to the proprietor. I had to cleanse myself, even for my own purpose, from the piss and dung that now covered me.

As I traveled along the road, to my relief, I came upon a small stream of considerable width. I laid my sack of supplies down and proceeded up to my knees and there I washed my habit and myself the best I could. The water not only cleansed the cloth I wore, but some of the anxieties of my mind.

As I left the creek, I saw a shepherd sitting by the tree consuming my supplies.

I wallowed in my wet habit towards him and said, "Brother, I wish to share all that I have, nevertheless this is all I will have for a long journey."

The shepherd looked up at me. He was a stout young man. In addition to the daily tasks he performed, he was much broader and stronger in width and height than I could imagine I would ever be.

"Ah! Brother Monk. Brother Monk! You take a vow of poverty. Now you can practice it. Ha! Ha!" he answered as he finished off the last of the wine in my gourd. He got up and stuffed the last piece of cheese into his mouth and walked off.

I could not believe anywhere people were of this nature. I could not believe there were such things as they were. However, it is not for me to question God's will or the spirits of others, but to follow what the dear Abbot asked of me.

On the second night, I approached a village. It was again in the shadow of darkness that I started to approach. As I entered the village, a man staggered drunk through the street in the same direction I was coming.

Once he stood in front of me, he said, "Brother Monk, give me coin for my thirst is not quenched and I have no more to feed my needs."

I looked and said, "Oh, Brother, does not one think moreover you have sufficed your craving?"

"Do not judge me, Monk. Give me coin!" he uttered once more. Now he was close at hand.

I replied, "All I have is water from the creek, a small crust of bread and two sovereigns in which the dear Abbot has given me for my needs to return from my quest."

"Your quest is now to give me the sovereigns."

I reached into my habit and pulled out the two sovereigns.

"Dear Brother, may we share? If I give you one and keep one, you will fulfill your needs and I will still have half of what I need to return to the monastery."

He did not answer with his voice but with his fist. Before I could reflect what was happening, the mighty blow from his fist hit my face and the blood poured out of my nose like from a puncture. I fell over backwards, stunned, only to feel the kicking of his unforgiving feet against my body.

He reached down and took the sovereigns out of my hand and said, "Do not be selfish, Monk."

I lay there for most of the night. Somehow, while the stars were still out in the heavens, I prayed and asked Almighty God to protect me with the Psalm of David, 'As I walk through this valley of death . . .' I repeated out loud to myself.

I felt bruised and battered as I once more started on my journey towards the quest of what the Brother Abbot had asked.

This night I had no food left, only water. On the contrary it does not matter. I had learned to fast many times in my life. In fact, in some ways, I have always found Lent to cleanse not only my soul but my body. As a result the discomfort was not one of hardship. This time though, I felt much safer with the animals of the forest than the people of the villages or dwellings. Therefore, I slept in the forest with the other creatures of God. I found a peace wherein I had not found since I left the monastery.

On the fourth day, well into midday, I arrived only to witness a young woman being prepared to be burned at the stake in the town square. I hardly needed to ask who she was. I had failed the Abbot. I have arrived too late. Her trial had been completed; her verdict had been the sentence of purification by fire.

As I made my way through the crowd of anxious spectators, I could not help but feel some form of cruelty of enjoyment of seeing someone other than themselves suffer.

Then the execution and purification by fire was about to commence. I looked into the face of this young maiden. Tears formed in my eyes for I felt that she was not guilty of the crimes in which they accused her of. My instant reaction, as the fire started at the base and the smoke already starting to rise, was to at least save her soul, if I could not save her body. I spontaneously reached out and grabbed the standard of one of the clergy with Almighty Christ at its peak and ran madly through the crowd pushing and shoving, trying to reach this soul before its end here on earth and eternity.

I was within maybe two, three, ah, it does not matter. I was close and I reached out and pushed my hands to the end of the standard. This virgin of Christ at least had His face to look into with her last moments on this earth. Only then did I feel a severe blow on the back on my head as I fell forward, never more to get up from my own doing.

I once more woke in the chair in which I had spent the night in. I could not believe what had taken place, for the last thing I remembered was looking at the portrait. My body was sore. I was totally and completely exhausted. I tried to move out of my chair. However, as I made the supreme effort to get up, I fell back into the chair and collapsed. It was then I realized I would need more than my own strength. I rang for my male servant who knocked. With all the effort I had, I yelled, but it was a whisper, to enter.

When he entered, he was totally taken back by my condition. In a whisper I asked if he would aid and assist me back to my chambers and help me into my bed. Without any question he did. Once back in my chamber and helping me lay in my bed, he asked what he should do; however, I could not answer him due to my weakness. The very best I could do was raise my hand in such a way for him to leave.

My body was wrecked. I felt as though I had been the one who had been beaten. My head throbbed as if I was the one who had that final blow which was received.

By the following day, I was feeling much better; however I still was unable to get out of my bed. By the third day, by the grace of God, I returned more to normal. I tried to explain what happened that night, not only to my wife, but also to myself. She had no more answers than I did.

So we agreed sometimes it is best if we try not to understand the unknown other than to put it away and hide it with the purpose of getting on with the present. This is exactly what I did. Before the week was finished I was back to normal doing my day-to-day activities and did exactly what I had chosen to do with the intention of putting this experience behind me.

The good Doctor stared as almost in a trance at the last page in which he had read. He was focused on the words; however he seemed reluctant to take his eyes off the book. The pages had become indelibly imprinted into his subconscious, with his conscious struggling to recapture his control. Finally, with extreme effort, he closed the book together with both hands to end the concentration his eyes produced on the page. Once the book was closed, he seemed to regain what had felt to be an insurmountable time away from his conscious being. He took deep breaths and as each breath filled his lungs with fresh oxygen, he sighed for the first time since he'd been reading the event. His hands then quickly reached for the clip which would close the book before he put it in the sealed container.

Once this was done, he felt some control back in his life and his purpose. He sat there gazing at the large doors with the intention of leaving this sanctum, the library of the great man himself. With the utmost effort he tried to reach for the bell with the aim of ringing for the butler to come and assist him from these premises. Although he was in control of his body movements, his mind was forced once more to the portraits above the mantle-pieces. Yes, he gazed upon the portrait with a vision that he had not witnessed before. There was at this time an aura of goodness and kindness, with benevolentness. An aura of peace with one's being. He found it enticed him to remain constant in its view. He literally forced his eyes by moving his head once more towards the doors to break the trance of the stare. Once more focusing on the great doors, his hands recollected his intent to ring the bell for the butler. Then, at this moment, his mind was once more distracted from its mission and was being drawn like iron shavings to a magnet, his eyes were forced to the opposite portrait, where he gazed with an element of concern along with horror.

This portrait looked down upon him with the reflection of anguish and distrust, also with ruthlessness and evil; opposite of the man's portrait who was so benevolent above the other mantle-piece. He felt like he was at the equator; divided in two and not belonging to either.

With a force he had not realized he had, he motioned his head with the strength of determination towards the doors and spontaneously rang the bell at the same time. In less than five minutes, there was a knock at the door and with a voice as strong as he could muster said, "Enter".

Once again the butler entered, "You rang, sir?"

"Yes, yes I'm ready to . . ." he paused. He had to catch his breath. "I'm ready for the chauffeur to take me back to my dwelling."

"As you wish, Sir".

It was only then as he got up to follow the butler did he realize that when he had entered the room in the afternoon, the sun was shining and it was lit by natural light. He had not been aware at all in which the shadows of darkness had crept through the windows so then he assumed by some automatic apparatus, the lights had turned on automatically. He walked through the long corridors with some anxiety of trying to get to the outside parameter rather than enjoying the antiquities and art which prevailed. He walked closely on the heels of the butler and shortly they came to the foyer. The doorman was waiting and rang for the chauffeur to bring the limousine around. He made little or no conversation other than courteous gestures to facilitate good manners to the servants.

Once in the limousine, then driving out of the long estate to reach the main arteries of traffic, he started to breathe with a relaxation that he hadn't realized until this moment. He immediately looked at his watch and for the first time he realized it was well after five o'clock. It would be somewhere around six-thirty or later before he returned to his home. Neither the chauffeur nor he had any desire to make any conversation as he looked endlessly out the side windows. Nothing seemed to approach his vision other than passing traffic on either side. He was anxious to return to his domicile. He felt exhausted, worn out. He had put in extremely strenuous days before, long hours, much longer than this day. Now, not only his physical being, but it was as if . . . well, it was as if his soul was tired, or his spirit. It didn't matter. It was weariness. Finally the minutes ticked away, as he approached his street. Once again heading up to his home, the chauffeur got out and opened the door then wished him well. He thanked the chauffeur for his services and went into the house.

His dear wife was waiting with open arms. "Oh, it's so good to have you home. I was starting to worry about when you'd return."

With this, she paused and looked at him. "Are you alright, dear?"

"Yes, yes, just a little tired. Sure could stand a glass of wine. Would you please join me?"

"Of course! My dear, of course! I'd love to hear all about your day."

"Yes", he sighed. "I'll be in the parlor."

"I'll join you shortly," came her reply.

He'd barely sat down in his favorite chair and loosened his tie when his beloved wife returned with two glasses on a tray with the decanter of red wine. She poured him a glass and was proceeding to pour hers when he gulped it down as a man dying of thirst. She looked somewhat in dismay as Dr. Sebastian never drank in gulps, but savored the nectar of the grape.

She looked bewildered at him again, "Dear, is everything alright?"

"Yes, yes my love. Please pour me another glass. I've had a strenuous day."

"Of course, of course my dear", and with the second glass he was more moderate but again finished it before she'd taken her first sip.

"This is most unusual of you, my dearest," she mentioned to him.

"Yes, I will explain at once. One more glass, my beloved, one more please." They both without hesitation sat and he was holding his glass rather than consuming the fluid in it.

"I did have a most extraordinary day. His Lordship is as elderly and frail as I anticipated. Nonetheless, he has even greater manners than I have ever met before. There is no doubt in my mind his days are numbered and he's well aware of that. He is everything in which one would expect of a man of breeding. His word is his bond. After a delightful lunch and modest conversation, he and his male servants escorted me to the study of his Great Grandfather. Once there, on opposite mantles, were the Portraits."

"Well, tell me more, dear," she pleaded.

"After a short period of conversation, his Lordship had one of his male servants produce the volume of manuscripts. It is richly bound in exquisite leather and has a lock and key, and only one of the male servants has access to a secret compartment of the room where the key is kept. I should have mentioned before one can see this volume, it also has an outer sleeve of the same discriminating leather as that covering the manuscript."

"Sounds like an exceptionally rare book, one might say," she once more added.

"I would have to say that is probably the largest understatement I've ever heard you say," he replied.

"Now, now my dear . . . please continue," she said encouragingly.

"Well, His Lordship, frail as well as being uneasy in that surrounding, said I would be left alone to read the book at my leisure and at any given point in time that I wished to leave, all I would have to do was to ring for the butler and he would make arrangements for me to return to my home, which is exactly what transpired."

"Well dear, if all went well, and from what you have indicated, why are you . . . well, why are you in the state you're in?" she asked in concern.

Dr. Sebastian once more took a long gulp out of his third glass of wine which was currently giving him some kind of false stability. He took in a couple of deep breaths.

"I read the first event one might say, or chapter, of this great man's life, and about the Portraits themselves. It wasn't what was written, but it was what I experienced as I read the words from sentences and then the pages, and somehow I was living in the period of Joan of Arc. I was actually seeing with my own eyes, as if I was a floating spirit hovering over this monk's life. I have never in all my life experienced anything quite as . . ." he paused once more, "unusual."

"I had set aside a specified time to leave for home and I was absolutely astonished how reluctant I was to leave that room. As if the hours I . . . it's merely nonsense my dear, absolutely nonsense. I've had a dreadfully long day and of course I was stressed in the first part of this morning. You know how much I was depending on this meeting with His Lordship for the museum. The gains of his priceless art works to the museum would be like having the chance to take over another museum's treasures as a gift. Enough nonsense! I wish not to go into it any more. What are we going to have for dinner tonight, my beautiful wife?"

"Ah yes, something special! I knew you would have a stressful day the moment you got up, so I prepared one of your favorite dishes."

"Moreover what . . . let me guess," he smiled.

"Yes, a rack of lamb. Of course, the mint jellies with the young asparagus to say nothing of your favorite yam that will give the dish a colorful appearance. I've accompanied your favorite salad of fresh cherry tomatoes and baby onions along with an extra special dressing. Furthermore, for dessert my dearest, I've prepared your favorite, a rhubarb cobbler," she added with pride.

"Oh my dearest beloved wife, you definitely are the jewel of my life, and I have had an extraordinary day. I'm sure the rewards will be forthcoming both to me and the museum."

With this, the good doctor and his wife went into the dining room where his special meal waited and the evening of delight prevailed.

WITCH IN THE EVERGLADES

—⁓—

Dr. Sebastian's secretary and His Lordship's secretary had been working very earnestly to set up another appointment for the good doctor to return to the mansion and proceed reading The Portraits. To neither one's dismay or inconvenience, finally the secretaries came to an agreement, in which it would be convenient for both parties to resume the doctor's reading. Now it just so happened the date was two weeks to the day he had first been to the mansion and read the Portraits.

The good doctor continued to do his cataloging and intricate work of supervising the massive staff that prevailed in the museum itself. New exhibits were planned as well as new articles coming from the four corners of the world. He gave little thought, if any, to the next appointment at the mansion. As the days found their way through his itinerary, the day soon arrived in which he was to be picked up by the chauffeur.

Once again he put on his best suit and prepared himself for the day ahead. This time he was more at repose and peaceful of mind and did not have the anxieties of the previous meeting. Also he was told that the secretary, rather than His Lordship, would be the one who would accompany him to the study and prepare all that was necessary for his pleasure. Promptly at the same time the chauffeur drove up, and it was a repeat of what Dr. Sebastian experienced the first time. The greeting, the efficiency, the drive to the mansion, the doorman, and then the butler were as before. This time the only difference which really prevailed was a secretary of his equivalent age greeting him for the first time, and escorting him to the aviary for some morning refreshment before the day started.

The conversation was light and neither productive nor evasive. He had learned the secretary had spent most of his life in the employment of His Lordship and was not only a dear and loyal servant but one could almost feel a friendship. After the refreshments, the secretary along with two male servants escorted the doctor to the library of the late Robert F. Edwards. The door was always locked and still had a musty, unlivable atmosphere in which he noticed the first time he had entered. It was probably due to the fact it was exactly what it was; unused. He had no doubt in his mind he was the last person who had been in the room since his visit two weeks before.

The male servant quickly went to the library to obtain the book of The Portraits while the secretary again asked if there was anything of his needs at the present. There would be lunch served at noon or if he wished another time and all he needed to do was ring the bell. At any given hour, at his pleasure, the butler would come and escort him to the appropriate dining area. Now the two male servants assisted, with the senior one who had the key, while the more junior one placed the book on the side table adjacent to the massive desk. The senior servant took the sleeve off once again and unlocked the binding. With little other conversation, the three men left Dr. Sebastian to his task at hand.

Once more, he was alone. He quickly gazed around at his surroundings, and then with almost a fixation, the portrait of the pleasant one's appearance cast a vision on him which held him quickly and then released him. He reluctantly turned his head to the diabolical portrait on the opposite mantle. It too held him, and he could feel the force of pushing himself away from the portrait. He took a deep breath, either from dismay or concern, nevertheless had a sensation he was not familiar with. He then addressed himself to the book. Once again the binding was beautiful. The leather had that rich ornate look which only leather can achieve with maturity. He went to the ribbon which he had book-marked his last reading. Yes, there it was; the new passage. He eased himself into the gentle chair and felt a comfortable position to start his reading of the second chapter "The Witch In The Everglades".

The days wandered through to the weeks and the weeks were captured by the months. As one month followed the seasons to another, the time once more approached. I was totally unaware of the anniversary, you might say, of the paintings of the portraits.

I resumed the full activities of day-to-day living and thought nothing more of it until once again I was sitting alone in the study, busy concentrating on the things that were important the day thereof, when it seemed like a flash of lighting had entered my head, with the aftermath of a clap of thunder, which blocked my actual being. I must have stooped forward in my chair as my head fell violently on the desk which took its impact.

Where am I? Who am I? What am I? All these questions came to mind as my mind focused and regained its presence of thought.

My God! I'm in a jungle. I feel so old. I feel like I must be a hundred or so.

Oh! Let me step out into the brightness of the day, from this dark pit in which I'm in.

My God! Have mercy on my soul.

Where am I?

As I walk towards the light that penetrates through the entrance, my first reaction confirms what my initial thoughts were. I was in a jungle, a heavily-treed swamp. That's right! It's a swamp. Of course, it's a swamp. The rivers, the smell of the earth, the moisture, the humidity, the oppressive heat; such as only a swamp, a stagnant cesspool can give forth. I am in the Everglades, where the new are born with the aim of life to live off the ones who had recently died. There are the smell of things, both animal and vegetable decaying in the heat of each and every day.

But where, oh, God, where? Then, it was like I answered my own question. I looked at my hands. They were long and thin, as well as being wrinkled and brown, like prunes which had withered in the long days out in the sun. I reached up to my face and that had the lines of age everywhere. They were deep as eternity itself. My nose and my cheeks had large warts. My lips were like thin slices of meat that aligned across a face that no one wished to look at. My hair, my God, it's long and straggly, like some poor animal;

mostly black with grey and white lines streaking across it, running like a river of darkness through its landscape waste.

I looked at what I'm wearing. They were rags. They have had their full days of wear long passed, their moment of glory long before my back saw them.

I tried to straighten up to look out into the swamp. On the contrary, I can't. My back is bent forward.

I am a hag. Yes, that's what I am. I am a hag. Oh, my God! How long have I been this way?

Then the answer came.

As I hobbled back to the hut, I looked around. Yes, I was not only a woman. I was a hag. Moreover, one of the worst with the aim of being put upon this blessed Earth. I was a Witch in the Everglades.

As I once more hobbled towards the small bench, then rested my weary body on its hard surface, I peered around my shack, my domicile. It had even scared me; for hanging from the walls, and if one could call it a roof, were the creepy, crawly things of the Everglades, the remaining skulls and teeth, dried-out parts, of what had once been the living things of the Everglades.

If it was a hearth, it was a poor imitation. Nonetheless, I guess, it must serve for my existence in this place so desolate to life itself and even more remote to any other living human being.

What have I done? Why am I removed from all others?

I sat in the shadows that were illuminated by the sheer light of the penetrating day. I regressed back . . . back . . . back. My thoughts moved back.

"Oh, yes, it's coming back to me," I muttered, "to me . . . Oh, no!"

I was one of the Seminole Indians. No, I am one of the Seminole Indians. I'm one of the ancestors of these proud people.

We were hunted down by the American soldiers. We were massacred whenever they found our villages, until we were forced deep into the Everglades to defend ourselves.

Yes, now I remember. The time was 1842-1843. I had no parents. My Father was killed by one of the raids of the Army and my Mother died giving birth to me, her only child. I was raised by the Elders of the village.

Oh, no. No. No. No. It can't be true. I know it's true.

I was born under an evil star. Though the villagers treated me well and the Elders tried to mend my ways, bad things happened. It was not my fault. Oh, yes, it was.

All I had to do was will my thoughts of revenge, of contempt of all the things to facilitate evil. If it was an animal, it would meet a violent death. If it was another child that I wished to play with, and they rebuked me or laughed at me, they would pay with their health. No, I had not reached the stage with the intention where life and death was in my palms at my will. Nonetheless, I could conjure up evil thoughts, spirits who exist in the night.

I was a night-child, not a day-child. I showed no enjoyment in the warmth of the day. Often at night, they would find me sitting, staring out into the darkness listening to the night-life of the Everglades. This is when I started to communicate with the evil ones who preyed on the living and their nightly quest for their life and their survival.

I guess . . . No. Yes. Yes, it was when I developed into womanhood and my menstrual period started, when my breasts became sensitive, then the aim of my powers increased. There's something about menstrual blood . . . No, it's about blood in which the evil ones enjoy the most. They grew stronger as my friends and my companions. As I became older, on the cycle of ovulation, they danced the dance of darkness with me.

Within years, maybe two at the most, the Elders of the village had finally reached the limit of their patience and tolerance of my behavior. The Elders held a Council and it was decided by one and all that I must leave the village; subsequently I must not contaminate others in our villages or other villages with my play-friends of the darkness.

The Elders decided, as a result, I must be taken to a remote area of the Everglades and there I should be isolated from all living the just and the good life. They took their dug-out canoes and searched for a place far away from all living things of the day.

Afterwards when they found this place, they built this shack, this dwelling; my home deeply hidden in the arteries of the unknown everglades. When they stocked it with sufficient food and essentials, they brought me with them and left me here. They told me hence I could play with my friends; but not to be a part of the good and the living of society, of the village, or of the human race. They told me they would come on each quarter of the year and feed me the essentials and clothing that I would require during my life on this Earth.

And so! Oh, God. Consequently, it came to pass and here I am; an old, old hag and they still come on each quarter of the season of the year. They do not come near me. Within the light of the day, they drop off flour, salt and coffee with cloth. The rest of it, I forage in the land of darkness and evil. I catch food of the Everglades whether its small crocodiles or snakes or birds, whatever is living in which I wish to feast upon.

Oh, I cannot remember what it's like to be with others. I cannot remember the village. It was so long, long ago. As a consequence, all I have now are my friends of darkness.

I do not know how old I am. I feel like I have lived forever.

Yet again, they come on the cycle of the anniversary of the ovulation, though it had ceased. Long since I can remember, we spend the days together and they teach me the new things of evil. They share their desires of hate and destruction. They told me of deeds they have performed for the evil ones who are even higher than them.

Their quest is always the same: to feast on the blood of others and to give the ultimate to the greater ones, the souls of those that they have feasted on. I, too, contribute to the greater ones. I, too, provide them with the feast of the souls. Not often, mind you. Furthermore, there is evil out there, out there where the white people live. There are evil thoughts and evil wishes.

There are a few who are bold enough, who have heard of my existence and know that somewhere deep in the Everglades I live. Not often, mind you. Nonetheless now and then, I get a visitor. One who has evil in his heart and revenge is his only relief. He usually brings me gifts like sugar and clothing. Some even bring me whiskey and tobacco. Those ones I give special attention to.

Their requests are always the same—revenge of another.

While they camp outside my little hut, I call upon my friends from the darkness of the night and together we weave a doll of revenge. We put the special items in which will perform the ritual as well as what has been requested and granted. Then, within two, three, not more than four days, the doll is finished, the exchange is made and the men with the evil hearts leave with the doll of destruction. Sometimes it's a woman, other times it's another man. Nevertheless the inevitable is always the same. They will meet a violent death, whether it is in a gunfight or whether they fall from a stairwell and break their neck. However, they will always die violently. That is what the doll's reward is to the one of vengeance. I have never, nor my friends, reneged on performing the act which has been requested.

Then, it is our turn. Of course, all of these visitors gave me a few tokens of pleasure. But, little do they know that those who seek revenge shall be revenged as well! For evil is complicated, and its ways are not understood. Like the opposite of good, evil has no conscience in taking more than its share.

Two years to the day that each visitor with the evil heart takes his doll away, my own special doll in which I have made of him is given to the greater ones to enjoy his soul. As a result, it's what is known as "pay-back time." All those who took the life of another, now my friends have their soul.

Oh, oh. Yes. The night is falling once more. It is my time to join my friends in the darkness. Ah, to be with them, and not alone, gives me the only pleasure which this existence has.

Oh, oh, the pain, my pain. Oh! I grasped my head as if it's going to topple off my shoulders. Oh! My body stooped and its form goes even further down on the bench. Oh, the pain, the pain, as I stooped forward.

At the same time as I hear myself moaning uncontrollably, I try to lift my head. I put all my strength on the desk and lift my head forward off the desk. I fall back into the great chair in which I'm sitting in. Once more I hold my head. It is pounding and violently throbbing.

Now with all the effort I can muster, I open my eyes. Oh, blessed be God. Blessed be the eternal life. I'm back in my office. I'm back in my library. I am back in my study. I am again too weak, far, far, too weak.

What seems like eternity, I wait holding my head. Afterwards, then with one hand I gently ring the bell for a servant to attend me. I'm too weak to speak.

Soon after my first servant enters the room he rushes out again and gets help. I'm literally carried to my bed where I stay for the better part of a week coming in and out of some kind of coma, the inducement of someone's subconscious taking over the conscious and then the conscious demanding the return.

Each day I seem to gain some strength and sanity. Oh, God, it's happened again. Oh! What a horrifying experience this is.

This time my wife and I sit after I recover and go through the steps of what has happened. Once is a nightmare. Twice is more than coincidence. Of what is this? What has caused this? What have I done or what has happened to me in my life when this is happening?

As I recover I am not content this time to place it on the shelf of my mind and leave it until it withers away. As my strength has gathered its full recovery, I now approach my regular physician and want some answers. He tells me he is a doctor of medicine, not a psychiatrist or psychoanalyst. He advises me that if I am obsessed with this kind of dream, as he calls it or an illusion that I could seek some advice from a more professional person in this field.

I bluntly come out and ask him, "Am I going crazy?" Then he laughs a laugh of security and says, "By all means, no; Of course not."

But somehow this tingling sensation in my gut does not relieve my mind's conviction of his truth.

It was well into two o'clock before Dr. Sebastian had finished the chapter and rang the bell for refreshments. The butler once more came and escorted him to what could have been a mini banquet with so many delights. The secretary, although he had eaten earlier, joined him for some of the refreshments. After a light conversation, the doctor expressed he had read the second chapter and was quite moved by what The Portraits had so far given him. He asked if it would be permissible to return back home a little earlier today rather than to start a new chapter which he was convinced he would not be able to finish and wanted to have the utmost involvement in each experience of the late Robert F. Edwards. Of course the agreement was made with the secretary, and without any further ado, the secretary asked when it would be convenient. The doctor asked if he could return to the study where he would just finish making a few of his notes, which he wanted to bring home with him. With both of them in agreement on this, once more the butler was called for and the doctor followed him back to the study. Sometime later, the doctor ring again for the butler to return and make arrangements to prepare the chauffeur for returning him home.

Without any hesitation, this was granted by the secretary and without further ado it was completed. Within the hour the chauffeur was driving down the long corridor to the highway and on to the freeway. Shortly after five o'clock, Dr. Sebastian bid the chauffeur goodbye and entered his house.

After the warm greeting from his wife and her asking how this day prevailed, he did not immediately reply; although he asked for a malted whiskey straight, then went into the parlor and sat down in his chair. When she came with the glass of whiskey, he asked her to sit so he could tell her some of the things he had experienced that day. With her glass of white wine and him with his malted whiskey, he took a larger than normal sip but seemed to have more control than he had on the previous day when he returned from the mansion.

"Oh my beloved, it was somewhat as the first meeting without the presence of His Lordship. However, once I got into the library of the late Robert F. Edwards, things proceeded very similarly. I did experience, one might say, a compulsive desire to look at both . . ." he paused for a moment, "both the Portraits before I commenced with the reading of the next chapter." He took another sip of his malted whiskey. This time he almost finished the two ounces which she had poured. Then, like a flash of lightning against the barren landscape, there was a pause in his mind followed by a loud clapping sound that follows a violent act.

He said out-loud, "Oh my God!"

"Yes my dear, what? What? What has happened?" she asked in concern.

"It's been exactly two weeks to the day I first went there."

After a long pause his good wife confirmed, "Yes, it is. Coincidence, isn't it?"

He finished the last ounce of his malted whiskey and went over to the decanter and poured another long shot into the waiting glass and took another sip before returning to his chair. He looked at her earnestly, "Is it?"

She smiled her warm, caring smile and replied, "You're not going to start getting superstitious at this stage in life, are you?"

He laughed his warm laugh and said, "Of course not, dear. You're absolutely right; just another coincidence, no less."

"Now, what was this one about?" she asked again.

"Oh, rather disturbing, my love. It was about a diabolical creature, obviously by the poorly-done Portrait". He wanted to say 'Evil' Portrait, however he corrected himself before the word came out. Then, on a second thought in his mind he added, I might as well say the 'Evil' Portrait which possessed the late Robert F. Edwards and tell my wife how I feel about this portrait. Nonetheless he would save this information for another time was his final thought on the matter. Now he started by telling her about the last chapter he read concerning a witch in the Everglades who possessed super-natural powers.

He then added, "If it has any credence, which somehow I have reason to believe it may not, this creature was of substantial age and her main purpose was to be isolated from other people. Nonetheless, now and then someone who wanted an evil deed done to another can always find some person to do the deed for payment of some kind. In this case, when the person got the witch to perform the evil deed, as well as paying her what she asked at the time, she agreed to start the act. When she performed the evil deed, it was not the end of the request. The person who asked for it to be done also, at some later date, would have sacrificed their soul to the devil on their death. A rather disturbing and diabolical event which probably would have caused the late Robert F. Edwards much despair and shock at this particular event. This concluded the day my love, with this behind me the secretary and I had some refreshments, then I returned home."

"I'm delighted to have you home, my beloved. I've missed you and hoped this one was going to be somewhat milder than your first one," she then replied.

"Well, you can see dear", the doctor added, "I'm nowhere near as nervous or . . ." he paused. "Well, I'm nowhere near as nervous, let's put it that way. Now, what should we be doing this evening to celebrate my return from The Portraits?" They both laughed hardly.

"Well, nothing quite as elaborate as last time, however it's better than the left-over's you had last night. I've prepared a salmon dish as the entree. After dinner I thought we could go to the theater tonight," she mentioned.

"Excellent choice my love, excellent choice," and so with that, the evening of happiness began and the two enjoyed each other's company as if they were newlyweds.

GENERAL IN OTTOMAN EMPIRE

—⚯—

THE DAYS WENT BACK to normal for Dr. Sebastian. The workload never ended and the long hours proceeded sometimes well into the evening, as his good wife would always be waiting with either a late dinner, or some light appetizers when he didn't want to have a full meal. His secretary went back and forth with His Lordship's secretary once more and the weeks quickly went into each other. His Lordship had taken a turn for the worst. His fragile health had deteriorated and all the staff at the mansion was more than concerned. They were diligently putting his health as their priority. After the secretary of His Lordship explained the fragile condition of His Lordship, this was related back to Dr. Sebastian who immediately sent a personal get-well greeting to His Lordship by courier. After what seemed to be almost a forgotten period of time of commitment, His Lordship recovered and his secretary resumed the endless business of making appointments and administrating the necessary agreements which were present and somewhat behind. Needless to say, one of them was Dr. Sebastian's re-appointment of coming to the mansion to continue reading The Portraits book.

It was ironic (or was it?), that is was one month to the very day the doctor had been there last. Unbeknown to the doctor, both his secretary and The Lordship's secretary agreed on the time. And so, once again, Dr. Sebastian, almost absent-mindedly this time, looked at his schedule to see the next appointment was slated for tomorrow to be going to the mansion. He knew well in advance that Lord Edwards III was not in adequate health to have an audience with him, let alone spend any time finding out his progress in The Portraits. It would only be the secretary who would greet him when he arrived. For a second time, it was almost like déjà vu. The chauffeur came at the same time, the greetings were the same, and of course, the drive to the mansion and then the doorman and at last the butler. All were as if it was a re-run of the times before.

The secretary once more greeted him in the aviary and after a refreshment of coffee and sweets; he was escorted in the same manner to the library. Once more the procedure took place as usual with the male servants producing, first the book of Portraits and then the key that would open up the contents for the next reading. With this procedure being completed, as before, the men left the room for Dr. Sebastian to begin reading the next chapter of the Portraits.

He quickly gazed around the room as he had done previously and it still had that musty air which never seemed to circulate, but lay heavy as dust upon the furniture. In addition to this, today there seemed to be a further chill in the air. He felt cold, even though he had his suit jacket on. He wished he had a sweater underneath his jacket. On the other hand, it seemed rather odd, as this morning when he left for the mansion, it was a warm summer day that was developing. He actually gave a slight shiver as he opened up the contents of the book to begin reading the next chapter.

Curious as to why this chill in the air, he walked over to the French windows leading out into the garden. Once outside, he immediately felt warm, and knew if things continued, it was going to be a hot day. Reassuring himself, he returned into the study only to find the air was definitely colder than outside. He knew without looking that this building did not have any air conditioning. In some discomfort, he returned to the chair and the contents on the table to commence his reading for that day.

As life would have it, the living must always go on and I am no exception to the rule. I have commitments. My day-to-day business is demanding. My life, in its social order, is demanding. I have many numerous things in which I must attend to or, they will undeniably attend to me.

Afterwards, even though I am plagued momentarily and regress back to these encounters, they cannot dominate my thoughts. I must return to what I have to do: to coexist in a standard of living in which I have and my family enjoys.

Furthermore on this note, I continue throughout the days that worked their way through the months and ever onward through the seasons. As the dates on the calendar indicate, not only the days were fast-approaching but the day of doom in my life, the anniversary of the paintings is now nearing. I am now more determined than ever to avoid the study.

I have my work brought to the atrium. For the next five days I will not go near my library. Whatever I need, I will insist one of my man-servants bring it to me. Absolutely under no circumstances am I going to set foot in there until after the anniversary of those paintings. I am going to be convinced once and for all, that if I am not present; I will not be captured into a nightmare of the past.

Significantly, as the days and nights fall to the day of mention which is now upon me, I become somewhat agitated, apprehensive and definitely edgy. And why not . . . ? Is it not human nature to try and overcome one's anxieties, only to increase them? Of course, I am now as obsessed with getting through the day and the night as not venturing into the study to see where the paintings are.

By the evening meal I have lost my appetite totally and ponder with my brandy over an open fire. I am in solitude of mind and thought. I'm presently about to retire, as I am alone with my thoughts. On the contrary then, almost as if in a trance, as if I was sleep-walking, hypnotized, oh, no, possessed, I walk to the opposite end of the wing hoping to enter into my boudoir. No, I returned to the study. I do not need the light, for the portraits—they need no natural or unnatural light, to seek out my soul.

I no sooner enter the room, and with the horror I know awaits me, I am struck down once more with the pain of a piercing, hot iron penetrating my mind. As the searing, burning effects my consciousness, I fall face down on the floor. I have no idea how long before, or when, I will recover. Though I stumbled around and found my way in the darkness of my mind I am now somewhere in a room I do not know. Where, or what place am I in? For all is dark and strange to me. Nothing is the same as I know it. Oh God, where am I, and who am I? Please Almighty God, help. Please, oh please, hear me, my God.

There was the knock on the door in which I responded to out of sheer recall and answered in a distinct voice, "Enter!"

It was when the door opened that so did my mind. I was sitting behind a desk, not one I recognized and neither was the room. It was plain and yet distinctively of authority. The figure that entered the room was dressed in a uniform. Though I was not familiar at the moment, I quickly established where I was and who I was.

Oh, Allah, divine human being of all who exist forevermore, where am I and who am I? These were the first thoughts which came to my mind.

I was now a General in the Ottoman Empire.

Now my head clears as if a fog is lifting from the night with the dawn and the mist parting on the light of day and so was the knowledge returning.

It is September the 16th, 1913. I am part of one of the greatest wars which will be recorded. In fact, it will become known as the "World War." It is the Balkan Wars. The expulsion, oh, my God, my heavenly Father, Allah, and the Prophet Mohammed, we are the civilized parts of this world that has ruled for over four hundred years as an empire, which is now being contracted. We, the brothers of Islam, the fathers of knowledge, the Prophet Mohammed, the Koran of the spoken truth of Allah, the Ottoman Empire is under attack by the infidels, the unclean, the unworthy.

Oh, Allah, what is happening to those who have served the great Madrassa of Medina, the fourth Vahideddin. Oh, merciful Allah, oh, my thoughts were of these, when the subordinate enters into my room and my mind.

"Oh, worthy General, I bring news of the front, of the battle that rages on with the infidels. My news is of great sorrow to you personally and to our beloved Madrassa and the Empire. We have suffered great losses and the enemy has taken great advances over the field of battle. Though our soldiers have fought gallantly, they have perished in their own blood."

I remain silent as if I existed but I did not exist, that I was and yet I was not. This messenger of death and despair continued. Though he was an officer of mine who I recognized, I stared beyond his eyes and beyond his figure.

I muttered, "Continue. What is the casualty count? What has the enemy gained and I have lost?"

He bowed his head as if he could not bear to give me the news.

"Oh, great commander, my General, it is your son, the Captain, who led the charge against so many of our foe."

My heart stopped, my mind glazed over as if some protective shield from destruction had given me protection. My voice was as steady as if I was on a parade square.

"Go on!" I commanded.

"He fell gallantly. Furthermore, his troops followed even after he fell to the endless fire of the enemy. They took the day in that part of the battle in honor of your fallen son, my General."

Somehow I heard my voice more than spoke it.

"Where is he now?"

There was a long silence, a deafening silence, one that penetrates the air and freezes all which is around it.

"He is still, my General, with the dead at the field hospital. I felt that you would want the news as quickly as I could provide it."

I answer in a strange voice, "It has been said. It has been done. You are dismissed!"

The moments which followed were in chaos, confusion, despair. In my mind I could not grasp my physical loss, my purpose of existence. My eldest, my love, my first-born, I have been told no longer exists in this world. He has gone from me and this world only to be returned to the Almighty Allah.

I bowed my head and clasped my hands over my head as if I could lift the thoughts with the intention of being delivered from them. As the moments passed and the hours moved, the reports came forth. The horrific losses of my gallant son with his brave men had suffered were enormous from the grueling blows of the advancing infidel forces. They were unmerciful and showed little of the word 'of quarter.'

It was then in my moments of grief that the captain who had come with the news of sorrow to my soul re-entered my office and my mind.

"Oh, my General, your son lies in the infirmary waiting your presence, if you so desire."

"Thus desire? What madness! What absolute lunacy can one want to see their first-born lying cold, wearing the mask of death? Nevertheless, alas, alas, I must fulfill what destiny has given."

Once more I dismissed the captain. At the present, once I have gained the strength of mind and body, I walk as one walks in their sleep or one who is already gone beyond and has become a zombie. I drag my feet, as though they are weights from hell, to where my son lies.

I reach the infirmary and drag my feet towards the form under the sheet which is on one of the beds. I go toward the part of the sheet where his face would be as he lies under the sheet on a hospital bed. His face is at peace; but it's cold like the icy hand of death itself. I touch his face and the life is no longer with it. I fall to my knees and the tears flow from my face like rivers which have no destiny or purpose. Some fall on the sheet which at this moment covers his beloved body. Others fall on his still gentle face.

My heart screams with the anger of a river of blood. My mind stands alone by itself from my soul. My body explodes with its inter-parts feeling an eruption of violence. My throat is raw as the flesh which has been torn away from my son's limbs. My mouth is like the great Sahara Desert sea sands. In addition to this, yet another pain flashes before me from my soul, the cries of the father of Hector in the Battle of Troy. What gods, regardless where or who they are, can show such vengeance upon a mere mortal who stands before them and looks down at his first-born, his child? Nay, no god or gods! It is a demon from hell whether it is that of Apollo who drags Hector around the encampment of Troy or these infidels who have destroyed the first of my loin, my first son, the one who was to inherit the lineage of my ancestors. My tears flow as if the river of sorrow can find no end to the screams from my body and soul.

I am helped to my feet by my orderlies and escorted back to my quarters. I sit alone in total grief. My mind floats to the time my eyes cast upon Omar, my son, my first child, my life.

As a consequence, then all the sorrow changed and twisted to form into another feeling, a feeling of hate with revenge, a passion stronger than the sorrow. All the professionalism of my soldiering was replaced by the barbarians and of what the bloodlust of revenge was in my body and soul. It built in me like the fire which rages beneath the Earth waiting to explode and throw its venom of lava upon the land above.

I heard somewhere in the distance of the back of my mind the sounds that surrounded me with another knock. It was my junior officers and my orderly.

Somehow I managed to mutter out of my total confusion of distant thoughts and new-found vengeance, "Enter! Enter as you will," in a voice that sounded unlike mine.

They entered my quarters and asked to share their time with me. I know it was for my sake and not for their need of company. After joining me the orderly prepared tea for us. We sat as equals and drank sweet tea with the Turkish heads. After we had spent some time and they did their best to console my spirit, I dismissed them.

There are a few times I have in the past indulged in opium which clouds my mind of thoughts that will not leave. This night was one of them. I reached into my private drawer and brought out the silver hand-engraved compartment which contained the white powder. I sprinkled it generously, liberally might be a better word, upon the remaining Egyptian apple tobacco. Afterwards, more in my thoughts I drew heavy on the water pipe. As Allah provides, there as does the opium forgives. The clouds that I wished to appear once more aided my thoughts.

Sometime during the night, there was another knock I was not present in mind to account for. As before, the white clouds of opium darkened the skies of my mind, and I found some form of peace. I have no idea when the orderly came who aided me to my bed.

It was in the morning, when a firm, muscular hand shook my shoulder that I stirred into consciousness again. The hand was from one of my officers.

"My General, though your sorrow is deep, our needs of command are great. May I aid and assist you in the days which lie ahead to get the orders of direction such as we so desperately need."

My head clears from the fog, the mist of the white powder which gave some form of forgiveness of the torture from my mind. I dismiss the officer as I informed him, "I shall be forthcoming to enter the briefing room."

I ring for the orderly to bring me fresh clothes. My uniform must be immaculate. I must show repose and discipline for what I am going to ask as a supreme effort of support from all my officers and every rank which falls under their command.

After bathing and dressing in a fresh uniform of my rank and my position, I then proceed to the briefing room. Though my mind is far from clear of what my heart and my soul possess in agony, I take command of the rank in which I own and the procedure I am going to ask of those who I command.

As I entered the room, all my fellow officers, junior in rank, stand at attention and salute me, then hail me, "El General!" "My General! ", as I return the salute and go to the podium.

"My fellow officers, my fellow citizens of the Empire, each and every one of us know that our enemy has delivered a serious blow to our line of defense. Our losses have been heavy."

I choked as I uttered 'losses' and each man who stood before me bowed his head. There was a moment of silence, for each officer knew my loss personally and one of their fellow officers who ranked high in their admiration, my beloved son, Omar, their Captain.

Once I was able to repose myself, "We are going to avenge those who have taken so many of us to the gates of Allah. We are going to take for everyone who has been sacrificed, take ten of theirs. Though it's a small token for the loss of our bravery and the quality of the blood we have spilt. Nonetheless, it shall be done; for this is the word and the wishes in which I ask of each and every one of you from this day on."

With this, I summoned them to the map room. After extensive briefing on our defense lines and our repositioning of the holding the territory what we still possessed, understanding the full significance of the reconstruction of our second front, I asked them to return to the briefing room.

"At this present moment, I understand where we are and where we will be and the losses we have received, both personally and to the Empire, but we shall avenge the Infidel. This is the plan and we will go forth. Tonight, I wish us to muster a false second front attack, full barrages of artillery, continuing for the next forty-eight hours. I wish the most alert and most skillful of commandos to be brought into as many groups you feel required capturing and bringing back as prisoners the highest ranking officers from their headquarters."

"Once this is completed I will give each and every one of you the maximum of seven days to reconstruct your forces for a major assault against the infidels. If you wish to call it vengeance, let it be said. If you wish to call it a counterattack, let it be done. Nevertheless, I will have my vengeance upon those who have spilt our blood."

I paused. I could not speak any longer. My throat closed as though a hangman's knot had found my throat. I bowed my head and I could feel my eyes become puddles of water, though I fought and gasped as if a man dying from his last breaths. Slowly, I composed myself once more. I looked upon my officers, ranking from majors down to lieutenants.

"Let it be said. Let it be done. Let Allah fulfill what I have asked for, dismissed."

They saluted me and then said, "Our General's wishes are our commands. They will be fulfilled by one and all of us."

We all left the room and went to do what had to be done.

As the night followed, so did the white powder and the water pipe which found a soul in total despair. I returned to the mortuary and held my son, my first-born, the purpose of my life, and the dreams of my ancestors' futures in my arms. I wept. I wept with sorrow as I'd wept with joy when he was first given to us.

By the second day, my wishes had been fulfilled. We had not only been successful in our bombardment creating a false counterattack, we had mustered the infidel leaders into their map rooms with their high-ranking officials gathered around like a flock of sheep.

Our commandos had done well. They had captured many. Furthermore, to my delight and surprise, it was not just one nation's officers. We had managed, with the skill in which we possess, to capture the English, French, Italian and Russians. Though they formed a sheltered group of officers from the men in the front lines, each and every one of them held a position higher than those who they forced to give their lives. The highest rank was a British Colonel and the lowest was a captain in the Russian Army, probably more of an advisor, or a communiqué, from the Russian forces.

I then called my men, my officers, back into the briefing room.

"What you are going to hear and witness is my decision. I have abandoned the etiquette of war. I have returned to the principles of violence in which accompanied the warriors of our past. What I am going to tell you may shock you. However, it will be done. I am going to bring these officers in to witness the torture and execution of their fellow soldiers, the men under their command."

"When this is completed, I am going to demand the commandos return these men, these officers, so they can tell all who I am, 'the butcher of Edel'. I will no longer be known as 'The General' of this front. I will be known as the person who has no mercy on an infidel. Shows no quarter for what he has taken from me and the blood of the innocents of my homeland, the fruit of my loins. I am going to avenge all of those who have fallen in Allah's name."

There was a silence that penetrated the room.

Then in unison, there was a roar, "Our General, your word is our wish. Your command is to be obeyed."

With this I saluted them.

"Dismissed"!

I had my orderly prepare a bath and a crisp new uniform. I had my junior officers muster the highest ranking officers of the captured group to stand in the midday sun. I wanted their uniforms to smell of their sweat. I wanted them to feel as dirty and unclean as their souls when I was to first greet them. I wanted to show them how a civilized officer lived. These barbarian pigs were going to witness their demise.

After six hours in the midday sun, they looked and smelt like the swine they were. I had them brought in to a briefing room. The first four in number were the British Colonel, the French Major, the Italian Major and the Russian Captain. I had them then bound to their chairs, both legs and arms behind them.

Facing them was a long table with chairs which would accommodate twenty or more in which were facing directly across from them. There was, of course, an officer as well as two guards on each side of the prisoners. Yes, officers they were and prisoners they are.

I entered the room almost as if I was an emperor. My uniform was crisp and immaculate. There was not even a crease, let alone a blemish from head to foot in my appearance. I looked as though I was prepared for a portrait rather than an encounter.

The ranks of the prisoners before me smelled of their own beastly sweat. Their uniforms displayed their rank as well as their filth.

I walked casually with a confidence and an air of cruelty to the long tables that were placed before them. The empty chairs were ahead of me.

I smiled as my swagger stick was held tightly under my right arm.

"I wish to introduce myself to you, distinguished officers of the opposing force."

My voice had every dripping moment of sarcasm and contempt in it. There was no mistake even though they may not comprehend what I had said. They knew it was a sneer against what they were.

"I am General Mohammed Caliph. I am the commander-in-chief of this line under the direction of my beloved Mehmed VI Vahideddin of the Ottoman Empire. What I am going to give you to witness is . . . ," and I paused, and then looked into each of their faces, "is the horror. Yes, gentlemen, the horror of war. This is what we have gathered for today and what we witnessed yesterday and the day before. However, today you are going to witness with me the horror of dying."

In the midst of this, I had my soldiers bring in twenty mixed prisoners of each and every nationality. They ranked as low as privates and went right up to lieutenants. Each one of them was escorted by two of my soldiers, and then tied to a chair by the waist and the legs.

I walked back and forth as though I was some animal stalking, waiting, pacing until the prey was in place and the moment was right.

It must have been an unnerving moment for the enemy's officers. On behalf of the senior officers, the only one who wished to make his presence known was none other than the British Colonel.

"My dear Sir, I wish you to know that we are to be treated as officers. It is under the Articles . . . ," and he never got the word out "War" for as his voice gave presence to the room, my swagger stick made its mark across his face immediately below his right eye. I returned my swagger stick under my arm as the eyeball fell like an egg in which was broken for an omelet down the side of his face. He was feeling the wetness and the moisture of his lost eye with blood on his face. Nevertheless, the shock would relieve him of the agony he would experience momentarily.

I smiled and then said, "Listen and pay attention. I wish not for you to discuss things. I wish you to learn about things that very soon you are going to witness."

I left the room when one of the junior officers of my army summoned an orderly with bandages and sedation to give to the colonel of the British forces. Once he was conscious of his loss as well as being in control of his pain, I returned.

"Ah! Gentlemen we meet again. Next, let me show you what war is, what the horror of war can do. Let there be no mistake . . . what you see today is the beginning of what will be tomorrow."

I turned to the twenty men who were strapped to their chairs and nodded to the soldiers who controlled their lives behind them.

"Let it begin! Let these infidel officers see how their men die."

With what was preordained, the soldiers of my army, one holding the shoulders of the victim or enemy and the other placing their hands on the table, quickly and securely nailed the enemy hands to the table. Once their hands and arms were completely immobilized by the nails securing them to the tables, their officer's eyes were wide open with horror.

I paced back and forth once more, as some of the younger men let out screams of pain as their hands were nailed securely to the table. The ones who could not stop screaming, I had gagged.

I turned to the officers with the benevolent smile of a demon who was enjoying a bloodlust blended with hate.

"Now in addition to having your attention . . . let me continue before I have any more distractions." I looked at the British Colonel who was doing his best to not pass out with his own pain.

I turned my back to the officers and nodded to my soldiers. They produced long, thin slithers of bamboo which they took and placed under the fingernails of these victims. Once the fingers on all hands were extended by the bamboo slithers I had them light the flames of the dry kindling. As the flames danced, the hands squirmed with the agonizing pain as they were nailed tightly to the table. More screams arose from the less brave and determined men. Now more throats were silenced by the gags around their mouths.

Once this had been completed, I paced back and forth as someone in a trance bordering on madness, filled with hate and a lust for vengeance. I stopped and looked at the officers of the opposing force. They stared with almost a blankness of disbelief.

Then I turned to the victims and my soldiers and nodded once more. Now they took large tweezers and removed the fingernails and the remaining parts of the bamboo splinters.

By this time, there was not one of these soldiers of the enemy forces who had not been gagged, for their screams had joined their comrades. There was a muffled sound of moans along with some regurgitation of fluid from their throats.

I did not feel compassion. I did not feel remorse. I did not feel anything but hatred for those who had destroyed the greatest empire, the longest-standing civilization in this period of chaos, these barbarians, these untouchables who reeked of sin and corruption.

Was it not Allah who had first given the word to Mohammed to forfeit the fermented juice, so that the mind would not be clouded and corrupted? Was it not Mohammed's teachings of the Koran that had brought the huge expansion of the Ottoman Empire? Was it not the justice and the culture of this Empire that spread enlightenment from its origin, like a beacon of light with hope for humanity and mankind?

They had not only taken my beloved son, but they were destroying the light of civilization. Though I did not have any compassion for those who were withering in agony, Allah has given us mercy. Furthermore, I, too, must show mercy.

I turned once more and paced back and forth looking into the hollow horror of the officers strapped to their chairs. I knew in their minds they wanted to say something, nevertheless fear controlled their lips.

I smiled a smile of someone who was diabolical, someone who was possessed by evil of thoughts and mind. Nonetheless, yet I spoke of Allah. Oh, Allah, Oh Allah, forgive me.

I faced the victims who were strapped to their chairs and nailed to the table.

"Let Allah show mercy upon you and yours."

I looked at my soldiers and nodded once more. Their long and sharp knives removed the heads of those who were suffering and placed them between their nailed hands. The dorsal jerked but the mind was no longer attached. There was a muffled scream of horror from the officers who had witnessed the total destruction of their men.

I gave them time to soak in the horror of what they had witnessed before I addressed them.

"At this moment, you know what the horror of war is. I am going to have you returned to your quarters. I want you to tell all of what you witnessed today, for this is the beginning. It is not the end of my vengeance against you, the infidels, the evil ones, the ones who have destroyed the light and hope of civilization."

I walked out.

I was informed soon afterwards that the officers, including the wounded English Colonel, were returned safely to their officers' quarters on the opposing force.

Within days there was a massive counterattack under my wishes. However, I was not longer there for I returned to my quarters at this time in the evening in full despair. I felt the pains and the hollowness with the emptiness of a soul who has departed from the enclave of its body.

Once more I reverted back to the white powder and the water pipe. I sat quietly consuming the aroma of the Egyptian apple tobacco with the strong opium from Afghanistan then waited for the white clouds to form in my mind.

The next thing I can recall was my manservant hovering over me and calling for help.

Oh, God, God, I've returned from the night of horror. I'm back in the land of the living. My breathing is labored. I cannot stand. I am literally carried back to my quarters, my boudoir. My dear wife rushes to my side in a total panic when she is informed. I am far too weak to respond. I can barely breathe. I am in agony. I am barely alive.

Of course, my doctor is summoned and comes immediately to my side. He gives me sedation and examines me then assures me at this time, if I did not have such a strong heart, yes, I would not have survived. He is bewildered but I am too weak to express anything other than gratitude of his presence.

Once again the days drift through. Then like the past, within a week, I have recovered. Yes, I have recovered from what?

No, I'm not normal. Now I realize I am possessed. It is not a nightmare. It is not ones experience. I have reconciled nowadays I am possessed. Yes, it is the Portraits.

Without hesitation for the third time of the anniversary of their creations, I ventured into another time, another place and, above all, another person.

As I recover, I have returned to the doctor for both a mental and physical examination. It is remarkable that my health has resilience in so far as it does, especially under these experiences. Nevertheless, I am blessed. I then asked the doctor for his advice. He is not only my physician, he is my friend. In addition to after thirty some odd years, he knows my secrets and my health better than my confessor.

He advises maybe I could seek a psychiatrist or someone who delves into explanations of paranormal behaviors or schizophrenia or some other mental disorder. I take his advice wisely and with prudence. But, I know my doctor and friend is no wiser than I am in what is happening.

After many sessions with different specialists and those also who deal with the paranormal, they all dabble with their own thoughts and expressions of what might be transpiring in my mind. They give some feeble explanations of why I am being self-induced, almost into a hypnotic trance, on the anniversary of the paintings. I take their advice and probably welcome it even though in some ways I doubt it.

Dr. Sebastian looked down at the page he just finished and regressed back to the contents of this chapter. His thoughts first went to the General and the great loss of his son, but then as he reviewed his thoughts more thoroughly he couldn't help but think of the many aspects of war. Dr. Sebastian had many degrees and one was being a historian, so he was well aware of the conflicts between man, nations, and culture's, to say nothing of religions. As words escalated into arguments and arguments went from that stage onto hostile actions; conflicts were inevitable.

His thoughts went right back to the time when the cavemen would fight over a water-hole, or some other important part of their day-to-day living, to the modern-day wars which we experience now. Men who fight these conflicts lose their lives and the people they are fighting it for are losers and winners but are never successful. People fail to realize that war, no matter whether a war of words at home, or blood being spilt on the battlefield for principal—there are no success stories, only failures. He had read on numerous occasions where war in a situation helped raise an Empire or civilization to greater success than their opponents, nonetheless he always knew deep down in his heart that if these two opposing forces had worked together to create and invent other methods than those of war, how great civilization would be today.

His thoughts drifted on in this direction, only for him to lift his head to glance at the diabolical portrait. Once his eyes gazed upon this portrait, he realized there was a lot more to war. It went deeper than just a personality, or a desire of one group of civilized people to destroy another; it was the character of the leader who wished his legacy to be written in blood. As he looked at this portrait, he understood that evil still walks among us.

He forced himself to find the bell to ring for the butler. Shortly thereafter the butler knocked and with the usual commitment of arrangements, both Dr. Sebastian and the butler made their way down the hall to the front door where the chauffeur was waiting to take Dr. Sebastian back to his home domicile.

His wife was waiting as usual with her warm smile and asking, "How was your day, darling?"

He put his arms around her and said, "I think I could have a glass a wine before I should tell you anything."

With this, she quickly released herself from his embrace and replied, "I'll be back shortly, see you in the living room."

It was just moments before she returned with two glasses and a fine bottle of Beaujolais wine. Once they clicked the glasses and found themselves comfortably sitting across from each other, she asked, "Well, are you ready to tell me now?" He was somewhat hesitant. "As you know, it was one of my days that I went to the mansion to read another chapter of the Book of Portraits."

"Yes, dear. You told me this morning," she replied.

He took a deep breath and then another large mouthful of wine. "I guess one would have to say that it was the less appealing portrait's chance to possess the poor writer," he added. "May I have another glass of wine before I give you a quick report of what's transpired in this chapter?" he asked.

Without hesitation, his good wife poured them both another glass of wine. He took another rather large mouthful from the second glass and then started. "Well dear, you know how much I hate anything to do with war and this was all about the day-to-day lives of what happens in extreme cases of war."

She looked somewhat puzzled; nonetheless he felt she still comprehended what would lie ahead.

"It's about the Ottoman Wars and a general who had just lost his son in a great battle that the Turkish soldiers were not successful in winning. It's about his great sorrow as a father and his vengeance as a soldier. I could go into greater detail, my dearest . . . , but it would neither serve you with a greater understanding of this chapter and it would only make me regress back to the evils of war." "Enough said, my darling. Now, please join me, for I prepared you a very pleasant meal," she acknowledged.

"May I be so bold as to ask what it might be?" he replied.

"You are only moments away from looking at the surprise yourself, so I will not spoil it with vocabulary," she replied. They both laughed and went into the dining room to enjoy their meal and a wonderful evening together as two people truly in love.

THE SCHOLAR

—⚊⚊—

Dr. Sebastian was busy as usual at the Museum. He had not forgotten about the Book of Portraits, but on the other hand, he had not put it as a high priority for his next encounter of reading another chapter. In fact, he had not done any follow-up whatsoever, as he was given the impression that it would be his Lordship's secretary who would make the next appointment in unison with his own staff.

He gave this no more thought, until his own secretary informed him that if it was possible, another appointment at the mansion could be arranged for next week. He confirmed the appointment would be adequate for his schedule and thanked her for her continual efforts to coordinate the times and places he was required to be at.

As time waits for no man, it definitely did not for Dr. Sebastian. The balance of the week flew by quickly. He had not forgotten about the appointment to the mansion, but was a bit taken back when the chauffeur arrived to drive him to the mansion. He muttered to himself, 'Oh! How time flies . . . Where did my morning go?'

Once in the limousine, they continued the route which had been taken the time before and in due course, they drove up the winding road to the mansion itself. As usual the doorman was there to greet him, and then the butler who escorted him to the library of the deceased writer, Robert F. Edwards. The two male servants assisted him. One got the Book of Portraits and the other servant retrieved the key from a hidden area behind the desk. He was asked if there was anything else he required. Do. Sebastian confirmed that everything he needed was available and he would ring when he was finished. Once the two servants and the butler left, Dr. Sebastian opened the book and looked at the contents. 'Ah! Yes,' he said under his breath,' a most interesting chapter, I assume,' and with this he started to read The Scholar.

As the months drift by, I come to different alternatives with the paintings. I now am becoming obsessed with their presence. I decide furthermore, I am going to destroy them as my best option. However, to my absolute horror, as soon as the paintings are removed from my library, I fall violently ill. I still order the paintings off the wall and somehow I am reluctant to have them destroyed. Nevertheless, at least, I have them put into storage hidden from the presence of any human being.

As soon as this is done, I fall into a coma. My condition worsens with each passing day. Out of desperation, my wife cannot stand it anymore. I have become little more than a vegetable, just waiting to exit life and presence from this world. She demands the paintings be replaced back over their original hearths.

To everybody's total disbelief of reality, in less than twenty-four hours I have recovered. I am out of the coma. I am feeling better. As well, within two days I am back to being normal. Ah, normal. What is "normal" anymore? My soul, my dreadful existence of life currently is nothing more than being controlled by the paintings of The Portraits.

I do not need psychiatrists. I do not need fortunetellers or soothsayers. I am possessed. How I am possessed, with the aim of God to answer and maybe to share when I leave this planet, this Earth, this existence.

What I fear most is what lies ahead on the anniversary of the paintings, the portraits. Oh, what experience awaits me on their anniversary? I try, like somebody in solitary confinement, to reminisce of happier moments, of a day of freedom, which I had experienced not so long ago.

Though the days are normal—what's normal?—when one waits as the calendar flicks the moments away. Then the inevitable, the month, the week and then, oh God, then the day. I will not fight it . . . for it is as much of me as I am of it.

My household knows what has to be done and what I face. What they do not know, and neither do I, is where. Nevertheless, we do know when. Before this day is finished, I will now be possessed by one of the portraits. No, I will not lock the door or try to hide like someone in an open field.

I return to my library to experience what lies ahead and to wait for my fate of what journey lies before me.

I suppose it is like life and death itself. Once one accepts one is dying, one can cope with the journey ahead. I find instead of forcing my strength of resistance, I am going to be subservient. I go to the large leather Chesterfield stuffed with horse-hair in my den. I sit patiently, as comfortable as possible, in its fine décor. I will lie here or slump forward in comfort rather than to fall like a stone on the floor, as I had in the past.

Then, as before, it strikes without warning. The pain, the flashing of light, the roar of an untamed ocean rushing against the cliffs of resistance of my mind breaks my will and darkness appears as I go through a vortex into another time.

Ah, where, oh, where am I? Moreover, my God, who am I?

As the mist which surrounds my mind and my soul, to say nothing of my body, dissipates, I look upon myself and the surroundings.

I am in China, oh so long ago, when the 'Terra Cotta Army' formed ten thousand strong. The dynasty of the emperor was powerful and demanding of all who served him.

Ah, yes, I am in one of the southern provinces. My age, ah, look at my hands. Yes, I am young, well, and maybe forty-plus. I touch my face. It is smooth, hairless. My eyes are flat like slits in paper. I feel my robes, my clothes, my garments. They are of a fine silk. Where am I?

As I raised myself from my lotus position and made my way to the shutters which have closed out the light of day and gently opened them, hoping against hope, I have found the kind of place to exist.

Yes, it is a beautiful courtyard with fine ladies sitting amongst the fragrance of flowers while the children play at their feet. It is a large courtyard. From my position behind the shutters I have no way of knowing the numbers which may well be up to ten. The children range from all sizes, from infants crawling to young girls reaching puberty. It is a beautiful sight. It is a peaceful sight. It is rewarding to see some happy faces on the children.

I turned and then looked at my dwelling. It is small but comfortable with an elegance of someone important or in the presence of someone who is important.

As the clouds dissipate from my mind and the fog lifts from my memory at this moment, ah, yes, yes, it is coming back to me. Oh, yes! I am Wu Fung, son of the great Fung family who served . . . . Served? Oh, no. No, we have fallen on sad times. Our josh has turned to darkness.

Of course, it is coming back to me now. My great Father, oh, Great Minister of the Interior, the enlightenment of the mighty Emperor. Oh, Father, Father.

How could such a wise and seasoned man of greatness make the mistake of not pleasing the Emperor? All our lands, our holdings, our great wealth have been taken away, including his life. Ah, no, no, no. It cannot be. Ah, surely, it is true.

Out of our great clan, only I and one of my brothers have managed to escape the wrath of the Emperor. It was only by the risk of one of our beloved servants that I was able to escape the great city, the 'Forbidden City,' under the mask of a peasant drawing a cart with a coolie hat and rags to wear. Oh, the hard journey working away further and further south while the storm of the Emperor grew stronger and took with it all that displeased him in its wrath. It was in Chia Yun that our beloved servant bid us to go separate ways.

We were educated people of the highest rank. We were one of five families who displeased the Emperor. As a consequence, at this instant, we had nothing more than our lives.

Our beloved servant gave us two instructions. One of us was to go as far south as Shanghai and the other to go even further into the Kunming. It mattered not to either one of us which was to go where. We hugged each other, my brother and I, which more likely was for the last time. I had chosen to go to Kunming and my brother to Shanghai. We hoped with the help of the gods and the kindness of what was left of life, to be able to find work or some position to fill.

As a result, on my journey currently I was alone. I struggled endlessly, as some pilgrim, not knowing what pilgrimage he sought but unquestionably a sanctuary was needed. The days moved forward and rotated with the nights. Then I reached a large city. Since I could do scribe work, and undeniably was more than educated to a fault, I had to be willing to do subservient tasks to hide my great skills. For if they would question me and ask to see my documents, though none would be demanded of lower servants, still upon discovering that I had no documents of such skills, I would be arrested and the wrath of the Emperor would breathe once more down upon my family. He would extinguish my existence like all others before my brother and me.

Therefore, I took on menial tasks of transcribing legal documents. It provided me with the substance of life and a small shelter. One might say the *yin* and the *yang* of my life was starting to show harmony. I impressed the benevolence of my benefactor by the quality of the work in which I produced. Though he questioned me on many subjects and many riddles, my wisdom and determination for self-preservation was forthcoming. My answers were, like his riddles, a question within a question, an answer with no answer. Nevertheless, my work and skills made it prudent for him to continue the services with his meager remuneration.

The years found their way and his understanding of my secretiveness and my quiet, reserved ways of life became accepted. It was then that, after many years of being a good servant, he became a good master and drew up documents for a new existence for the rank which I would hold. I would hold the rank of a scholar of the arts of the 4th degree. This would permit me to seek a better life and a greater remuneration. I will always be grateful to my benefactor for my life and for how he improved upon it. My joss was lifting the clouds of darkness and the shadows of the dawning of happiness was upon its rising.

I believe it was in the Year of the Dog, however it was a long time ago, when my benefactor called me to his chamber and smiled as an older man smiles upon a child who he is pleased with. I knelt before him and kowtowed.

When he said, "Rise," I lifted myself into a kneeling position with my ankles stretched backward to support the weight of my thighs.

"I have news which will enhance your life," Master Hsueh Pan smiled. "One of the great magistrates, Lord Cheng, of this district is in need of a tutor for his children and to aid and assist them in the skills in which will be required by the status of his family. Many of his children have reached the age in which time is of the essence. You will be respected there. Your life will be better than it is here. Before three moons have lifted and passed in the sky, one of his servants will come and take you and your belongings to your new home. I have done all I can for you, my child."

"Oh wise and benevolent foster parent, I will always be grateful for my life in which you have given it meaning and purpose. May the gods bless your house and all of your children's, children's children . . . for I, a poor soul, who has suffered greatly, you have become my salvation. There are no words in any language to facilitate the gratitude in which I have for my life and for your continued benevolence in making it worthy of existence."

Therefore, true to his word, a male servant, accompanied in a fine cart with horsemen and a carriage, came to fetch me with the small bundles of belongings that I had accumulated over the years. After three days and four nights, at the beginning of the dawn of the fourth day, the great city that this magistrate ruled over came into view. Like so many cities, it had a large protective wall protruding around its perimeter with turrets at each end; of course a great gong at one end and bell at the other, signaling as a result the great gates were open for one and all to enter.

As the cart rumbled through the gates, I looked in amazement, observing the wealth and prosperity I could determine in my first moments here. My benefactor had been true to his word. This was a very rich magistrate and with great power.

My mind was divided like the day is to the night. One was seeking a much better life and the other the darkness of my past. I knew this magistrate would have no qualms, or even second thoughts, if he thought I was a refugee or a fugitive from the great

Emperor; to turn me over to those that would bring about my end. However, with my new documents looking as authentic as any which could be produced anywhere in China, I was sure my silence of the past would remain my secret of the present.

On top of a great summit was the magistrate's palace. Ah, yes, it was a palace. It was more than a mansion, though they call it a mansion. It, too, had large, decorative walls in which surrounded its exterior. As we entered into one of the open courtyards where the servants' vast quarters were, I was amazed at the number of doors which were assigned to servants. It would be impossible at this time to even guess the numbers that were needed to support and look after the needs of this great magistrate.

This was a great moment in my life. No, it was not what I had been raised as a child in the wealth and prestige of the Forbidden City of eternal hope and happiness. Nevertheless, I recognized the wealth which had been accumulated either honorably or with conniving. Lord Cheng was definitely in favor of the Great Emperor Himself.

I was shown to my quarters which were, as they are today, comfortable and rewarding, looking out on to the garden of peace and the children which I would teach the knowledge that I have. I was treated and elevated to a place of importance in the household of Magistrate. As the days continued the doors of the great mansion opened to me more with the supervision and guidance of different servants who had access to these parts of the quarters.

A moon had come and gone before my duties were explained. Then, as if I was to enter into the sanctum of a god, I was dressed and prepared in the garments to which would be appropriate to my station while being in this mansion. The day of being presented to the magistrate was upon me.

I felt a weakness of fatigue and dizziness, a lightness of head in which one could only feel when one is breathing hard and yet the air is not being received. I worried that I would give something away, something that would displease the moment of his assessment.

After being received and kowtowing then waiting for an endless period of my life, he said, "You are the new tutor of my children, my heritage. Tell me more about your skills and what you can contribute to my house."

I lay prostrating myself before the magistrate in his great hall. I did not look up, but had my head buried firmly against the tiles. He spoke in a low, growling voice, however at the same time, non-threatening. He asked me questions of my educational abilities and what philosophers I had studied, what economics I knew, what political structure I was aware of, what astrology and other sciences of alchemy and anything to do with the academic world. He never asked of my family's name, or my background. Nor did he question what my intentions in life were. I could not help, even in this kowtowed position, but feel the intention this magistrate, this ruler of this state, this province, had wisdom unto himself.

For, if he had asked me questions about my family, I could not have denied him the answers and he would have then shared my great fear of being discovered and his family would have perished like mine. As he had not asked, he had no way of knowing. It was the same as what my intentions were: simply to survive and to endure another day in exile with another day of life.

It seemed to me an eternity, but was merely a matter of a short time that I was in the great hall. I waited in silence for the next question, although it never came. Instead there was a clap of his hands and the mighty doors to the great hall opened when two of his servants entered. They kicked me, gently, but still the same, to make my way up and all three of us backed our way out, bowing to the great magistrate. I was then informed, by a private servant, immediately I had been elevated to the position of scholar throughout the mansion. Now I would have the privilege and access to most of the great parts of the mansion, with, of course, the exception of the great hall, the magistrate's private quarters, and without saying, his wives' and concubines' quarters. All else would be mine to explore, be present at any given time of day or night. Also those there would respect me and my wishes.

I was then escorted to my new quarters which, to me, were astonishing. They had the elegance and breeding not of the same quality or grandeur as my home of the past in the forbidden quarters of the city of the emperor; however just the same, they were breathtaking and showed presently even in the provincial outpost, there were different classes of people: those who ruled, and those who were ruled. I, too, had servants now, and my wardrobe had changed to the position of a scholar, of a learned person.

In the days that followed, my servants introduced me to the different parts of the great mansion, everything from the massive kitchens in which supplied the continuous and endless varieties of gourmet foods to appease the ones in favour, to the stables, to the work areas and to what would be my teaching areas. I found from my servants now the great magistrate was in his sixtieth year and, by all accounts had relatively good health. He had a zeal for life and a passion for love, physical and otherwise. The arts were something unknown to him, but the administrative, sciences and even philosophical views, were as keen to his middle eyes as his vision of the future was for his dreams.

His children at this time, though many, were limited by only six of the male gender. The other fourteen were of the female sex. For the female gender he had little other than to show them the breeding and the protocol with etiquette of higher courts in the more affluent provinces, and of course, in the Forbidden City itself. For his boys, the oldest being ten, this was a dynasty he was building for them, to educate them to accept the responsibilities in which he would pass down to them and recommend to the provincial governors who came to visited.

For this reason, the days past, the months found their way, the seasons moved from each other and the year of the Dog vanished, only for my total amazement, how soon it returned. How could over so many moons have passed without me realizing? By now the young boy of ten was twenty-two. The children of the magistrate had swollen under his groin to thirty-eight. I had never had a desire to take on a wife, or as far as that goes, a concubine, though many were offered to me from time to time. I had always managed to decline. One might say it was for many reasons, nonetheless when it came to the final decision; I could never put another human's life into the danger of being associated with me and the death sentence of the Emperor. So, I enjoyed the mansion with all except the sexual fulfillments that accompanied it.

I was not only the scholar; now I was the chief advisor of the magistrate. It was more than an employer-employee relationship; it was more than a master and servant association, it was two men who shared visions and looked to the future. I had found a friend in the magistrate, though he continued to never ask of my family name, nonetheless he knew it as well as I did. He knew of my past as well as I did, however though the words were never uttered or spoken by either one of us, he protected his future, his family and their dreams.

I should maybe, for the sake of no other, share some of the experiences of these last twelve years. Some were extremely happy moments, like when another son was born and how it would elevate that wife's position with the wives and concubines, when she would always have more favours and privileges for producing a male. Or the great celebrations in which took place when the magistrate again had won prestigious moments over his peers and was accelerated with honours by his elders.

There were sad moments. One in which I should mention was a young girl, barely into puberty. I have never been allowed to share the reason why she was a gift from her parents to be a concubine of the great magistrate. However, on the night of conception, her virgin flower did not open and he felt that this was evidence of his not being the first to penetrate her. He immediately cast her out of his quarters and the next day they found her hanging. She had brought shame upon her family and she disgraced his bed.

Another unhappy moment in which I can recall was the punishment I witnessed, not that long ago, maybe a year and a half, not two though. There were three brothers. They were what one would call unreliable in their duties and had no respect for others. They had been recommended by quite a few of the senior servants of the magistrate. Not only had they been tardy with their duties, they were known to continuously go to the village and buy large jars of wine. Their faces would turn red and all knew what they had been doing. They would scoff and become belligerent. However, the day they stole to facilitate their needs of the wine, this was more than the other servants would cover for them. Consequently, on this day one of the senior servants informed the magistrate.

The punishment itself has always remained in my mind. The three men were brought into the great hall by three servants and after all of them kowtowed to the magistrate, he clapped his hands and six more servants entered the room. Now, each man was escorted on either side by a servant, while the third servant carried what looked like a small paddle. It could have been even used as a large spatula for stirring. The magistrate then once more clapped his hands as I sat below his throne in a lotus position.

The servants with this paddle removed the lower garments of the three brothers. The other servants on either side quickly made them bow into a position almost close to touching their toes. Then the punishment started. At first it almost looked like a game with a swing of each paddle on each buttocks being applied in a rhythmic motion. Not large swings, au contraire, exceptionally small, but continuous in a rhythmic movement. These burly men stood their ground and the punishment was one hundred paddles each. Long before midway, the men were moaning and muttering in pain. By three-quarters of the way, their buttocks had become swollen and piercing red as scarlet, and then the moans became screams. Long before the hundredth stroke arrived on their buttocks, the cheeks had burst with blood and it spilt upon the tiles as the men screamed and screamed, begging for mercy.

Of course, there were a few unpleasant times. However, on a more happy and memorable moment, not only had the elder son reached adulthood, but some of the others had been accepted to the great college. It was the first major step to becoming a magistrate and then onto a governor. The old magistrate was nowadays beside himself with joy. He continued with every courier's news of his sons' progress with success in their education in which I had once provided, to celebrate with great gusto, along with feasts which would last for weeks. It was always a good time for everyone, not only currently in the mansion, for the colossal abundance of food to facilitate the feast was provided along with the delicacies that went with them, were provided from great distances, and always gave the local villagers something more than scarcely a feast. They shared the remains of the banquets. The delicacies they had only fantasized in their minds, they often had the privilege of at least participating in small quantities, in what was the taste of such gourmet moments of gastronomically pleasures.

It was sometime in the Year of the Snake, that I too, received a surprise second to none. The eldest son had returned home. At this time in his mid-twenties; it was told there was a great concern and upheaval in the Forbidden City, the great Emperor had died. There was confusion among the family of who would be the next emperor of China. There was talk of civil war with great armies mustering in different portions in different provinces to support one emperor over another.

The magistrate immediately called all of his children from the universities back into the mansion. Once safe and sound, he sent couriers out to get information. The new Emperor was the younger brother of the old Emperor, something highly unusual. To make things even more odd, he was not an Empress's son, but a senior concubine's son. Unbeknownst to me, the magistrate, under total secrecy of one of his senior servants, and couriers under pains of death, went to the great Forbidden City. They learned not only all of what happened, but knowing that the young virile Emperor of the day had opposed a great many of his brother's decisions, they presented long briefs of documentation in which my father, my family, had not committed a treasonable act. Furthermore my father had been wrongly accused by his enemies and all his lands and family had been unjustly removed from the empire.

It was with this newfound information in which my magistrate then approached me and informed me of his findings. He confronted me for the first time in our long relationship with who I was and what a grand noble family I had come from. For the first time in our relationship, he asked me rather than commanded me, to provide the information so he could reinstate my family to its glorious prestigious past. I was absolutely beyond words. I could not have contemplated in my wildest thoughts of something transpiring of this magnitude. I begged him to let me have the rest of the day, and if possible, the next, to grasp what information he had provided me with and what request he had asked of me.

He nodded with acknowledgement of my decision and my request. For the next two days I could think of nothing else. I went through the motions of what I had done for the better part of twenty years at once, and yet my mind always returned to what I had been told. It was not of what I was doing or what change in life would transpire. It was the great longing of knowing my other brother had survived. Up until now I had dared not mention that another living soul of my family had escaped the wrath of the Emperor. Nevertheless at this point, maybe by the grace of the gods, and this incredible magistrate, I too might find the secret which has avoided me all this years.

The next day, in our private meeting, I requested if it was possible, if he could enquire about my younger brother. I had taken him aback. He had always assumed I had been the lone survivor. After I explained the little I knew from so long, long ago, of us parting company . . . of me going into the interior and my younger brother going into the southern provinces, he said, "Let me grant you your wish, and let destiny give you your answer."

It was sometime in the last moon of the Year of the Snake, in which to my great pleasure and surprise, my younger brother had been found. No, he had not succeeded anywhere near as graciously or as elegantly as I had done all these years. He had still kept an obscure lifestyle as a mere labour. Nonetheless, he was alive and had a wife with six children. He was absolutely beside himself when they told him I was alive. They did not tell him that our family had been pardoned, for you see, I was the elder brother, and it would be my benevolence to give him whatever I felt just of our family's reinstatement.

Furthermore, upon the return, with even more benevolent news, immediately I was summoned by the magistrate. He looked at me with a somewhat peculiar manner. His aging had taken a heavy toll, and one might have to say, somewhat to his lifestyle. His health had deteriorated in the last years to being merely acceptable, rather than of quality. Nonetheless, he was anxious to continue his quest for the future of his family as well as now and in the future.

At this time, the future of my family was considerably more in favour and had greater wealth and influence than he ever dreamed of, or his children. Things had almost turned about. I was the superior and he had become subservient to me. Nevertheless our relationship, our friendship, never changed. He asked me what my intentions were, and I informed him without hesitation I would like my younger brother to inherit all the wealth with prestige of my family.

He was shocked. Not surprised, literally shocked.

He asked, "And what of yourself?"

This was when I smiled, the smile to an old face and old friend I replied, "I'm with my family."

I had never seen the magistrate so emotionally moved. I knew he was beyond words for the tears trickled down the old round face and landed on his Manchu moustache.

When he had gained his repose, he answered with, "I have had many sons, but no brothers. You are mine."

With this, so it came to pass. The proper documents were signed and the seals immediately were registered and my younger brother returned to the great houses and wealth of our family.

I wish I could end here; however, it would not complete what happened. So, with a heavy spirit, I will continue.

The following year brought sadness to the great mansion and a great loss to me personally. My benefactor, my friend, my magistrate, died. His older son took over the position in which he had been groomed for, by both his father and me all those years ago when he was starting his tenth year, and now he was in his thirtieth. He welcomed me as his father and the guiding force in which he had lost and was suffering from missing. He honoured me far in excess from the position of a scholar and so did the others in the mansion. Afterwards, the years went by and the children's children who I taught became adults. My strength and my youth were now replaced by the aging factors of reality. I taught no more, though the youngest children would gather around me and plead, as if I was some kind of wizard rather than a scholar, to tell them stories of their father and of their great-grandfather.

So this is where I had spent the better part of my life, the best part of my years. Like all things, one night I returned to my quarters feeling more tired than most days with my aging body. Once in bed the peace of the night and darkness forever more joined me.

The next morning, I woke as usual, disoriented, and slouched on the couch. I had long kept the doors to my library opened and, once again, my servants assisted me back to my quarters. My beloved wife nursed me back with the doctor, who brought his new assistant to witness such a bizarre event in which took place on the anniversary of the Portraits.

It was well into the second week before I started to resume my daily duties. It seemed to me and the Doctor that I was taking a longer period of time after having an experience with one of the portraits. Yes, of course I am getting a year older each time these events take place, nonetheless I feel weaker much longer after each event.

I've given up trying to understand the complexity of which one will rule the night of the anniversary and medical science seems to be either null and void with being very elusive why these paintings would have such an effect on an exact date. Nonetheless, life must go on and I must say I'm prepared to meet the task which confronts me now that I'm more back to being, I was going to say normal, which is not true, so I will have to say the way I am at the presence. It is now that my strength has returned and I'm joining the rest of my family at the dinner table and resuming my duties in my office. I try to put those moments of possession behind me. Each anniversary seems to be more challenging to my well-being or again, it could just well be my imagination. I'm grateful to how I feel these days and I'm looking forward to being productive in the days which lie ahead.

Dr. Sebastian looked at the doors which would open as soon as he rang the bell. He paused a moment and quickly flashed a look at the disagreeable portrait and then gazed upon the one who had a pleasant appearance. He then returned his eyes to the last pages of this chapter.

He had been to China many times; in fact, if it be known he was one of the first guests to enter China as a curator. He'd always been fascinated by the different dynasties of China and this particular chapter reminded him only too well the many hours he spent reading not only about the different dynasties but some the great works of authors who told of the times in the different periods of China. He was familiar with not only the caste system, but favors of the Emperor who ruled as their god. He was fascinated by the pages in which he had just completed. It was like, yes! It was like living in that time he thought.

He was very reluctant to close the book; however, he eventually rang the bell for the butler. Shortly thereafter the chauffeur was driving him the great distance back to his home domicile. After greeting his wife in the normal way, she was most interested in how it went at the mansion. They both joined each other in the living room with a Chardonnay glass of wine.

Without hesitation this time he wished to express this particular chapter and how it related to his knowledge and interest in the dynasties of China. She was only too well aware of his vast knowledge of this country and its long tradition of dynasties lasting hundreds of years. Nonetheless, he elaborated more on what he had read in this chapter of the intimate parts of one man surviving when his family was out of favor with the Emperor, which was very interesting for her indeed. When he concluded, his dear wife mentioned how she had learned a great deal from her husband in the past and this was to be added to the knowledge he had already given her of this particular country.

As usual, she had dinner waiting and seeing the night was of a pleasant nature, she asked if he wished to take a stroll with the dogs through the park after dinner. So it came to pass, hand-in-hand with their two Cairn terriers tugging on their leashes, all four of them strolled through the majestic park of ancient trees.

THE GERMAN BLITZ

—◊—

ONCE MORE, DR. SEBASTIAN was attending to the day-to-day needs of being the curator at the Museum. Things were moving relatively smoothly, and though he was not on top of everything, as this would be an impossible feat; he was nonetheless keeping on top of the day-to-day operations. There were plans in the work for a large exhibition to becoming one of the main attractions in the future. He had put out many feelers to other museums that had exceptional displays of antiquities of various civilizations. Until now, nothing had been confirmed so he had very little to report to the Board of Directors in which direction he wished them to pursue.

Later in the afternoon, when he returned from lunch, his staff informed him that his Lordship's secretary had made arrangements for him to attend another reading of the Portraits the following Thursday. He gave his consent, thanking Emily for a job well done and then returned to his own office.

He was on his way home went he realized that each time he was scheduled for a reading, that it was always on the same day of the week. Maybe not every two weeks, or even a month would lapse, but somehow the day was always the same. He wondered if it was mere coincidence or if it had something to do with his consistency of reading chapters at the mansion. Without too much further thought on the subject, he arrived home and was greeted by his wife as usual.

The days followed quite quickly and soon the time arrived for the chauffeur to pick him up. When he did arrive at the mansion the procedure was the same and greetings became routine, until he finally was left alone in the library of the late writer.

He made himself comfortable and set to the task at hand. He opened the book and looked at the ribbon marker from where he left off. As he gazed down at this chapter, he was wondering in what direction it was going to lead this poor unfortunate writer (and now him, the reader) and by which portrait would possess the words and the events in which lay before him.

Oh, how the time flew. I can't remember how fast the days moved until this dreadful moment arrived once more in my life. Yes! It was drawing to a close, the day that the evening would take over my soul once more. One of the portraits would possess me and throw me back into another time, another place, another moment in which I had been a part of in this long journey of my soul.

I'd never got used to the anniversary of these terrifying moments. I had tried many things to induce the good portrait or the benevolent one to take me on a journey, though I wished to take part in none, I had little or no choice. It was the diabolical, or for lack of a better word, evil portrait that I feared for my very soul, as well as my life.

It possessed such moments in which my entire body was often reduced to nothing except fragile remains of the experience I'd experienced during that period. And so, tonight it would take hold once more and I would be the victim of one of the portraits. I'd long since stopped fighting or trying to avoid the inevitable. I'd even, finally, relinquished the idea of having the portraits replaced at either end of the study, giving them equal distance to my desk and the two hearths and mantles that they had.

Now as darkness covered the courtyards and the servants retired for the night, I prepared for the inevitable. It mattered not what I'd done the day before or during the day, or, what my thoughts were. Without warning, probably like a stroke or a heart attack, one minute I am alive and well, or so I think, and the next minute, I am gasping my last. I felt that it might be best if I retired to the leather sofa; at least when it came, I would be able to, well, maybe fall into whatever was going to happen and my poor mortal body would tilt forward or better sideways, and lie upon the leather. If not, it would be the same as many other times: they'd find my withered form on the floor in some kind of comatose state.

Yes! This would happen, sometime this evening, on the anniversary of the paintings.

Oh! It's happened. I'm lying under the bed. I'm with my grandmother. My mother's on the other side. I'm a mere child of 6. There's a wailing, howling, eerie sound screaming out into the night air. "Lie still! Or the Bogey man will get you."

"Where is he now, grandma?"

"Don't—make—a sound. The Germans will come and take you away."

I cuddled harder into the arms of both my mother and my grandmother which were wrapped around my small body. They were scared. Somehow, without being told, I knew where we were and what was happening. It was London, England and it was during what was known as the Blitz. This was the time when the bombing of London from the Germans took place. We were at war. And they were coming. The sirens howled their screaming sound to warn us, the British people, the Londoners, to get into the bunkers, the bomb shelters, and hide in our homes in some form of safety. It wasn't really that long as the sirens kept howling and screaming their warning as the great lights roamed the skies looking for the enemy above.

One could hear above the sirens, the moaning, groaning. It was like a thousand—maybe a million—insects coming; that humming, buzzing sound of the engines of the planes. Yes! They were upon us now, along with the sirens and the buzzing sound was a new terrifying sound, and flashes of piercing light. The anti-aircraft guns were shooting at the sky, hoping to find a target of the enemy. And then, we would hear another sound. Almost like a shrill whistle and when it stopped, there was a huge bang.

The next day, one of the buildings where your friend or your mother and father's friend lived; it was nothing but a pile of rubble. It happened, of course not every night, but definitely quite often. Especially on a clear night like tonight the Germans would be flying over London. And so, the hours would pass, all three of us huddled under our beds, hoping and praying that tomorrow we would not be dead.

My father and grandfather were fighting in the war. Yes! It was not a good time to live in London town, except that's where our home was. And, so at last, the night came to an end. Well, not the night, but the sirens and the great searchlights which were looking into the skies. We all crawled out from underneath my bed with both women putting me back in my bed and tucked me in well then wished me good night. How could one say "good night" after all had just happened? However that's the way we are.

Before very long, the morning came and it was fitting another day, off to school. As the days moved from one to the next, and somehow life became somewhat normal, if one however could call the times normal, I would return to what I'd started to do so long, long ago, it seemed.

Well, who knows, it was probably when I was really young, like five. I'm six-and-a-half, well, really six-and-three-quarters, so it was a long time ago. It started when I couldn't sleep one night and I started looking at the ceiling. In fact, I actually started to look at the shadows on the ceiling and then it happened.

I was on the ceiling, looking down at myself, in the bed. I could move around, nonetheless I didn't move in the bed. I was free! I was floating! I was on the ceiling! I really was scared the first time. As soon as I was scared, I opened up my eyes in the bed and I was back in the bed and all that was left on the ceiling were the shadows. It was the first time that I remember. After, it became easier and, to say the least, I became a lot more adventurous. I wouldn't do it every night. There was no point. Sometimes I would even forget about it. Then again, sooner or later, I would return to doing it. A lot of times I would just sit at the top of the stairs and listen to my mother and grandmother talk while they had a last cup of tea before going to bed. They would always be fiddling with the radio and saying something about trying to get the BBC.

This last while, it was when the bombings where still taking place, that I started to venture out and what a moment it was; what an experience. Many times after my mom and grandmother would put me into bed, I once more would hit the ceiling. It became easy. Before long I was on the ceiling once more, and without any effort at all, I was then outside. Once outside, I could do anything. I would fly over the rooftops, dipping and twirling and moving about, seeing whatever there was to see, and doing whatever I wished to take part in. Sometimes my curiosity was so great I would race ahead towards the English Channel and catch up with the fighter planes that were defending the island. I would be sitting right beside the pilots and they didn't see me.

Those were very, very exciting times and scary too. There were also very bad times when I would be beside the pilot and there would be return fire from one of the large planes. And then, they would get that funny look on their face, and slump forward on the stick and the plane would start to twirl in its death throes into the sea.

Of course, I would always just move on. It was nothing for me. I felt bad for the pilot. He was such a young man. Or, another time, I would be in the enemy's plane. And they'd be trying very hard to get back to where they were from and our fighter planes would be shooting them down. The pilot would be speaking German, and to my surprise, I understood what he was saying. He would be telling the gunners to starboard, to port, to aft. He would be requesting to break formation, and on and on it went. It was like—no, it was—being in the war.

I kept doing this consistently. It was something that gave me some kind of release of all the things which were going wrong around me. All the fears of other people seemed to matter little to me. For I always was able to escape. All I had to do was lie on my bed and look at the ceiling.

It was so easy. And so enjoyable! And so exciting! I would travel all over London and then, I got older. I started travelling all over Europe. I would swoop down and look at different cities and what people were doing. Mind you, it always had to be at night. I could never do it during the daytime. I tried, but I couldn't. I think it had to be something to do with the shadows on the ceiling. I don't really know.

Nonetheless then, the ultimate: I started to travel into Asia and where the Japanese were fighting. I watched great naval battles. However like all things, I made a mistake one night. Not a small mistake, but a large, large mistake. It was just another average night with me travelling around. I wasn't even really that far away. I was travelling up around Russia where the German army and the Russian army were fighting.

I watched and I—oh—I made such a stupid mistake. I stayed up too late. Or maybe, one might say, too early. It was daylight. No matter how hard or fast I tried to get back to my house, to my room, the sun was up and the darkness had retreated. I knew, even in my small years, that it was the worst mistake of my life. I had given up, in fact, my life.

Well, it might have been the way it was, when I was six or seven years old in London Town. However, it was morning in my library. And once again, my servants had found me in a half-prone position, as white as new-fallen snow. If there had been any blood left in my body, it definitely wasn't present and accounted for in any form of my skin. I had a gaunt look and a glazed eye. I was incoherent as usual. My breathing was shallow and raspy as the aide carried me back into my bedroom.

I had survived another encounter with the portraits. I would find out later, in the week that lay ahead, my good friend the doctor would always shake his head relentlessly after these incursions with the unknown, and would say, "Your poor fragile body cannot take another one." Nonetheless somehow, my time had not found its end. I endured another anniversary of the portraits.

Dr. Sebastian took a deep breath as he read the final pages of the German blitz. He could not help but think of the young boy as well as the writer, who in many ways was one and the same. He regressed back to his own youth and his last name Sebastian. Yes! It is a German name; he was of German descent. In fact, if it be known, he was only the third generation of his German ancestry who lived in Canada. His great-great-grandfather had fought in the First World War under the German flag and the German monarchy. He thought like so many; this was the time in what would become known as trench warfare. It was a different kind of war than anyone had fought before and for good reasons he thought.

For a moment he entered into his historical profession rather than his relatives' location. The First World War was the introduction of the new and devastating war of the world. It was the first war the soldiers could stay for long periods of time in the front without needing supplies of food or other such things as medicine. It was the introduction of canned foods and became known as the food of choice of soldiers who called it bully-beef. The second most significant thing that this terrible war contributed to its long devastating loss of life was the machine gun, and last but not least, the first introduction of the war in the skies. Yes! His great-great-grandfather did fight as a soldier in the trenches of this terrible war as a German.

He looked down again at the pages and then around the room, he did not spend much time other than a casual glance at both of the portraits, then again regressed back into his own thoughts of his own family. Oh yes, the second great war, World War II, his great-great-grandfather lost his life during this period. It was between the First World War and Second World War in which his great-grandfather, upon returning to the war-torn country of Germany made application to immigrate to Canada.

Once his great-grandfather reached maturity, so did the world once more engage in conflict, World War II. His great-grandfather fought under the British flag as a Canadian soldier. He distinguished himself not only in rank but being with a regiment of super commandos. He lost his life during the campaign at Anzio, Italy.

Once more Dr. Sebastian leaned back in his chair and now looked at the great doors, where shortly he would ring the bell, and the butler would enter from. As he stared aimlessly at the doors he could not help but think of his own family involvement in war. He had the same name as his ancestors and yet they both fought on opposite fronts during their history. For his family, what a waste it seemed of the individual life. In many ways, he still thought of himself as a German descent and a Canadian citizen. What would have happened to him, God only knows if his great-great-grandfather had not taken the mammoth steps of immigrating to Canada. He stopped to say a silent prayer and how grateful he is to be a Canadian.

Once his thoughts became more current, he quickly reached for the bell and rang it. In a very short time the butler once more arrived. As in the past, the procedure was repeated as before. It was a very short time before Dr. Sebastian was once more being escorted back home by the chauffeur. The usual goodbyes were expressed by both and once again he entered the home to greet his beloved wife who was waiting with open arms.

"Well, my darling . . . how was the day?" she asked.

"Oh, not too bad, my love. I did a little soul-searching at the end of this chapter, and had dreadfully few answers for myself," he replied.

"Well, now could I entice you into a glass of wine, to help express some of your thoughts of the day, or would you prefer me to tell you how mundane mine was?" she chuckled.

"A glass of wine would be most enjoyable, and I'm sure your days are never mundane. Nonetheless, whoever wishes to go first, let it be said, let it be done," was his reply. And so it came to pass once more, he shared his experience at the mansion and enjoyed a pleasant meal with his wife and another wonderful evening they spent together.

THE GEISHA

—ᴍ—

Iᴛ ᴡᴀs ᴀ ɴᴇᴡ month and Dr. Sebastian couldn't believe how fast the year was progressing. He accomplished a lot of things this year, both at work and at home; on the other hand, the end of the year was fast approaching, and he should at least have one vacation. If this didn't take place within the next three or four months, it would be like so many other years—he would build up a contingency of holiday-time, or like in other years gone by; he would take the monetary policy and stay on the job.

Nonetheless, he did owe a holiday to his beloved wife, who liked going on cruises the best of all. He had been doing a bit of research on cruises and had tentatively booked a cruise to go through the Panama Canal. His wife was in all favor of it, due to the fact she would only have to go on one flight to Fort Lauderdale and the cruise ended back in Canada which pleased her immensely. Yes! Tonight he was going to surprise her; he was going to announce he had booked two tickets for the following month. It was going to be a relatively long cruise for they would be gone at least three weeks; mind you, he had much more time coming to him than the mere three weeks he would book off.

All the same, he was reluctant to take this much time off in the immediate future. There were still commitments coming from other museums to put exhibits into the next year's enticement for this Museum which would attract both its regular patrons as well as the tourists who would be coming through the city. He was just about to ring for his secretary to book tickets for the cruise, when he was interrupted by her to inform him that three weeks from now, she and the secretary of his Lordship had made arrangements for another reading of the Portraits. He quickly looked at his calendar and agreed the time would be sufficient for him to make it possible. He realized it would be tight, nevertheless he still could go on the cruise and so then he requested her to make it so.

The next three weeks vanished with the day-to-day drum beat of work and administration, until the morning arrived when His Lordship's chauffeur repeated the trip back to the mansion with Dr. Sebastian in the backseat. It was the usual, which he had now become quite accustomed to; both the greetings from His Lordship's secretary, to being escorted by the butler and male servants to the library. After the Book of Portraits once more was placed in its usual position, Dr. Sebastian took his regular seat and he dismissed the servants.

Before he opened up the book, he casually looked around the magnificent room with its columns of rare books and the memorabilia that Robert F. Edwards had brought back from the four corners of the earth. As he gazed around at the interesting artifacts, including the two portraits on either side of the room, he could not help but feel anxious. Why would it be like this he thought for a moment? Then he realized once again, the air was different. Yes! That's what it was . . . once he left the hallway and entered into this room, it had stale air—even though he'd asked for the glass-doors leading out to the garden to be opened by the servants. Maybe it was nothing more than his imagination, but still the air remained stagnant . . . . not even the faintest breeze from outside entered this compound. Without any further ado, he set to the task and once more opened the book to the marker he had left for his return. He then looked at the heading waiting him with the words, "The Geisha".

Oh, how quickly a year vanishes and the days seem to be so far ahead when one starts the year. Then, they vanish like the morning sun as it sets in the evening. I have no idea how the days have dissipated into the weeks and now the weeks have lost their supremacy against the months. Of course, the time has come again when The Portraits will take my destiny in their ways, as the evening fast approaches; their time of domination is at hand.

As in the past, I have at this moment given up any devious ways of escaping their time which possesses my life. I have accepted this by the grace of God and all which is present and accounted for, that I may endure another period which one of The Portraits dominates. As I sit peacefully—such a fruitless word, "peaceful"—anticipation, fear, anxiety, apprehension. Any of these would be better than "peacefully".

I have removed myself from my mammoth desk and any requirements of the day to sit leisurely on the large leather couch adjacent to my work station. Periodically, I glance in the direction of both mantle pieces, my eyes raise up to the portraits that dominate their settings. Which will it be today? Which will possess me tonight?

As the afternoon drifts into the shadows of the first of nightfall, it happens. Without warning! Without any preparation! Oh. I am here once again. But, then again, where? Moreover, who am I?

Oh! As the present passes my life into what at this instant is the present, I am—yes—I am a young woman. Indeed, I am a little blossom of happiness. I am a Geisha. I live in the time of the Ox dui no tsaki 24891011 sho no tsaki 1356712 of the Japanese lunar calendar. However, in the Western calendar it is the spring of 1805. I live in the House of the Seven Clouds of Happiness. I am one of the Geishas who are being trained, groomed, to fulfill the true destiny of happiness that a Geisha can provide. I should actually start a little earlier.

For when I was still of single numbers in age, I believe it could be eight or nine, my father fell on hard times and the mouths to be fed were too many. I was not only of an age which could be betrothed, but I had great potential of beauty. My father was not a peasant, but of middle class, if one could say of these times that there was a class who was not of Regent Blood, nonetheless he was successful in the ways of merchants and trade.

As these times were difficult for all in the district, the region that the Lord Prince of this part of Japan was the Shogun, my father chose me, his eldest daughter, to become a Geisha.

Upon this period, he approached a Mama San of the Seven Clouds of Happiness to accept his gift and his desire for my destiny. She willingly accepted me after she had done a full examination of my body, and my mind with my possibilities.

As a consequence, at the present time (a decade later), I have reached the second rule of enhancement of the Geisha. I have still one more to complete before I will be a full Geisha and will entertain the men in their worldly pleasures and fulfillment of their physical needs. Ah, of course, I must be more precise: their sexual satisfactions and fantasies.

At this time, I am still intact as a virgin, or a flower which has not bloomed. Yet, there is so much I have gained at this very moment than when I first entered the House of the Seven Clouds of Happiness.

I was exceptionally fortunate because I did not have the feet of many of the lower class concubines and prostitutes. My feet were small, petite and frail; as if I had walked on clouds for the years before I entered my vocation. Seeing as I started with my feet, I will continue in an upward motion to complete what one would see with the eye. I am small and fragile.

Many of the elder Geishas call me the Porcelain Child. I look frail and even now as I have reached womanhood, I look like the dawning of youth. My legs are slender and well formed, however not extremely long. The only hair on my body is a soft down which trickles around my womanhood. The rest of my body is smooth and soft as a texture of delight, to be seen and to be touched. My belly is flat, like a harp waiting to be plucked.

Moreover I have reached to the maturity of my womanhood. My small, firmly-developed breasts have piercing points to delight the touch. My head rests squarely on my shoulders and now my face—ah yes, it is like the moon, round and inviting. My chin only gives the smallest of the beginning of the fulfillment of my lips; my teeth follow the form of my mouth in a perfect array of pearls which are neither chipped, nor dented, nor discolored. My nose does not distract from the beauty of peace and contentment as one who gazes on the moon-beams which radiate from it. My eyes are like shadows which never distract of being open. I am blessed with long strands of silk so far to cover my head and adorn the infinite patterns to facilitate the creations by the hairdressers of the day.

This is my being with the purpose I have tried to let one and all have a glimpse of what men—and women—look at when they enter or I am present, in the House of the Seven Clouds of Happiness.

This is what I have been graced with by the Creator of Japan through the Shinto faith. I am—when I enter the Shinto temple—the reflection of goodness and innocence in the eyes of the reflection of the mirror of the Shinto faith.

Nonetheless there is more—and there is, much more—for I am gifted with a voice! When I sing the ancient songs of our ancestors and especially of the ancestors of the Shogun of this region, I have been told that my voice has the pitch and the clarity of a nightingale singing at the break of a dawn for its mate. I can hold the pitch longer and better than any of those senior Geishas in this house.

My fingers are exceptionally long for the rest of what they are attached to. As well, I am able to pluck the strong strings of the instruments of the Japanese yokobiwa and once again my musical talent has not gone unnoticed or untrained. I am always being rehearsed and corrected, I may add, for the slightest imperfection.

My legs are strong and slender, which gives me the privilege of performing in pantomime the great feats of the warriors and the mythical paths which they were faced with.

It is said that when I am fully dressed in my kimono and my hair is done in the tradition of performance, and my face has the porcelain appearance with the makeup, then I look and float like a porcelain doll performing the great acts of the past.

It is only now, this last year, with the intention I have been studying and preparing what the senior geishas and periodically the Mother San herself in the ways of fulfilling the needs of a man who will penetrate my maidenhood.

This is the beginning. Now, I stand at this time to continue what lies ahead in the future for me and my destiny. It is not more than a hand-full of nightfall's when the Mama San summons me to her quarters. After performing the manners appropriate as required by any Geisha, she gives me permission to sit in the traditional Japanese position with my feet crossed and my buttocks to rest upon them as a stool, with my back straight and my face waiting for the instructions.

She informs me I have been her choice to entertain an important dignitary of the community. He and his servants will choose other concubines for the evening, however I will be the one who will perform the rituals and provide the pantomimes to facilitate his requests. She gazes into my eyes which show wonderment and a million questions with countless anxieties, then once more she reassures me with the intention her training has reached the place in which she feels comfortable that I can perform accurately to the standards in which—then she lets it slip—"The Magistrate" will be present for.

My placid innocent moon has red flashes of color which penetrate into the cheek area. Certainly, I am blushing. To have such an honor to perform in this way for a distinguished guest, a person of such high rank. Once more, I do the traditional bowing as she realizes there is nothing more to be said and I wish to retire to perform in my mind every possible pantomime that I have ever been taught.

I return to my quarters where my maidservant awaits. She sees at once I am flushed and asks if I am well. I reply I am and I wish to have some rest to prepare the matter for me to take on my thoughts.

As I lay there, my mind flashes up dreams of grandeur and intrigue and hope beyond most Geisha's minds. Once again I think, 'Oh, if I could only be required when I perform the greatest of all pleasures by a noble. To become a magistrate's . . .' and once more I could feel the burning which penetrates my skin on the cheeks. A Shogun, a Regent, to be one of his concubines.

Oh, I almost feel like my head is going to topple off with such thoughts of grandeur for such a humble servant. I must rest and so I wake with the peace which is required to prepare myself for the evening. I will take the usual modest nourishment of rice and tea with a few vegetables and dried fish.

Ah, the moment is immediately at hand with the purpose I am to prepare—and be prepared—for the evening with the intention of maybe lasting two hours or until dawn. As I put on the sacred silk garments, to facilitate what I will perform in and the hairdresser styles my hair to perfection with the enormous brushes and combs to become the most advantageous to performing the pantomimes.

My face now becomes hardened, like the mother of pearl, the inlaid pearl, of the lacquer dishes. It is expressionless and my large kimono shows nothing of my hands. I have become the symbol that will produce thoughts which are requested by this elegant guest and his servants.

As I enter the room, there are Geishas of lesser stature than myself catering to every need possible of the servant, and of course, the master, by feeding them whatever they wish at the banquet table. A more senior Geisha is stringing lullabies and melodies of the ancient ones by request of this magistrate, my honored guest. As I enter the room, I look like a beautiful butterfly that has floated into the presence of all who are witnessing it.

I hear the command of the senior Geisha: the first pantomime. It is extremely easy. It is something that was my first to be taught, and definitely one which I have mastered. It is of nature and how nature provides the needs of all that exist. When I am finished, I know I have pleased the magistrate for he looks at me and waves a gesture at the Geisha who is wishing him to drink sake.

The next pantomime is depicting one of the great battles of the warriors against an unjust act of their enemies. Again, I know this one well and perform it with all the gestures which make it a classic amongst its time. When I have completed these two, I am feeling somewhat fatigued after four hours or more—since my continual practicing of these particular pantomimes, I know roughly what time has expired.

I was hoping I had pleased this great master. There is silence for the longest time, and my heart pauses. I became motionless. The senior Geisha had stopped playing and waits for instructions to dismiss me and continue playing soothing music. By now, the feast at the table is gone and only the drinks of sake remain.

The great guest himself then personally asked almost the impossible of any Geisha. I was to perform in pantomime the creation of the great faith of our ancestors. I could feel the strings on the instrument tighten as the senior Geisha ripped through her mind at the incredible beginning of such an attempt. Then the music started, with the whining and piercing of each chord straining itself against maximum efforts to retain it. I had to begin.

After three hours of performing this most difficult request ever asked, it came to an end. The magistrate grunted and then the Geisha on either side wiped from his face the tears of happiness that he had experienced. Both the older Geisha and I were then instructed that our presence was no longer required.

Drained with exhaustion, I went back to my quarters and was helped by my maid to retire to my bed. I had no idea what had transpired. I only feared for the worst. In this period, one cannot help but obey and pray to the Shinto gods that one may live to see another day.

As the days followed, our routine took on its normal agenda. I neither had the privilege nor the slightest will to ask how the evening went. For it would be unheard of to inquire if satisfaction was given, or god forbid, the thought perished in my mind, if there was displeasure.

The days past with the weeks and I continued with my studies of reaching final enlightenment of being a Geisha. Little did I know this mighty and powerful dignitary was the head magistrate of our city of Nagasaki. For one to know, we do not; certainly as Geisha, and as Japanese, venture outside the street in which we dwell, unless there is a direct command from one of our superiors.

Nonetheless, before the full moon saw two of its risings, the magistrate had to report directly the progress of the city to the Regent Shogun, or prince. During this period, he always brought gifts and encouragement that all was as it should be for fear of failure would cause seppuku, or the tearing of the belly by suicide.

As his audience was in progress and nearing his completion of success, the Regent asked, "Is there anything of interest which you have seen since your last report?"

The great magistrate thought earnestly for a moment and dared not ignore the request, for to forget something is equally as unforgivable as a mistake.

"I wish to let you know on one night, I enjoyed my station by going to the House of the Seven Clouds of Happiness for entertainment and there I witnessed a performance which brought such emotion to my body so as I shook, and my face became wet."

"So! So! Hi, Hi," the Regent commanded, "go on; go on."

"With your permission, I will return and ask for more information of this Geisha and have the report brought to you as quickly as it is obtainable, if this pleases your Regent."

"Hi. Hi," was the reply from the Regent.

Now the Regent nodded and immediately the magistrate was dismissed. Upon returning to the city, before he returned to his family, he went to the House of the Seven Clouds of Happiness and asked who I was, and what station I was as a Geisha.

To his amazement, and sheer surprise, he found I was a perfect choice for pleasure for any Regent. I had reached the cultural happiness which few would ever achieve as a Geisha, a true Geisha, and I had not been spoiled by another. Therefore, with what Japanese function at best is obedience, he made the report available as quickly as the scribes could write it with perfection and then had it delivered to the Regent henceforth. While all this was going on I knew nothing nor did my Mama San.

After another full moon had found its way to its rightful place, a reply came from the magistrate that the great Regent wished to have a private audience at his palace with the Geisha named the Little Blossom.

THE GEISHA

With no hesitation, my Mama San prepared for my journey. It would be the better part of two weeks before my entourage would arrive, and my Mama San had quickly started to prepare the list of things which would be required and the gifts that our humble house would forfeit for such an appearance.

Before the moon had found its place of fullness, I was ready with a large contingency for this arduous tour. It is extremely difficult to travel any distance. For over half my life, I had never left the House of the Seven Clouds of Happiness.

My Mama San had given her personal carriers my luggage and requirements. The gifts of both the magistrate—who now had taken complete charge—and the Mama San's poor gift by comparison, nevertheless generous offers. They contained everything from the best silks, to the finest lacquer dishes with inset pearls, sugar and other gifts of lesser value too numerous to mention: a hundred lacquers of silver. I was in wonderment. I was in total fear of what lay ahead. Then, like a leaf dropping it came without warning.

Within seven days I would perform before the Regent himself and his guests. Three of my senior Mama sans who had come with me on this trip were given the instructions of the pantomimes which I was to perform. It was a small venue compared to what I was expecting and preparing myself.

There were two songs: one of a warrior's cry of victory, and the other of the anguish of loss of love. The pantomime was the easiest and simplest, nevertheless somewhat powerful. It was again of growing up and facing the challenges of adulthood.

I was somewhat—no I couldn't say . . . yes I can, for nobody will read this, for these are my thoughts—I was somewhat confounded, and disappointed. I wanted to be given at least something the House of the Seven Clouds of Happiness had told me that I'd performed exceptionally well.

There was no doubt in anyone's mind, including mine; the Regent knew everything that took place in his realm. He would know which pieces I had performed and which ones would honor his presence the best. Therefore why these simple ones? Everyone who was to prepare for this night stood in some bafflement, and awe, nevertheless still it is not the way to question. It is the way to perform without showing unhappiness or thought into such an honor.

I was far too emotional to hope in any possible way to take on nourishment. I took a little tea to appease my needs. I was washed excessively until I thought I looked and felt like a prune which had been well done under the scalding waters. I was rubbed with oils and flower fragrances. Everything with the purpose of enhancing pleasure was thought of.

As a result, the final moments came and I performed. I performed like one in a trance. One who had been transposed into another plane of thoughts. My voice, even to my ear, had never sounded as pure. The notes that were so difficult for a human chord to reach, I sang out as pure as the creator had intended.

When it came to the pantomiming, my feelings of my childhood years of learning the ways of a Geisha transposed the pantomime into a personal deliverance. After the completion, I was dismissed. I was nervous and so possessed to perform successfully, that I barely saw the Regent. I never once looked directly at him. For rudeness is unforgivable and intolerable in the times I live.

For the other guests who were present, they were all of rank far in excess of even what my Mama San had witnessed in her long, arduous career. I, this Geisha, of the House of the Seven Clouds of Happiness, was successful. I had brought a great honor to be in the presence of the great Regent.

I returned to the quarters which were assigned to us and remained there with no communication of when I could return back home. The days continued, and the weeks vanished. Even now, the months of spring had given way to the leaves of autumn. I had nowhere to go and no understanding of what would transpire. I still had no knowledge of the night in which I had performed, and only once did I perform.

Then, without warning, I was summoned to perform again. This time, they were difficult pieces. They were of the highest quality of the historical events of the Regent's ancestors. It was his ancestors victories over their enemies; their family lineage and along with their loyalties of their allies. I knew my life and all that had entered into it, was resting on my frail little shoulders.

However what could I do? His wish was my command. It was said, immediately it had to be done.

At last the evening came. It was so different from the one I first experienced. There were only his personal servants and the vast needs of his selective concubines to perform the rituals of his dining. Once again, I came to the stage and performed the first act. Without hesitation, he signaled, or had one of his servants signal the concubine with the instruments, to give me the instrument and to sing the praises of his ancestors.

He caught me off guard. I was prepared for the pantomime; my mind was locked into the emotions I needed to perform it. Not to sing it. Yet, it came as a request and all those who depended on my success for their lives, was now in my hands or more precisely in my voice. I was quickly summonsed to the position in which the other Geisha was positioned with the instrument and took the instrument in my slender fingers and felt the strong chords.

Once more, I felt the ease and tranquility and peace, as I became familiar with the plucking sounds of my fingers. I started to sing the songs of his ancestors' successes. I lost myself in the lyrics. The notes—both from my fingers and my voice—united into phrases that filled the room with emotion.

When I finished, I felt my inner kimono wet from my own perspiration. My breathing was controlled like my life; nonetheless my nerve endings were twitching like the entrails of a deceased animal. I remained silent, gazing at nothing and dare not look in the direction of the Regent. Then one of his servants commanded I perform the last; the one in which was extraordinarily the most difficult. Not because of the intricate parts of singing it, or reaching the notes, however one slip of an accent, one mispronunciation, could be an insult to the loyalty of his ancestors, to the great Emperor Shogun.

This was the final test. This was the final moment. For the first time, my fingers felt the fatigue and strain of the endurance they had been through for hours. My mind knew the price which would be paid if the last minute was not perfect. As a consequence, my mind floated into a trance; to remember the little knowledge I possessed to describe the great sacrifices and losses of the ancestors.

I started to sing about the moments when the great Regent Shogun of this province was granted the lands in which their family still possessed. I told of their great compassion during the 200-year civil wars when they remained focused to Tokon, the great Emperor and the great descendant of the Shinto religion and the god of the universe. I went on as someone who was being guided by his ancestors' personal experiences. I was relating both their anguish and their success.

Time did not exist in my mind. I had become absorbed by what was taking place in my mind and coming through pure with the string instrument guiding my voice to levels that no-one, including myself, had ever heard. When I finally completed the last and the most difficult of all, the Shogun himself commanded me to come forth.

He then looked at two of his concubines and said, "To my quarters."

As a result, they escorted me to his chamber. I was bathed once more, vigorously with the hottest water, close to boiling my skin. I was then rubbed with oils and fragrances and all the makeup and hair for the ceremonies was now placed in a natural form of the beauty wherein the Great Doma of Shintoism had blessed me with.

The two concubines tried their best to set me at ease, sensing from my body language that I was lacking in confidence. They knew that although I was a Geisha, and I had reached the last stage of perfection in the arts, I had not felt or received the piercing of manhood in my maiden's nest. They assured me accordingly the senior Geishas and the Mama San had prepared me well for the moment.

I dare not ask about the Regent, my lord, for it would be both imprudent and unacceptable. Therefore I was like a receptor of knowledge, yet to pour anything back into the unknown. They sat on one of the many cushions that were scattered about in the enormous boudoir of the Regent. The room was rather sparse in contents, nonetheless rich in heritage and with the warmth of the surroundings, I noticed that the rice-paper partitions separated the vastness, which opened up to be far greater in size than the House of the Seven Clouds of Happiness which housed over 50 Geishas and their maidservants.

I had gasped at the sheer mammoth size of this one room for just rest and entertainment. The hours twinkled by and it was less than halfway through the darkness when a runner of one of his servants came and informed us his master would be at hand. Quickly the other two concubines left—oh, I have just had the impertinence of assuming I would be one of his concubines—rather than a Geisha for the night.

Oh, how false my pride and how dangerous my dreams are. The two concubines left this humble Geisha who waited to please this great Shogun of his physical requirements.

I was prepared on the tatami mats and lay like a porcelain doll in the sheerness of the night. It was not long before the master of the realm entered into his room of delight and slumber. He took his time, looking and examining what lay awaiting pleasure for him. I knew the moment was fast approaching with the intention of all that I had prepared for—this moment—and the instructions of giving great pleasure and need of man's requirements was at hand.

I neither felt panic or despair. I only felt anticipation and a tinge of uncertainty. I would be the vessel with the purpose of servicing his manhood which would be penetrated and satisfy his needs both physical and mental.

He had his servants disrobe him. After they left for us to be alone, he lay beside me and said, "Please my thoughts and you'll become one of my wishes."

Then as a result, exactly what he asked, I did the best I could. I soothed his manhood as I had been taught and played as if it was a magical flute. I caressed it with my palms and milked it into the stiffness of desire and passion. It was then that he took command, first touching the points of my tiny breasts and then reaching down with his manhood and the guidance of his great hand, he entered where no man had entered before.

I reared up, not with passion, but with pain. I gave a muffled cry as I bit deep into my lips. And then, to my surprise, the rhythmic motion which persisted became more than acceptable.

It became enjoyable. I started to both remember my instructions accompanied by my passions. I could not believe the pleasure I was giving him, nevertheless he was also rewarding my knowledge.

As we reached a crescendo, he too moaned and then he laid his full body weight upon mine. He was considerable, much larger in all aspects than I would ever have comprehended with my first encounter of a true man and his physical needs. I too, felt the moisture of our bodies and had experienced what was a new pleasure for me, and the enormous fulfillment of his needs for him.

We rested, both breathing deeply and both lying face upward, looking at the ceiling and enjoying the cool refreshing breezes which made themselves welcome to the heated moment. I have to confess I felt a relaxation in which I had never experienced before. I also had a desire to go into a slumber though I resisted as much as I could, my body demanded this after the strenuous performances of the earlier part of the evening. I was at this moment fulfilled and my body demanded its rest. I do not remember if my slumber was long or short.

All I remember was scarcely before the night gave up its shadows and the day that lay in waiting broke; the Regent, this great prince, once more wished his manly needs to be satisfied. I enjoyed this more than the first time and couldn't believe my own fulfillment was being satisfied in pleasing his. Shortly after, once more the fulfillment of his needs, we returned to lying facing up only for him to pull a cord shortly which gave the immediate response of his servants.

He said, "Let the concubines prepare to return to take this Little Blossom to her quarters."

My heart fell like a stone into the oblivious seas only to hope there was a bottom. It seemed less than a blink of an eye, the two concubines who had prepared me for his wishes, returned and took me forth. It was not back to my quarters where my servants waited and all my things in which I had brought were present; it was to the quarters which were totally different in the area of his concubines.

Could it mean that I had at this instant joined one of his fruitful enjoyments? One can never question, for to question is to be disobedient. In addition to be disobedient one must be punished, either by the individual committing seppuku, or to bring shame and loss to all others who are in their family. The two concubines left and it was not much longer as I sat gazing through the window as the darkness had been replaced by another day, when servants who I had never seen entered.

They told me this was my new dwelling in the great palace and they were now responsible for my well-being. I had come as a geisha. I am now a regent's concubine.

In the days and months that followed, on more than one evening, I was asked to perform and after completing the performance, I would be taken to the regent's quarters. Others days, I would remain isolated in my room, or my quarters, with my servants. I dare not ask of what was transpiring with my servants or the geisha's who accompanied me. It was not my place any longer, though I cared in my heart deeply. I had brought great honor to the House of Seven Clouds of Happiness. I had fulfilled my destiny both as a geisha and a child of my ancestors.

As the weeks fell into the months and the months moved forward into the cherry blossom times, I once more enjoyed the many frequent nights in my master's bedroom. My clothes had completely changed. I now wore some of the finest silks with the rich embroidery of gold and silver weaving. The artistic works of the creators was present in all I wore. I was treated with reverence and respect and enjoyed a certain amount of companionship with other concubines.

There was one thing which somewhat amazed me and even to this day gives me some bewilderment. My great regent, my master, was of an age in which my father had yet to see. He was exceedingly virile and my pleasing him in his needs must have been fulfilling, for I became with modest acknowledgement, his preferred concubine.

I have no way of knowing or sharing why, only being grateful that it was to persist and hence as the moons in their fullness came to the sky and then retreated for another period, the winds of fall and the autumn of the year was fast approaching.

It is a time of great preparation, for after the lunar year, the great regents, or princes of their noble families, once more have to return to Kyoto to pay homage and bring gifts with tribute to the greatest Shogun the Emperor. There is always a great amount of preparation before the actual expedition or journey is taken place, just to gather the enormous supply of gifts required to present to the Emperor.

It is also a time of excitement and anticipation for my Regent. It would be his turn to remain in Kyoto for one year with his family, who then has to remain there permanently. One of the great customs of our land (to protect it in a lasting peace against the evils of civil war) is that the great Emperor demands the wives and the children of noble families remain in the holy city. It is not for me to judge, it is only for me to remind myself that I will never see the city. For any woman who enters past Osaka en route, must remain in Kyoto forever.

As the days came closer to the departure, to my total amazement, I was told I would accompany the Great Regent on his journey. Much had gone into preparing for each day in advance, for staying at an Inn or a temple en route, and many runners were sent back and forth. At last, the caravan was assembled for the journey which waited it. I was in a grand lacquered carriage, more splendid than any I had ever seen. My robes were of the finest silks. I was accompanied by two of my personal servants as our long procession started its journey towards Kyoto. On this long journey, massive pots were constantly filled with tea to refresh those of us who neither walked, but were carried. Each night we would reach the designated accommodations, some days were as short as ten hours, and some as long as eighteen hours. Nonetheless, each day brought us closer and closer to the mystical city of Kyoto.

I had no idea where my destiny would take me, or what lay ahead. Mine was to perform with entire pleasure for this Regent all that was required for his needs. The days went into weeks, but the timing of the journey needed to be perfect. We must arrive either before, or at the date on which the Great Emperor, the greatest of Shoguns, was willing to have an audience with his subjects. There seemed to be an organized agenda in which the least inconvenience would be nothing less than acceptance of death.

As we reached the great city of Osaka, I had never seen anything I could describe to myself. It was huge. The governor had already prepared for my Regent's needs and requirements for his stay. It was only now that my master's personal servant told me I would remain here until the caravan returned without my master. Now, I knew that I would never see the city of Kyoto and, therefore, I would never have to remain there for the rest of my life.

To know when I would return to the palace again, was not for me to know, but for me to wait until I was told. It was well after the fullness of the moon once more was on its downward slope, that the great remains of the caravan returned and a servant informed me that I would not return to Nagasaki.

I was then told the news which shattered my life, shattered my very existence of purpose. I was to join a caravan of the Dutch upon entering the city of Osaka, and I would go with a Dutch doctor to fulfill his needs as I had the Regent's. There is a moment when one's heart breaks and the soul leaves to go beyond. Afterwards then, it is pulled back by an anchor of agony to the body in which has not let it be released. This is what happened to me. Once this servant left, I fell upon my tatami mat and sobbed uncontrollably. I was unquestionably preparing to commit seppuku, suicide. It was one of the other concubines of the first night who came to my aide and my help. She comforted me and asked me not to be so judgmental in life but to accept each moment as the presence of being with the great provider of the universe, of the Shinto faith. I was somewhat inconsolable even with this.

Nevertheless, what can one do when their destiny has already been written in time?

As we reached the perimeter of the great city in which my family and my regent controlled, my lacquer carriage broke away from the caravan and proceeded to the small island where the Dutch traders were. We had one of the finest interpreters address the Dutch doctor.

Through the thin rice paper I could see that he was as unaware of what was happening as I was. After many hours of discussion, I was escorted to his quarters before he entered. He was so different than my master, my Regent. He was definitely a foreigner. They were few in numbers, I was told, for I had never seen one before. He was much taller than my master and his face was covered with hair, but not like mine, or anything that I had seen before. It was red. His clothes were so different and unbecoming; probably the most noticeable thing which came from him was the odor, the smell. He smelled like the droppings of a boar. I held back, waving my fan frantically so I would not produce any type of gagging, though I was totally nauseous. He had few words in Japanese in which were laden with a sound that I had never experienced before.

In his awkward ways of communications, he told me that I was a gift to him from the Great Regent; for he had saved the Regent's first wife by foreign medicine. I knew full well how important this great lady, the first wife of the Regent was. Not only was she from an important family of a coalition in which had been arranged by the Regent and her family in marriage, but far more important, she had borne the first of his sons who would be the next Regent of his mighty empire.

I could now understand why a gift of greatness had to be given, and I am honored to this moment and will be until the last breath gives me thought of the sacrifice my Regent made in presenting me as his gift.

My life was completely different. It was different when I was in the House of the Seven Clouds of Happiness to the elegance and regal surrounding of the castle of my great Shogun, my Great Regent. I was now living in humble quarters, with foreign objects and all foreign men. Only the scribes were ever seen of my people. Yet, on a more notable thought, though they were far inferior to my stature, the prostitutes of honorable houses were permitted to stay with these foreign Dutch men. Many of them, long before my moment of entry into their lives had borne children and as I became allowed the freedom that I had never experienced before, I was able to communicate with them. They told me more about the ways of these foreign people and how they too, fell under the rules and laws with customs of our great land. That they too were restricted to our customs and to gain permission for all in which they wished to seek.

Again, no matter how hard they tried or the man now who owns my body and my being, to communicate, I could not understand or even wish in many ways to accept: the way they ate with a knife as if they attacked the food, with a weapon, this totally confused me. They used a pewter mug and plate which rattled and was most distasteful to lay food on. Even how they rested and performed their manly desires, this was on an elevated platform.

As the years passed, I found this man to be a gentle soul, so different than my father and the Regent, both in his needs, his desires, and above all, his behavior. He wished to spend time with me. He wished to communicate with me. I was no longer just a vessel to fulfill his needs.

For the first time in my life I felt the tingle and swelling of life in my belly and there came a child, the first child of four. He is a son and I too changed from a woman into a mother. My owner, my ruler, my Dutch doctor not only bore the hair of fire, but my offspring did also. I could only wait until he grew longer and bigger to see if he would inherit what his father had, not only a beard of red; but a body covered in hair like some animal. I had never gotten used to it; I don't think I ever will. It is so un-human.

Once my womb of happiness found life, it was soon afterwards that I gave birth to a second son, and then a third. Then a few years past before my last and final contribution to life was given and she was a daughter. During these years I had grown much more accepting to my new role of life and what lay ahead of it. I also had a fulfillment in my children, a love, with a devotion that never changed, but had changed me forever.

I took on leadership roles in the small enclave of the few women who remained with their children. I taught them the manners and the pronunciation of the Japanese in the great ports. I taught them the customs and in many ways I became a teacher as well as a mother. The doctor on occasions would leave the compound and go into the city to aide and assist our medical doctors. It was known throughout the small community that at any given time their rulers would call them back to their homeland and it was also without exception their companions would remain the subjects of Japan.

As my children grew and I grew more used to the customs of a foreign land, between a deep commitment by this man and myself with the help of scribes, we started to communicate verbally with each other. He had started to write medical journals for his Japanese colleagues and on three distinct occasions he was granted permission to fulfill this work. As a result I was blessed by the Shinto gods and his foreign god that he stayed longer than most of those who were of his race.

It was during this period the Great Regent who had given me such a moment of glory passed into another world. His son, as predicted, took the reign and to continue the succession which had not been broken for hundreds of years, for the fear of the remembrance of the great civil wars.

Not many more calendar years passed and my child, the firstborn, had now reached maturity. Then the dreaded moment arrived when my great foreign companion was told by his Emperor that his stay had come to an end. I could not help but feel all the pain of loss as he had so long been part of my way of life.

Also, there was a great anticipation and fear of what would lie ahead. This foreign doctor, this man with whose seed I had born life, promised me before he sailed he would always provide food and shelter for my existence and that of his children. They were noble words and I had seen others of these foreign men give truth to their word. There was nothing else I could do. There was nothing else which was allowed to be done.

Once again, the full moon acknowledged another period and my heart prayed the ships that carried the cargo trade would not find misfortune but the shorelines of Japan. As one wish and those wishes do not come to pass, hence was my wish. On a day like every other day, it changed forever. A ship was spotted, a foreign ship, far out to sea. One never knows, or one can never tell, if it is a Dutch ship or a hostile ship or one in distress.

I had lived on this shoreline only too long and too well to know that all kinds of ships enter into this safe water and ask to trade, to ask for help, or to abuse our laws and customs. Nevertheless, as this ship continued its course, directly to our shore and our shelter dwellings, it was distinguished as a Dutch ship. It currently would be a matter of how many moons before the father of my children would leave. With a heavy heart, I watched this foreign ship wait for permission to enter the harbor of safety.

Within two days, the request was granted. The days that followed were filled with activity, as one cargo left and another one was being purchased to return. Soon a message was brought directly from the captain that my children's father was to return with no exceptions, to the land where he was born.

It was during this time of excitement and sorrow; there came a request from the new Regent, new Shogun, my benefactor, and my first lover's son, to the doctor to come to his palace before departing. At first my thoughts were that for the short period left in our lives to be shared even the Shogun, the great prince of this region, did not let me have. My thoughts were sour rather than joyful. It would take weeks before my children's father could return to this small island; nonetheless a request from a prince is a command that cannot be ignored by anyone who has their footprints upon this land.

My companion made the preparations and once again with a small gathering of his needs and gifts for the Shogun, he made the journey to the great palace. It was a time which was an interlude to the life I would at this point remain in, alone in a compound of prostitutes, their children and foreigners. I went about my duties and requirements as if the day had not changed, only the time.

Shortly before the moon acknowledged its fullness once more, the father of my children returned. After all the customary requirements and protocol were made between the Japanese and Dutch, he then returned to the quarters where I awaited him. Of course, his children were the first, and rightfully so, to welcome his return with a glee of happiness which I could not share fully, knowing well this could be one of the last times they would be given this opportunity.

Nevertheless, such is life, such is destiny. After the children were fed and retired for the evening, the doctor sat once more and we were alone. He dismissed our servants and looked into my eyes with all that his vocation provided the kindness and the consideration of life itself. I am not capable with the art of clarity of what he said, word for word, but to the best of what I can, I will share.

As we sat, he reached out and I thought it was his manly needs that needed satisfying from the distance he'd been away and the distance he would be away forever. This was not so. He took my hands, each in his and he looked into my face and at this moment I will try to tell you what he said.

"My dearest Little Blossom of happiness, you have truly brought to pass what your name has told others of. You have given me all that a man wishes and I must tell you all that has happened and why.

When I was in the great city of Kyoto so many years ago, the Regent's first wife was being looked after by the greatest doctors, including the Shogun's, Emperor of Kyoto. But still, her life was starting to dwindle into the next world and I was summoned to the quarters.

I realized that she needed an operation and I sent back a courier to fetch my instruments of trade. Two days after I operated, (under the closest scrutiny of the most learned doctors of the land), she started to recover. Before I left to return back here, the great Regent sent his personal servant plus the scribes and translators to explain that such a reward commanded such a gift in return; as a result he gave the happiest concubine of his palace to me. I, even then, knew enough of the customs of your land, that I could not jeopardize everyone around me by refusing his gift.

The translators described in depth the importance of what I had been able to do, what I had been able to give, not just to the Regent, but to the very stability of two great names, two powerful families of Japan, to maintain the peace and laws of this land and, therefore, the gift had to be (though not of equal, nevertheless at least), of immense significance. This was what you and I were part of."

He paused, and I remained silent.

Nevertheless my eyes filled with moisture as little waterfalls trickled down my face. He squeezed my hands tighter and almost in a whisper added more.

"I have returned from the present Regent, the son of the man you knew. He again told, in extreme depth, of not only the significance of me performing the operation successfully, but also how grateful for all the years his mother had been given, and always spoke of the noble one," and he bowed his head in modesty, "that gave her life and let her see her children grow into maturity."

My doctor held his breath to control his voice as the cascades of wetness continued to flow down my oval face.

"Because of this; you and our children are to return to the palace and regain the stature in which his father had given you under his reign, and your children are his children."

I gasped. I felt weak, almost without substance of life. I took away my hand and reached for my fan in my kimono and waved it hysterically to give me the life-giving air which my body needed to remain conscious. Of course, being a doctor, he knew and being a companion for so many years, he knew the significance of what he was telling me. My children, his children, our children, would be as the Japanese. My people refer to them as the "coral children", but now would have great honor and respect and privileges. I was being returned as an elder concubine of the palace of my Regent.

Oh destiny! Why do thou not share merely a glimpse, either through the gift of astrology or sooth-saying, where one is headed and where to look? It was less than half the cycle of the moon when the ship which was first sighted sailed on the tide with the foreign doctor, the father of my children.

A few days later, a great procession of carriages and servants came and took my children with myself to the palace of the Regent. Now, this is where I am; this is where my children are. This is where I will wait for some other day, to know when the cycle of life has ended for me.

I woke. Or I came out of the trance, the obsession, still sitting in the same position as I had been taken away to that other time, that other life. I reached up, weak and exhausted as I always do, then touched my face.

It was wet with tears. Oh! Merciful God who controls my destiny! Who am I in eternity? Please, let me always be your servant!

I stared out across the massive desk to the gardens where it had broken the first light of day. I had lived through the night of The Portraits once more. I had returned to the living. With a supreme effort, I rang the bell which would bring my trusted servants, as before, to assist me to bed. Then, as always, I fell into an exhausted state until the days that were forthcoming returned me to my strength in which I would enjoy for another year, until the anniversary of this night of The Portraits.

Oh my God how many lives have I lived before? How many more will I be able to continue to exist before The Portraits end this one that I am living now? Yes! Only You, My God, know . . . and in truth, maybe The Portraits too. Nonetheless this servant of one and the slave of the other can only be in waiting to know.

Dr. Sebastian finished the last page and looked around the room with an impartial quick glance at its contents and then went to the French doors and looked outside. It was a beautiful autumn day with the leaves having turned into rainbows of colors, with the gentle breezes bringing the leaves down to carpet the grass and beds of flowers that they came to rest on. He was overwhelmed by the beauty which presented itself in front of him. Without any hesitation, he opened the French doors and walked out into the landscape waiting his presence. He gazed at nature and all the beauty that was presented at this time of year.

In his mind he quickly returned to what he had read about the geisha girl, in that long, long time ago of the Japanese Empire. It was the time of the Samurai. Yes! He knew it was the time in Japanese history to conserve peace against civil wars. This dynasty isolated the island from its neighbors. It became a culture unto itself with its disciplines of severity for anything which would cause disruption or with the fragile peace of shoguns and their wishes to rule the Empire of Japan. He thought of the long period of the dynasty which existed of the samurai for over 400 years.

His thoughts now returned to the present and what his eyes were witnessing. There was a small pond with ducks finding peace and sanctuary in their midst. His mind shifted gears to the present and how dominant Japan was in today's society. It was the second largest economy in the world. It had grown out of the ashes of the Second World War into the most aggressive and successful country of Southeast Asia. It had achieved success in marketing and inventing products that the general consumer throughout the world found superior to others that were representing the same products.

Nonetheless, their culture had remained somewhat of a mystery to the outside world. Their mannerisms, their requirements of food, their way of living a communal life were all different and mysterious to the Western world and other parts as well. Yes! He said to himself under his breath, 'there is no doubt that this period of the Samurai's still persist today in the modern-day Japan'.

With this, he looked longingly once more at the beautiful grounds and realized it was time to make his exit; not only from the grounds but from the mansion itself. Without any further ado he returned to the study and rang the bell for the butler. The same procedure took place as it had been in previous engagements. Within two hours, he was once more saying goodbye to the chauffeur and saying hello to his beautiful wife. The evening again was nothing more or less than one he and his wife enjoyed each night and the day ended.

THE PILOT

—⚍—

THE LAST MONTH FLEW by and in Dr. Sebastian's world, he couldn't believe the month had already come and gone with him now into the first week of the next month. There was nothing unusual taking place, but being the curator of such a large Museum, there was never a dull moment. His secretary Emily was doing an efficient job as always, keeping his schedules far enough apart that if something came up immediately, or one task lasted longer than the other, she wouldn't have to reschedule his entire week or perhaps month. He glanced at the long list of things which had to be done today and what was pressing for this month.

Lo and behold, sure enough on the exact same day of the third week of the month she had scheduled him for another reading of The Portraits at the mansion. It suited him fine, as he was making good progress on the book in general and realized by now that each encounter the writer experienced was totally different and in diverse times in history. In fact, it was more than possible, at least by Dr. Sebastian's recollection, this could well be a reincarnation. This regression was only for a matter of 24 hours or less. However, it seemed that The Portraits were an extremely important part of the enigma in which the writer was induced into the past, that perhaps he had really lived at one time.

As the week vanished, the day's work was not completely done by the good doctor, even though he always was doing his best. At last, the day did arrive when Dr. Sebastian would once more make the trek to the mansion and continue to read the Book of Portraits. The procedure was exactly the same as the past; the chauffeur would come and drive him to the mansion, then he would be escorted to the study where the book would be placed as before.

He opened the book to the beginning of the new chapter, to start to venture into the next possession of Robert F. Edwards through one of the portraits.

Ah, of course. How fast a year passes. Moreover one has to again face the moment which is inevitably going to exist, sometime during tomorrow and throughout the night. I have come to accept, if not ever being able to comprehend why; nevertheless, tomorrow will be the anniversary date of The Portraits.

It is long past nowadays that I have tried to avoid what is inevitable. I am thoroughly convinced without any reservation or exception if I or any other person were to destroy The Portraits; my life would be extinguished instantly.

It is better to endure one moment of unpredictable explanations each year which has drained me, not only of my physical strength, my mental capacity, but my moral existence of the present and what lies in the future. As the morning drifted into the apex of the midday, I had spent the better part of my commitments and duties in my office, my study, my sanctuary, with the exception of each portrait being at opposite ends of the grand room.

Over the years, I've noted that this part of the mansion looked somewhat like a cross. The huge doors at the farthest part are the entrance to this magnificent study, my sanctum other than on the anniversary of The Portraits I am at peace here.

Each portrait commands its position and place within this room and in my life over their own designated mantelpieces, an enormous desk, with the vast library of books and memorabilia in which I've collected in the years gone past are present for my comfort and my enjoyment of 363 or 364 days a year.

Nevertheless on this anniversary date of when The Portraits were painted, one of them once more is in total possession of me. It was scarcely after teatime when the servants came in and lit the fires, and the warm crackling sound of the embers of alder gave me a false sense of security. I had completed the tasks in which I'd assigned myself for this day and retired to the leather couch facing out into the vast gardens behind my desk.

I reached for a book of poems, always hoping, that maybe, just maybe—I would find something which would influence the beautiful portrait over the evil one. I took the beautiful words of Wordsworth to scan which poem I would select, and then, almost like a fog, a mist, the backlash of smoke, entered my mind and filled it and then clouded it.

When I refocused, I was no longer in my study. I also was no longer in the period of life in which I clung so desperately to.

The date is June 13, 1943. I am in a uniform, a British officer's Air Force uniform. Once I start to familiarize myself with my surroundings, I realize I'm in one of the local pubs. It is completely full of servicemen, and close to where Central Command had positioned one of our air fields, so we dominated the pub and probably the local economy with our air force personnel.

It was neither quiet, nor loud. A few of the boys were trying to make an attempt of singing some old Gaelic songs. Others were throwing darts. Most of them just sat around, nursing a pint or two of the local ale. We Air Force officers had taken it upon ourselves to drink Guinness as the favored beverage of the day; however, it was really a choice still.

My squadron—oh yes—my squadron! For I am none other than Godfrey Birmingham, Squadron Leader. I've reached the ripe old age of 28. I have 68 successful completed missions under me.

I have advanced in this short span of joining the RAF, to the present, being a co-pilot at first, and now a squadron leader. My crew, who accompanies me and the squadron, are second to none. Frederick McDougall, better known as "Freddie", is my co-pilot. James McGregor, who we call "Black Mack", is my bombardier. Percy James is my navigator; so his nick-name is obviously "Mapper". Bernard Jones or "Tiny Tim" is the front gunner. Raymond Sandstone, better known as the "Backpack" is the rear gunner.

Yes, that's us: the crew of the old Mother Hubbard, our Lancaster bomber. Backpack was in city times, a commercial painter. Our front nose of the Lancaster bomber is painted on two sides. One, a big boot kicking the ass of Gerry; and on the other, Old Mother Hubbard's shoe, with each one of us as a crew leaning out of one of the windows of the lace of the boot. Yes, I guess I would have to say we were not only a crew who had done over a third of the missions together, which I'd been personally involved with them; we are much more than a team.

We are somewhat—let me think for a moment. We are something more. We are like the companions on a checkerboard, against the other odds . . . no, no, no! Absolutely not; we are far more complex. We are much more intricate; much more complicated. We are powerful pieces on a chessboard. We thought and acted and responded to instant situations without any hesitation and in more than one case, probably more like in every case, we had gained the reputation of being invisible.

Yes, we'd taken some heavy KK fire from the Gerry's. The belly of our beloved Lancaster had some air conditioning that wasn't in their design plans. Nevertheless we always made it back. Yes: back home completing our mission: successfully, I have to add.

Once I had reached the rank of Squadron Leader, Freddie was supposed to be the captain of another Lancaster. The commanding officers had approached him on more than one occasion. Of course, he wanted to be Captain. If nothing else, it provided more pounds for a few more pints. He'd have his own crew.

However, when push came to shove, Freddie always declined the promotion and requested that he stay with the crew of the Indispensables. Our reputation grew on the base as being something more. Other pilots requested a standing list when being rotated to join our squadron. In many cases, we had taken on some of the more difficult missions, but always returned as a complete squadron.

It was like we were blessed. Or—who knows. It's war. I don't think anybody's blessed! Neither the living nor the dead I think is blessed. You just do what you have to. However, we had one heck of a reputation to beat.

Therefore, as we super-heroes of youth waited for . . . I was going to say Central Command to give an order, for another mission . . . but it was actually more the weather report. We'd been socked in now for the better part of three days.

Then, if all went well, and there was a break in the weather, we'd be off in the wide blue yonder once again. We'd been briefed— every day—on the same mission. It was going to be a five-prong approach on the harbor of Hamburg, Germany. Our squadron was going to be the last, which is always . . . well, a high-risk one. The first and the last have the most difficult times facing Germany targets. The first announces our arrival and the direction in which we are coming.

With night-raiding, of course the search lights scour the skies like shooting comets, and then, the endless KK fire or anti-aircraft fire from below from the Gerry's. Both at night, and with the odd day-raid we always had fighter support crossing the channel. Then, depending on the Gerry's attitude, let's call it, or readiness, with the fuel consumption of the fighter pilots, they would escort us quite a ways into France. Other times, coming under severe combat attack with the Focke-Wulfs, the Gerry's fighter planes, they engaged in dogfights and left us to fight our own battles.

Accordingly, this one was no different. It was going to be an excessive amount of bad eggs on Hamburg. That's our non-technical name for bombs. Yes, our rotten eggs would land on that poor city with those factories as well as refineries and shipping lanes. We had full intentions of giving Gerry more than just a backache. We were going to break their stronghold and their back.

So now, we had to wait. Wait for Mother Nature to give us the weather to complete our tasks. Each morning we would get the briefing and be on Red Alert, until cancellation. Tomorrow morning would be no different than the last three consecutive days. We had a pool going to see how long it might take before we got back to doing our job: whooping the living daylights out of Gerry and his rotten attitude.

Each night was spent in the pub, with the proprietor saying, "Okay lads, you know the run. You don't have homes, but we do.

Our family's waiting for us—and prayers for you. Therefore, drink up and toddle on home to your bunk!"

And each night, that's what we did. The following morning at 8:00 hours, once again we were in the briefing room. Even the instructor looked somewhat exasperated when he started pulling down the screen maps and rehearsing what all of us had pretty well memorized from the previous days.

However, that's what military chain of command is. You listen, and they tell you; even if it's the same thing. After the briefing, and the general report, we continued to wait. By now, the cancellation of this mission today was running 80 percent in favor on the pool. Nevertheless, like so many things in life in general, there's always a twist.

But, at 15:00 hours, we got the green light to suit up. We were going out. Yes! The crews were assembled, fuelling had been completed for the squadrons and the bomb compartments in the huge belly of each of the Lancaster's were full of rotten eggs. The last minute preparations were given. At 16:00 hours, we did our first inspection of our craft. As always, the maintenance crew had done their job, and it was our job to make sure that it was done right. Then we all entered into our positions and waited for instructions to take off.

When you have in excess of 100 aircraft, and a hull loaded with explosives, it takes a while to get them airborne. Nevertheless, by 18:00 hours the fighter pilots were escorting us across the Channel.

Yes, we were going to kick ass once more. Things were quiet across France. The escorts got almost to Paris before they dipped their wings and wished us well as we went on to Hamburg. I checked the rest of the squadron and we were in perfect formation. There was little or no doubt, this was going to be another routine mission: in my mind, and in the crew's with our fellow air-ships of the sky.

It seemed hardly moments before our navigator announced we were approaching. The first wave had already gone in and dropped the eggs. One could see the puffs of explosion and the skies being ripped open with high-powered searchlights trying to find the location and formation of our presence. So, there we were. The last to go in and ours was to drop our eggs right square smack in the harbor. I turned the plane over to the bombardier, who now is in complete control of the ship.

With that I heard, "Bombs away". The large doors opened and our payload found its way waiting to deliver its force on the grounds below. I was given the signal that the bombardier doors had been closed and I was once more back in control of our ship. Yes, absolutely. There was considerably more flack, KK fire.

I sincerely believed they'd figured out where we were and were doing their darned best to make sure at least some of us couldn't get back home.

I heard from the bombardier, "It's getting nasty back here. They're shooting bloody holes in us. It's time to move on, don't you think?"

I replied, "We're already leaving. Get those gunners ready and we'll be at the Channel before you can figure out how successful this mission was. Over! Roger."

Now we started our long, perilous journey back. Yes. This time Gerry was ready. I don't know which landing field their air force was at. I don't think we'd even reached the French border before their planes were in the sky. Those Focke-Wulfs were not only good fighter planes, but their pilots wanted a taste of revenge for what we'd been doing.

Our gunners were down in their turrets. Backpack and Tiny Tim in each of their turrets were ready for the Gerry fighters. We were taking it. They were both in their moment of pure joy, both men circling around like a bubble, spitting fire at the enemy.

They had to be good. Our whole lives depended on them. It wasn't long though. Luck had to change, and it wasn't in our favor.

Backpack got it. Gerry was trying to take us out for sure. He had taken out our tail gunner. We just had to hope and pray that those big Rolls Royce engines kept purring, no matter how much we got shot at. It seemed like eternity and then I heard the bombardier,

"Cap, you better get back here; we're in more than a little trouble. Over!"

"Roger." I gave the yoke controls to Freddie. "I better go back and see what's going on. It doesn't sound good."

No. It wasn't good. There were gaping holes in the fuselage; by more of a miracle than anything else, Backpack was still alive. Pretty shot up in the chest and the bombardier had put a bunch of sulfur packages on his chest, and then had given him as much morphine as he could.

When he said we were in trouble, he wasn't just marking out a tune. We were in big trouble. I ran back halfway and ripped a couple of air tanks off the wall to make the breathing easier in the back.

A moment later, just then, as I started to make my way back to the cabin, the ship rocked. With that it started to roll and rock once more. As I got to the cabin, horror had struck me across the face. There wasn't much left of the instrument panel and there was even less of Freddie. His upper part of his dorsal and his head had covered a good portion of the cabin. It was a horror that froze in my mind, and chiseled its way into my soul.

Then I saw a headless form holding the control as the ship rolled and rocked against all odds. I gave a heave as my stomach turned and wanted to twist out its contents. I reached my seat and grabbed the yoke. Number one engine was on fire. I managed to turn it off and hoped on all that was holy and sacred that the remaining fuels in the wing would not deprive the other engine of what we needed desperately, and not catch on fire.

It probably was the only lucky thing that happened that night.

In the meantime, Tiny Tim was no longer firing. His bubble had been burst, like cracking an egg.

I yelled back to the navigator, "Get in here!"

He got up from his small position behind the partition, only to start wrenching profusely the contents of his stomach.

"Take Freddie off the wheel. You're going to have to take the controls. It's going to take everything I have to hold this plane in the sky."

He gagged and gorged the contents that remained once more out onto the deck, and muttered, "I can't".

I snapped back. "I'm not asking what you can and can't do, I'm telling you—take those remains off that co-pilot's seat and sit there. This is an order. Now!"

One thing the armed forces had done is taken men's freedom of decision away from them. Even in this day of modern war, we are commanded by discipline to obey rather than to debate. He continued to throw up, dry heaving, as he took Freddie's remains away from the seat and then, he sat there. Frozen!

"Now take the throttle."

"Yes, Sir!" He gargled out.

I hadn't done much better than him. My bombardier jacket wore what I had in my stomach. The cabin smelt of everything that was putrid. Also we were flying solo.

It's a rule of the skies: you let the dying and the disabled to fend for themselves. The squadron is much more important than hanging around trying to do something that wouldn't be successful anyway.

I think the only saving grace, if you could call it that was the Focke-Wulfs had figured they'd done us in and it was just a matter of time before we would fall out of the sky, and they wanted to catch up with the rest of the squadron to see if they could increase their percentage of drop-outs. We'd lost so much altitude; keeping off the ground was a challenge.

It has always amazed me, and probably others, that under extreme pressure, impossible feats can prevail. It was more than just a miracle that I had the supreme strength to continually pull this dead machine from falling from the sky. All the time yelling instructions to the navigator above the force of the wind penetrating the massive holes in our cabin. We had done it. I could see the water. We were close to the Channel, somewhere.

I literally screamed, to be overheard by what was around us, "Get a bearing. Get a bearing, for God's sake, man!"

I took over the control throttle once more alone.

He left the co-pilot seat and staggered like someone who was in a comatose state only to return and say, "4 degrees, South by Southeast, maintain the course."

"Get back in the seat!" I cried out.

We were still on course, give or take a few degrees. Then, I never wanted to scream, or cry so much in my life. I heard the sound of the Spitfire. They were bringing us back; all we had to do was hold on.

For God's sake, take this torn Mother Hubbard and her children's boot home. Each second became eternity for the remaining part of the crew.

The bombardier now had replaced the navigator and had the controls, still pulling like Hercules, holding the gates of Heaven open.

"2 degrees, South," came a scream from the navigator.

Then I saw it. Yes! I saw it and so did the bombardier. The runway!

We had no running gear left. The undercarriage had been completely torn and the struts were like torn limbs that had nothing left to support our landing. I didn't have to tell anybody to brace themselves.

We were all dead men waiting for the moment of eternity. By some miracle, once more, we did a belly flop somewhere on the runway. Another engine fell off and spun itself somewhere and the emergency crew's loud sirens tore through the air as they came to rescue us, if they could. Fire hoses were pouring foam and water and God knows what else as the ambulance crews tore away the doors and hoped for the best that life was still inside.

Tiny Tim—there wasn't much left of him. Backpack was still alive. As for Freddie . . . there was the larger part of his remains on the cabin floor. Bombardier, better known as Black Mack and Mapper our navigator were being helped out of what was left of Mother Hubbard.

I took one long look at what little we landed in.

I walked out of the plane like somebody who didn't know where they were or why they were there, only to fall face down as two medics took me to the Infirmary.

The next day, under sedation and in a clean uniform, (my orderly made sure that I was presentable as possible), I was to report to the commanding officer. It was when I looked into the mirror that I couldn't believe it was me. Yes, it was me alright. I wasn't 28 years of age any more. I was more like—my God—twice that age. My golden-auburn hair of youth was now spotted salt and pepper with the entry of white hair. The lines on my face had removed my youth with my sure-footedness as I made my way to the Commanding Officer's room and knocked.

He said, "Enter," with his tough, rough Scottish brogue.

I made a feeble attempt at coming to attention and a salute. He looked up. I don't remember much.

All I heard was, "My good man—at ease! Take a chair."

I started to . . . stammer might be the right word; garble, might be another. Somehow he seemed to understand the verbal report I was giving of what happened, until I came to the part of when I returned to see what was left of Freddie at the wheel.

I broke down and started to sob and cry hysterically. I tried my very best not only as a commander, but as a military man. Nonetheless, all my fortitude and all my discipline were in vain. I sobbed and sobbed and sobbed.

I felt a strong hand on my shoulder and a deep Scottish voice, "Well lad, you went to hell with death, but we got you now. You're back with us."

As I sobbed uncontrollably, two medics again come and helped me back into the infirmary. They sedated me and that, oh no. No! No! I'm back; I'm back in my study.

I'm on the floor. I'm covered in my own vomit. How I didn't aspirate to death is an unanswerable question in itself. I don't know how long I have lain there. Again, as always before, I was far too weak to even contemplate or visualize how to gain help.

As pre-arranged, if I had not reported before a certain time, my trusted servant with the aide of others knew to come and check on me. Once more, I stared into his eyes, as a man who tried to focus back from the horror of another time.

I remained in bed, secluded from the rest of the living world for days on end. Oh, oh, how many more of these events must I live through before my end?

Dr. Sebastian stared down at the last entry. His mind was confused at the ending of the pilot, did he survive, and was he discharged, what happened? These were the questions which were running through Dr. Sebastian's mind along with the horror of what the pilot had experienced. Yes! Once more Dr. Sebastian returned to the years of World War II and his family's personal experience of the loss of his great-grandfather during the war. He couldn't help but feel a connection with both the pilot and the writer's words which expressed their feelings in these tragic times. His mind paused for a moment, and then continued to think that it was always the old men with their political ambitions that the young man gave their lives to try to accomplish for these old men's dreams.

He broke his thoughts away from concentrating on what he had been reading and did a quick glance throughout the room, then rang the bell for the butler. The procedure was the same as had been in the past, with at last the chauffeur's driving him back to his home domicile. However, as he was looking out the window, not concentrating too much on the traffic going both ways, now for the first time he noticed a large graveyard.

He looked at the arrangement with the diversity of the tombstones as well as the crosses which marked the deceased military personal from different periods. He stared as the limousine continually made its way past, and his eyes followed the view until he could no more see the graveyard. It was then he regressed back to thinking of the thousands, no, more like tens of thousands, or possibly hundreds of thousands of military personnel who lay in these pits known as graves. There were millions in the last two great wars who lay in unmarked graves along with the citizens which perished in these conflicts. His mind continued to think of these melancholic times and the tragedies everyone who was involved experienced, and for what, he asked himself.

Once arriving home, his dear wife was waiting for him with a smile and a hug. By the very look on his face, she could tell he had not had a pleasant experience.

"May I get you a glass of wine, my dear?" she asked.

He replied, "No, I think I'll have a large glass of malted whiskey, straight, please."

"As you wish, my dear. I'll be with you in a moment," she responded.

"Don't rush, my darling. I'll just sit here waiting for you in the living room," he answered.

Shortly thereafter, she returned with his malted whiskey and a glass of red wine for herself. "Would you like to tell me about your day?" she asked.

"No! I would rather you go first this time," was his reply.

"Well now, let me see what I did, besides get out of the house," she tried to lighten the mood. "To start with, I did all the errands which were required and came back, and had a modest lunch with my friends. Also, I took the dogs for a walk through the park. I guess I must've done something else, but it doesn't seem very important now that I try to recall it," she added to him. "So, I see it must be your turn now, my darling" she replied.

He took another large mouthful of the malted whiskey, and then said, "As you know, I read another chapter of the Book of Portraits at the mansion."

She acknowledged by nodding her head in a positive manner. With her acknowledgment, he started to express his feelings about reading this chapter and its contents.

"It was about the Second World War, in which a young pilot had a horrific experience on one of his missions. Yet, it left me with a dreadfully melancholic feeling of all the people, both military and civilians, whose lives were changed forever in these conflicts of violence," he added. "I tried to shake the mood before I left the mansion," he added," although I regressed back when I passed a graveyard on the way back home," he then looked at her as if he was finished. He was really asking the question to himself, but now sharing it with his wife.

"Why, if we are supposed to be so civilized in today's society . . . yet the only difference of bygone years of war is each time we become more sophisticated in the ways of destruction of others cultures and their citizens? Will it never end?" He was asking himself as he once more looked for the answers.

She looked sympathetically at her husband and answered. "I don't think it will . . . . Not in our lifetime. Nonetheless don't give up, we have a long civilization and although the Homo sapien is increasing in numbers, perhaps one day we'll find a way to stop killing each other." She then looked at him and asked, "I think it's time to have a date. How about inviting me out for dinner and the theater?" With this, she was able to break the spell of melancholy which persisted ever since he read the last chapter.

"What a great idea, my love. You freshen up, while I have another malted whiskey, then off to dinner and the theater of your choice," he acknowledged her suggestion.

With this, she got up and changed into evening attire while he was waiting in the living room for her to join him once more. After a delightful meal at one of their favourite Italian restaurants, they enjoyed an excellent play of Agatha Christie works. The evening soon came to a close. He was so grateful his wife was able to turn his mood of depression into an evening of delight and enjoyment. As they retired for the evening, he smiled directly at her and said, "You are the very best I could ever hope for. Thank you for being you, my beautiful wife, and good night."

THE SHOEMAKER

—∽—

FOR DR. SEBASTIAN THE weeks vanished and he was well into the second half of the next month. He had given little, if any thought, to returning to the mansion to read more of the Book of Portraits. The new displays had been approved for the upcoming season in the Museum, and were being arranged in the appropriate spots. He found himself as busy as ever and not being distracted by anything that wasn't pertinent to the Museum itself.

This particular morning, upon entering his office to meet the challenges of the day, he started to review the memos on his desk, along with urgent phone calls and other pressing commitments. This was when he noticed there was an appointment made for next week by his secretary for another visit to the mansion. It was not that he didn't want to complete his commitment to His Lordship, and abandon the idea of having this precious volume donated to the museum; it was just not the best time to do it. There were so many other commitments more pressing. Nonetheless, if His Lordship found time for him to carry on reading the next chapter, who was he to change it?

On the day in mention, the chauffeur was waiting outside his house. After the usual greetings, the drive to the mansion commenced. Dr. Sebastian actually was in deep thought on how the displays would come together to command the attention and the patronage of those visiting the Museum. Keeping these thoughts, it wasn't until the limousine turned up the long driveway to the mansion itself that he realized they had arrived. After being escorted to the library of the late Robert F. Edwards, Dr. Sebastian once more was in his usual position about to start the next chapter in the Book of Portraits. One thing he had never done, and had no intentions of doing, was looking ahead at the chapters which were yet to be read. It was not in his habit to do this in any form, whether it was a text book, or just the daily documentations which came across his desk on a regular basis. He always disciplined himself to follow through without taking any shortcuts of what he was about to acknowledge. And so with this in mind; he opened at the bookmark of the chapter in which he was about to read, 'The Shoemaker.'

Oh all right, why not, it's another year that's past. I find the years move faster as I get older. Or, maybe I'm not moving as fast as they are. Nonetheless, once again, the day has arrived, or more correctly, the evening is fast approaching on the anniversary of The Portraits. This year I've tried different approaches to abandon my obsession or anxieties periodically, as I enter my library that I spend so many hours in. I have grown accustomed to walking straight to my desk, rather than looking at the two mantles holding my fate on this anniversary. I've even taken up other challenges in life, like painting some of the places and things which I've seen throughout my travels. My little studio is littered with my attempts to express myself in another medium other than writing. Yet, they too seem to reflect my being from one time to another; from being exuberant to being pessimistic or melancholy, reflecting my moods. Oh fair enough; the shades of day are diminishing and the darkness of the night is blanketing the horizon.

I decide to take one long last look at the gardens which prevail through my window. As I walk over and look out, the sun is once more giving quarter to the darkness of the night. I feel the pains of apprehension piercing my well-being knowing that when the sun is no longer present, The Portraits will have their way. Oh God . . . oh God, our Heavenly Father, which one shall possess me tonight? Oh Father, who art in heaven please let me endure one more of these treacherous possessions that overtake my well-being. Let me not die on these diabolical journeys which I have no . . . yes . . . no control over of either of my mind, my body, and above all my soul.

As the last rays of the sun fade into the sunset, I return to the leather couch which I find has provided solace for me in the past, rather than lying on the floor or bent over with my head on my desk when the next morning arrives. I feel the urgency of finding a comfortable position, to await my fate.

I do not dare look at either one of The Portraits, for fear I might influence the evil one, or abandon the benevolent one from taking me on a journey that I do not wish to participate in.

Oh God, it is happening. At this moment, I'm sitting with two of my best friends at a pub in Liverpool. We are enjoying some fine ale and conversation. Frederick, the candle stick maker, is better known as 'Freddy the stick', and Jamie has learned the trader of a weaver, for myself, they all call me 'Bobbie's Cobbler'.

We had not planned on going out for a few pints of ale to-night; however, Freddie had made a strenuous effort to complete his tasks at hand, and then said he would treat us to a pint or two on his success in business this week. Soon, the three of us were sitting in our usual spots, indulging in a pint of ale.

It was in the shadows of darkness of the night, when the pub's doors swung open and six rough and ready men came in. There was no doubt in anyone's mind, these men were sailors. This was a surprise, as though periodically sailors did come up the lane to our pub, they usually stayed closer to the waterfront and those pubs which accommodated their trade. These men were loud and boisterous, obviously having more than their share of grog to drink.

They ordered drinks for all us in the house, which numbered somewhere around fifteen or more, counting them as well. We all accepted their merriment as well as their generosity. As the evening progressed, gradually the regular patrons finished their drinks and returned home. Freddie and Jamie and I were in good spirits to start with, but far from being intoxicated.

At this point, these boisterous sailors were telling tales of their adventures on the high seas and some boasted they had sailed the Seven Seas. Being good story-tellers, they intrigued us to stay on for another one and another one, including the drinks in which they provided. Three of the sailors, now impaired by the amount of grog they had consumed, stumbled outside, to expel what they had drunk before returning to either the ship or lodging they were staying in.

As we started to finish off the last pewter of ale which the sailors had generously insisted on buying, we too, were starting to feel the after—effects of an evening of excess. We bid the sailors who remained in the pub a 'goodnight', and in jolly spirits started to make our way home. The darkened streets were abandoned now by even the light keepers. Little did we know that the three sailors who we thought were so intoxicated, where there laying in wait, while the other three blocked our passage from retreat. We were no match, either in strength or in numbers, to overcome them. After a severe beating and being dragged to God knows where, our fate lay in their hands.

It was not until the next morning when we found ourselves in a hold on a cargo ship. We had been captured by a chain gang, a press gang. We were the victims of a ruthless procedure where the crew mustered men for the next sailing. We could feel the rocking of the ship. God knows what it was or where it was heading. All we knew by our limited experience of the ocean was it must have cast off with the tide. By mid-day, a couple of slop-buckets were lowered along with another two buckets, one with water and the other with dried biscuits. To our surprise, we found that we were not the only victims of this brutal kidnapping; there were a total of eight of us now in this hold. It was dark, except for the grate high above our heads which showed whether it was day or night.

By the next day we had gathered together as victimized comrades. We had no plans of action, yet all of us wanted to find out at least where we were headed and what the next port of call would be. The now empty biscuits and water buckets were pulled back up and refilled. We started to panic, thinking that maybe this wasn't a press gang, but a slave ship. Panic possessed us, now feeling the greatest fear we had experienced yet. The eight of us huddled together, and tried to either pacify each other or add more fear than we already had.

It was on the third day, close to mid-day when the grate was removed and a rope was thrown down. We were told to grab hold and we would be pulled up, one by one. The mid-day light was blinding to each one of us as we were removed from the hold. Once on deck, we were roughly manhandled to form a line. The ship was under full sail and there was nothing to see, except a blue sky above with a darker blue ocean surrounding the ship. Slowly, I was able to focus in the bright light. I realized I was standing on the lower deck.

As I glanced upwards to the wheel-house, there stood a rough and tattered man who felt much of his success around his belly. This man had a mean look on his face, showing no compassion or mercy for anything or anyone. There was no doubt, even in my befuddled mind that he ruled the ship and the high seas as a captain. There were three other men who stood on either side of him. Including the rest of his crew, we now numbered eighteen.

The Captain bellowed out, "Now, hear ye mates, hear ye . . . and I don't repeat my words twice. I am the Captain of this fair vessel, 'The Forgiveness', and I am going to introduce you to the First Mate, Bradley . . . the Second Mate, Bennie . . . (and, he looked sort of puzzled at the third one) . . . ah yes, Harold. These men are my arms and my legs that will give you the orders which I demand, and the punishment if you do not deliver them."

One man from the hold, I still don't remember his name, stepped forward and asked, "Captain, would you be kind enough to tell us what port we're headed to?"

The Captain's face turned even uglier than his first appearance. "I ask the questions," said the Captain. "I do not give the answers." He turned to hail the third mate and said, "Teach this man and the rest of this naughty crew a manner with twenty-five of your best." The Third Mate came down on the lower deck, waved a hand for two of the existing crew to assist him, and quickly took this man and had him strapped to the rod irons. His shirt was ripped off his back and a cat and nine tails took pieces of his flesh off as the twenty-five lashes were given to him.

He screamed for the first two and then he moaned for the five, but by the fifteenth he was unconscious; and his back looked like some wild animal had torn it to pieces. He was quickly cut down and again the two regular crew members who had tied him to the rod iron threw a bucket of salt water on his back. The captain witnessed the entire procedure for his shear enjoyment of what had transpired.

He said, "Does that give you the answers to what was the question?" and there was not a mutter or a moan, not even from the still unconscious person.

This was the beginning of our training to become sea-faring men.

We had absolutely no idea in what direction, let alone what port we were headed to, and in many ways, it really didn't matter for our hands were at the mercy of a ruthless, sadistic captain. In the days that followed, we were served the basics of dried biscuits and salted mutton for food, twice a day. We learned how to climb up the ropes to the tall ship masts which were carrying the large sails, then by working our way quickly and securely, as best we could, to the canvas which blew us forward and onward to wherever captain wished. We learned to do our watch and all the chores of being a crew at sea.

I was rather fortunate in my trade of being a cobbler. Although few of us had shoes, at least the three mates and the Captain, of course had boots. Being handy, I was also given more responsibility in working with the carpenter. Freddy had the worst of the three of us. Being a candle stick maker, they had no need of his trade, so he got to clean up bilges and some of the more distasteful jobs. Jamie, being a weaver, was once again assigned to mending the canvas and checking the rigging.

It was well into the second week, short of a fortnight, when a gale came up. We were torn and tossed by forces of nature in which I could not comprehend existed. I could not believe any mortal man would be asked to climb the catwalks and reef in the canvas. This was when I realized why we were nicknamed "tar babies", learning from the more seasoned crew members who had experienced this unforgiving force of nature. They had put tar in their hair, so when they were well above the tall sails they could grab on to the rope and still reef in the canvas by pulling some of the tar from their hair.

I had never experienced anything as terrifying as this storm from hell that produced a raging attitude of nature's rebellious ways. More by a miracle of God's forgiveness than nature's benevolence, we managed somehow to get the sails reefed in and secured. At this point only the bare poles continued to take the full force of these unforgiving winds and frothing of the sea that wished to totally engulf all things which floated upon it.

Days and nights became as one. Whether it was my imagination or whether it was true, I think the storm had raged for the better part of four days or maybe even longer. It mattered not, for once it did subside, even the Captain who was on the bridge, seemed to assess that something greater than him had prevailed over our destiny. With the storm over, we started the task of trying to establish what damage had been done to the sails. Also, unbeknownst to us, the Captain and the First Mate were trying to establish where and how far we had been thrown off course. We gradually heard through the grapevine that the ship had been thrown off course well over seven hundred nautical miles. Instead of heading towards the northern part of North America, somewhere around a place called New Port, we were heading towards the Caribbean.

Even though the captain had turned the ship around and by his bearings, the Forgiveness was sailing in the direction of her original port of destination; we now were faced with even a greater problem. The easterlies which were to bring us to New Port were no longer available, and no matter how much tacking we did, or corrections he made us do, the ship lingered, slowly agonizing towards correcting her course.

To make matters even more disturbing, we found after assessing the damage of the hull from the storm, a large portion of our food supply and fresh drinking water had been destroyed by salt water. We were now restricted to rations that a prisoner in a prison cell would not find sufficient to continue to live long. Nevertheless, we had to do the labor of men of iron.

The ship languished and lingered trying to correct her course, and she should have been renamed the 'Ship of Un-Forgiveness'. For at this time, we were becalmed. The sails of the great tall ship lay like shrouds on a picture of blue stillness below. The heat of the relentless sun poured down on the decks to shrink this ship of despair as the days followed the nights. Still, the sea stayed calm and even the air at this point was hard to breathe. We poured salt water continuously on the drying decks as the weather took its toll on the ever-shrinking wood which was the only salvation between us and the sea. Scurvy started to break out, along with the dysentery we all suffered, and still nothing, only the slapping continuation of the sea licking the hull. We were too weak to lower the life boats and row our way out, which was futile at best.

When life was at its lowest ebb and the crew had started to make their peace with their maker, finally there was a breeze. Then, there was a ruffle in the shrouds that had total control over our destiny. When the next morning broke, those ruffles started to fill and flap the sails like great white angel-wings and the ship started to move forward.

We all fell on our knees in glorious praise that we had been spared an agonizing death. Though the rations did not improve, in fact, they were continually being diminished; we felt that we were given a second chance to once more enjoy a life other than a watery grave. It was then that Freddie, my wonderful friend, my companion through all the years of my life which now numbered into my thirties, died of scurvy. Each day more numbers of the crew would join him in his watery grave.

Often, at night I would sit on deck in an isolated area to think of my past and weep for my beautiful wife, my childhood love and my two wonderful boys. My life which had been as perfect as any man could ask; had been snatched away from me in a moment that I did not provoke. My closest and dearest friends of childhood had come to this same fate as well. No matter what destiny lies ahead for Jamie and me; Freddie will never be rejoined with his precious family. If only one of us could return to Liverpool, England to at least tell what has happened to the others, God would be merciful to our families. What despair, what anguish, what torture our families were experiencing? Our wives who were dedicated to us as much as we were to them, how could they know we would have vanished on the morning that they kissed us goodbye. As the days move forward, I continued to pray we would see land somewhere, anywhere, any place in the world with terra firma.

It was less than nine days when the man in the crow's nest yelled clearly, "Land ahoy! Land ahoy!"

As he pointed in the direction, all of us ran to that side of the ship to look longingly at something each man in his heart wished to hold. Within the next watch, we too could see the land. It was the next morning before we could see the shore line and it took us the following day to arrive at a port. To our total amazement, it was the port of call which we had so long ago been destined to—New Port. The Captain, with his total belligerence and inconsideration of life or the safety of others, had not only corrected the hundreds of nautical miles off course at the price of his crew, he had not stopped at another port to take on supplies.

We dropped anchor and there was not a man among us that was not eager to touch the land which he treasured so much. The Captain and his mates demanded us to be on deck.

"Yea, you scurvy bunch, no help from you. We have found the port of call. We will rotate shore leave accompanied by a mate, so you don't lose your way back to the ship."

We had no idea how long it would take, but we did know that sooner or later this ship had to be de-stuffed and it would be pulled into the wharf for the unloading of its cargo. At the end of the week, the Forgiveness was given permission to dock at one of the wharves. As the de-stuffing took place, Jamie and I made a plan. We'd been so grateful on our first shore leave to put our feet, then our hands, and then our whole body back on solid soil, we swore an oath to each other, as well as to God as our witness, we would not return on that ship. We would not be sailors of the sea. We would at all costs of life, find a way to let our wives know what had happened and what we were doing.

As the de-stuffing took days, we planned an escape. One moonless night, Jamie and I lowered a rope from the deck and slithered down into the water, then swam under water as much as possible away from the ship. Once we were a fair distance from the ship, we swam ashore. Obviously we didn't have much baggage, one might say. We had a pair of shoes, a knife and the clothes on our back. Once upon the shore we made our way inland. We felt like fugitives in an alien world. But, we'd broken away from the irons of imprisonment and bondage from a cruel captain and an unmerciful agenda. This was our very first progress since that agonizing night so long, long ago. We had finally broken through the shackles which had bound us in a liquid prison.

After resting and gathering our bearings, we realized that we would have to wait until daylight to get a sense of direction. There was at least one saving grace, during the little privileges we had going ashore, we realized the New Port settlement was an English port and therefore, we at least had the advantage of being able to communicate with someone, anyone, in a common language. When daybreak finally rose we found ourselves somewhere in a forest with trees we had never seen before. We tried to find trails or paths, but we did not want to go back to the settlement. If nothing else, the Governor would probably turn us over to the Captain and the only difference from at the present to yesterday, our backs would be scarred with an everlasting remembrance of disobedience, if we survived the lash.

With this thought in our minds, we worked our way further and further into the forest, always hoping to find either a meadow or an opening. By the end of the day we were quite hungry, though our stomachs had shrunk considerably from the parsimonious diet we'd been on for weeks on the ship. By the second day we were lost. We didn't even know which direction we should be in.

Then, it happened. We were captured once more. We were captured by weird, unruly looking people. Men who had dark skin, black hair, and were half naked. They had spears with axes and made threatening gestures. We both huddled together and then fell on our knees hoping to get one prayer out before the end would come. Instead, these men started yelling and screaming at us in a language we could not possibly comprehend. They then forced us back up on our feet and made us walk through a path which we wouldn't have found on our own. It was a short walk, when out of nowhere came a clearing. In the middle of this clearing there were not huts but some form of tent. It was a village of some primitive nature. Something no one's imagination, no matter how great it was, could comprehend at least, not in my lifetime in England.

We had heard about natives. We'd heard about the spice routes and other wonders of the world, nevertheless to come face to face with these people was unexpected. We were not roughly-treated, but our hands had been bound and once we got to the village, there was a King or leader who appeared from one of the larger dwellings. He too, spoke loudly but we were unable to understand. He squatted on the ground and forced us to do like-wise. He pulled out a knife and he drew a picture in the dirt of the village, and then threw the knife into the middle, indicating where his tent was.

It was a new way of communicating. Both Jamie and I pondered for a minute, and then we started to understand. He was drawing us pictures and asking us to do the same. Having my hands released from their bindings, I reached for the knife but he quickly snatched it back. I then tried with my finger to draw in the dirt two small holes and pointed to me and Jamie. The Chief at this moment knew we had a common communication. He signaled to one of the other men to get a stick, and then I drew the tall ship in which had imprisoned us. The Chief nodded. I drew stick men, Jamie and myself, who ran away from the ship. Again the Chief understood. He then put his hand on his chest and opened his arms to us. We were welcomed. We had been saved, by not only strangers but people that lived a way of life far different than anything we had ever experienced or had access of knowledge to. Still, here was their extension of friendship.

I don't know what made us do it, but we both put our hands on our chest and than opened our arms. From this moment on, in the days that followed, we were looked after. We helped with the menial tasks of the village. We were fed with equal amounts of food as any of the villagers. In some ways it was a peaceful way of living, and equally rewarding. Three months (they referred to moons) had passed. As days became shorter and the nights grew longer, the days were still warm but not as hot as before, with the evenings grew colder and colder.

It was during this period that both Jamie and I were not only adopted by the villagers but we had made a supreme effort on our behalf not to express the way we did things, but to adapt as quickly as possible to their way of life. We learned to hunt and fish with spears. We even became adequate in hunting deer and elk with bows and arrows. We learned how to do trapping of the small animals like beaver and muskrat. These were things in which the men did. The women of the village gathered berries and had small gardens of some kind of tubular vegetables. The elders would look after the children and tell many stories of the village and it's past. We in turn, with every opportunity that arose, would try to learn their language of communication. As we gained more knowledge of their expressions, we were able to able to tell them of our past and where we lived, our families, our wives and children. They shared with great interest and care. In many ways, it could have easily been the Promised Land. Everything was self-sufficient. They needed or wanted for nothing. I might even go as far as to say it could have been what Genesis said was the Garden of Eden.

It was during the fourth moon, when the weather started to change considerably. The green foliage in the forest had started to change to yellow and oranges then bright browns. The leaves were dying. They told us it was the cold time, the sleeping time for the soil; that the earth needed to rest and this was when it would go to sleep. Shortly into the fifth moon, I woke up one morning and went out and to my wonderment, the earth and the trees and everything else was covered in white. The air was crisp and cold.

Long before this, the men had put on tunics which fell well below the knees of their pants. Their shoes, though of soft soles, were warm and durable. The women had always worn long dress with the same foot wear, but now added blankets around their shoulders, and heavy cloaks to keep themselves warm when out in this new winter or sleeping period. The days that followed were colder and the nights grew longer. The only tasks of any importance were providing food and fuel to keep warm. It didn't seem to bother anyone except Jamie and myself. It was as if, as they said, the earth was resting.

Well into three months of this bitter cold, I fell ill. My health had never quite recovered from the endurance in which I experienced on the cruel ship. As far as that goes, neither did Jamie's. Nevertheless, at the moment it was even more serious. I developed an endless coughing and no matter what he was called, a doctor or spiritual advisor of these villagers, came and performed ritual after ritual on me, while the women would have me drink different forms of medicine. The cold on my chest would not break. If anything, it started to produce a rasping sound when I was breathing. One of the elders and the Chief told Jamie they had no medicine, spiritually or physically which could help me and told him that in all probability, I would join my ancestors in the spiritual world.

It was then that Jamie asked if they would do us a supreme favor and take us to the outskirts of the foreign village. We were well aware that these villagers, though small in numbers, probably less than twenty, had had a bad experience with the foreigners. They'd been treated poorly and abused. Both Jamie and I could relate only too well to the way men of our race have treated each other, let alone a people that are foreign in looks and behavior, as an alien from some other world. We fully comprehended what they must have gone through. These gentle people who were kind to each other had obliged us, by their manners to care for others less fortunate than themselves. Nonetheless, the villagers knew my life was no longer in their hands, of helping or contributing to my existence.

After Jamie had pleaded on more than one occasion as I grew worse, the Chief finally consented that he would send four of his men with a stretcher for me and take us both to the outskirts of the foreigner's village. They had in more than four or five years, relocated and re-routed trails so that the foreigners would not find their village or interrupt their culture or their way of life. Still, in concern for my health with Jamie's pleading, the request was granted. In the next few days we all were prepared for the journey. It would take four to five days of their skillful navigation to get us to the outskirts of the village of the foreigners.

They covered me with heavy blankets and fur pelts and continually gave me warm broth along this journey. My condition deteriorated and on the last night, during my coughing spells now for the first time blood sputtered out. Jamie would have to drag me the better part of two miles, give or take, to where the houses of the foreigners were.

Before midday arrived, he had succeeded in dragging a dying friend.

With much apprehension, he entered the village. Yes, they were British. After talking to some of them, Jamie was directed to the doctor in the area. Once I was admitted to the doctor's home, he immediately recognized the condition I was in. I had what he pronounced was consumption which later in years would be known as the dreaded tuberculosis. Between himself, his wife and his older daughter, they managed to save my life. It was spring when I'd finally recovered well enough to start to perform the most menial of tasks like walking and sitting at the table.

By summer my health had recovered substantially and the villagers were more curious about how Jamie and I had spent time with what they called 'Indians', than they were about our returning to England. They told us there would be ships periodically bringing supplies from England and God knows when they would return to the motherland. At last, I was able to help another cobbler with the trade I had learned so long ago and Jamie found a variety of jobs which provided us both with shelter and food, but very little savings.

It was during this period that the Governor of the region, along with a large entourage, came to the village. He was rather interested in our stories of being on a ship which practiced the ruthlessness of press gangs. He took sympathy on us and provided us transportation back to New York. It seemed so long ago however it was no more than a year that under the darkness of night, we arrived in New York. After being established in a rooming house and gaining employment, the Governor said he would advise us when the next ship arrived that would be returning to England.

The months passed, the spring brought the flowers, the summer brought the warm weather, and both Jamie and I wrote letters at every given opportunity and handed them to captains of any ship sailing near our homeland. Hoping against hope, by any chance, that our wives would know we were alive and we were in the New World. We waited, that by the grace of God, we could one day return on a vessel, homeward bound.

It was late in the fall, and once again the trees had returned to the rainbow of colors, when a ship which was a naval vessel of the British realm, dropped anchor. The captain had recently finished circumnavigating or charting large portions of the coast-lines and was re-stocking his ship to return to England with his reports. The Governor asked the Captain if he would consider taking on any civilians. Of course, being a military ship, and commissioned by the King himself, it was absolutely absurd. The Governor, having a warm heart and a kind disposition, was going to entertain in the good manners of hospitality, the Captain and his officers at his dwelling.

He also sent an invitation to us, and to put on our best garments as well as our most respectful behavior, for the Captain of the vessel had already refused passage to us. The Governor was hoping if we had the opportunity of being present and the Captain heard our discouraging and deplorable story, he might show some interest in the realm of the natives who were first in the region.

After waiting the better part of a fortnight, the vessel had been re-stocked and the guest list had been sent out to the appropriate people who would be invited, which included both Jamie and myself. The evening was robust and reflecting the quality that the British aristocrats know how to perform in the true manner of our growing empire. The captain was gracious and of good-breeding. His officers were equally of good breeding and all came from aristocratic families. Before the evening was to conclude both Jamie and I had the opportunity to tell some of our amazing events to each one of the officers as well, briefly, to the Captain himself. They were amused by our tales of these people who lived such a remote existence in the middle of a forest. One even mentioned he felt their way of life was extremely primitive, to say the least. On the other hand when we told the officers of the benevolence and kindness we received from these people, there seemed to be a genuine acknowledgement of interest.

We both returned to our rooming-house, disappointed and expecting nothing more than a fine meal at the Governor's house. Two days after the event we received another message asking that we return to the Governor's house. We asked for permission to leave our employment early and go to enquire what the Governor had to say to us. We heard that after leaving the dinner the previous evening with the officers, the good Governor brought the subject of us up again. He had personally asked the British Captain to escort us, at his expense, back to England so we might be able to tell the appropriate authorities of the events which we had experienced with the local natives. The Governor personally felt it would be beneficial, not only in the welfare of the realm, but for military purposes which may arise in the future. In contrast to some of the other natives, these ones may become allies if a rebellion or a situation arose with the French further north.

Reluctantly, the Captain concluded this assessment had value and he would arrange for appropriate quarters aboard his ship for our return. We could not believe what we'd heard.

Though we had been able to save very little money after providing for our immediate expenses, once again the good Governor said, "I've already paid your passage as gentlemen and in return I expect you to write a full report of your findings and your experiences to the appropriate authorities back in London. This will be the repayment I require from both of you."

With a deep admiration and a renewed belief in humanity, we waited for the Captain's permission to come aboard. Though the quarters were rather crowded, they were of a luxurious manner compared to what we had experienced on the Ship of Forgiveness. The food was what the Captain and his officers ate at their table. The wines or the beverages provided were of standards of the British Navy. We were treated as gentlemen, as guests of the Royal Navy.

The days that followed were a different experience for us on the high seas. The discipline was rigid. The rules were obeyed to the 'nth' degree. Nonetheless they were just, they were fair, and the men were treated with respect. There was a professionalism of even the lower seamen who had never experienced anything like what the crew of The Forgiveness had received, let alone been under the commanded of that type of Captain.

After a fortnight, we were mid-way across this vast ocean. The winds had been forgiving and the expertise and seamanship of the navigation demonstrated first-hand why the Royal Navy commanded the high seas. It would be another fortnight give or take, before docking in South Hampton. The rest of the voyage continued in a professional manner, well navigated and right on schedule. It was a few days after the second fortnight when we arrived in South Hampton.

The voyage had taken a greater toll on my health. Though I had not deteriorated to the state when my life itself had been threatened, my health was still fragile. I was a mere shadow of the man who had left only years before. Jamie had fared a little better and once we had disembarked at South Hampton, we made arrangements to get passage to Liverpool. I had barely boarded this commuter cargo ship when my health declined rapidly. Before three days out to sea in the channel, I started once more coughing and heaving, unable to keep anything down. By the fifth day, nearing Liverpool, I had grown much worse. The first symptoms of the dreaded consumption had returned. I had started to cough up the liquid blood that controlled my life.

We landed in Liverpool and with the help of my trusted friend Jamie, we made our way homeward bound, heading to the street that we had lived with our families so long, long ago. I looked like a ghost, with sunken eyes, as if soot had been painted around them to blacken them as coals. My hair was straggly and thin, tightly-stretched skin wrapped this bag of bones.

My wife barely recognized me. Upon receiving me the best she could do was to weep. Tears of joy were followed by those of disbelief. That night, laying in my own bed at long last, with my sons and my wife around me, the doctor came. He asked to examine me alone. I'd been spewing large portions of blood up whenever my strength would permit.

He looked compassionately at me and said, "There is nothing I or any other mortal man can do for you. The hands of the Lord are all that are left for you."

I smiled a warm grateful smile back which startled the good doctor.

He asked, "Why do you smile at such despairing information?"

Then with a weak whisper, I answered, "What greater gift can a dying man have than to lie in his own bed, with his family around him?"

That night I left that world and like the nights before, the dawn had come up and I opened my eyes to find myself weak and on the chesterfield in which I'd sat on the night before.

Once more, I tried to focus on my surroundings, and was able to establish that I had returned to this time. I said a silent prayer, being grateful be back in my own time. I lay there on the Chesterfield too weak to make my presence known. It was well into the first hour of sunrise before I was able to ring the bell. Two of the male servants arrived and immediately assisted me back to my boudoir.

As before, my wife and the Doctor were summonsed as the servants placed me upon the bed. After the good Doctor examined me and gave me a large sedative, I looked longing at my wife and tried my best to smile. Before the sedative took effect, I reached out to hold her hand and in my confused state, I tried to tell her how much I needed her and was grateful to be back with her. I never took my eyes off her, until the sedation took over and I was no longer conscious.

I don't know whether it was my age or this last encounter, however I felt weaker than I had in the past and it took me longer to recover. The weeks vanished and it was well into the third month before I was able to resume my normal activities. Nonetheless I am very grateful be here in the present and well enough to take on my daily responsibilities.

As Dr. Sebastian read the last paragraph of this chapter, he looked directly ahead at the large doors in his vision. He did not have any desire to turn his head either to the benevolent painting or the more sinister one. As his mind pondered over this last chapter, he could not distinguish which portrait had possessed the writer. With these thoughts still in his mind, his hand automatically reached for the bell which would bring the butler, and start the process of returning home. He spent little time looking out the window in the limousine, for it was now very repetitious, and his mind was focused on the many projects which were taking place in the Museum. Deep in thought, the time passed quickly and he only realized the journey had been completed as the chauffeur stopped in front of his home. With the usual farewells he once more entered his home into the arms of his beloved wife waiting.

"Well, you're home early today," as she gave him a great hug and looked up into his eyes.

"Yes! Yes, I could've stayed longer and maybe even tried to do another chapter. Still, I think if I can complete one chapter at a time, I get the feeling more of what the writer had gone through during his detainment in another time with one of the portraits."

"Are you going to tell me what it was like in this chapter?" she asked.

With a broad smile on his face, he replied, "Only if I can have a glass of wine to quench my thirst."

Nodding in agreement, she replied, "Make yourself comfortable and I'll bring a fine bottle of Merlot with two wine glasses at your service."

He settled himself in his favorite chair in the living room before his wife returned with two glasses and a fine bottle of the grape.

"Now! It's my turn to listen as you tell me about this latest chapter," as they both clicked the glasses of wine.

"Let me see. The chapter that I just completed; it's about a man who was a cobbler when the tall ships were still moving cargo back and forth from Europe to the Americas. The remarkable thing about this event is a man and his friends were captured into a chain gang and taken aboard a cargo ship. This tale is about their endurance. It also is about the writer's knowledge in this period. I get the feeling that it was the native Indians in this case that had a more civilized behavior then the colonists."

"Oh, how interesting," she acknowledged, and then added, "Did all end well?"

"That is the part which puzzles my mind; the cobbler returns to his home in England to die in his own bed surrounded by his family."

"I do say . . . it doesn't have much of a happy ending, could I be right in saying?" she asked.

"I haven't really been able to distinguish which portrait possessed the writer at this, but yes, I agree; it is the endings which is somewhat baffling to me, whether it is happy or sad."

"Would you like another glass of wine before I start dinner?" she said to break the mood.

"I would most enjoy another glass and being informed on what we are going to have this evening to entice my appetite," he replied.

They both have a jolly little laugh before she informed him that it was going to be one of his favorite fish-dishes; bouillabaisse soup that she'd been working on all afternoon and accompanied by a freshly baked loaf of French bread. As for dessert, she'd prepared one of his favorites; bread-pudding with a cinnamon top. He nodded in approval and declared that he would try to restrain himself until she was ready to serve the dinner. The evening stretched into the late hours as they both enjoyed watched one of her favorite Agatha Christie movies before retiring for the night.

THE FOG

—ɯ—

Dr. Sebastian was busy cleaning up the last little bits on his desk before leaving for the weekend. In the last three months he accomplished a great deal. Many of the artifacts which had been in storage for some years now had the chance to be on display; while others which had dominated the space for many years were now back in storage. The entire Museum had taken on a new excitement with the changing displays, not only for the employees but most importantly for the visitors to the Museum, whether they were locals or from out of the country. It was seldom that Dr. Sebastian felt as satisfied with what he had accomplished and to have most of the immediate demands under control.

With these thoughts, he started to look forward to the next week and what may lay ahead which was pertinent to his immediate attention. As he was going over the schedule, he noticed an appointment was made for exactly three months to the day of his last visit to the mansion. He'd given up wondering if it was coincidence that his secretary was making these continuous appointments on the same day regardless of what month. Truthfully, it gave him an eerie feeling of something more sinister or unexplainable that was taking place on his visits to the mansion. After examining the rest of the priorities in the next week; he closed up the memos and proceeded to leave his office. After saying good-night to his secretary, he quickly drove home to enjoy the weekend with his wife.

On the day designated, as before, the chauffeur arrived at Dr. Sebastian's home. The procedure was always the same. The hour and half drive to the mansion did not deviate more than a few minutes from previous visits. As usual, the butler would escort him once more to the library. And as usual, the two servants in charge would present him with the Book of Portraits. As they left the room, Dr. Sebastian opened up the book to the next chapter. As he looked down the words in bold print were 'The Fog.'

Oh! What have I done this year, it has vanished so quickly? What have I accomplished in this time that I face this night which awaits me in horror? Now, the shade of light is being replaced by the darkness as I sit alone once more in my library. I now have abandoned my desk and moved over to my couch. In the past, I found sitting waiting for the unthinkable to happen on my couch was the best place for me to be. I gaze beyond my desk to the windows which shield me from the outside. Now the shadows of darkness are growing larger as my eyes continue to focus on their advancement.

Soon, my destiny will be placed in the power of one of the canvases, either good or evil which will hold me in their entrapment, amidst another place in the spirit world. Again, one of these canvases will take my soul to one of my past lives and the time in which it took place. I've survived more than one of these encounters with sheer perseverance.

Oh my God, my greatest fear is that I will not survive one of these encounters and I will be left in the past. I have abandoned the idea long ago that I am the victim of a demented person in the past or hallucinating that I have fallen back into a time warp and being possessed by another person. No, this is not true . . . for it is my soul, my karma of the past times. At times, my soul was kind, benevolent and worthy, and then like the left-hand versus the right-hand, my soul has experienced being cruel, ruthless and unforgiving.

These are the thoughts I'm having in my mind before the time approaches that I will be possessed. There is no need for artificial light to illuminate this room, for after the God-given natural light of the day diminishes and I fall into the darkness of the night, the time will come. The last glimmer of light is vanishing and the darkness of the night is waiting its turn as I stare out the window to wait my fate. Oh! Oh the pain is unbearable. I will not be able to endure! Help, for the love of God, help!

I am running for my life on a path along the coast which is narrow. When I started my walk, it was a beautiful day and now the mist from the sea has turned into a fog that is chasing me from behind. I have fear, for it is not the fog itself, but what I feel is *in* the fog. I am running so fast and the fog is catching up to me and what is in it.

Oh, please God, do not let me fall or stumble, please! Thank you for saving me.

The mist that precedes the fog is now ahead of me. I am losing this race against those in the fog.

Oh, at last! At last, in the distance, I see the bell tower of the church. The distance is not that great, but the mist now has reached the church and I still have a way to go before I achieve the same. I must do it, I can do it, and I will do it! For my life is in danger, at least, I feel that in my heart. I am now close to the churchyard and so is the fog. The fog is engulfed the church and is ahead of me.

For the first time, I hear something . . . Yes, I do hear something . . . it's voices. My intuition was right, there is something. No, they are human voices in the fog and they are screaming. They are just behind me. I swing open the gates to the churchyard and run towards the doors of the church.

Oh, God, thank you for saving me. I reach the doors of the church only to find that they will not open. They have always been open before. And then my mind reaches inwards, of course . . . . every time they were open when I was going to church, it was Sunday or some other service.

I turn to face my adversaries. But, by the grace of God they have not reached the church steps, yet I can feel their presence gathering closer and closer as the seconds pass. With fear sharpening my mind, I remember the Vicar's house is just behind the church. In speed, I run towards the Vicar's house and am soon banging on the door.

Now the screams are closing in on me. I find myself screaming as well as I bang continuously on the door like a mad person. My hands have become too sore to bang any further. I am preparing to meet my fate when the door opens and a housekeeper looks out.

She looks bewildered and asks, "What do you want child, what do you want?"

I cry out at the doorway, "Please . . . . for the love of God, give me entrance, please!" In a high-pitched voice, almost hysterical, I repeat, "Give me entrance, I'm in great danger."

The elderly woman looks out at the fog which has engulfed the Vicar's house and then opens the door wider. I enter the dwelling. I am gasping for air and look around the room as my lungs breath deeply for the air present and my eyes see sanctuary. The elderly housekeeper directs me to one of the chairs in the kitchen.

With reassurance, she keeps on repeating, "You are going to be all right, dearie. You're going to be all right, just relax . . . just relax, dearie."

I start to cry uncontrollably between gasps of air. What seems like eternity to me, but in reality is only a few minutes, I start to gain some repose and start to look at my surroundings.

Now that I have gained some control of my breathing, the housekeeper asks me, "What's wrong, dearie?"

Then she recognizes me and I recognize her. I tell her I live in the Manor and I was taking a walk along the sea path to the village to see my aunt. My parents are Lord and Lady of the Manor. We are well respected in this community which pays tribute to our farmlands and we are held in high-standing in the village itself. My Father, a leader in the community, is always willing to participate in any worthy cause, and contributes both his time and money at any given request. My Mother is no exception in her many works of charity, whether for young or old, it matters not to her, in aid to serve all people in need. My two brothers and I have been brought up in a loving family. We have a few servants; two chambermaids that overseer the domestic requirements, a faithful cook that provides our dinners, and, of course, the gardener. Oh my goodness, I forgot the stable help. As one can see we support and look after more than just the five of us.

I have just turned twenty years of age. I was only seven years old when my first brother was born, and then followed by my second brother when I was the age of nine years old. I've always taken on the responsibility of being their guardian. Of course, we had nannies and tutors as we grew older. But, in many ways I took it upon myself to be more than a sibling, I had a motherly instinct to ensure my brothers developed by not only my standards, but that of my family. My Mother, being an aristocrat, was extremely busy in the affairs of the village and surrounding areas.

I became the disciplinarian with a firm hand for my brothers. It has always been taken for granted that I was their guiding force in their upbringing. I've always treated them fair and with kindness, but I've always been the leader, well . . . maybe one might say, more a ruler. Of course, it goes without saying; I never suggested or made them do any girly things. My Father was in complete control of the manly things in their agenda as they grew older, like hunting and riding, as well as boy's activities of sports. I enjoyed the more feminine activities of embroidery and musical instruments, to say nothing of writing.

The housekeeper then said, "Its okay, dearie. It is all right . . . you are all right. Would you like a nice cup of tea?"

I looked up, and then replied, "Yes, that would be very nice. Thank you for your kindness."

We were a happy family! Oh! Oh, why have I used the past? We are a happy family. All of these things are going through my mind, racing from one moment to the next.

With the help of a strong cup of tea from this kind and generous woman, I have regained my repose. By the time I have finished my second cup of tea, the good housekeeper is still holding my hand and asking me "What happened, dearie?"

When I attempted to answer her question, I returned to weeping. Half an hour passed, and with her patience and my supreme efforts, I was able to answer some of the questions she has asking. I told her that when I started my walk, the weather was pleasant and it was a clear day, so I decided to walk to the village to see my aunt. I was approximately midway to the village when the mist surprisingly started to form along the sea cliffs, only for the fog to follow closely behind. At first, I was not concerned, even when the mist swirled around me, and the fog was much thicker behind me. But, due to the weather conditions, I started walking faster. It was only then I heard crying, screaming in the fog.

The housekeeper looked at me, still holding my hand and asked," You heard what in the fog? Did I hear right? Did you say cries and screaming?" the housekeeper asked me.

I was still looking at her, though my voice started to quiver, "Yes, I heard cries and screaming in the fog behind me. They were screaming for help," I added.

"Well dearie, why didn't you stop and help them?"

I looked directly into her eyes and realized I had no answer for either one of us.

Then, in a whisper I replied," I had a great fear . . . a great fear of these people. I have no answers for you or myself. It was in my heart and my soul, this great fear."

I really don't know why I had a great fear. I looked towards the window as if I was waiting or expecting someone to stare through the window but there was nothing. By now, the fog had lifted somewhat. I could see the church and then I looked back at the housekeeper, with her warm smile and understanding of youth.

"It's all right, dearie. It's all right," she no sooner got the words out and the Vicar himself came into the room. He was somewhat taken back that he had a guest without his knowledge, but after the housekeeper quickly explained my fear and dilemma, he too, was comforting me.

He moved towards me and put his hand on my shoulder to assure me and then added, "If you wish to talk about this, I'm hear to listen and may have some understanding of your situation."

He was a little older than my Father and had been the Vicar of our parish ever since I can remember.

He then said to me, "It might be better for us both to go into my office and I will hear what has happened to you, both physically and spiritually, that has caused you such distress." Though I'd been to church on every occasion that was required, I've always been with my family. Even when my brothers were tiny, I had never been alone in the presence of the Vicar.

Although I am a woman, I still have the shyness of a young girl and the obedience, I may add. Without hesitation, I got up from the chair. Then, looking at the housekeeper, I thanked her for all her kindness. With this completed, I followed the Vicar. His office was nowhere near as elaborate as my Father's. However, this could also be said about the rectory compared to our house. The Vicar returned to his desk and I sat across from him. He then asked me how the family was and what progress I was making in my music, along with my embroidery and writing. On yes, my writing, I love to write poetry especially on a warm spring day. With the skill of being a person of the cloth, he delicately guided me.

All my words flowed out, as I felt the comfort and ease in his presence. I told him everything.

"I was walking along the path which comes to a part where the cliff reaches down to the sea and works its way towards the small hamlet to visit my Aunt's house. As I continued my walk by the cliffs . . . that was when the fog started to roll in."

When I got to this point, I could feel a tightening in my throat and the restriction again in my breathing, even though I was at ease and secure in the house of the Vicar, and the presence of Almighty God. I then proceeded to tell the Vicar of my fear and hearing the voices behind me, screaming for help in the fog. Somehow I knew with the confusion in the fog, if they caught up to me—I would join them.

The Vicar asked me, "Who are they?"

I then replied, "I do not know." I repeated, "I do not know."

With this, the Vicar now turned his head and looked out the window. He asked me to join him. To my amazement, the fog was lifting. I could see the skies return to their blue beauty with the sun shining above.

He turned to and said, "The fog has lifted, all has returned to normal. I will have the stable boy escort you home." He then added, "Maryanne, please give my best regards to your family and as always, I'm looking forward to seeing all of you at church this Sunday."

He then excused himself and left the office as I remained standing by the window. It was a very short time when he returned and summonsed me to follow him, which I obliged without hesitation. As we returned to the main hall, he opened the front door and there was the stable boy waiting to escort me back to my home. Without further ado, I thanked the Vicar and his housekeeper, and then followed the stable boy.

We took the same path which less than an hour ago had been blanketed in fog; now there was barely any mist on it. He led the way as I followed behind him. He was not talkative and I was in no mood to encourage conversation. It seemed the distance was much shorter than when I had begun my walk hours before. Soon, my home was in sight. I thanked him sincerely with all my heart, for being a gallant young man and escorting me to safety. Now with our goodbyes behind us he went on his way and I opened the door to my home.

As I entered the hallway, I felt safe once more; then it entered my mind whether I should share my experience with my parents. It had never been the habit of our family to withhold information from one another. Even when my brothers were much younger than they are now we would always have family discussions and share our experiences. Now and then, there were sad moments which we wished not to relive; nevertheless both our Father and Mother encouraged us to be forthcoming.

With this thought, I sought out my Mother to tell her of my experience. Well, this is not quite true, for the first two members of my family that I shared my experience with were my brothers. Both of them seemed disinterested, to say the least. My brother Lloyd asked me if I thought I'd really heard ghosts.

I replied, "I have no idea."

With this response, Lloyd had no further questions or thoughts on the matter. The best I got from my other brother Harold was the odd look up from the book he was reading. After having no further interest, they both looked at me as if it was time for me to leave.

Now I did find the room in which my Mother was in and without further delay, I asked if I could interrupt her and share my experience this afternoon. My Mother is always willing to stop anything she is doing, at any time of the day, to listen to us children. I really shouldn't say children; for we are young adults, by all accounts.

My Mother listened closely to my experience in the fog, and then asked, "Do you the really think it might not have been your imagination running wild on you, walking in the fog?"

I have always had the highest respect for my Mother's knowledge and being able to say the right things at the right time. I concentrated on the question in earnest, and then I replied to my Mother, "No, not in this case."

I then repeated, mostly to myself, but was looking at my Mother and repeated, "No, Mother I heard voices. I have no idea why I experienced the fear I did, nonetheless; I did hear voices."

My Mother gave me that knowing smile and said in her warm loving voice, "You're back home safe and sound and that is really all that counts." We both put ours arms around one another in that wonderful moment of a Mother knowing her daughter is all right and her daughter knowing that she is safe in her Mother's arms. With this, I took my leave and returned to my room. I needed some peace and solitude before the evening meal.

The hours passed quietly as the servants were preparing the dinner for our usual time of eight o'clock. During the evening meal, none of us brought up the subject of my experience in the afternoon. We carried on the usual conversation of events that were coming up or ones that we had missed. As always, my parents listened and made slight comments or suggestions on the itinerary's which were forthcoming. After dinner, my Father and brothers went to the billiards room. My Mother and I retreated to the living room and sat around the fireplace doing needle-work. The routine was what we practiced every evening, and by eleven o'clock, all of us retired to our designated bedrooms.

The next morning started as it always did, with family conversation around the table as we shared our breakfast meal. I did not mention the past experience, nor did any of the other members of my family. I came to the conclusion that if I couldn't explain what happened to myself, let alone others, it was best to put it behind me, and get on with the present.

I went about my morning activities, writing some poetry and thinking of peaceful thoughts as I passed the time away before I realized the mid-day meal had arrived. We all met in the aviary to enjoy not only the food which was present but the surroundings that enhanced it. Once again the discussion of what we had been doing in the morning hours and our plans for the afternoon were the subject of the conversation by one and all. After lunch was thoroughly enjoyed, we went our separate ways. I stopped by my room to pick up a long overdue book that I wanted to finish. I then returned to the aviary on this warm pleasant day to be surrounded by flowers, and soon fell into a peaceful mood.

It was an hour later when my Mother appeared. She smiled and said, "I thought I might find you here."

She then asked if I would be obliging to accompany her to my Father's study. I looked up somewhat surprised, but not overly concerned, and asked if there was anything wrong.

She replied, "No, we just want to go over a few things that you brought up the other day."

It was then that I realized what the subject matter would be about. Without any hesitation, I got up from the chair, placed my book on the small table beside it, and replied, "I'm ready now, Mother."

With this, she once again smiled and said, "Follow me."

As we both entered my Father's study, he was busy as usual sitting behind a large desk, with a massive amount paper before him.

"Please sit down. I will be with you both in a minute," my Father replied. We both settled into two comfortable chairs, and after a few moments passed, my Father spoke.

"First, my dearest daughter, I believe you know how important you are to your Mother and me. We love you beyond any doubt in our minds. We've always involved you and your brothers in all the activities of this household. We have loved you from the first day, to this very present moment, with all our hearts and devotion of being parents. You were, and always will be our first child. Nevertheless, today I have to share with you something which we have kept from you on purpose. The greatest hope we have is that you will not feel we have been neglectful withholding this knowledge from you.

We felt it unnecessary to think about this matter; let alone bring it to your attention. All the same, yesterday, when you experienced your fear in the fog, we felt it was time to share this information with you, even though it may be troublesome and incomprehensible to you at this moment. Still, it may clear up some of the questions that you have in your mind of what you experienced during your walk to the village when the fog came up.

I feel with this knowledge, you may have a greater understanding of what may have transpired to date.

Exactly twenty years ago yesterday I was walking along the same shoreline that you were. It was there, when I found you in a basket. I returned to the house immediately, and without any hesitation both my wife and I took it upon ourselves to become your ever-loving parent's. From that day forth, we have always been and will always be your loving parents. Furthermore, the community has and will always recognize you as our first child."

I was totally stunned. I was trying to understand what I was hearing, but I was in shock. I sat straight up in my chair with both my hands gripping the armrest. My eyes never left my Father's face, however my breathing was shallow and if possible, I was perspiring under my garments. All I could do at this time was wait and listen to what further prevailed from my Father.

My Father paused. The silence was deafening, at least to my ears. It as then that my Mother took her position and spoke, "When we first found you as a bundle of joy that entered our lives you would have been at best, two months old. The first few months after receiving this wonderful gift from God in our lives; we, as responsible people, did our best to seek out and identify your natural parents. As we searched for answers to questions in our minds, there were no results. One of our theories was that you might be the child of an unwedded mother."

She looked straight at me with a serious look I had only seen a few times in my entire life.

"The day before the great gift from God, you, my child, came into our lives; there was a great tragedy at sea."

My Mother's eyes started to water and again it was one of the few times I've ever seen my Mother so emotional. She took a deep breath and then silence came once more. My Father was the one to speak of the tragedy at sea. A few pieces of the shipwreck were later discovered to be all that remained in that fatal storm.

He looked at me sad and forlorn, "One of the ships lost at sea during this terrible storm had set sail for the New World and was carrying pilgrims. To the best of our knowledge, from the seafaring people in this area, the ship was caught in the gale, and thrown off course, then caught in thick fog, only to be shipwrecked on the rocks. The men of the sea searched the entire area diligently but did not find any survivors, only a few pieces of the ship itself. To this day, no one has been able to recover more than a few pieces of wood as evidence of that fatal day."

"So now we are sharing the day that you entered our lives. In the days that proceeded, there was no evidence to substantiate that you are associated with any of the lost lives of that shipwreck. The reason we are sharing this with you, is our family has never had any hidden secrets with each other. My dearest and most beloved daughter, the reason we are even sharing this moment that you became part of our lives, is to let you know your Mother and I take everything seriously on what happens to anyone of us. When you heard the screams in the fog, both your Mother and I felt it our duty to share this information with you."

My Father had stopped talking and the room became silent. Both my Mother and myself continued to stare upon my Father. He still remained silent. I have no idea how pale I looked to them, but if it was any indication, I felt like a ghost myself. I was sure my hands were as white as the new fallen snow, followed by my cheeks being as red as the fires of hell. My breathing was rapid and shallow. I had difficulty getting sufficient air in the room, my head became light-headed. I felt dizzy as if I was going to faint. The tears started uncontrollably running down my face, the only sign that showed I had not frozen in time. Both my parents were by my side holding my hand. I got up out of my chair and put my arms around my Mother, sobbing. I could feel my Father behind me, holding me and giving supported.

Is this the beginning of what it's like to be an adult? Being scared out of one's life one day, only for the next day to be informed that you did not come from your Mother's womb. Between heavy sobs, I muttered how much I loved them both and how dear they were to me. Both of them reassured me of the love and devotion they had for me. They both continued to stress that they would always be my parents and I would always be their first child, their first love.

Once I was able to gain my composure, I asked for permission to retire to my room. As I returned to my bedroom I looked around at the familiar belongings. Now somehow, they seemed distance or foreign to me. I lay on my bed and gazed up at the ceiling as my mind drifted over the events of the last 48 hours. Being confused would be an understatement of my thoughts.

The remainder of the day was like so many of the previous days before in my life. When we all gathered for dinner, the subject matter was the same as the days before and what was the most interesting thing that happened to each of us today. Of course, my brothers took control of the conversation while the other three of us listened. I was in no mood to make any contribution to the conversation, in fact, in some ways I was like a distant bystander to the whole dinner itself. As the meal finished each one of us retired to our favorite rooms, my Mother and I returned to the living room with the warm fire. For a prolonged period of time we sat together and said nothing to each other and concentrated on our embroidery.

At last, my Mother mentioned our discussion this afternoon. She assured me the only reason they had brought the subject up was to let me know they did not believe it was my imagination or I was hallucinating. All the same, other than the association of my arrival in their life, they had no idea why or what I had experienced on the path in the fog. Like all other evenings, as the clock ticked its way towards eleven o'clock, we all retired to our rooms.

The sunshine was beaming through my window as I still lay curled up in my bed, reluctant to start the day. Finally I got up and went to the window and saw what a beautiful day was present to enjoy in life's fullness. After doing my toiletries, I joined the others for the morning meal. It was as normal as could be. The days that followed were as if nothing had changed in my life or with my family.

Even I started to question myself about that fateful day in the fog. By the time a fortnight found its way into our lives everything remained normal, even the weather. I had wondered by this time; if the fear of being alone in the fog, had maybe let my emotions capture more than was real. Maybe, just maybe, it was being isolated and somewhat disorientated by the rapid advance of the fog to say nothing of its density. Perhaps, my mind had played a devilish role of my fear, especially not having a companion to share my situation with. Had it been nothing more or maybe less than my creative mind conjuring up an idea which would put the fear in anyone? Who could or would create such a work? Oh! Who knows . . . who knows? Only God knows for sure.

By the end of the month I had returned to my normal ways and put this experience in some small alcove of my mind. Maybe not quite forgotten; but nevertheless, out of mind for the present. The months then followed like the days before, and finally the festive season was upon us once more. The sheer enjoyment and merriment which goes with the Christmas time and all the things it brings was shared by one and all. At last, a new year entered. This would be a very special year, for I was going to be 21 years of age and an adult at last. Life was good for the whole family and exceptionally good for me.

The planning of my 21st birthday party was very elaborate. Everyone from my good friends at school, at church, and now at college were invited to participate in my moment of becoming a full-fledged adult. Yes, even my brothers' friends were at my party, and it goes without saying that my parents' friends and relatives of the family were also present and accounted for. This was a Gaelic event and I was extremely happy. To make things more special, there was one young man who was from a good family who was making overtures to 'yours truly'.

He had one of our mutual friends introduce us and after the friend parted, this handsome young man continued to make small talk with me while his parents and mine mingle with others. I must admit that I was flattered (as well as attracted to this young man), however more importantly, he was able to carry on a conversation of diversity which did not concentrate strictly on male subjects. I was pleased with the time we did spend together, though it was not of any great length.

It did not go unnoticed our parents. The first person to mention this get-together by the two of us was my Mother. She always will be the more inquisitive and observant of my parents. She brought the subject up about a young man showing an interest in one of her daughters. With all the humor and happiness I was experiencing that day, I could not help but laugh and ask how many daughters do they have? As my humor was well received, my Mother then asked me what my feelings towards this young man were. I told her that I felt considerable admiration and respect for this young man in the short time of our conversation. And so this day ended on one of the great highlights of my life; first, I become an adult and secondly, I had an admirer.

In the following days my Mother, like always confided everything that she showed an interest in, and of course, especially her children with my Father. She told my Father of the conversation I had with this young man, and my thoughts and feelings towards his interest in me. Later that day, my Mother asked me to join her in my Father's library. On normal occasions, my brothers would be involved in any subject matter concerning the family. It was not the case this time. As the three of us sat in comfortable chairs, my Father took the lead in the conversation.

"Your Mother and I have knowledge of an interest you've shown towards a young man of good breeding. Asking as your parents, would you like to further this involvement on a courtship basis? Before you give me your answer, I've had a letter from his parents. They are asking on his behalf, if there would be any chance of him pursuing a courtship. Now, my beloved daughter, what are your wishes in this relationship which is developing?"

My answer was forthcoming, "Father, if it pleases you and Mother, I would definitely like to explore the avenues and opportunities which this young man presents himself towards me."

"Then, I would suggest I formerly invite him and his family along with some mutual friends to dine at our home at a convenient time for one and all," said Father.

I agreed immediately and thanked my Father and Mother for their wisdom and approach in this matter. The arrangements were made and all the right people were invited. The seating arrangements were planned well, not to be conspicuous, but on the other hand giving James the opportunity to make direct conversation to me without drawing undue attention. The dinner went well, and by the closing of the evening my parents and his parents spent time talking on a one-to-one basis. Towards the end of the evening, James asked me if it would acceptable by my parents and myself, if he could call on me at my convenience. I accepted his invitation unconditionally.

That night was the beginning of a true courtship of James and me. As the weeks moved into months, we were in each other's company at every opportunity which was available. James and I enjoyed the moments of horseback-riding, playing tennis, or just walks along the path of the cliffs. Of course, we were always escorted by a chaperone, for our family would not have it any other way. It was obvious to one and all how happy we were in each other's presence. It was becoming rare to see one without the other. We were anxious lovebirds, waiting for our freedom without the prying eyes of all around us. It was commented on by everyone that we had a romance of once-in-a-lifetime.

My life was picture perfect. I was being courted, and in love, with a young man who was suitable to my station. I also felt a warm affection I'd never felt before towards any man. As the time passed, we found not only the attraction and love for each other was growing, but like my parents, we wished to spend time sharing our thoughts together.

There was no doubt in our minds about our wishes to be together in holy matrimony. But these things are not quite as simple as it would seem, for it was our parents' decision on the final outcome of our relationship. The two of us were apprehensive when his parents invited my parents and a select group of friends for dinner. As the evening progressed, with one toast after another, it was becoming evident that this was my betrothal party. My beautiful James stood up and asked my Father and Mother if he could have my hand in marriage, before all the witnesses who were present and accounted for. Oh, my beautiful James was so elegantly polished and felt so comfortable in this aristocratic environment. Then my Father stood up and looked directly at me, and then directly at James, and gave his consent. The rest of the evening we were definitely the centerpiece of the conversation with congratulations. It was a day I would always remember, as a highlight of my live. James and I were ecstatic on how well things went throughout the evening.

The next days were a whirlwind of excitement, in some cases, even disbelief. I kept thinking of getting one of those daisies; 'he loves me, he loves me not', but it didn't really matter. Whether I plucked the petal 'he love me not' off the flower, or whether I questioned everything that I could possibly think of as negative, it always came up that 'he loved me' and I loved him. I found myself in a state of intoxication, not believing I could be this happy. I found myself, instead of walking dignified like a young lady should, often to be skipping along like a young child. As far as my poetry, I was so prolific that one would think I was rushing to have a publication due at any moment. My life now was at its phoenix for my life couldn't get any better. Sometimes I felt my heart would burst wide open with pure joy.

It was one of these days with my heart full of joy that I decided it was long overdue to visit my aunt. With happiness in my heart, I started walking on the path along the cliffs by the sea. As I walked briskly, humming to myself, the sky above was blue with gentle breezes moving the puffy white clouds.

I was more than halfway to the village when the sky became overcast with a mist rising up from the sea. As I glanced towards the ocean, I could no longer see the shoreline. Remembering what had gone before; I did not want to experience a bad moment with such great happiness in my life. With this thought in mind, I quickened my pace, barely just short of running. Every so often, I would stop and look out to the sea. The mist had now been replaced by fog.

I did not feel apprehension or fear. All the same, I did wonder as only moments before, the day was so pleasant. I quickened my pace further, not wishing to be present as the fog came in over the cliffs. I knew that when the fog was as thick as pea soup, one could only feel their feet touching the ground rather than see them. Still, the fog was rolling in thicker every moment. Now, I was running. The fog had engulfed my retreat back home.

I concentrated on the path leading to the village, knowing the fog was growing thicker behind me. Then, I heard the screams. No, I was not hallucinating nor was I imagining, I did hear voices screaming in the fog. Now I had real fear; for the voices were real and they were from real people, somewhere in the fog.

I started to run for my life, only to see the bell tower of the church. I said a silent prayer to God to help me make it to the Vicar's house. As I continued to run, the fog now engulfed me. Overtop of the screams, I now heard the pounding of feet running behind me. Only by sheer perseverance, I reached the church gates and flung them open.

I ran down the path toward the doors of the church. Even in my panic, it was the first time I've ever noticed the tombstones were leaning one way or the other, away from the path. Others still further away were fallen over backwards, as if to avoid the forms in the fog, or so I thought. Foolishly in my panic, I'd forgotten the previous time I had run to the doors of the church. 'Oh God, the doors of your house must open' for I hear the foot-steps close behind me. Only to find the doors were not going to open their heart, to give sanctuary to me.

I had no choice but to turn around. There they were, just a short distance away. They stood there like ghouls in the fog. Their clothes were wet and covered in seaweed. Somehow I knew they were the people who perished on this anniversary of the day the ship went down with all hands and passengers that were lost. These were the souls coming back from the dead, to let me know what their story was and how they had lost their lives at sea. I was frozen like a statue before the church doors. Two of these spirits moved forward from the rest. They were dressed in typical garb of the Puritan faith; he was in a tall hat and black attire while she had a bonnet and long dress. Both, like the rest of the ghouls were covered with algae and seaweed.

They were young. They couldn't have been more than a few years older than me. As they came closer, I stared directly at them. Their skin was white, with almost a scaly look of fish. Their eyes were black and hollow-looking. I was frozen to the ground.

Then the man spoke and claimed me to be his daughter, and added, "You are one of us. We've come once again to take you back with us, where you belong."

I screamed as loud as I could, but nothing came out. I stood there helplessly, as the man and woman came on either side of me and took each one of my hands and led me back into the crowd of ghouls.

I came out of my trance. I was helpless as I laid there on the couch. As always before, in previous sessions of the portraits, I was totally exhausted. I've long given up in the past trying to call for help, or ring the bell for my male servants to aid and assist me. I have given instructions to the male servants, when the dawn has arrived, to allow at least one more hour before entering my study. At that time, to come in and help me return to my boudoir.

I feel today, as I have in the past, if they enter too soon . . . if I had not returned from the past which I was experiencing, I will not be able to return to the present. Further, I feel which-ever canvas possessed my life would claim it for evermore. At the prearranged time, the servants entered my study and helped me make it to my boudoir. As in the past my beloved wife and doctor are waiting for me. After examining me in my semi-conscious state, the doctor gave me some sedation and other medications which would aid in my recovery. My beloved wife then sat by my bed and held my hand.

The long days ahead once again gave me back my life that I enjoy for the rest of the 363 days of the next year.

Dr. Sebastian lifted his head from the manuscript and as always it had drained the strength from his body. Once his breathing became normal, he rang the bell to summons the butler. From past experience in reading different chapters of The Portraits, he was learning to control his emotions. Yet, it was with extreme effort for his one hand to reach for the bell, and compose himself to return to a normal way of life. He forced himself once more to look at the benevolent painting and then the diabolical one. He couldn't help but feel how Robert F. Edwards felt when one of these paintings possessed him and took him out of his control.

The butler assisted Dr. Sebastian to the front door where the chauffeur was waiting as usual. There was little or no reason for conversation on his trip home. After an hour of driving, he was escorted to his front door and he thanked the chauffeur for his support.

"Oh darling, you're home. I was hoping you'd be home early."

"Yes! My beloved, I am home," Dr. Sebastian answered.

"And how was your day, may I ask?" his wife inquired.

"Well, one might say I'm getting used to these ventures at the Edward's house. Even so, this chapter has left me emotionally drained. Well, my beloved, what are we having for dinner tonight. Anything special?" Dr. Sebastian asked.

"Of course, my dear," was the reply from his wife.

"Do you wish to surprise me, or can I guess?" he asked.

"Whichever is your pleasure, my darling."

"Then I am going to guess it is baked salmon."

"You always are a good observer, and almost read my mind," came the reply from his beloved wife, and then added, "Let's join each other in the living room and share a good vintage of red wine."

Once settled in, they looked across from each other. She asked, "Would you like to tell me about your day?"

He thought for a moment and then replied, "I am sure it would be a more enjoyable evening for both of us if you told me what transpired in your day."

They both chuckled with each other. She agreed, "It was the usual, doing a little bit of gardening and walking the dogs and then preparing the evening meal."

He replied, "It sounds absolutely delightful. I wish I'd been with you."

THE REMITTANCE MAN

—ᴍᴌ—

As Dʀ. Sᴇʙᴀsᴛɪᴀɴ ʟᴇғᴛ the house, he looked forward to starting a new week. With all that he had accomplished in the past, he was quite sure that this would be an easy week to complete some of the more mundane tasks which waited him at the Museum. With these thoughts running through his mind, he greeted his staff with a cheery 'good morning' and settled into his comfortable chair at his desk. He took a moment to look out the window. Yes, it was another beautiful fall day and he promised himself this year he would spend more time enjoying the long, warm autumn evenings.

He then addressed the challenges which lay upon his desk. After going over phone calls and memos and all that would arise during this week's challenges, he noticed his secretary had given him another appointment at the mansion on the following Thursday.

As the days wandered from one to another, he enjoyed the evenings walking the dogs with his beloved wife. The week vanished and the next week arrived. On the day in mention, the chauffeur was waiting at the appropriate time to take Dr. Sebastian once more to the mansion. He had little thoughts of what would transpire and even fewer thoughts on what would lie ahead in the Book of Portraits. In fact, his thoughts concentrated on the other tasks which had to be met before the weekend would arise. With his mind on other matters, the trip seemed less arduous than the ones previous.

Once arriving at the mansion, the procedure was the same as previous times and without further ado, he was escorted to the library of the late writer. Once the staff left him on his own, he opened the Book of Portraits to where he had left off. His eyes cast themselves upon the chapter ahead, 'The Remittance Man.'

How fast the days move from each other as one enters the challenges which lie ahead. Even so, this day is different than the ones of the past months that I have enjoyed . . . for this day marks the night that I will encounter another experience of being possessed. Tonight, I have no idea, like the nights before, which portrait will possess my soul and my mind, then throw me back into a previous period in time.

I continue the progress of examining documents and contracts while sitting at my desk, as I wish to have a productive day no matter what the night leads to. With this mighty determination to complete a full day's activities and progress in my life as it stands at this moment, the afternoon has come and passed with the night quickly advancing. I have tried numerous ways of approaching this night of treachery and events which drive me back into a past that I have no recollection of. All the same, I am always trying to find ways to have more control over at least which portrait will possess my soul.

Tonight is no different. I will try this new approach and only tomorrow, if I'm fortunate enough to live through this journey once more, which in the past I have had no control of it, I can share this is a solution or alternative. I've been the principal participant in these journeys that I've been tested in, and I had tried to avoid or change them in many different ways, only to no avail.

The night is fast approaching once again. The shadows of darkness continually push the sun towards the horizon. I get up from my chair, and gaze through the large windows to view the losing battle of the sun as it diminishes from the sky. I look out into the gardens of tranquility and peace, which has taken many years to achieve such colors of beauty, which now in contrast are changing into shades of silhouettes. All that remains of the day is the glow of the red/oranges sunset highlighting the few clouds which prevails. The last moment of natural light is banished from the skies, as the darkness dominates.

I have no idea why I continue to stare into the garden, with only silhouettes in the darkness, waiting for the inevitable to take place? Oh yes! Oh yes! There it is, the first star I see tonight.

'Star-light, star-bright . . . first star I see tonight, make a wish, make it right. Oh God! Please, Heavenly Father make my wish right.'

I continually look out the window, gazing into the blackness, now the only natural flame of light is in my heart. It's happening! Oh my God, it's happened. I am no longer looking out the window of my study.

I am gazing at the breaking of the dawn. The stars that once dominated the skies only a few moments ago are now drifting back into their hidden positions. As I continually gaze through the window, the light of another day has begun. Already the sky has turned into shades of blue from the black ink only moments ago. I seem to be fixated, unable to move from this window of observation. As the light takes over from the darkness, the landscape before me is foreign to my eyes.

As I survey from one direction to the other, I cannot get a bearing on the location of where I am, or what world I'm in, as far as that goes. As I continually search for some familiarity, apprehension rises to a new fear. I may not even on the planet Earth. I force the window open and then extend my head further out in both directions.

Oh, my God! Merciful Lord! There, before my eyes is a large mountain in which the top has being sliced off, leaving what was once the peak or the column missing. My mind races like a fast galloping racehorse, in the moment he sees his victory against all others.

The answer came to mind, could this be . . . is it Table Mountain? Could this be Cape Town in Africa? I step back from the window and survey my surroundings. Yes, they too are as foreign to my noble surroundings as the landscape outside. As I survey the furniture, as well as paintings and other works of art, I realize that I must not only be in Cape Town, but in another period of history. I tried again to get my bearings of the time and period, studying the antique furniture including the canopy bed.

I am distraught when I look at the attire which I'm wearing. I am dressed in a long white robe. No, it's not a robe, it's a night garment. My goodness, what am I, or who am I? I see in the room a full-length mirror which I immediately start to walk towards. Standing before the mirror, I realize, I'm not only wearing a sleeping gown, I have a sleeping hat or cap as well.

I now try to clear my mind so that I'm able to take a better survey of my surroundings; there is no doubt, this is a largish room or sleeping area. The expensive furniture and other items are for only one kind of room—a very elegant boudoir. I am now wondering who I am and why I'm here. Immediate questions which come to my mind are—why I'm in Cape Town, Africa and what year would this be? As I sit down in one of chairs and review these elegant accommodations, I survey the surroundings inch by inch. After an intense inventory of what is contained within these four walls, I observe a large cord or tassel attached near one of the bed posts.

With this knew-found knowledge, I get up from the chair and walk over, then pull it vigorously. I had no expectation of what the results would be. Shortly thereafter, there was a knock on the door in which I immediately called out, "Enter."

Upon entering the room, there was a male servant who greeted me by saying, "Good morning. May I be of service?"

I stare at him, knowing full well that he recognizes me in every capacity and I have absolutely no idea who he is, other than he has come to do my bidding. I look bewildered, as I stare directly at him, with all the arrogance of an aristocrat and ask, "What day is it?"

He quickly replied with, "It's Tuesday, Sir . . . the day you go to the Club."

"Yes! Yes! Of course, I know what day it is, for I was bluffing, of course. I'm referring to what year, the month and date. Do you understand?" I bellow out, as if he was incompetent and not me.

"The day and month of the year, Sir?" he replied, looking bewildered.

"Do you not understand English?" was my answer.

"It is June 4, 1859, I believe, Sir."

"You know, or you don't know. Now, are you correct or not?" I snarled.

He then answered, "To the best of my knowledge I believe it is to be correct, Sir."

In some way, he must been used to my ill behavior and eccentric ways, for he still was waiting for my next command.

I obliged him immediately by saying, "Bring my breakfast to this room. I wish to dine in bed. After you accomplish that task, set out my clothes for what I'll be wearing to the Club later."

As he was about to leave, I addressed him once more by asking, "What time is it?"

"Time, Sir?" he replied.

"Of course, the time of day, are you daft?" I answered him.

With this, he fumbled in his waistcoat and produced a pocket watch, looking at it carefully, he said in the clearest voice possible, "Ten minutes after eight o'clock, Sir."

"Well, leave me now and do my bidding," was my last command before he left the room. I sat in the chair, staring around the room, again trying to identify the new character identity I have assumed, feeling the arrogant, over-bearing, aristocratic attitude somewhat obnoxious.

After my man-servant returned to my quarters with more than an adequate breakfast of juice, coffee, meat and eggs accompanied with different breads, I told him to come back within half an hour to prepare my toiletries for the day which lies ahead. After completing the breakfast I found most enjoyable and to my liking, within the half hour my servant returned to prepare the water for the bath and then proceeded to shave me.

During this period, I kept on asking questions which led him to become more confused, and looking at me as if I had changed from one person to another and only my form remained. As my clothes were laid out, once again I questioned his intent for my attire to go to the club.

Now being completely confused, he responded, "It's your usual attire, Sir. However, whatever you wish to wear today, if you will advise what it is, I will prepare them for you."

Again my arrogance and ill-behavior surfaced with, "Just get on with it, I haven't got all day."

Once being prepared for the outside world, I left my boudoir, only to discover how large this dwelling was. It contained many rooms and to my knowledge, two servants were there also to do anything at my bidding. The apartment area consisted of two additional bedrooms, a large study or library and an exquisite fireplace in the parlor. The dining area would easily accommodate ten people at one sitting, then of course, the toilet facilities. In one of the wings furthest away from my living quarters were the servants' quarters, with the cooking facilities for the maids and cook, which I assumed were there. The rooms in which I personally observed at my leisure were elegant and consistently furnished in the Victorian period.

After fully observing both the quality of the place and its setting of items in each individual room, they were inferior in quality to the Victorian period in England itself. Nonetheless, I would think they were more than adequate for the setting in Cape Town. Often, it was the impoverished aristocrats that were sent to these outposts of the empire.

The study appeared to nothing more than a clutter of papers and memos strewn on top of the desk and everywhere else which would accommodate their existence. At first glance it gave me a further concept of how I behaved. As I pondered over the scattered amount of letters and other documents in their helter-skelter positions, I realized now what I was.

Oh dear, my goodness . . . I am a remittance man from dear old England. My dearly beloved aristocratic family disinherited me and of my inheritance; then removed me from their presence and my great position, only to be in this desolate point at the end of Africa.

As I continued to rummage through the documents and several unflattering letters, I gained the knowledge that on a regular basis, I received a liberal amount of remuneration. This was on one condition; that I remain in the present location and if I ever made any attempt to return to England, they would disown me publicly. I was not only banned from communication with any of my relatives, I would be further banned from participating in any event of a gentlemanly status.

My goodness, I do say, I must've done something rather naughty to deserve such treatment. As I sat at the desk opening one letter after another, I came to read what seemed like a document of legal description. Oh, it definitely is a contract drawn up by solicitors. This agreement leaves me no alternative, but obedience for the sake of money. It takes several readings to decipher the legal jargon before I came to the crux of the contract or agreement as such.

Well! Well! This gives a thorough description of myself, and what my rightful heritage was. I guess, one might say I was a scoundrel when I was young. Even so I'm not that old now, I am at best in my mid-30's, handsome, with an athletic body and I would have to say a good sense of humor, with the right kind of people, of course. Yes! Oh yes, here it is. I did manage to accumulate large gambling debts; nonetheless my family could well afford my unfortunate bad luck. Furthermore, the ponies did not add to my success, resulting in greater losses at my family's expense.

I suppose there is always the straw that breaks the camel's back and this may very well be the straw that did it. I was and will always remain a ladies man. Ah yes! I had many interludes with charming young ladies of my class and stature in society, only to leave them after I plucked the blossom from her womb and was not overly popular when in the same company of their families. I had overstepped my boundaries when the latest conquest turned out to be the wife of a Member of Parliament. She was an adequate mistress, but sooner or later, like all my interludes, I tired of her and then abandoned her. There's an old saying—'there's no revenge like a woman scorned' and in this case; she told her husband of my poor manners and behavior in her presence. When he confronted me of my misdeeds and accused me of being nothing more than a rogue, I challenged him to a duel.

On that fatal day that we met to settle my honor, such as it was, as we were pacing off, I could not wait for us to be addressing each other and simply shot him in the back. Of course, my family asked me not to associate in their presence. They did not fare any better in public, definitely not in the circles we were accustomed to being in. Fortunately, I was not a very good marksman, and had only wounded the Member of Parliament. My elder brother, who was in the Upper House of Lords and considered one of the more important members in the House, was able to influence the courts and this Member of Parliament not to press charges. I'm sure there were concessions made which were adequate for this dismissal.

Last, but not least, my Father, I will never forget that bloody day before him. He had me summonsed to his study where I remained standing before him while he dressed me up and down, lashed out at me with every possible insult with his endless vocabulary, ending with the phrase 'if I was any other Father, I would take you out to the carriage house and whip you to within an inch of your life'. This was followed by him getting passage for me on a ship loaded with criminals, heading to an outpost in the Empire, with the intention of purging dear old England of its scum. It was a rather nasty meeting of minds, one might say.

All the same, my older brother once more came to my rescue and of course, my dear Mother was able to aid and assist me by providing me with some means of support in this remote part of the world. Oh yes! It all comes back now. I've been here an agonizing five years, five worthless years, wasting away.

No wonder Morris, who is my male servant, looked bewildered at me this morning. He must've thought I was indulging in one of my many distasteful habits which I've accumulated out of sheer boredom. No, I was not this particular morning indulging in eating the clouds by having an opium substitute which is one of the many entertainments that is available here.

Well! Well! I shall go down to the club for lunch at least to see what awaits me there. In all probability, my good friends François and Hans would be there waiting for my arrival. We have one thing in common along with probably many others, but we are all remittance men.

Once more I ring the bell-cord in the study for Morris. What a lazy Negro he is. One can't expect to get any kind of good domestics in this part of the world. As Morris enters the room, I look at him with contempt then tell him make arrangements for me to go to the club and "Get on with it," was my command. "Snap to it, man. I want to get there early." He irritates me by his very presence.

"Yes, Sir. Right away, Sir" came his rely.

I returned to the window and gaze down at the street below. The streets, my goodness, I'm being more than generous and complimentary by calling them streets; for they are nothing but wide dirt paths filled with cargo wagons drawn by oxen or mules. What am I dwelling in—a warehouse atmosphere? The people, my God, the white trash I'm witnessing below is horrible, worse than the common man which are detested in England. For that matter, these men are like vagabonds, dressed in someone else's discarded garments. These unspeakable creatures are riding horses on these dirt paths, causing clouds of dust. Dear God, what have I got myself into? It couldn't possibly be happening! Those Negroes are mingling around on the streets as if they were equals. My God, what kind of place is this? There are savages precisely outside my door steps, how much worse can things get? There is no doubt—some days one should never, and I repeat never, get out of bed. Things only get more disgusting. Where is that damn Morris? I pull the cord again with disgust.

Morris enters and asks," You rang, Sir?"

"Where's that damn carriage, Morris?"

"It has not arrived as yet, Sir."

"You did make proper arrangements to get it here on time, didn't you?" I screamed.

"Yes, Sir. I did, Sir" was his rely.

I have been here all of five years, three months and six days, in this rat's nest at the end of the world.

Morris enters my presence once more only to inform me, "Sir, your carriage is waiting."

"Well, it's about time, nothing ever seems to go right these days," as I acknowledge this information.

"You are right, Sir." Morris replies. "May I ask if you will be dining at home this evening?"

"No I won't, don't bother," came my reply.

As I descend the flights of stairs to ground level, the doorman opens the door to my carriages which is waiting.

"Take me to the club," I commanded the driver, as we rolled through the dust, passing hastily built shacks to contain the necessary supplies of hard goods and food for this desolate environment. The distance to the club was short in this small city. However, at least it was a building that stood out amongst the rest of the debris, as more elegant quarters for men of means. Once the carriage pulls up to the door, I get out only then do I realize how horrible the conditions are in this outpost with sidewalks of wood. My good Lord, how primitive. At least, this place has a doorman who speaks well enough, and is not quite as barbarian as the others.

"Having a good day, sir?"

"Take me to my usual place in the club," I replied.

"As you wish. Please follow me," in his crucifying the English language.

The facilities seem to be accommodated all on one floor, nothing like the clubs back home. However, then, what is home after five years of abolishment? As I enter the sitting area, tiny in size compared to the ones that I'm accustomed to, there are leather chairs of a mixed assortment, obviously cast-offs from the better parts of the Empire. As I peruse the room, at least I see gentleman sitting periodically throughout in the proper dress attire.

"Over here! Over here!" As I looked in that direction, I see my two fellow companions, François and Hans.

"We were having our doubts that you would arrive in time for lunch. All the same, if you missed that part of the day, we were looking forward to at least you joining us for bridge."

"I would not have missed either for the world," was my reply.

As I made myself comfortable in one of the chairs and looked at both them, I then asked, "Is there anything new since the last time we were together?"

They both smiled and it was then that I realized it probably was more meant as a joke than an inquiry from me.

Nonetheless, my German friend Hans was the first to answer by saying, "What in the world could possibly be different in this place from one day to the next?"

What he said was a truism, at least for us remittance men. His family was not as affluent in his homeland as mine, but all the same, he had the breeding and the means from an aristocratic family. He was relocated to this desolate area of the world due to his violent nature. When he found somebody disagreeable, he would challenge them to a duel. Having already been dismissed from the Army for his lack of discipline as an Officer he still chose the weapon of leadership, the saber. Of course, most of his opponents had little knowledge of swordsmanship, let alone the use of the saber and consequently, Hans would lame them or injure them in such a way that they would never have the use of a full body. Along with this distasteful behavior, another aptitude which accompanied his dismissal from his family was his large gambling debts. His accumulated sum of gambling debts even exceeded my enormous amount. Still, there is a saying, 'birds of a feather do flock together'.

Oh yes; my other companion François is French, even more so—is Parisian and comes from a noble family of long heritage and wealth. His reputation as a ladies man made mine pale in comparison. One of his less respectable moves when luring the opposite sex into coupling with him was a nun of one of the cloisters. He could have easily been excommunicated for this encounter alone, but the disciplinary acts of the church did not impede his sexual desires. However, things came to a head when a fellow aristocrat and a high member in the Parliament returned home; only to find François in his boudoir, not only making love to his wife, but his daughter as well, the three of them frolicking in merriment.

This was the breaking of the relationship with his family. His Father up until then had made good on his gambling debts which far exceeded his allowance and paying off men to keep quiet and not scandalize his family when François's loose behavior with either their wives or daughters became known. All the same, this last escapade was far too great for any further understanding from his father and he became a remittance man in this undesirable place.

One might now say that the unholy threesome enjoyed each other's company, for we all had the same common denominator of expulsion from our station in life. Our conversation continued on our activity later today at the Bridge tables in which we would entice some of the locals to participate, so we could cheat funds from them to humor our dull lives. It was not only the challenge of getting away with it by removing funds from these unsuspecting fools; it also provided us with a subsidy for our funds from our homeland. With this in mind, the three of us ventured off to the dining area for a small but substantial lunch. After lunch, we went out and participated in some outdoor activities and sports to pass the tedious hours of the day. Then, on to play Bridge with fools waiting to give us their money. This was, and is a typical day of being remittance men in this hell hole.

The days that followed fluctuated very little from day to day. Even so, the evenings did provide a variety of events. On more than one occasion we would be invited to other family's entertainments that would bring in people of some talent to perform in their homes and impress their guests. Also, the governor was always trying to find an excuse to celebrate some kind of event and we would always receive an invitation, regardless of anyone else.

A few months past, and by now there was gossip in the air as well as on the grape vine of a man called Cecil Rhodes. God knows who this man was and for that, God is the only one who cares about him. As the gossip of Cecil Rhodes trickled down, piece by piece of his activities as well as what he was proposing to do, it became almost like a myth. The talk of his accomplishments and achievements had finally reached the club itself. At least, this provided us three comrades with something interesting from our usual activities in this lost outpost of despair that is our existence here. This person Cecil Rhodes was an adventurer and had travelled into the Transvaal to God knows where and was on his way to return to Cape Town.

His adventures went further, so it is told, then even the Boers or Afghans who were here long before us British. As the gossip continued to expand the story; as he travelled this uncharted area of the Transvaal, Rhodes had come across a native, one of those black bastards who was starving to death. Apparently this self-appointed salvation of mankind gave this black bastard some food; which is disgusting in itself. Nevertheless this savage in return gave him a stone or a crystal of some sort which later, again so the story goes, was a diamond the size of one's small finger. By now, of course the exaggeration has managed to identify its size as ones thumb; all the same, in every tale there is always the substance of truth.

This bit of news captured the attention of one and all in Cape Town and as the tongues wagged, the tales of Cecil Rhodes grew. As the months went by this person returned as living proof that he did exist, and as he became more popular he was invited to join the same circles of the upper class in which I had to endure. In due course he was invited to one of the Governor's balls that the unholy three of us were also attending to relieve ourselves of boredom. On this particular date, my friends François and Hans with myself were present to see if there might be some better pickings of the opposite sex.

Our hopes were dashed when there were no new arrivals since the last poll. Therefore, the only females one could plausibly feel any sexual attraction to were the daughters of the upper echelon at these functions. There were quite a few government officials that had been drawn into the net of serving their Motherland's interest in this desolate hole, someday hoping against hope that they would be elevated to a higher rank. Even so there were only five highlighted ladies that were available and the pickings were more than slim, nevertheless the longer one endured the limited facilities of any sort, one's standards diminished as well. For the few spinsters of reasonable age who were available, there was not a wine cellar that contained enough flavor of the grape to make them acceptable for merriment in any capacity for a night of sexual fulfillment. As far as the brothels that existed, one would have to be one of those Afrikaans to lower one's standards to endure such company to appease their sexual needs.

Back to the subject at hand, this man, Cecil Rhodes did finally arrive to attend the evening facilities. During the evening

I had the pleasure, my goodness, did I say, I meant to say I gave him the opportunity to engage in conversation with me. He was unquestionably not a man of my breeding or standards; nonetheless he was an ambitious chap who was extremely focused on achieving his aims which would not be limited by having anyone get in the way. In all due respect, his determination accompanied with ruthlessness gave me the opinion he was not just an ordinary commoner and as the conversation continued I have to confess I gained an approval for him. Though we spent a short time that evening in conversation, he left me in no doubt that he was a visionary and focused on accomplishing his means by any way possible to his achievements of getting ahead, both financially and socially. This short time I realized, by fair means or foul, this man was going to make a contribution one way or another to the Motherland, so that he would be accepted by the upper crust of society. After the evening came to a close my other two comrades made comments of their encounter with Cecil Rhodes throughout the evening. We all came to the conclusion of the common denominator he was a visionary, he was extremely focused, ruthless and determined to return to England and share a position with the aristocrats.

As the months drifted by and the New Year managed to find its way into our lives, François and Hans as well as myself kept close observance, at a distance on the activities of this Cecil Rhodes. We also, in our own way, kept track of his activities and the rumors of his next adventures. Though we kept at arm's length distance from personal contact with this individual, we were able to acquire the information that he was planning another expedition much deeper into the Transvaal than any other person had before.

He sincerely believed this diamond he received from that wretched savage was nothing more than a token of the vast wealth which lay ahead. By midyear, my comrades François and Hans with the help of myself created a scheme, one should never say scheme, merely a business adventure in which we would form a company that the investors would put up the capital to venture into the Transvaal and seek out the fortunes which lie in this unknown area of the world. In turn, the investors who put up the capital for us to go into the Transvaal with an expedition, we would get 60% of all the wealth which we would find and the investors would get 40% of the rewards after, of course, expenses were taken off. It took considerable months before we could put together a suitable business plan which was acceptable by us, and the year was drawing near to an end before we were close to having formed our company.

Our New Year's gift to the community was introducing them to the opportunity of becoming shareholders in a very lucrative venture. Of course, being a guiding force in the club and in good standing with all the government officials of the day, we were in an excellent position to be accepted as knowledgeable on how to conduct a proper business venture compared to these poor beggars of common stock. Shortly after our introduction to our plan, these investors were lapping at our heels for an opportunity to join our company. One might say it was harder to take candy from a child than to take vast amounts of money from these so-called businessmen.

Eventually, by the spring of the year we had accumulated sufficient amounts of capital and we were in full progress of launching our expedition. The supplies consisted of 10 fully stocked wagons pulled by 20 oxen and 12 Afrikaans, whom I detested the thought of, let alone having to take 30 some odd savages who would do the physical labor that was required. The enticement for the Afrikaans was when we three returned safely (as emphasized over and over again in the contract) in return they would receive 5% of the profits, after expenses. As for the natives, the blasted savages, we offered them food and shelter with a small token of return for their villages which in my spirit of giving was more than generous.

Even so, they would only receive these rewards if they were both loyal and hard workers with doing all the tasks which were required. This would consist of cooking and caring for our basic needs, such as setting up base camps, digging of latrines, and to caring for the animals. Hans, being the most proficient and having the best leadership qualities in organizing was put in charge of supplies, and accumulating everything that would be required in the expedition. François's position of responsibility was to make sure that each phase of the expedition would reach its achievement in an orderly and congenial fashion. My responsibility was to negotiate and continually assure our new-found shareholders of their position and to control their expectations for our return.

The months dragged on and things slowly changed from the planning stage to reality with assembling of the goods in the warehouse; to contracts with the Afrikaans and the natives who were now preparing to launch the expedition itself. We chose the month of March, just after the rainy season, to commence this venture. As we continued to enjoy the modest accommodations and lifestyle in this hell-hole that barely provided our needs, we knew that once the trek commenced, even these modest concessions would be removed and the hardships would be enormous. As the days followed each other and the weeks accumulated their time, the three of us were starting to appreciate the small concessions of Cape Town from the accommodations we had once taken for granted in our homeland. As the chosen date for the trek was drawing closer, we knew we would be facing insurmountable hardships with endurance only a true adventurer can conceive and still look forward to. As the weeks continued, two of the commitments that were required were completed. First, the funds which we had received were in excess of what we had hoped for from our shareholders. Second, the supplies we required for this trek into the wilderness had been gathered and stored in the appropriate warehouse. The Afrikaans, as well as those black devils had been signed on, now completing the last part of the assembly. One might say that we were arriving to the third part of this business plan which is to proceed into the unknown. Now we were ready and we felt pompous enough to hire a band and committee to ensure our expedition had a grand send-off.

Our 10 wagons were loaded with supplies and items we felt were appropriate to trade for any unsuspecting moron's diamond. With 30 natives who were required with 12 Afrikaans and one might say the unholy three, the column wandered through different arteries of the city deliberately, so one and all could witness the depth of the new company's commitment to its success.

We had traveled less than two days and were commencing on the third when the isolation and civilization vanished from our vision. As we continued to make our own way on virgin soil we were experiencing landscapes that I could not have imagined in my most vivid moments. One could misconstrue his location and direction in this wilderness by turning around two or three times, and then would be totally lost. The three of us were well aware now that we were completely in the hands of our employees. With an iron hand at the helm and a steel fist in the other hand, the natives soon learned the discipline in which we expected and the Afrikaans respected our attitude as well.

As the days came and went and the weeks followed, the three of us had no idea whether we were making good time, adequate time or any advancement of all. The landscape continued to open up into the vastness of earth, sometimes covered with grass and periodically a tree or some shrubs to break up the monotony of this endless landscape. As we continued to penetrate further into this unknown landscape, we came across variations; from dense forests and then again the vast openness from the flatlands, to hills and valleys. The vegetation also fluctuated and though none of us had any interest in biology or botany, we were curious enough to ask the Afrikaans about what we were witnessing. The wildlife, whether it was in the air or on the plains had as many varieties as the vegetation itself. We witnessed what look like horses that were black with white strips, or the other way around; we were told they were zebras along with lions, giraffes, and elephants just to mention a few. In the air the variety was even greater; some of the wingspans of these birds' were at least four or maybe five feet across. The weather also changed in the high plateaus, it was hot and dry and in the low valleys it was hot and humid.

It was during this period we came within range of one of the villages that some of our savages had relatives or connections with. We set up a campsite to reposition ourselves for the next few days. When we were preparing to disembark, we discovered three of these black devils were not accounted for; now we had a dilemma. The decision to pick up and continue the expedition without their presence would show weakness and leave us vulnerable to being abandoned by any, or all, at any given time in this no man's land; or to set an example. The three of us concluded we had no alternative—simply to track these devils down and bring them back, and then use them as an example to one and all on our attitude to desertion.

It was just shy of a fortnight before the Afrikaans found these devils and dragged them back to our campsite. After questioning them extensively, they showed a defiant attitude towards responsibility and commitment. Their only explanation for their behavior was they had forgotten the time and were enjoying it with their families and relatives. We had the Afrikaans inform these three bastards that the next time they would be able to see their relatives would be in eternity. We then had the first one strapped to a wagon wheel, where we took turns whipping him to death. It took an excess of 150 lashes before he took his last breath. The next devil, we tied to the wagon wheel, facing us. The three of us proceeded to throw knives at the outer extremities of his body and after having received numerous knives in his arms and legs; we moved up into the dorsal area and finally hit a vital organ. After he was cut down, the third and last one again was strapped to the wagon wheel, facing us. Once again, the three of us took out our pistols and proceeded in a similar manner that we had with the knives. This procedure was to be more agonizing before he entered eternity.

The three carcasses were laid side by side with all present to witness the punishments that we administered to those that broke their contracts. The savages took on a new view of our cruelty and even the Afrikaans showed expressions of uncertainty and possibly fear of their rulers. One and all had witnessed the ruthlessness and cruelty we were capable of administering for disobedience and that night all the natives were shackled and hand-cuffed in their resting places, so that they couldn't possibly congregate together. As the following days proceeded and the nights came upon us, this procedure of shackling the barbarians became the rule of thumb, and needless to say there were no more desertions.

The next month, we continued to proceed further and further into what was known as the Transvaal and periodically we would come across small hunting parties of savages. The Afrikaans would take a few savages from the expedition who may have knowledge of these other tribes to hopefully communicate in some form or another as to where we were. But, we gained little or no information from these sources. As we continued to proceed in the direction which now seemed to be endless, we came to an area which was dominated by a tribe called Zulus, which we'd never heard of. All the same, the Afrikaans and the natives were aware of their existence.

The entire expedition took on a different attitude, as well as our surrounding areas of landscape. Our natives (pardon me, the black scum,) informed the Afrikaans that this tribe or mob of savages was very powerful and large, as well as feared. Our scum savages became more apprehensive and quieter as we kept venturing further into Zulu country. We kept hearing from our black scum, over and over again, about the warlike attitude of the Zulus.

At the beginning of the fourth month of our expedition we were well into Zulu country when it happened. We were traveling deeper and deeper into their territory on this particular day when a hunting party came out of nowhere. We made every effort possible to communicate, first by the Afrikaans themselves and then by dragging our black scum to the hunting party. They tried to communicate, but we found that there was no common language whatsoever. After a considerable length of time, we communicated by picture graphs on the bare ground and body language. The message from the Zulus' was that we would need permission to stay on their lands. We were then, for a better word, escorted to an area outside one of their larger villages.

We awoke in the morning to find ourselves surrounded by a circle of warriors that had gathered throughout the night. At dawn, the three of us as well as three Afrikaans were escorted by the warriors into the village. It was then that we realized the warriors outnumbered our expedition by two hundred times, at least. At this point, I would not say we were their prisoners, but all the same it could well happen that way if we could not convince them that we were just visiting guests.

By the evening they were putting on some kind of ritual or performance. The six of us had no idea what the purpose was. The dances performed by the warriors were both primitive and ruthless in their endless gestures of performing acts of horror as well as immoral gestures. By now, their entire bodies glistened under the lights of the fire with their own perspiration. Then, the women started to join the frenzied movements, aided by some warm fermented beer and other substances of intoxication. To witnesses this was terrifying as all of us sat in apprehension of what possibly could take place next.

Only then was the leader or ruler carried out on a litter or platform. He was a huge man, possibly in excess of 500 pounds. I do not believe I would be exaggerating, for his weight was so excessive that his legs would not provide the support needed for him to stand up. The dancers continued their frenzied movements around the various fire pits, but he was the center of their worship. Then, other women gathered around him to scoop up large amounts of animal fats from containers and started to smear his entire body with this lard. When this was completed, young virgin girls wearing only a small cloth between the genitals danced suggestive movements before him, as they placed precious stones embedded in the fat of his massive body. His large massive body looked inhuman as the virgins continued to dance their exotic movements, while other women came forth to serve food and beverages to him.

The feast continued far into the night. It was almost the breaking of the dawn of another day when the group of warriors who we had first met came and surrounded us, making gestures for us to get up and follow them, which we were only too pleased to accompany their suggestion. They lead us back to our campsite and made gestures that none of us were able to comprehend. All the same, at least we had the comfort of our own surroundings and the protection of our few weapons so we could defend ourselves. The day was just about over when all of them got up and left.

The following day, the same group of warriors returned, and this time accompanied by a witch doctor or shaman. With an extreme effort to communicate on both sides, it was understood vaguely what we wanted to transpire. For us, obtaining the stones from them and in return the goods that they would accept in exchange in the transaction. There was an infinite amount of time haggling over the machetes and the extra rifles with ammunition. These were the only things of interest that they were willing to negotiate in exchange for the stones. As for the beads and trinkets, along with the pots and pans that we had dragged half way across this continent, we might as well have buried them in the dirt. In return for the best items we had, the bartering became ridiculous. We would receive very few small diamonds which would barely cover the expenses of the supplies, let alone any profit for us or anyone else. No matter how long and vigorous the negotiations took, they were inflexible.

At last, we realized it was of no use to continue. We settled on the meager amounts of stones they were prepared to give, in return for the vast amount of rifles with ammunition and the machetes that they were going to receive. It was then the three of us stepped aside from the bartering to discuss the idea of finding a weak member of this group of savages, then having one of the Afrikaans approach him to suggest he would receive a special gift if he wished to further barter with us.

In return, all we would ask was the direction of where the stones were found. There's always a traitor in every crowd, and one of savages returned to our campsite that evening. This black barbarian was highly motivated for material wealth. Under candlelight, we did receive adequate enough information from this traitor and informant by him drawing a map in the dirt, along with picture language, giving us an idea of how many days and in which direction it would take to arrive at this given spot. He also indicated that during the night of the feast celebration, we had received permission from the King to stay in the land of the Zulus. With his ill-gotten gains of a pistol with ammunition and machete, he slithered back like the snake he was to the pit where the rest of them dwelled.

The next morning, we broke camp as quickly as possible, as we had no intentions of returning but going forward in looking for the precious rocks. After four days in the direction this savage indicated, sure enough, we arrived at the location in which he described on the dirt map. After a long agonizing trip to the location, we set up camp. By the following day, we started to do an exploration of where these precious stones were that we trekked across this continent of hell to obtain. The next few days, no matter what direction we chose or how long we followed in that direction, simply the rewards were less than acceptable. The little that we had found in this rugged terrain were small insignificant diamonds, approximately the same size as the ones we had bartered our guns, ammunition and machetes to obtain, but no encouragement of a mother lode.

Without warning, out of nowhere, an insurmountable number of Zulu warriors came down and surrounded us. From that day forth, we would never sleep soundly again. We retreated as quickly as possible to our main campsite, trying to defend ourselves as these locusts continually bombarded us with their spears. The Afrikaans and ourselves mowed down as many of them as possible with continual rapid-fire. At one moment the Zulu warriors regrouped, and we gave the remaining amount of rifles to the black natives that had accompanied us. The battle raged on; it was no battle, it was a massacre. One could not step out of the parameter of the campsite without tripping over the dead or wounded Zulus.

This bloodbath was on both sides in its variants, we had not fared any better than the Zulus. Of the natives who we had brought with us, none survived. By the fourth day, four of the Afrikaans had joined their ancestors. Our greatest loss was François; of the unholy three, now only two remained. The wagons and oxen which pulled them were among the casualties of this conflict. More by good luck than anything else, somehow the horses had scattered and were still standing. We had no idea how long we had before the conflict would resume, so in all haste we managed to round up the horses. Before the ruthless Zulus returned, we had no choice but to look after our own dead. With the help of the remaining Afrikaans, we buried their comrades and our dear friend François.

We then took the remaining horses and packed as many supplies of food and water that they could bear. The ten of us surveyed the carnage we were about to leave, and with little hesitation moved out like dogs running with their tails between their legs. As night fell, we had nothing, no tents, no blankets; we slept upon the ground while one of us stood guard on a rotation basis. The days that followed which had taken us months to get into the Zulu territory now only took weeks as we worked the horses beyond their endurance. We continued this pace of exit from the lands of the Zulu and when the horses were exhausted and could no longer hold our weight we would walk alongside them as quickly as we were capable of, all the time knowing we were being watched. There was no doubt by either ourselves or the Afrikaans that the Zulu warriors could and would attack and finish the job they had started back at the digs.

We considered the reason we have been spared and got this far out of their lands was to return with the message that we had received—to tell all others to stay out of their lands or face the same consequences. Finally, with perseverance and determination, to say nothing of our mortal fear, we finally reached the boundary of the Zulu territory.

Oh my God, what a cost in human life in a lost dream. Now we had the challenge facing us of torrential rains, wild animals and insects as we continued our trek back home. During this time going south on this continent of horror was the rainy season, and we tried to find shelter the best we could, but I caught malaria. What seemed like an eternity, at last the rains let up sufficiently so we could continue in a southerly direction.

It was during this time that we came across a native village, and the Afrikaans were able to persuade the natives to provide us with food and shelter, to allow me to recover somewhat. The witch doctor performed rituals over my withering body, yet in all probability, it was the ghastly concoctions provided by the women, forced down my throat that helped to relieve me momentarily of the chills and fevers.

Stopping at this village could have been one of the worst decisions we had made, when these villagers came to realize that some of the natives who we had commandeered for our expedition were their relatives. Furthermore, the stories spread in the villages of the natives that we had disciplined by putting to death; we were none other than those white men responsible for those evil deeds.

We needed to move on quickly. My health had recovered somewhat though I was still weak, I was able to keep up with the rest of the group. No sooner had we gone by another village when we encountered our second conflict in this expedition. The village warriors had gathered together to seek their revenge, not only of the men we had brutally put to death, but also the other savages that we had dragged with us to suffer at the hands of the Zulu. The numbers they had mustered together for our annihilation were not as great as the Zulu's, nor were they as warlike. Nonetheless, their vengeance was as fierce and determined as any Zulu and after the massacre, there were only two of us left. Hans had met his maker along with the remaining Afrikaans.

The last Afrikaan and I took mounted the two remaining horses, all that was left of the entire expedition. With perseverance, each day we made our way back from whence we came. There was nothing other than the hope of survival we shared with each other as we continued to inch our way back to Cape Town. My health deteriorated rapidly, to the point where I was no longer capable of staying mounted on my horse. The Afrikaan rigged a stretcher to my horse and dragged me from this.

I had no idea what day, or even what month it was when we two remaining survivors of the expedition arrived back in Cape Town. The Afrikaan dragged me back to my dwelling and my male servant immediately acquired a doctor and nurses to be by my side. I was convulsing with the fever, and then shivering uncontrollably with the shakes of cold as malaria took to its full wrath.

The small token of our rewards were still in my possession and I knew it would only be a matter of days I would be able to survive before I joined my comrades in eternity. With this impending doom, I had my male servant contact the general manager of the company and requested his presence as soon as possible. Upon his arrival at my bedside, I relinquished the small gains of stones which we recovered from the expedition and informed him of what had transpired in our long absence from Cape Town. The next morning, the nurse on night-watch informed the doctor that I had passed away some time in the wee hours of the morning.

I gained consciousness, or returned to my time in this world lying on the floor, shaking and shivering with my clothes soaking wet from my own perspiration. It seemed like an eternity, but in reality was less than an hour before I had gained enough strength to crawl like a dog to where I could ring for my male servants. By now, they entered in haste knowing full well what to expect and they were not disappointed or surprised. They came prepared from previous experiences with a stretcher and other servants to aid and assist.

Once they were able to put my shivering, frail body on the stretcher, I was carried to my boudoir and placed on the bed which was waiting. On each side of the bed, as before, my beautiful wife was waiting and on the other side, my doctor. I looked longingly and tried to focus on my beautiful wife's face and say something, even though I was barely coherent. After the doctor examined me, he injected a strong sedative which would give me the rest to possibly regain some strength that I've lost during this night. My wife sat by my side for the rest of the day. The days that followed were repetitious of these anniversaries. I grew stronger each day and tried to forget the events of the horrible experience, this possession of the night. I have been always grateful when I return to this side of my life. As the days gave way to the weeks, once again I was able to return to my normal life activities, until I had to face the possession of the portraits again.

Dr. Sebastian looked at the last page of this chapter and then turned his head to see the portraits over the mantelpiece. He then got up from the chair and walked over to the French windows, and went outside to look at the magnificent landscape which prevailed. As he gazed at the complexity of beauty by both man and nature, he gained repose of his own time and place. As his eyes wandered over the manicured garden of beauty, he could not help but return to some of the words he had read about the sheer vastness of Africa itself. Though he had never been to Africa, many of the artifacts in the Museum came from different parts of this peculiar and unusual continent.

He returned back to the library and rang the bell for the butler to make preparations to return to his home. As the chauffeur was driving the long distance between the mansion and his home, he once more drifted off into what he imagined Africa would've been like when the Remittance Man did his expedition. In many ways, Dr. Sebastian felt Africa was still a dark and foreboding continent which practiced many barbaric acts against humanity. He was only too well aware of women being forced into sexual activities with men dying from AIDS. To say nothing of the young boys who were kidnapped from their own villages to serve as unscrupulous soldiers of death and rape. He wondered how much more barbaric it was during that period of time in the last chapter he had just read. Maybe, the conflicts were few and far between until the white man tried to civilize them.

His thoughts were interrupted as the chauffeur drove the limousine up to the front door, and once more to be greeted by his beautiful wife.

"Well, dear, you are home early, or at least earlier than I thought you would be," she replied.

"Yes! All things went well, or as well as one can expect and I'm getting through the Book of Portraits finally."

"You don't sound too happy about your progress, or as far as that goes, the chapters which you have now put behind you," she commented.

"Oh, no . . . it's nothing like that, my dear, it's just . . . well, it's just I always feel somewhat melancholy or depressed being in the library itself, let alone the contents of which I'm about to read," he answered.

"I think it's a little early, but nonetheless, I do think it would be appropriate for me to serve you a nice glass of wine and listen to the day's events unravel, if that would please you?" she asked.

"Well, you're right about the time, but yes, I'd be more than happy to share your presence over a good glass of the grape." With no hesitation, he went into the living room, as his wife brought in a bottle of Chardonnay accompanied with two glasses.

As they sat together, she said, "A toast to my beloved husband and the story he is about to reveal, or maybe just merely the day's events, which-ever will please him".

With somewhat of a chuckle, he said in a humorous voice, "Let my tale continue of what I read this day. The chapter was known as the 'Remittance Man' which takes place in South Africa and parts of Zimbabwe. To get to the crux of the story, it's nothing more than about a man and his companions who had disrespect for all other living things, which led to their demise, and all three ended up dying," he finished.

"Oh, my goodness, not a very happy ending, to say the least," she replied.

Once more they be filled their glasses of wine and continued to talk about the things which she had done that day. That night's dinner was of modest means and after enjoying a few hours of a detective story on the television, the day finally came to an end. Both retired to the bedroom and as they were falling off to sleep, told each other once more of their great love for each other.

THE JESUIT PRIEST

—⚡—

A NEW WEEK FOR Dr. Sebastian was at hand. As he made his way up to his office on the third floor, he was greeted by many of the members of the staff. When he arrived in the outer office where his secretary Emily was already at her command post, he greeted her with a 'good morning' and received one in return. It seemed to him that he had hardly left the office even though he had a most enjoyable weekend. The end of autumn was fast approaching and the cold days of winter would soon be at hand. Nonetheless, he was in a jovial mood, for this was the season that the Museum was decorated to celebrate the Christmas season.

It was always a time of year in which Dr. Sebastian had mixed feelings; he would reflect on what little was left of the present year and on the other hand, felt optimistic for what lie ahead in the next year. As these thoughts danced across his mind, he started to look at the week's agenda ahead. Sure enough, next Thursday would bring him to the mansion and another chapter in the Book of Portraits. He had long ago given up on the rationale of somehow always arriving on the same day, regardless of the week or the month. It meant little or nothing other than twigged his curiosity.

When the day in mention arrived, the usual procedure took place. The chauffeur would drive him to the mansion, he would be escorted by the butler to the library, the two servants would open up the Book of Portraits, and he would commence with his commitment. Upon being alone once more, he took a few moments to wander around the room that both intrigued him and yet, he was always glad to leave. He salivated for a few moments as he brought into focus the many artifacts and paintings, along with sculptures and memorabilia the writer had brought back from the four corners of the world to display in this room; the many hours he must've spent here, came to Dr. Sebastian's thoughts. Once more he took the challenge at hand and opened up the ribbon which marked the next chapter. He would now find out which portrait tormented this poor writer in his hours of need. Looking down at the page before him was the chapter, 'The Jesuit Priest.'

As always, this date runs up to me like a thief in the night and captures me unaware in the closeness of the time that these portraits will come to haunt me again.

This has been a pleasant year in which I've been able to accomplish many of the things I've hoped to do with my life as the years are now coming to the twilight zone of my existence. Here I am, once again in my study, reconciling to the time in which I will be possessed once more. I have been plagued in my thoughts for many years now that one of portraits will possess me.

Tonight I've searched in every possible corner of my mind which portrait will possess me on a journey long ago in the past. I have never distinguished whether it is my karma or a reincarnation to some distant past existence. Regardless of which one of the portraits takes on this night of possession, I am an unwilling partner in their game of fate.

Over the many years of these experiences of horror and despair which are totally against my will, I have never found a way to avoid them. All my attempts have failed to achieve their aims or even come close to accommodating some of my wishes. The portraits themselves seem to have their own agenda, whether it is one on the right or on the left.

I am going to try a different approach, though I've tried many in the past and have not been successful. Tonight, I am going to spend my time in prayer. I've also brought a rosary with me to aid and assist me in concentrating on communicating prayers to God. I will keep saying Our Father's and Hail Mary's with the Glory Be to be assist me as I await the moment of horror which will surely come. I'm also going to try to avoid contact with the room itself by turning my swivel chair and facing the windows, so I may gaze upon the tranquil peace of my gardens. By now the Sun is giving up its position in the sky. My fingers move from one bead of the rosary to another and I repeat the prayer while my eyes watch as the sun gives up its position of the day with the darkness of the night that lies ahead.

I watch as the majestic ball of fire diminished upon the horizon. The darkness now starts to surround the enchanting colors of orange, yellow and turquoise as this orb of hope slips deeper below the horizon. The last glow of colors are being replaced with darkness, to own the night.

Oh! Oh! I'm in a small chapel. I am kneeling before a small altar. I'm all alone. As I take my eyes off the altar to quickly scan the rest of the chapel, yes, I am quite alone. The hour is late and the only light available is the dancing of the small candles, as they flicker in their containers below the statue of the Virgin Mary and St. Joseph. At the altar, large candles burn before our beloved Jesus Christ, hanging from the cross above. As I look from one side to the other, the Stations of the Cross are clearly visible in their relief as they dominate the small chapel. Kneeling before the altar, I return to deep prayer,' My Holy Father, who art in heaven and all the Saints. Oh, Jesus Christ, my Lord, my Savior and Holy Mother of God. Please help me in my hour of need.'

Once more, I feel the mist clearing from my mind. I'm a novice in this monastery of the Jesuit fathers. Oh yes; I am coming close to the time of my ordination and the years have gone past quickly. As I continue to pray, I repeat in my mind and my heart to Jesus Christ, my Savior, that I will be, if it is his will, a father of the cloth and worthy of that in which he represents in this world.

I gaze once more at the altar and then apply my hands in prayer; yes I am definitely wearing the cloth of a novice. I am now focusing on the present and a little of the past. Once more, my eyes return to our beloved Jesus Christ hanging on the cross, for all of us sinners. I feel the strength of the railing as I lean forward, putting more of my body weight on my arms and clasped hands in prayer.

As a flashback in my mind's eye, I return to my childhood days so long ago. There are my brothers and sisters, which numbered 12 including myself. I am now in my mid-20's and I am one of the five eldest. My younger siblings are just starting their lives. My older brothers and one sister are all married and have children. Oh, my dear parents, what an influence they have on all of us. My beloved father worked as a laborer and continues even in his senior years. My dearest mother takes in laundry of others and goes to other peoples' homes as a charwoman, to help bring a little more to the table. They are the salt of the earth and the pride of the Spanish Basque community. And most fortunate for me, my beautiful family lives seven or eight hours by cart from the city where the monastery is in, Ávila.

This is a remarkable city where I am taking my holy orders, for it also where St. Teresa and Her Order has been the centerpiece in great contributions to the Order and for helping millions. This wondrous city has represented Holy Mother the Church and Her Saint's, even when the heretics were present and gathering followers to be unfaithful to the Church. This city stood out from many others during the Inquisition, removing the unfaithful and cleansing the city of the heretics. This was a terrible time in the history of Spain for the faithful to Holy Mother the Church.

My faith is constantly burning like the wee flames which are flickering in the candles, day and night, in this tiny chapel. These tiny flames from the candles which burn all the time in chapels, churches and cathedrals throughout the world represent the faith that I hold in my heart, the true faith of Jesus Christ and Holy Mother the Church. I realize the time has come for me to return to the dormitory and prepare myself for the classes for the coming day. I am so reluctant to leave this peaceful place which gives me tremendous happiness. As I return my eyes to the altar, I reverently make the sign of the cross and genuflect. Slowly, I stand up and make my way through the doors which will give me entrance once more to the dorm.

I would not say my days are repetitious, but vary little in pattern. My day starts as all the others, at five in the morning with mass followed by a meager breakfast of porridge and then on to classes of philosophy, with a short break to share our thoughts of the lesson which we've learned from one of the good Fathers.

Midday in the monastery is when we share another meager meal of vegetables with bread, and this is then followed by classes of theology and once again when the classes have finished we have an open discussion of what we have learned in this class. Then, when the first shades of evening are starting to form, we return to the chapel for Vespers. After this is completed, we have the last meal of the day which is usually accompanied with some form of meat and more vegetables. We then return to the chapel for meditation and consultation by one of the Jesuit priests. This completes the day, like most days I have spent becoming a priest in the monasteries of the Jesuit order.

For almost seven years now, I have progressed in my studies and the meager substance of food is enough to nourish my body and stimulate my soul. It has been a wonderful life and a most rewarding experience. My teachers are Jesuit priests, very learned men, and most of them have Doctor's degrees in their chosen field, be it languages, social behaviors, medical practices or numerous other studies. Many of the Jesuit priests who teach philosophy and theology explain the significance that the studies will have on us, to understand the greatness of Holy Mother the Church and the Saints.

In my academic studies, I am adequate and nothing more. I hold or possess little of the knowledge which is given to me by these gifted men of learning. I speak with the local dialect of the Basque in Spain and now I am my trying my best to adopt more of Castile Spanish accents, but with great difficulty. As for Latin, I can pretend to understand most of what they are speaking to me. However, the written form with declensions makes mastering the meaning of Latin a complicated language for me. I would make any senator of the Roman Empire realize that I was from one of the provinces.

God does not always give the gift of knowledge freely, nevertheless what I lack in academic achievements; my teachers have acknowledged to me personally that I have a God-given gift of communication. They have also said that my devotion to Jesus Christ and Holy Mother the Church is second to none. It is with these gifts that God has enabled the teachers and professors to have the patience and determination to help me achieve the requirements in these long years of becoming a priest. It is difficult to say who has the greater patience and determination, to force, piece by piece, the knowledge which is required for priesthood into me. Still, I've come a long way from my beginning and now I'm nearing ordination.

As the months float by, the day draws nearer to my greatest achievement at this point in my life; taking the Holy Sacrament of priesthood. When the day arrives, there are five of us who are going to be ordained as priests. From this day forth, we will be able to say the Mass, hear Confessions and perform all the duties of the Holy Order of priesthood. To be a Jesuit priest, we will take the vow before Almighty God of chastity, obedience and poverty. Today, throughout the city and the monastery, there is a great excitement shared by one and all, especially us five young men who are now going to be priests.

My family and those of the other men will be present and accounted for on this glorious moment in our lives. From this day forward, the five of us will never be the same; for we will be priests, we will be Jesuits and we will walk in the shadow of Jesus Christ and Holy Mother the Church. Today, for the first time in my life, my father and mother along with my siblings and all others present will address me as Father. I have worked vigorously towards this day, to complete the qualifications which are required for priesthood and now a milestone in my destiny. The next day is another great moment of my life. I will say Mass at the Cathedral, with my family and friends present. With emotions that are hard to express, my feelings are exuberant beyond anything I've ever experienced by giving Holy Communion to those around me. This is the greatest day of my life. I can only thank God, my parents and the Jesuit professors for letting me experience the fulfillment at this moment in my life.

For the next two weeks, I am granted a leave of absence from the monastery. In this precious time, I return to the small village of my up-bringing, and share with my family and friends merriment and reminisce over the many times I've spent in my father's house. The local priest of the village welcomes my new Ordination and lets me say Mass every morning, and each Sunday not only saying Mass but giving a sermon to the congregation. These new-found privileges of Jesus Christ and Holy Mother the Church both have filled my fondest and greatest dreams. I have an exuberant feeling of happiness and contentment which I have never felt before and am very grateful to my Lord. I am in constant prayer, that if it's the Lord's Will, and Holy Mother the Church, I will be assigned a position somewhere close to my family and this village. If this is God's will, I will have the opportunity to see my family and enjoy the moments that they have with their children. However, this is not meant to be, for when I returned in two weeks to the monastery, my posting is anything but close to my village. In fact, it is in the other end of Spain itself.

Due to my limitations in academic abilities, I am not even aware of the districts in my own country, let alone the empire of Spain. I find to my amazement that posting is in the province of Seville, which is in the southern part of Spain. I gain this knowledge of my posting from the libraries in the monastery. If I had been qualified as a historian, I probably would have salivated on this assignment; for this region of Spain which was under the Roman Empire and then at a later date was dominated and controlled by the Moors. The Moors were finally driven out, after many strategic battles with the Knights of Christianity.

This area of Spain did not have the long duration of Christianity as the area that I'd grown up and studied in to become a priest. I am genuinely confused on this assignment, especially being my first experience in priesthood. All the same, one does take the vows of obedience and I must not question it in any form, including my mind, and must accept it as God's will and the will of the Holy Order of priesthood of the Jesuits.

A little disheartened, I ready myself for my first assignment, to be at their beck and call. Within the next few days I was summoned to the prefect's office. He informed me it was the decision of the monastery to send me to Madrid and I would get further instructions from the Jesuits there. The time spent in the Madrid monastery could be anywhere from two to three months, or more. They would find appropriate passage for me to continue on for me to reach my final destination and posting. And so it came to pass.

Within the next few days, the prefect of the monastery had secured passage in a carriage to my first destination, which was Madrid. The carriage driver eventually dropped me off at the monastery in Madrid where I was greeted by the gatekeepers and a Jesuit priest who were expecting me. As I quickly glanced at the enormous size of this monastery, my imagination had been inadequate in what my eyes saw before me. The complex was so vast and so magnificent that I felt like I was looking through the eye of a needle at the world. The great cathedral attached to the monastery was towering above everything else, as it reached towards the sky.

As I had entered the city, I remarked on seeing the steeple of this great cathedral so far in the distance. Now, close to it, the cathedral engulfed everything which surrounded it and dwarfed them by the greatness of its presence. As I gazed around me, I became like a child in a fantasy world. The good Father who had greeted me at the gate had the patience to let this humble priest from the provinces stand and gasp at the significance of these surroundings, where the founding fathers of the Jesuits Order first made their mark, not only in Spain but now throughout the world.

After I gained some balance of my new surroundings, the priest encouraged me to follow him to the secretary's office. He dismissed himself as the secretary looked over my documents and then assigned me to a cell for visiting priests. My surroundings were so different than the monastery where had I studied my priesthood; not only was the monastery so enormous and prestigious, it consisted of many priests. As one day followed the next, I learnt they were all ordained priests, and were of extreme importance, not only to Holy Mother the Church but the Jesuit Order itself. Each priest had a specific assignment for improving the knowledge and continuing the expansion of the Order.

This was the very hub of the Jesuits. These men of knowledge were guarding the Order in so many different fields. They were the greatest minds congregated together in one area, to coordinate the destiny of the Order in Spain and the nations throughout the New World. These Jesuits were just as important as the Conquistadors in expanding the empire of Spain and planting the seeds of Christendom.

For the next three months, I was more a guest than a participant in the activities around me. I volunteered to be of assistance whenever possible; however there was few times that my offer was accepted by these great academic minds. Though I was anxious to serve in any capacity, I was only given the most elementary assignments.

Finally my stay at the monastery was completed. I was informed that they had secured passage on a transport caravan which would take me to my final destination. Within the next few days, I joined the caravan as it made its way from Madrid to Seville on its first part of the journey. In the days which followed, great distances were achieved. Each nightfall, we would enter a suitable area then find shelter in one of the inns. In some cases, we were able to stay in the guest houses or the monastery itself. We were always welcomed as honored guests. I experienced much happiness along this journey itself, for I never missed a day saying the Mass. Also, I was able to give those around me the Holy Sacrament of Communion and absolution, as well as comforting and counseling. This was a new experience for me, which opened up the crevices in my mind of darkness and gave me new light as well as experience in my ordination as a priest and how to serve my almighty God. Life itself was so different in every aspect of what I had served for half my life in the monasteries; now I was experiencing a whole new world.

The very landscape is different than anything I've ever experienced. To say nothing of the men and women, even their mannerisms and dress are foreign to what I have seen in my village and the city where I took my Holy Orders from. Their very way of speaking Spanish is difficult for me to understand, let alone converse with them. Also, the way they prepare their food and the variety of dishes is again foreign to my taste. Since I've lived a modest and pious life in the monastery, I know very few luxuries or diversity of food, other than on feast days. Both meats and fish are prepared with different spices, but the most surprising is to experience the vegetables and fruits that I have never even known existed until now.

At last, we entered the city of Seville and I became childlike mentality in the world of wonderment. The city itself is so different than Madrid and anything else I've ever experienced. The buildings, I was told, are of Turkish design, unique in the colors and materials for their construction.

Many of the buildings which still stand are a result of the Moorish people living here. After the defeats of the Moors, the churches were redesigned from mosques into proper places of worship of our Lord Jesus Christ. The more I saw, the more my mind reached out for answers. There were freestanding towers, and when I asked what the purpose of these was, I was told they were minarets for the use of the faithful in the Islamic faith to prayer. I was astonished these unbelievers in Christianity had been able to conquer our land, settle here, and our people. My homeland now seemed so much larger than had been in my mind before. From the little history I had studied, I understood the contribution of the Roman Empire. But of the Moors themselves, I had little understanding of, other than their conquests. My limited knowledge consisted of Moors believing in Allah and the Prophet Mohammed. I have little understanding or tolerance for anyone who did not believe in the teachings of Jesus Christ and the Holy Mother the Church and of St. Peter the First Pope. To all others, in my simple mind were heretics. There is consideration in my mind for these heretics which should be purged from the lands of Christianity. Here I am now, in the aftermath of those who invaded our land and the people here are the descendants of heretics.

After another two weeks of traveling, I arrived at my final destination, the monastery of Cordoba. This enclave of the Moor's still shows their presence to this day in the architectural designs they left behind. Everywhere I looked, there was a reminder that the Moors had occupied this part of Spain and if we had not driven them out, we would not have what is known today as the Spanish Empire. Once the carriage arrived at the monastery with the few belongings I had brought with me, I was dropped off at the front gate. I was met by one of the priest's and shown to the cell which I would be occupying. It was after Vespers that I discovered not only the monastery was the smallest of the three in which I had been present, there was only 10 priests who occupied this monastery. Of course, there were other people who were present and accounted for on a daily basis. These people had employment from the monastery for services they specialized in, as well as the nuns who prepared the meals from a nunnery a short distance away.

The prefect was well along in age, but strong both in body and will. As I expected, I was given the junior positions of responsibility. What was one of the responsibilities I welcomed with zeal was teaching the younger grades of boys, who would be made into responsible citizens in the future. As the days passed and the months arrived, I soon developed a pattern similar to my years at the seminary when preparing myself for priesthood. It was hard to believe the months passed with the seasons and to my amazement I had been here almost a full year. By now, the priests had accepted me as an equal and many as a friend.

On the day of my anniversary of entering this monastery, the other priests (with the help of the nuns) had prepared a small feast to celebrate my one year in their presence. I was still astonished that a year had vanished in my life and what I had learned in every aspect of this year; with the ways not only of this monastery, but the lifestyles of this district in Spain. How quickly without realizing it, I had woven my life into their ways of doing things, from the smallest things such as eating fish in a different manner to the way we would celebrate the feast days of our saints. I'd received so much knowledge and understanding of all the people around me that I felt somewhat guilty in the little I had been able to contribute in return.

As the years vanished, my happiness continued and I was well into my third year. By now some of the priests who I had met on my first days so long ago had been reassigned to different monasteries and even two of them to different countries. Now I was in a senior position to the newly ordained priests as they came from receiving their Holy Orders, and I had not quite reached my 30th year.

One day, the prefect, a gentle man who I considered a friend, called me into his office. As we sat across from each other, we talked about the children and their progress in their studies, as well as the day-to-day matters of the monastery. As we continued the conversation, I could not help but feel there was something more on his mind when he invited me into his quarters to have a fireside chat. I sensed he had something important to say. At first, I thought he may have received information that he was going to be transferred to a different monastery. How wrong I was. After a friendly conversation, he informed me that I was to be transferred and would be returning to the monastery in Madrid for further instructions. I asked him as a friend, if he could enlighten me more as to where my destination would lead.

He smiled his fatherly smile at me and said, "My dear friend, you are asking only the messenger. I have no more knowledge than what I've given you."

I was bewildered and uncertain of the events that were taking place in my life. Nonetheless, when one takes a vow of obedience, the questions one has must remain unto themselves. In the small community such as this, the word had spread upon my leaving the perfect's office. The questions I was asked were the same one-sided as I had asked the prefect moments before.

His answers were the same as the priest's, "I have no idea, and am no wiser than you".

The days ahead were filled with uncertainty and anxiety, yet a curiosity of what lie ahead. There was a melancholy to give up these enjoyable years here in my new-found home. I reflected back not only on the students themselves; but also on the people who I had assisted in their spiritual needs who were my friends and I was more than just a priest. In many cases, I had become a guiding inspiration in their lives and they definitely were the rewards of mine. Before the month came to an end the arrangements had been made for my transportation to return to the monastery in Madrid.

As I set out on this journey, I thought it was as interesting as the first time, watching the landscape change and staying at different inns and monasteries along the way. Now, in reality the only thing that had changed was me. In these four short years, I have gained so much more understanding of all the things around me. I have become more grateful each day in the profession that I chose. Oh no! No! God has chosen for me.

Upon arriving at the monastery in Madrid, I was once again totally dwarfed by its size and complexity. I was overwhelmed by the number of other Jesuit superiors, but also visiting priests and bishops from Holy Mother the Church. As in the past, I was greeted by a priest assigned to be my guiding force, to assist me to be at the right place at the right time in the coming days. He showed me to the cell I was assigned to while I was staying at this monastery. It was well into the second week before I was informed to attend the tribunal of superior Jesuit fathers. These men are the greatest philosophical and theologian minds of their time. They have the foresight and vision to guide and rule the destiny of the Jesuit Order and the priests who served it throughout the four corners of this world.

By now the time for my appearance before them had arrived. I was granted permission to enter the room of these three wise men, who sat elevated in high-backed chairs with a long oak table before them. There was a single small stool below them in which I was to occupy. Their ages reflected years of achievement in their success to be able to hold this position which governed and ruled over all under their realm. As they gazed down on me, in my humble position, I felt I was nothing more or less than a lump of clay molded for their inspection. The eldest of the three and most superior was the first to speak.

"Today we have summonsed you in our presence to inform you of your new assignment and vocation to represent the Jesuit Order and its' presence. We have received a thorough report of your progress since your ordination as a priest. Your development, as well as your shortcomings and limitations are all know to us."

By now, I knew my face was blushing and I had no control over what my physical appearance was portraying. My Roman collar was tightening around my throat, as if it was a noose waiting for my execution. I lowered my eyes to the floor, when the superior priest spoke again.

"Do not look at the floor. Look at us, for we are going to only say this once to you, so now listen well."

Immediately my head flung back as if a lash had been put on my back. I looked straight ahead at the figures before me. All the same, my eyes were blurred.

Once again, the priest who was in the middle of the tribunal spoke, "Your communication gifts from God have been accelerating, Lord be praised. Nonetheless, your growth in achieving higher standards of education is limited." He continued by saying, "You will never achieve any elder position in philosophy or theologian doctrine."

Then, the priest on the right spoke to me. "You will never achieve any significance or contribution as a teacher in this Jesuit Order which is a teaching order."

I continually looked straight ahead. I could feel the moisture drain from my eyes to my cheeks. My very being, my existence was always to be a priest. I thought of nothing else since my earliest childhood. I am ordained into the priesthood, and now these superior fathers are telling me that am I not worthy of being a Jesuit priest. For the first time in my life, I felt the deep sorrow of pain in my heart such as I've never experienced before. The silence in the room was deafening, at least to my ears, as I sat there like a child humbly waiting his fate.

At last, the priest on the left spoke and when he did, he said, "You been given by God the gift of communicating with others, in delivering comfort and contrition to their souls. Therefore, you will best be serving God and the Jesuit Order by going to the missions in the New World. You will do the best of your ability to practice this gift which God has given you and to represent this Order."

Again, the priest in the middle looked directly at me and asked in a softer voice, "Do you have any questions, Father?"

I looked directly into his eyes and replied, "Yes, Father. I have but one. When do I leave?"

For the first time since I entered their presence, the three of them looked on this block of clay with kindness.

The one in the middle replied, "We will make arrangements forthcoming. From this time forth, we are giving you permission to return to the village where you were born and enjoy the moments with your family and friends."

I knew the interview had ended and with this, I stood up and looked directly at each and every one of the three priests. With all the strength I could muster in my voice I spoke.

"You have given me and my family a great honor by allowing me this opportunity. I will not let God or my vocation down. I will represent God and this Order every day, to the best of my abilities and with the help of Almighty God," and then I bowed.

The middle priest said, "Go in peace, may God bless you."

With this, I bowed once more and then went to the large doors which were opened for me from this chamber. I did not return to my cell, but went to one of the many small chapels which were situated throughout the monastery. I have no idea how many hours I spent, nor did it matter. I found peace and contentment, communicating with my Redeemer. I had neither sadness nor feelings of despair; I just needed to be consoled and reassured of my presence. I knew I was going to leave my homeland, my place of birth, to never return. I also knew that any dreams I may have had of being relocated closer to my family and friends were abandoned now forever. I regressed back in my mind to my first assignment and the anxieties that I experienced. This one was equally as challenging and demanding. Even in my mature mind, I was having a difficult time comprehending what may lie ahead of me in the New World.

At the evening meal, many of the priests asked me questions about my new assignment. The best I could inform them was it was going to take place somewhere in the New World. I asked if any of them had ever met a priest who had returned from the New World or read letters with information from the missions throughout the New World. Their answers to these questions were vague and lacked substance in their answers. Many of the priests surrounding me gave with words of encouragement and positive thoughts that they had received from others in the New World who had converted many natives to Christianity. Nonetheless, as they continued providing the scanty information which was available to them, they also told me of the hardships and the disease that was present, resulting with early deaths of the priests who went to the missions. They assured me the records which were available through this monastery were very limited and majority of files and information would be in the Vatican.

I did not mind giving up my life for Jesus Christ. In fact, it would be the greatest honor and reward of His gift, to let me be worthy of being a child in the light of Jesus Christ. After the evening meal, I returned once more to the chapel. I remained in prayer throughout the night. I have always found peace and consolement in prayer, on my knees before the altar of Jesus Christ. As the hours vanished, I found what I was looking for in Jesus Christ, My Redeemer and My Holy Father in heaven, and the Blessed Virgin Mary. Throughout the evening, I prayed to the saints, but I seemed to always return to the Immaculate Conception and the Holy Trinity. As the morning sun acknowledged another day had begun, I left the chapel rejuvenated and was looking forward instead of backward.

Within three days, one of my fellow priests' informed me that they had found passage in a carriage going to Ávila. Once more, I would be at home with my father and mother, my brothers and sisters as well as my friends. The next weeks were a blur of traveling by day and staying in inns at night. With the next morning arriving, there would be a change of horses and we would continue on to our journey, always proceeding north through the countryside of Spain. As this journey continued I was arriving closer each day to the land that I knew and I was born in.

At last, one day we arrived at the doors of the monastery in which I had studied and completed by priesthood. Once inside the monastery I was greeted by my fellow priests and made to feel welcome. One of the priests showed me to the cell which will be my home until I found passage, or one of my relatives could come and take me to my family. I had the privilege of saying Mass and conversing with some of the professors who were still there teaching. In the evenings, group of priests would sit with me and I became the authoritive person on what the monastery and the people of the southern part of Spain were like. Though I would never qualify as a theologian or a historian, I definitely was a lecturer, and was able to share my experience and personal knowledge of the southern parts of Spain. I've been given an opportunity of gaining knowledge, not from books but from practical experience and personal involvement.

Within the next two days, my eldest brother had received word that I was staying in the monastery at Ávila. Without hesitation, the following day he harnessed up his cart and made his way to the monastery. Oh, what a joyous moment, when my eldest brother arrived at the monastery and I came out to greet him. We held each other as close as Siamese twins and we both wept.

Once I got my personal things and returned to the cart where my brother was waiting, we started the journey back to my village, my home, my place of heritage. Upon arrival, my brothers and sisters were waiting. My parents had aged and were being cared for by one of my sisters'. It was then that I started to realize how the years had vanished. My youth was no longer with me, and it was the twilight zone for my beloved parents. I visited and enjoyed the moments with my precious brothers and sisters, as well as their husbands and wives who introduced me to the new children who arrived in my absence. I spent time with my parents and looked at both of them with all my love and devotion. My poor father looks so frail; as if a bad storm came he would be the victim of the aftermath and might very well be taken to the other side. My mother had weathered the aging process somewhat better; all the same, the lines that covered her face were the road maps of life and were deep and unyielding. Her hair was parted exactly the same as I remembered in my youth, however now there were few strands of dark hair. All that remain was the snow-cap of age which covered her head. My father was as thin as a reed on a river bank, while my mother had widened in many ways, yet looked sturdy and healthy. My younger brothers and sisters had drifted through puberty and now as adults had taken up professions and trades which would aid them for the rest of their lives. There was only one of my sisters left who had not found a suitable companion. Even so, she was being courted at the time. I asked about my eldest sister who was in the convent at Ávila. I was told by my siblings that she was happy in the nunnery and found her vocation, as I had mine.

As each day vanished, another two weeks have penetrated into a new month. Each morning, I was given the privilege to say Mass in the church that I had been baptized and confirmed in. The same priest who had given me my first Communion

remained as the pastor of this church. He had the kindness of matured good wine and now let this child from his past give the sermons in the pulpit each Sunday. The congregation who had accepted me as one of their own in the past, now recognized me as a member of the cloth as I stood before them in the pulpit and read the Holy Gospel and delivered the sermon. On one of these occasions, the good father asked me if

I would like to join him for lunch, which I accepted immediately and acknowledged the honor he gave me. We talked about my past; when I was a child and my exuberant ways of expressing myself even then. We also talk about the days I became eligible to become an altar boy. As we moved from one subject to another, the reminiscing came to an end. The secular priest looked at me more as a father to his son, with kindness and love, knowing in the very near future he would never have the opportunity of looking at me again with his eye.

"Oh, my son! You are my son!" A soft voice came from within as he looked upon me. He then said to me, "I was such a young priest with zeal for life itself, with an ability to communicate with this congregation, to accelerate their altitudes of achievement both spiritually and physically, which I have tried to do in all these years." Then he added, "You have the gift; yes . . . the God-given gift of communicating with others. Why would you not consider giving up the Order of the Jesuits and become a secular priest; maybe becoming the deacon at this church itself?"

He never took his eyes off me and then added, "Within a year or two, I shall retire or join my ancestors and this congregation would be your flock."

As our eyes met, I was astounded by such an offer of generosity. He was offering his congregation, his flock to a young humble priest. My eyes watered like two pools ready to burst their banks; however I never took my eyes off my benefactor, my friend, my spiritual father. Once I gained some repose, I spoke almost in a whisper, more to myself than to him, "This offer is overwhelming. Would I seem ungrateful to ask for a few days, to gather my thoughts at such as generous gift?"

He continued looking at me with that same loving smile that I had experienced in my childhood and his ways which have influenced me into the life of priesthood, then said, "Of course, my son. I thoroughly understand that this is a great decision. Regardless of age or experience, to make any decision instantly would only be a folly. Please, make your decision in your own good time and convey the knowledge to me when you're ready."

For the next two days, every moment I had to myself, I returned to the cathedral to kneel and pray before the altar and doing the

Stations of the Cross; to help my thoughts clearly forth come in what purpose I was to best serve Almighty God. On the second day, well into the evening came the answer and the understanding of what decision I should make. I was kneeling before the cross at the altar, looking up at My Divine Redeemer and remembering the temptations which were put before him during his ministry. Then, I realized my good friend, the priest who had heard my first confession, gave me my first communion, had been the temptation to what my heart wished to have, at the price of my soul, when he offered me his congregation. I now had the light of guidance to remember my three vows of chastity, obedience and poverty; the vows that I took the day I became an ordained priest, as God was my witness. I could not abandon the vow of poverty, no more than I could abandon any of my vows God witnessed that day. God had given me the greatest gift I asked for in my life, and that was to be a priest.

Now, I will fulfill in every possible way this great reward while I'm on this earth. I may have been tempted physically but I have not yielded spiritually. I know I must go to the New World as it is to be proclaimed as my destiny. As soon as this decision had been confirmed in my mind and my soul, a great load was removed. I felt a new happiness and contentment in my heart, and was full of joy once more.

I was informed within two weeks I would report to one of the seaports cities. The days which followed vanished as quickly as the years of my childhood and finally the day came for me to depart from my father and mother, my brothers and sisters and of my friends, for the rest of my life. I then started to take the journey to the seaport city in a part of Spain that I'd never seen before. This city has a rich heritage as a seaport, import in trade and commerce, also defending the land from sea intruders. As I gathered knowledge of the past, I learned that the Celtics, Romans and the Moors occupied this part of Spain with even some reference to the Greeks and the Pillars of Hercules, so this city has a genuinely rich past as well as a present. For me, I enjoyed this as being one of the enclaves for the first Christians.

While staying a short time in this city, I met the captain and his first mate. The first mate and I would be sharing the same cabin going to the New World. Both men were pleasant enough and gentlemanly in their manner and behavior. The captain informed me at this time the ship was nearing preparation with its cargo to be completed within days and there-after we would cast off to the New World. In two days hence I was informed to board the ship with the captain and his crew on the evening before, as we would sail out on the morning tide. For me, this was an entirely new experience being by the sea alone, and watching tides coming in and out, and the endless view beyond, nothing but water.

For me the whole experience of witnessing such an event was exciting and unpredictable. That evening was the first time I did not have terra firma under my feet. Like the good Captain had predicted, at first light we left with the tide going out to sea. I stood on the deck looking at the land further and further away from my vision. My eyes were fixed upon the land of my birth which I would never see again as it slowly vanished before me. By the second day, all that was in view were shades of blue, one darker with ripples and the other lighter with puffy clouds. The gentle winds bellowed the canvas on the large masts far above my head.

It was then when I realized what the term 'land-lover' meant. After I said Mass and gave Holy Communion, my stomach started to roll with the ocean below and it took all my will power not to regurgitate any substance I had taken in. As the day wore on, so did my presence at the railing as I expelled all the liquids in my stomach. By the evening, I was far too sick to get out of my bed to attend the evening meal. As I lay there on my bed, I sincerely believe that the phantom of death had woken and I would join him in eternity. By the next morning, more by the grace of God, I somehow managed to rise to the occasion of saying Mass and giving Holy Communion to the crew. I swear my condition did not improve. In fact, it could be said that it worsened, because I was already at a critical stage. However, by nightfall the crew had managed to rig a bed on the deck which aided my stomach contractions of urging fluid that no longer existed in my body. For the next two weeks, I persisted to survive to the end of this voyage on the sea.

My companion, the first mate, had been a cabin boy at the age of six; one could say he had the salt of the sea in his veins. His year's now numbered a little more than mine, for he had less than four years before his 4th decade would start. He was a gentle man, but firm and decisive in the direction of himself and the orders to the crew. The captain was a true seaman of his time. He knew the winds and the charts as if they were the thoughts in his mind. My experience aboard this vessel was an endurance of sheer determination to once more plant my feet on terra firma. If I longed for my home-land, this was a great deterrent for I wished never to set sail upon water again.

Upon arriving at the port, I was escorted by military personnel to the garrison and met the priest who served this base. After I got a bearing of my surroundings, I came to realize what an outpost in the New World was all about. Its function was practical, efficient and nothing else. The buildings were functional, with furnishings inside that were sparse in quantity and poor in quality. Outside the garrison itself, in the hamlet, are residential dwellings, as simple in appearance as those in the garrison. In the following days, I experienced the local natives of the region whose appearance is simply different than ours. Their skin is much darker, almost chocolate-like in color and their build is short and sturdy. The men wear something like a skirt while the women wear a full dress. These local natives have adapted not only to our Spanish ways but can converse modestly in our language. These people do our tasks, such as the women preparing food and keeping the dwellings clean and the men do the heavy laborious tasks which are required throughout the hamlet and the garrison. The regent, officers and the soldiers are treated as aristocrats in the courts of our King.

In the next few days, I started to realize why Europeans call this part of the globe the New World. The garrison, as well as the dwellings in the small hamlet were constructed of an adobe-type material. It consisted of a clay mixture with horsehair and then a final coat of lime. The fortification was made of stone to support a modest amount of canon power. The complement of the entire garrison numbered less than 30, including the officers. The hamlet consisted of a few merchants, and docking facilities for both the garrison and the local community. The landscape itself was as foreign to me as anything that I had experienced, the trees and bushes, even the flowers I could not recognize. The overgrowth outside the parameter of the hamlet was far denser than any forest I'd ever seen. One of the soldiers told me that they called this forest a 'jungle', for when the rainy season is upon the land, the humidity is very high and all vegetation grows at a wild pace.

When I dined at night, there were very few dishes that I was familiar with. The few foods that I recognized from Spain were limited and served in small portions. Both the fish and meats were of varieties that I was not accustomed to, along with the different vegetables and fruits that grew abundantly in this region of the New World. As I ventured into the different cuisine presented before me, I found some of the dishes most enjoyable, while others were less appealing to my palate.

Before the week ended one of the officers of the garrison informed me that in the following week the caravan would be ready to depart to the mission where I had been assigned to. The trip would take in excess of the month to complete. This officer has a pleasant nature, nonetheless one recognized the coarseness of his command of the Spanish language and his general appearance made it evident that whatever regiment he would belong to, the best he could achieve was the rank he had in one of these outposts throughout the empire.

As one day found the next waiting, I came to realize the limitations of being in the New World. Other than the pure necessities of furnishings as well as personal belongings being very limited, the people who are living here are on a day-to-day basis are the lowest-class Spaniards trying to better their lives in their new environment. One might say they are opportunists who had left nothing behind to gain a much more prosperous life in the New World. All the same, I'm sure there are advantages and opportunities in this part of the world, even though there are far fewer luxuries here than even the commoner has in Spain.

This officer once more came and joined my presence and then also advised me it would be in my best interest if I would consider riding a horse rather than accompanying a driver in one of the wagons. I was astonished that he would suggest such a thing when he had no idea of my horsemanship. He explained to me that these were cargo wagons and were not carriages, besides there were no roads but merely trails which would guide us to our destination.

The cargo wagons were difficult to sit in and endure the long distances required each day throughout the journey. I realized the importance of riding a horse over the torturous hours on a wagon. My horsemanship skills were very limited for I only had the privilege of riding a horse in my youth.

At last, the day finally arrived with all the supplies being assembled in the wagons so the expedition could commence. Early that morning, the six wagons with their oxen were accompanied by six soldiers on horseback. As well, there were 12 natives who would walk on foot ahead of the column and to complete the entire company there was an officer in charge, with one lonely Jesuit priest.

In my imagination (which I consider to be good at best) as well as the information I had received before leaving for the New World and now conversing with the soldiers at the garrison, still all the same I was ill-prepared for what lay ahead. One of the first things I found unbearable was the intense heat accompanied with humidity. We had only gone a very short distance before my habit was soaking wet with my own perspiration. The natives were ahead of us breaking open trails with machetes to clear the way since the last expedition had been six months before. On both sides of this narrow trail were canopies of trees which were a great distance above us.

I had never seen plants of this nature before. The trail itself was overgrown by ferns and other vegetation that had sprung up in the short span between supplies going to the mission. Jungles had another meaning in my life other than dense forest and overgrowth vegetation, there were sounds coming from everywhere and in all directions.

My horse became nervous, as well as the officer I rode beside. He informed me there were many birds and beasts in the forest that he had never seen in all the years he'd been here. He warned me of the many insects and snakes, to say nothing of ants that were deadly with their poisons. However, I now understood why riding a horse was so much more preferable than being on one of the wagons, as the natives cleared to re-establish the trail, there was evidence of broken wagons that had gone before us.

As the days followed, I prayed constantly I would live to see the mission itself. The sheer endurance of those who had managed to carve a way through this wilderness was a feat only second to discovering this New World. This continually dense jungle was like an endless tunnel in which we were traveling and even when we stopped at nightfall to pitch our tents, the openings were still narrow and surrounded by the density of the landscape.

However, as we went further inland, each day the humidity dropped and the forest had openings where one could see something beyond their face. It was difficult to ride a horse up these inclines but it was the carts that had the most difficult time. The natives now had to push each cart from behind to get them up the inclines.

Though the weeks at the garrison had revived my physical body from the weakness I experienced when crossing the sea, I did not seem to have the same strength or endurance that I had left when leaving Spain. By the grace of God, and the determination of the men around me, we continually moved forward, day after day, week after week, to accomplish the journey we had set out to achieve. Even after these endless weeks, I felt I would never grow accustomed to the heat, the density of the landscape, and the heavy rains which would appear without warning only to vanish shortly thereafter.

I would never feel at ease, day or night, in these dense forests with creatures hidden from my eyes, just waiting for their opportunity. The snakes and other reptiles which carry the poisons were always around us but never seen. Also, there was the danger of mosquitoes which carry malaria and yellow fever as gifts in exchange for one's blood, and the afflicted victim had a long and agonizing death with no cure.

Our rations were modest, and the dishes were prepared by the local natives, to their knowledge and liking rather than our taste. By the fourth week, the heavy overgrowth became sparser and the altitude was higher. Now, the climate was similar to a summer in Spain. All the same, few men from the garrison had been here before and only the local natives had any understanding of what direction to take. This is both eerie and alarming. If one was to venture off this trail, one would be lost in any given direction.

The trees canopies were so high and dense that one could not determine where the sun was.

I was so grateful on the fifth day of the sixth week when we had entered a plateau opening and this dense over-growth was behind us. In this higher altitude, the temperature and humidity is pleasant, along with the openness of the surroundings. Even the air itself seems light and pleasant to inhale.

By nightfall, we had reached our destination, the mission itself. I had a concept of what the mission would look like, but still was not prepared for what I saw before me. As we entered the compound, three priests came out to greet us as if we were their salvation. And rightly so. Without the supplies that these braves soldiers and natives had brought with them, it would only be a matter of time before the mission would recede back into the jungle from which it'd been carved. Outside of the monastery's protective walls were small wooden dwellings. They were made with branches bound together, by what looked like pieces of a bark and the cone-shaped roofs were covered with broad leaves from plants in the surrounded area. The natives who had been converted to Christianity lived in these dwellings, around the mission.

In the days that followed, I came to understand the daily life of this mission. The native women did all the necessary cooking and looking after the priests' domestic needs, while the men labored around the mission itself. The priests, on and above saying the Mass, are the teachers of the natives and their children. I was greeted as one that was dearly needed to assist and help with the overburdened work of these holy fathers of the Church. The priests were overjoyed to see the caravan with the supplies which were so desperately needed for them to continue their work.

For myself, I felt as if I was some kind of dignitary being honored in their presence. Each priest independently came up and thanked me for having received my vocation and instructions to join them. Almost at once, I realized the importance of my presence here. Now, I would relieve some of the burden in their long hours of labor for God and Holy Mother the Church. The Prefect was definitely the youngest I've ever met; there was only a difference of two decades between me and him. I was assigned a cell which had been added to the mission once they knew that a priest was coming to join their congregation.

I was shown around the small mission's facilities. There was a small chapel, but more than adequate for the congregation. The common area was where the priests would have their meals. The courtyard was the centerpiece, with a well-designed garden where the priests would pray during the hours away from their duties. There was a small room used as the infirmary where the priests would do their best to assist the sick or dying. Next to this was a large covered area that housed the supplies which would be needed for the next six months until the next caravan came. The rest of the small rooms were of no great significance.

The moment we arrived, each of the priests was anxious to talk to the soldiers and ask them to share their experiences at the garrison and the world outside their mission. They were saving me for last, to personally share all that had been taking place since their presence in the homeland of Spain. Each day, the priests seemed to have a list of questions that they put aside for another day to question me all over again. I had never been in the presence of anyone coveting as much information as these priests did. On one of these days, the officer handed over a large box which, to my amazement and astonishment, contained letters not only from the Jesuit monastery in Madrid, but personal letters from family and friends of each priest. For the first time since leaving my homeland, I did not feel isolated with no hopes of communication with those who were so important to me. Yes, the distances between us would be immeasurable and the communication would be sparse; all the same it was available to both the giver and receiver.

By the third day, the priests had the native women prepare a feast in honor of our arrival. The food was prepared in a manner that I had never experienced before, to say nothing of the different varieties of food which I did not know even existed. Some of the dishes I found pleasant to my taste while others I was grateful that the portions were small. Many of the names of the fruits I was unable to pronounce, even so they were enjoyable. The meat and fowl, and some type of deer served at the meals were all different tastes for my palate. It goes without saying that the best wine served at this meal was brought on the wagons. I found it sinful as the meal continued and eaten with robust appetites of the soldiers, that there was still an abundance of food left over. The good Prefect saw my concern, and then informed me that any food left over from this table of plenty would be taken by the native women back to their homes, so nothing would be wasted.

For an entire week, the small mission was full of activities as the soldiers spent their days with the Jesuit priests. However, one week to the day, the soldiers and the natives prepared themselves to return to the garrison. That morning, the priests, including myself said Mass and the soldiers received Holy Communion and each one of us gave them our blessings for a safe return to the garrison.

In the days that followed, now the four of us started to get into the routine previously done by only the three priests. Each one of us was designated to doing things we were best suited to, according to our abilities. One priest was academic, and responsible for teaching the natives the doctrines of the church, catechism, theology and the Holy Bible. He also taught the children to read and write in Spanish. Another priest excelled in leadership, and with this ability, he oversaw the general operations of maintaining the monastery. He delegated the workloads both to the men and women, and supervised the maintenance of the gardens and fruit trees in the surrounding area.

The Prefect was the greatest of leaders. He oversaw the entire mission both inside and out, with such a congenial and outgoing spirit that he gave all others the feeling of wanting to cooperate with him and their fellow human beings. He was the guiding force who kept the community outside the mission expanding with new people who came and wished to stay. However, with all these talents there was one that was very important; he was the one who had the best knowledge of helping those who were sick and aiding them in getting better.

For myself, I shared the workload of all of the other priests. I enjoyed the diversification and welcomed the experience that Almighty God was giving me as a Jesuit priest, and to serve his people here in this mission. My gift of communication that the priests at the Jesuit monastery in Madrid had acknowledged was put to the test. Another gift I did not realize I possessed was the ability to learn and understand different languages as well as dialects. Within six months, I was commissioned by the Prefect to be in charge of all communication with the natives. I was the go-between with the other priests and the natives who did not understand or comprehend their instructions, whether conversion to Christianity or tasks which were assigned to them. I became the centerpiece of communication.

As I extended my knowledge, I realized why this mission was in such an isolated area of the New World. It was not only to convert pagans into Christianity, it also was a sanctuary against the Portuguese and (I'm sad to say) the Spaniards who would raid villages and took the natives to be sold as slaves to the overseers of plantations.

My first year vanished as the night relinquishes to the day. In that time, another supply-caravan came and went. To my delight, not only were the supplies welcomed, but also we received instructions from the Jesuit monastery in Madrid and personal letters from our families. I was rewarded by three letters from my brothers and sister. The letters contained more questions than information; all the same, the link of communication had been re-established, even in this remote outpost in the jungles of the New World. In return, I wrote letters in great detail of living conditions and what I was experiencing, which was probably far beyond any of my siblings to comprehend.

Word had spread throughout the region and even distances far beyond, of our protection and sanctuary for all natives, with the only requirement being that they had to convert to Christianity. Conversion seemed a small price for them to receive the protection of this enclave against the brutality and an early death of slavery. Not only did the surrounding village grow, we definitely needed to expand the mission itself.

Our first priority had to be the small chapel which was now totally inadequate. We started to build a large church which would enable us to serve the village, but also to accommodate the expansion we would be experiencing in future years. The church itself was a mammoth size and could hold in excess of 100 people. This was a monumental task which involved the extreme efforts of all the native men each day. The Prefect was required to give reports on a regular basis to the Jesuit monastery in Madrid, and they started to realize the significance of this mission. As the years fell away, the dear Prefect received a letter from the Jesuit monastery in Madrid that we would be assigned two new priests to aid and assist us in our success. Once the news was shared with the rest of us, we were all elated to have two new priests to assist us in this massive undertaking we were involved in.

It was déjà vu all over again for me. When the priests finally arrived, we questioned them endlessly, day after day, even into the weeks of what was transpiring in Spain and the Empire. We asked questions, as a child with an endless appetite for knowledge; anything from what was happening in Rome, to the political arenas of the known world, to small things like the habits and dress of the common people. Our thirst for information was endless as the new arrivals shared their knowledge as well as patience with us who had been isolated for so long.

Years vanished like a rainbow in the sky. My youthful years were behind me now, a decade finished and another one followed. Now I had been here twenty years. I came to realize how fulfilling my life had become and I would not want to be anywhere else than here in this world. My dear Prefect was in the twilight years of his life and had accomplished so much in his life. He had taken a vision by the Jesuit order to create a mission in unknown territory. Now, this is one of the largest mission areas in the New World.

We've grown from the first lonely members of the order, counting three to now over twenty priests at the mission. It was difficult for me to comprehend that I was no longer a junior member of the mission, but a senior with vast knowledge of the region. I also was somewhat confused and astonished at the same time, when I was considered to be the next Prefect of this large mission. I was humbled that the Prefect would consider me, of all priests, to be his successor, especially now that the mission had reached such a gigantic size and the responsibility was enormous.

As I was able to spend more and more time in the larger villages surrounding the mission itself; all who were present realized I had a God-given gift, not only of communicating but acting as the glue or adhesive to bond our community into one. I was able to visit each family on a rotating basis. During these years, my communication abilities were recognized by one and all. It did not matter to me if they were a child or elderly; they would always want to listen to my thoughts and my recommendations, with my unrelenting motivation for them to love Holy Mother Church and Jesus Christ.

By the end of the next decade, our dear Prefect had reached the golden age in which he was eligible to return to the monastery in Madrid for retirement. The command of the burden of responsibility that had grown with our success had taken its toll of his physical well-being. He was more than willing to see the approach of being retired from this burden.

The new priests arriving confirmed that the recommendation of the Prefect's choice was approved by Madrid. I gratefully assumed the duties and responsibilities of being a Prefect. In the years that followed, we took on the responsibility and obligations of the greatest expansion the mission ever had undertaken. The surrounding areas were now villages unto themselves covering large areas that had been cleared from the overgrown jungle. The number of priests that had been sent from the motherland now numbered more than those that were present in the monastery that I was first at.

It was now practical to erect churches or chapels in each of the surrounding villages. The priests would rotate on a regular basis to spend a fortnight in the village of that area; so the congregation was able to attend Mass every morning and receive Holy Communion and to have a priest look after their spiritual and physical needs without them having to come to the mission. Our success was used as a prototype by the Jesuit fathers in Madrid, who adopted our ways in other missions in the New World.

Time did not stop advancing on my body and soul. My body became weak and tired; long ago my dark hair had turned to snow white. My face was the road map of both my knowledge and the years that accompanied them. Though I had never been physically strong, my body became frail. I stooped forward as I walked to greet people. It was now time for me to appoint my predecessor. Both the Jesuit fathers in Madrid and the Holy Church in Roman accepted my recommendation. Though I did not wish to relinquish my duties and responsibilities, the time had come. In the next two months, my body became extremely weak and I was not able to do the bare minimal of my priesthood responsibilities; let alone be the Prefect of the mission. My voyage of life was coming to an end and within a fortnight, I deteriorated to be receiving Last Rites. During that night, two priests stood vigil at my bedside while I left this world.

Once more, I returned to the present time in my study. I was extremely weak and exhausted as I had been in the previous times, but this return was not accompanied by fears or anxieties like most of the transitions of the past. For the first time, in all these possessions of the portraits, I found I had a place in that time in which I was reluctant to return and join the present.

Though still weak with exhaustion, I was able to ring the bell which summoned my male servants to my study. As usual, I needed help getting back to my boudoir where my wife and the doctor were present. As before, the doctor was waiting by the bedside to administer medication which would be required to aid in my recovery from this transition. My beloved wife was by my side, holding my hand. I was too weak to speak or show any physical expressions other than smiling through my eyes.

As the weeks passed, my strength returned. Like the past, I was obsessed during this time to regain my faculties and determined to return to my duties and the enjoyment of being alive and in the present time.

Dr. Sebastian took his eyes from the pages of the Book of Portraits. He couldn't remember ever feeling quite as well after reading one of the chapters in this book. Still, he felt weary and somewhat exhausted as he looked at the great doors straight ahead. After regaining his composure and familiarizing himself with the surroundings, instead of being reluctant as in previous times, and almost feeling forced by the paintings themselves to gaze upon their presence, this time instead he took it upon himself to look directly at the portrait of kindness and goodness. As he gazed into the portrait, he had a moment of feeling that he wished he had been one of the priests at that mission that he had just read about.

Returning his gaze to the great doors, he then reached for the communication bell to advise the butler to return to the study. As for the procedure, it was similar to all the times before. The butler entered the room and his request was the same as always, he wished to make arrangements to return to his dwelling. Soon, the chauffeur was waiting to return him to his home. The hour or so driving home was uneventful and relaxing as he watched the landscape roll before him.

Once arriving home, he thanked the chauffeur and opened the front door to the waiting arms of his beloved wife. She was always apprehensive upon his return, due to the fact she never know what kind of effect the chapter of the portraits would have on him each time. To both her surprise and gratefulness, Dr. Sebastian returned in a peaceful state of mind. In fact, she observed for the first time that he had returned from the mansion in a jovial mood. Grateful to be united once more, they entered into the living room and joined each other with a good Chardonnay. After sipping the rewards of the wine grape, he proceeded to tell her about the remarkable chapter he had just completed, and shared a pleasant evening with his beloved wife.

MADNESS

—✺—

ONCE MORE DR. SEBASTIAN was in his office, however this time he was looking out the window at the street traffic far below. His mind drifted to the activity below and became fully aware that another year had started and was well into its second month. He looked at the dirty snow, which had once been pristine white; now there was nothing more than mud-piles mixed with snow, ice and gravel.

Yes! He said to himself, 'I can't wait until spring arrives' and then on the other side of his mind, the logical part came into play, and said, 'there's nothing you can do about it'.

With these thoughts, there was a smile on his face as he returned to his desk for the challenges of the day. Things were going very well at the Museum. Everything was on schedule and being prepared for the summer displays which had been approved by the Board of Directors. Dr. Sebastian felt he was not only in charge but in control of the activities going on around the Museum. It was such a nice feeling. So many times in the past he wished he could've been cloned at least 12 times, just to meet the immediate responsibilities at hand. As his eyes glanced over the monthly schedule of meetings, he noticed the following Thursday would be the next prearranged trip to His Lordship's mansion.

And so it came to pass. Thursday arrived, but this time he had the chauffeur pick him up at the Museum rather than at his home domicile. Once arriving at the mansion he was only too familiar with what was expected and what transpired. The butler once more escorted him to the study of the late writer where the Book of Portraits was waiting with the other servants for his arrival. After the usual formalities had taken place, Dr. Sebastian got down to the chapter at hand. He was taken back a little by surprise. Although the previous chapters in this book had always been unexpected, this chapter's title was Madness. He concentrated on the word of the heading and could only feel that this might not be one of the benevolent portrait's chapters. However, without further ado, he started to meet the challenge and positioned himself to read this chapter known as Madness.

Once more, I prepare myself to go into my study later this day filled with apprehension and anxiety. I have tried to avoid my study and have spent most of my time in other parts of the mansion. For the last week or two, I have tried to shake off this melancholy of what is going to take place on this night, when my soul once again is going to be possessed by one of the evil moments of one portrait, or maybe a less miserable experience by the more benevolent portrait.

My black mood has contributed to my ailing health in these months. I may well be gone by next year at this time; of course, God willing that I survive tonight. I am now at the age when youth is only a memory and old age is a reality. My eyes grow dim with the setting of the sun and I need artificial light, as well as glasses to grope in the mist I experience constantly. My ears, one has a cricket chirping in it, while the other sits with a stone in it that gives me no sound at all. I no longer stand tall or straight, but stoop forward as the cycle of the earth becomes longer. It matters not what I consume, large or small, my size grows larger around my dorsal. My hands are like branches in the autumn, shaking the leaves from their bondage.

Yes! Yes, moments of happiness are far and few between; along with my dreams and hopes of the future which are nothing more than mist in the night. I am experiencing a most negative psychological state this day. I spend most of the afternoon in the aviary, trying to focus on all the beauty that God has created in every form of plant with the diverse color and fragrances that surround me. I have maybe indulged a little excessively in the juice of the grape-vine. Even so, I have never been intoxicated on the night of the anniversary of the portraits. I wish not to experiment with anything that would be inappropriate for me, knowing what lies ahead on this night of anticipation, which is inevitable.

As the daylight relinquishes its place to the evening, I must also relinquish my freedom from this place of beauty. Now, I make my way wearily and with misgiving to my study, now that night is fast approaching. I ask one of my male servants to accommodate me and place a burning fire in both hearths. All the same, the room still has a cool chill about it. Is it my mood of misgivings about deeds which are best not known, or is it my disheartened thoughts that I have brought to these surroundings? I once more sit in my favorite leather chair, so when I retire into the night that awaits me, I will sink deep into its comfortable assurance.

I dare not look at either side of the room, for if I gaze upon the portraits, the one I fear the most will lock onto my soul. The silence of the night is interrupted by the grandfather clock which keeps ticking, ticking in the room. The hour is marching towards the dreaded moment. I reach out and ring the bell for my male servant. As he enters the room, he asks what service he could provide for me.

"Please put on every light in this room. Do not spare any, for I feel the shadow of darkness over my shoulder," I requested. After completing the task, he asked if there was anything else he could do for me. I replied with a weak smile," No thank you, I require nothing more". As he left the room my eyes followed him and I wished with all my heart and soul I too could join him in leaving this room which possesses me. I've have tried many different approaches to avoid this moment on the anniversary and none of them have been successful.

My body moves deeper into the chair for comfort of my mind and my soul. All the same, as I try to focus my mind on the benevolent portrait, I dare not look anywhere other than straight ahead. Nonetheless, like a hangman's noose, I have to look toward the painting of dread. With my entire mind focused and determined to try to close my eyes, the force coming from those diabolical eyes stares down from the portrait of evil. My eyes are locked into those staring down upon me. The penetration is unbearable. And then, oh, my God, it is happening!

I am standing alone. It is a cold bitter night, accompanied with coal dust that lingers in the air. The hour is becoming late. I am growing weary and tired of standing out here, on this cold isolated street in Soho, London Town. I'll endure another half-hour, at most, for the streets are empty. Most of my kind and the Johns' waiting for them have returned homeward. I will then take a bus and return to my dwelling and to my room where my parents live at Letterstone Road in Fulham.

I've given up hope long ago of ever achieving a relationship or marriage, as far that goes, or being any sort of lady other than 'one of the night'. Oh yes! I wish I was a lady, for now the best I am is a woman of the night. The bloom of youth is fading on my face and in my heart of dreams. Now, I'm in my mid-30's and the only gift God had given me was my beauty. I look what I am, and I am what I look. I don't know how it started. Of course I do. It was that young boy who penetrated my womb and my desire for love. I was barely a teenager and his needs were nothing more than lust. From that day forth, love has assaulted me and I only receive the demands of man's need to satisfy his lust. My faith in mankind and the kindness of the opposite sex is nothing but an illusion for me. By my late teens, I was more than capable of satisfying the sexual desires of men and my reward was, and is, financial.

Oh, my God, it is cold! My very limbs are weary and feel the bite that's in the air. I'm going to start to walk towards the bus stop, enough of my penance for a pound-note here. It is not a night even for the lust of man to satisfy his needs. Maybe my endurance of this purgatory, in this foul weather will bring me a reward after all. Here is a car coming and it is slowing, with the window down.

"And how are you tonight, Sir? Do you now seek the company of one kind and fair?"

"Get in the car and we will discuss the terms. If they're suitable to both, we will continue."

"It is my pleasure Sir." As I get in the car, I look directly at him and ask," What are your dreams or desires of pleasure tonight, Sir?"

"Well, I do not know whether one would call them dreams or desires. Nonetheless, I would say it's more of the business agreement, or a mutual understanding that I seek," was his reply.

"I am always in search of pleasing one of the opposite sex. In fact, it's my trademark."

"It is obvious to me, by the lateness of the night and your appearance in this district," was his reply.

"Now, Sir, would you like to know my name?"

"If you wish to give it to me, so be it, but it's no concern of mine."

"My name is Annabelle; my mother's grandmother's name was Annabelle."

"So be it. Though it does not matter, you can call me Henry," he said. "Well now, isn't that a nice name."

"Now, I have a request for a person of your profession."

"And what would that be, Sir?"

"Would you considering 100 pounds for letting me carry out a theory of mine on human nature?"

"You talk funny, Sir. Could you tell me what I'd be obliged to do, for such a large sum?"

"My first request would be that you could not return to your dwelling and I wish you to stay with me throughout the night."

"That can be arranged," I replied loud and clear.

"My next request is that you accompany me to an underground bunker which was used during the blitz."

"As you wish. I can accompany you to this place, Sir."

"Once we arrive there, I would like you to explain to me, in detail, your feelings of what you are experiencing when I play certain kinds of music, as well as different lighting facilities."

"Oh! Yes, sir?"

"As we see how this plays out, I might ask you to engage in physical coupling, if I so desire."

"Am I correct in saying, Sir, that if I perform these requests, you are prepared to give me the sum of 100 pounds?"

"I have never welshed on any man or woman and have always honored my obligations. Furthermore, if you agree to meet these conditions, I will give you the sum in advance," came his reply.

"I'd be delighted to share an evening with a gentleman such as yourself. I am looking forward to what transpires," was my answer.

"So am I! So am I, my Annabelle."

It was then that I felt a slight uneasiness. Even though he was of an upper-class, my clients would usually take me to a halfway house to quickly fill their needs and I would receive a couple of ten pound-notes for my services.

We then started to drive towards an older district which was further away from Soho and even further from my home in Fulham. Nonetheless, he assured me that he knew where he was going. At last, we arrived at what had once been an industrial area near the docks. We both got out of the car in a deserted area. He took my hand as we walked down a dark and lonely corridor between old deteriorating buildings. In what was probably less than five minutes, we had now entered an old bunker, deep into the bowels of the earth, using a torch to find our way. By now, I was dragging backwards as he was pushing me forward.

He stopped and said, "It's not far now, Annabelle," as he opened up the door and turned on the light. It was a rather large room with basic amenities of a bed, a washroom and modest furnishings. There was one other door which led to God knows where. I started to relax and hoped I had made a decision wisely.

I watched him take off his hat and overcoat, then reach into his suit jacket and produce a wallet. True to his word, he took out five twenty pounds notes and handed me the amount which I quickly put in my purse.

With this, he looked directly into my eyes and said, "Relax and we will have a couple of glasses of sherry before we start tonight."

"That would be very nice. Yes, that would be very nice, "I quickly answered.

He filled two glasses and handing me one, saying, "Cheers."

He must have slipped some kind of drug in the glass I was given for I barely finished half the glass before I was no longer conscious. When I did regain consciousness, I was shackled with chains just long enough to reach the toilet facilities which were available. I was still groggy and incoherent in my thoughts and was reluctant to speak. The gentleman who I accompanied here was nowhere to be found. I called out his name, hoping he was probably in the other room, all the same my request was not granted.

I returned to the bed where I first gained consciousness, with a throbbing piercing pain in my head. I looked at my watch, oh my God; it was midday of the next day. I started to panic as I realized my situation. I got off the bed and went towards the door we had entered and banged hysterically. As I continued, it wasn't long before I realized the inevitable; it was all for naught. I then proceeded to the opposite side of the room and tried to open the door, to no avail. I was locked in a room below ground, chained and shackled. I sat down in one of the chairs and started to weep. I had no desire to search the room for anything that may help my situation.

It was late in the afternoon when I heard a noise from the door and the gentleman I had accompanied the night before, entered the room.

I addressed him immediately, "What is the meaning of this? What kind of man are you?"

It was then that he smiled a sinister grin which made my blood run cold and my heart pounded so heavy that my bosom moved in and out as a cold sweat covered my entire body.

Then he came forward, reached out and grabbed my two hands and looking directly at me said, "Now this is going to be one of the lessons of my theory. Don't you remember about the music, lights, and a few other things?" his voice rang out.

When he let go of my hands, I immediately went over to my purse, reached in and produced five of the twenty pound notes. "Here is your money back! Just drop me off anywhere, just anywhere and I'll find my way home."

"Dear Mademoiselle. I did not renege on my part of the agreement and I expect you not to either," he spoke in a soft voice that scared me even further. He then started to explain to me what we were going to experience together in the next little while.

"Sir!" I snapped back with a reply, "An evening of merriment does not go on for a fortnight of endurance. Furthermore, you did not imply any length of time that I would be here, or in the condition in which I found myself at midday."

"My dear Mademoiselle. You seem somewhat confused. Let me say, you will take part. Now, without further ado, I will start to explain my theory and the part you are going to play. I want to find out how long it takes a person of your character to become completely insane."

My eyes widened in disbelief, as if I was condemned by the Inquisition for my crimes against God's Will and the Commandments before I went to meet my maker.

In a whisper I replied," What did you say?"

"I realize now, that with your limited ability and knowledge, you did not fully comprehend what I just said. So, Annabelle, I will explain to you again, I am going to study how long it takes before you will become hopelessly mad."

He then looked at me with contempt and said, "I will start my theory by music." Without further ado, the music started, loud and screaming with demanding trumpets, then with the accompaniment of drums. There was a complete orchestra in tight confinement. The music was changing with each instrument demanding attention. Becoming louder and louder, the veracious sounds filled the room. Without warning, he left. This incessant noise filled every capacity of space. No matter where I was, no matter how I tried to plug my ears, the unbearable sounds continued.

It could have been the second day or third day of my confinement, for I had no idea of what time. There was no way of keeping track of day and night, let alone remaining calm and trying to have a moment's peace. Time became irrelevant, only this insidious noise continued. No matter what I tried to do to drum it out of my ears, if anything, it seemed to become louder and louder. I tried wrapping my head with garments, putting pillows over my head; it only intensified the instruments beating within my mind. I was at a breaking point, in another moment I would start screaming uncontrollably at phantoms.

The door opened. This man, the devil of my demise entered the room. Unsuccessfully, I had searched every possible place to reveal the switch to turn this terrible noise off. He did it with ease, the secret knowledge only at his disposal.

By now, my balance was completely gone. I remained on the bed as he approached me. I was completely incapacitated as he stripped me of all my garments.

In a sinister voice, he said to me, "This is only the beginning, my dear. Only the beginning."

I lay there exposed to his view. After some time, with an effort I tried to raise myself to at least a sitting position.

Once he realized that I was somewhat stabilized in my condition, he said, "I've replenished the food supply and drink. All the same, you don't seem to have indulged much in either these past few days."

With a supreme effort, I tried to focus. I put my hands over my ears to get some equilibrium back in my life. I started to mutter words, even though I couldn't understand the meaning myself. My mind was pleading mercifully to the little humanity left in him to set me free.

The silence was broken as he spoke, "I see you didn't find the music suitable to your taste. I have another suggestion of entertainment which is totally different. This time we'll both see how you respond."

I was bewildered, but managed to stabilize my body enough to put my feet over the bed and bear weight on them. I was able to stand up and took a few baby-steps towards him. From nowhere, he turned on the switch that immediately produced a blinding amount of light; psychedelic, lasers, black lights, all swirling around the room in different angles. I tried to block my sight to this bizarre cruelty of light as I heard the door slam shut and lock.

I've lost all concepts of days and nights, even weeks, as far as that goes. My mind was no longer mine. For now, I have no idea what is going to happen. It seems like I've been trapped for years. The noise and bizarre sounds I had endured have disrupted my hearing and balance. Now, the lights are doing even more damage to my sanity. I tried to cover my head with my own garments, but could not provide the darkness I needed. One day, I even tore open a pillow and stuffed my head deep inside its contents. But still the lights prevailed, already embedded in my mind. By now, I was screaming hysterically and out of control. I stumbled around the room, crashing into the few pieces of furniture which prevailed.

Even in my madness, I heard a door click open. My sight was distorted. Even though the lights ceased in reality, they still prevailed in my mind. My vision started to adjust to different shades of darkness. My eyes were starting to focus on this diabolical man, who now found a use for my profession. As I lay there whimpering, shaking my head uncontrollably back and forth, he used my body and their openings as I've never experienced before, in all the years of my profession. Even in my befuddled mind, I couldn't comprehend the abuse I was experiencing.

What was even more terrifying was what he said to me in my fog, "My dear little Annabelle, when I'm finished with you . . . no one will ever know that you ever existed in this world. For in that room you do not have access to yet, is where your remains will rest forever. When I'm finished with you, you will be introduced into a bathtub full of sulfuric acid, until there is nothing of your remains left. Keep these thoughts in the forefront of your mind. As you continue to endure my wishes, which in the end will induce pure madness, these thoughts will always remain in your mind and how you will end. Keep in mind that when I am finished and satisfied with your existence, the room next door awaits you, my dear little Annabelle. So, for now, let me enjoy the pleasures that await my desires and your madness."

I did not know if I was hallucinating or if I was hearing what he was saying, for nowadays I was far beyond knowing what was real and what wasn't. I crawled like an animal off the bed and lay in a fetal position on the floor. He sat at the end of the bed while I lay helpless on the floor from being abused in every possible form of my body, my mind, and my very soul. I felt broken, physically and mentally and in total despair. Darkness overcame me. At first, I thought I closed my eyes and then I realized this man of evil had left without my knowledge.

I remained on the floor in total darkness, which at first was a relief to my troubled mind and my aching body. For a length of time, I do not know, my tormented mind had peace and tranquility in the complete blackness of my surroundings. I sensed what total blindness might be like. As I gained strength in both my faculties and muscles, I made my way around the room in my limited capacity with the chains of bondage.

A remarkable event took place in my mind, as I started to clear the cobwebs and confusion with the hallucinations of the little grey cells. I started to make a plan, if not to free myself from this hellhole; I would at least let this diabolical man know what revenge is. Let my name be woman. My mind cleared further. My thoughts went to whatever I could use from the food that was left for my survival. However, there were no utensils or plates, and the water to quench my thirst was in plastic bottles. I realized there was nothing in this compound in which I could in any way hurt myself or any other person. As I groped in total darkness, I realized for the first time that even the chairs were anchored to the floor. The washing facilities were nothing more than what water could be used to flush the toilet. I penetrated the darkness inch by inch, foot by foot. I tried to recall, in my befuddled mind, the time when I entered this place of horror. I soon realized there was nothing more than my bare hands that were all I had at my disposal to seek of my vengeance.

The days, what would I know, whether it was day or night. In this blackness, it could very well be a week or even longer. I have no way of comprehending time at all in this existence between logic and madness. There were moments when my mind returned to thoughts of being saved; maybe my parents would notify the police to search for my whereabouts, which would be my saving grace. At other times, I would realize the futility of being rescued from this hell. Even if my parents and my few friends discovered that I was missing, how in the world would they ever think of searching in a place like this? I soon realized in these terrible moments that I was totally alone and helpless in this situation, with no aid from the outside world.

I would have to wait long periods of time from hallucinations and madness that were present in my mind before a little clearing of moments of sanity. In these periods of sanity, I would try to remain logical in the little time to which these moments prevailed. Then without warning, I would return to the sounds of screaming noises and instruments bellowing out of torment. I knew the sounds were nothing more than the penetration of madness in my mind. Nevertheless, I would fall on the floor and cover my ears, rolling and tumbling around like some demented animal which had been afflicted by rabies or some other diabolical disease of the brain. Then when the screaming sounds in my inner ears would ease, I would return to the unbearable lights. Lasers, strobe lights, flashing in an array of colors far exceeding a rainbow were endlessly dropping their powerful hallucinations in my mind.

Time has no meaning in this nightmare in which I exist in total darkness. And then there were times that my mind returned from hallucinations of madness and again I examined every possibility of escape, yet nothing prevailed. Knowing my situation was hopeless, vengeance was my only thing left. If I was to going to be exterminated in a vat of acid by this monster, I would have at least left the marks of my vengeance upon him. My plan was simple. If I could retain my faculties, I would try to subdue my madness the next time he entered this chamber of horror. I would try to remain sane and approach him in the manner of the trade that I had practiced all my adult life. With my arms around his neck, I would caress him and then quickly like a cat, strike to pluck out his eyes. Oh yes, I kept focusing, in my moments of conscious behavior of this procedure over and over, to pluck out those pieces of coal from that diabolical face which has only lust for my body, my mind or my soul.

Without warning, like the times before, I was no longer in total darkness. The evil one, my tormenter, was once more present. I was grappling on the floor with the contrast of what was total darkness moments before, and now I was in the presence of light. My eyes, and more importantly my mind, tried to focus on the new source of light. As my eyes started to adjust from darkness to light, there he was standing before me, looking down at me with disgust. There was a moment of clearness in my mind, knowing by now that I must have lost at least two stone. Though my figure was of maturity; now I had been reduced to a bag of bones wrapped in skin, compared to when he first feasted his lust upon my body. I realized what my body must look like, but just the same, I was determined to achieve my revenge as I slowly stood up.

Never taking my eyes off him, I reached out with both my arms, hoping to place them around his neck. As I made my final approach, his reflex actions were quicker than mine, the best I was able to do was fall short of my mark. Though I never reached my goal of his eyes, my nails dug deep into the fleshy part of his cheeks, raking down towards his jaw briefly before his hands reached out and grabbed my arms with crushing strength. The next moment I received a blow which was so significant, flinging me across the floor. I lay there stunned, floating between moments of unconsciousness, then consciousness.

The next thing I saw was he had returned with handcuffs. He brutally put my hands behind my back, then raising me from the floor; he attached me to some kind of hook-apparatus from the ceiling. I swung back and forth, being suspended like a side of beef waiting to be dissected by a butcher. Now, in his possession was a whip, a lash and a riding crop. As I dangled, suspended above the floor, I could see I made my mark upon his face which had invoked anger and hatred in his eyes.

"I see, my little Annabelle, you are still in the possession of your mind. Therefore, I will teach you a lesson in obedience and manners. I will introduce you to the lash first, so your body will have the mark of the sailors of old, who thought they were bold."

He started whipping me unmercifully on every part of my body as I rotated on chains that suspended me from the floor. The lash tore away at my flesh, my body rotated to receive more of this supersaturated pain. I screamed in agony, without any mercy or consideration of my situation from the monster that was enjoying this new form of torture that he was imposing upon me. I was able to endure it no more and passed out. Only when he realized I was no longer conscious did the abuse stop. I have no idea of how long I was passed out for, as time does not exist in my world. I do remember having cold buckets of water thrown on my raw flash to revive me.

"Annabelle," his voice came from somewhere. I did not see but only was able to hear. He continued by saying, "Now that you have revived back to consciousness, I will now introduce you to the whip."

This time with the whip, he was slow in delivering the blow so I could anticipate the pain. I cannot give an accurate count of how many of these wicked blows I received before my mind once more found unconsciousness. With this, he would stop whipping me and introduced the buckets of cold water to revive me to consciousness again. Once in this state, he chose the part of my body he would like to introduce his vengeance of the whip to. I would scream out uncontrollably in agony. He would wait until I had nothing left but small whimpers before he delivered the next blow for his pleasure. This purgatory was repeated, over and over, until my body was covered with the marks of his abuse.

The last time I recovered consciousness, I was no longer hanging as a raw piece of meat dangling in the room. I was once more on the bed with my arms and legs stretched out, shackled to the four corner bedposts. Endless buckets of cold water continued, to bring me back to consciousness.

"Now! Now, Annabelle you are once more with me, so I can introduce you to the riding crop. When the horse fails to meet his masters' wishes, she will be reminded who the ruler is." With this riding crop he chose the small areas of my body which had not received the brutality of his first two administrations which were mostly between my legs on the inner parts and the same with my arms. For now I had only moments in my mind which were present to this terrific abuse of the remaining flesh of my body. By his diabolical methods of managing to keep me conscious, I felt no part of my body had been left without the welts and the removal of my flesh from the abuse of the whip, the lash and the riding crop and by now my entire body felt the agony of the abuse of these weapons.

I lay there in my exhausted state, too weak to even whimper. There was nothing else that this monster from hell could possibly think of to torture my body, my mind and my soul. Oh how wrong one can be, when they are in the presence of the demon that has linked his soul to the devil. Now, he introduced objects that were indescribable in size into my openings. The one he introduced to my mouth, he rammed it down my throat with six or more thrusts of up-and-down strokes until I regurgitated the little contents I had left in my stomach. Meanwhile, my other two openings were equally abused with objects so large in content I could not believe they could penetrate my body. Now my internal organs were experiencing the ravishing of this diabolical sadist who was delivering agony to my insides. My whole body was now one mass of raw flesh on fire.

How does this devil from hell keep my mind conscious, even though I do fade in and out, to my great relief? It seemed like eternity before I finally was relieved of the agony of my flesh, passing back into unconsciousness.

When I finally once more returned to consciousness, I found myself in isolation. The unbearable noise from my first agonizing days of entombment had returned, with every instrument known to man playing difference sounds. I was horror-struck in my position, unable to believe they were now accompanied with lights in every conceivable form. Flashing lasers, strobe lights, black-lights; and so many others that were beyond my capabilities to describe.

The inevitable happened. I was incapable of getting out of the position I was on a bed. Then I entered in to madness, hysterically crying out, no one could hear me. My mind had finally gone over the last leg of sanity and was in an abyss, a free fall into insanity. I continued screaming until my throat was unable to produce any sound. I lay motionless in agony, both inside out. My body had no purpose in living. I managed to put myself in a fetal position as I lay there in my sanctuary of madness from lights and sounds. I was no longer able to return to any form of sanity, breathing in and out as the madness that now possessed me was all that was left. This monster from hell has accomplished his goal. There is nothing left but my soul; for now my body and my mind are one with pure madness. My mind has now joined my body in pure agony and torment in this world.

It was during this time that the demon from hell returned to examine his experiment and theory. I have to confess I was totally unaware of any change to the sounds. He must have turned them off, but they still remained loud and clear in my mind. As far as the lights, I'm sure they also were turned off at the same time, but not in my mind. I felt hands that were not my own, in my fetal position. My sight was oblivious to anything which was present in this world. I uncontrollably drooled from my mouth. I may have screamed, as I felt my chest move up and down. I am not sure whether the sound was reality, or nothing more than the comfort of my madness.

In this powerless state, I felt I was being picked up and carried to some area, unknown in my present condition. I entered into the beginning of something cool; a cool, cool liquid. At first, it was my arms and legs, then my entire body. It started as a welcome relief in my madness, however shortly thereafter my entire body was on fire. My very flesh was being eaten away and dissolving. In my moment of death, I realized I was in the bath of sulfuric acid. My last thoughts were 'I am free'.

It was well past the hour that I had instructed my servants; if I had not rung, to enter the study and expect the worst. Following my instructions, they almost did find the very worst. My greatest fear is that they would discover my death had occurred under the spell of one of the portraits with their transition of my life to their chosen time.

My servants found me on the floor, unconscious and in a fetal position. With all haste the stretcher carried me to my bedroom where the doctor and my beloved wife were waiting. This time I was placed on the bed, still unconscious. I've been informed that the doctor did not really know what to do, but my wife's facial expression said it all in horror. As one day followed the next, I still remained in a coma. Within a week there were signs I was coming out of the coma. In the weeks that followed, I regained consciousness but I was still too weak to communicate. It was well past a fortnight before I started making some form of recovery. During the daylight hours, my wife was constantly by my side, with nurses rotating the night shifts. After two and half months, some progress was being made, but I never totally recovered. Whether it was during this convalescent time, or during the possession of the portrait, my doctor discovered I'd suffered a stroke which left my speech impaired as well as my left side.

The aging process has accelerated; I am fast approaching my 70th year. Up until this last encounter, I have always been anxious to return to the challenges of my daily life. Now, the brightest of my moments have become the yellow and orange leaves of the season of autumn. In my melancholy mood, I am the brown, rotting leaves which had already fallen to the ground and are starting to decay, to return to the soil of life. For now my dreams of looking forward are like the trees which lay bare; their life source of existence is gone. The days are no longer welcome but endured. My zest for life has been diminished, from the sparkling star first seen at night to the black holes of eternity in the universe. No matter how hard I try and am determined, the best I can achieve is to see a few sparkling stars in the night of life.

I am not only feeling my age physically, but more importantly, I am reluctant to face many more encounters with the portraits. As the months progress, I seldom enter the study and only when absolutely necessary. Yes, this last encounter has left me not only physically impaired but mentally shattered. I doubt that I will ever recover physically or mentally from this last evil encounter. Oh God, my Father in Heaven, please let me die in my own time.

Dr. Sebastian stared at the last pages; he could no longer go on. While reading this chapter, his stomach regurgitated its contents more than once. As his stomach settled down for the fourth time, he once more gathered the courage to look down on the pages which presented themselves to him. His inward thoughts spoke loud and clear in his mind as he uttered, 'Oh dear God, please do not let me throw up on these pages.'

As he gathered his strength, he managed with a supreme effort to get up from the chair he was sitting in and stagger towards the French doors. As he groped for the handle, his stomach regurgitated once more its contents of his breakfast. Once outside, he engulfed himself in the fresh morning air as he stared out into the landscape before him. With a supreme effort, he tried to focus on what he was looking at, rather than what he had read in the previous hours of this diabolical event which possessed the poor writer.

"Oh, my God!" he muttered. "Oh, my God," as his stomach continued to roll like a roller coaster entrapped inside him.

He stared, always trying to focus on the landscape which presented itself before him, in a majestic and manicured style that Capability Brown would have been proud to put his stamp of approval on. By means of this concentration on the peaceful view he was looking at, he was able to assemble some tranquility back into his life from the horror which he had experienced in reading the previous hours.

As he gazed out upon this tranquility before him, he had no idea of the time passing by. He only understood it was giving him the courage to return to the library. As this tranquility continued, his stomach eased its demands to expel its contents. He ventured back into the library and returned to the chair he was sitting in. He realized what the writer had experienced in his terrifying return to his present time. He dared not look up from the manuscript, for he feared that the hypnotic trance of the evil portrait would possess him too. He fumbled around like a blind man trying to find the bell, so the butler would come and relieve him from this place of damnation.

On the long drive back, the good Doctor tried to concentrate on the traffic, buildings, landscapes and any diversion that he could look at as the kilometers past before him. Nonetheless, his best efforts were interrupted periodically by his mind retracing the pages of the horror in which he had a short time ago read. At last, he was once again home, with relief. Once through the door, his beloved wife was waiting as usual.

Though, this time she looked upon her husband and said in a gasp, "Oh, my God! What is happening to you? Your face, it is stone white!" and grasped his hands with hers. As hers hands made contact, she looked up into his eyes and said, "They are as cold as a glacier, my love. What has happened?"

Now being with his wife, he realized how much the last chapter of the portraits had affected him. With a feeble attempt at smiling, he asked, "My dearest, would you get me a glass of whiskey? I sincerely believe I need one and a good strong drink, for therapeutic purposes, if nothing else." His good wife returned with a glass of at least two ounces of malted whiskey which he took gratefully.

"My beloved, could I have another, please?"

"By all means, my dear husband. I'll be right back," she replied.

By the time the third glass of malted whiskey had penetrated his stomach, the ill feeling he had entering the house with was now being replaced by a warm glow throughout his body.

"Oh my dear, I must apologize profusely for my behavior, for it was this last chapter that has left me so emotional and in such great despair. I cannot share, or even if I could, it would be better if you did not have any knowledge of what I have experienced in this last chapter of the portraits. I believe I'll go upstairs to have a shower, and then put on some fresh clothes before re-joining you, my dear."

"As you wish," came her reply, "and while you're doing that I will start to prepare the dinner."

His wife had prepared a rather modest meal, more a collage of appetizers than a full course meal. Accompanying this nourishment was a good bottle of Burgundy wine. With the evening progressing, the conversation lightened as he discussed his work for the following day, and she shared her gardening activities. Both he and his wife were being entertained by their beloved dogs, helping to lighten the moment of his melancholy mood. Still, as the evening moved forward he realized no matter how much alcohol he could consume, it still would not give him the peace of mind for a restful night. With this knowledge, he then informed his wife before he went to bed he would take a sleeping pill.

Now with a sleeping pill along with the large amount of alcohol he consumed it started to show the effects of the combination of the concoction which made him both mellow and in some ways incoherent. At this time his wife assisted him up to their bedroom and then helped him to retire for the night. She was unsure whether it was the medication or the alcohol combination, nonetheless she had confidence that once he was able to retire to the bed he would find maybe not peace, but at least sleep. This was the case; for once he found his body upon the bed, before he could say good night, he fell into a deep slumber.

THE MOUNTAIN MAN

—ᴍ—

THE FOLLOWING MORNING HE woke up somewhat confused and distraught. Nonetheless, the day had started and he must do likewise. When he looked over at the other side of the bed, it had already been vacated. After his usual preparations for the day, he made his way downstairs.

"Good morning, dear. How are you feeling today?" came the cheery voice from the kitchen.

"Oh! I've had better mornings, but thank you very much for your patience and understanding of last evening."

"Your coffee and breakfast is ready whenever you are," came her answer.

After the usual goodbyes, he made his way to the museum, and went directly to his office. 'Oh, my goodness', he moaned to himself, as he looked at the pile of work that lay upon his desk, and the endless messages which awaited his direction and commands. It was always a busy time in this position he held. However, for some unknown reason, maybe it was his imagination, the burden seemed even greater and the demands almost unachievable. As he met the challenges facing him this day and probably many more to come, he did not want to neglect his obligation to His Lordship about completing the Book of the Portraits. Nonetheless, it'd become customary that his Lordship's secretary would channel another reading upon a mutually agreed schedule. When his Lordship's secretary did phone the next week, on this occasion he asked if he could speak directly to Dr. Sebastian himself. After the usual greetings, he came directly to the point.

"Dr. Sebastian, on behalf of myself and the entire staff of his Lordship, we have a request that we wish you to consider as urgent." There was a long pause and then the secretary continued, "His Lordship has taken a turn for the worst, and as you are well aware, in the past his condition was fragile, to say the least. Nonetheless, now he has deteriorated to the point where he is bed-ridden. Both doctors and the team of nurses are at his side constantly, monitoring his condition. His Lordship constantly asks how much progress is being made on the Book of Portraits. In his present condition, it well might be hypothetical, still, we have a feeling he is hanging on with all of his remaining strength just to hear your closing remarks on Book of Portraits itself."

Dr. Sebastian entered into the conversation by enlightening his Lordship's secretary that there was more than one chapter to complete in the reading of the book itself. With this knowledge, the secretary requested that with all speed, would the Doctor consider returning to the mansion and complete at least one more chapter at his earliest convenience.

Dr. Sebastian answered, "By all means, whatever it takes. Can you advise me when would be the most convenient time to meet your request?"

There was a long pause on the other side of the phone, before his Lordship's secretary requested a meeting tomorrow morning. Dr. Sebastian was somewhat taken back, yes, he realized the urgency and the timeline which was closing, except he was not free to grant this request.

His mind raced like a horse going to the finish line and then said, "I will do my best, but I must have my secretary rearrange my schedule differently. I will get back to you at the earliest convenience. I hope this will meet with your satisfaction and request."

His Lordship's secretary replied by saying he thoroughly understood the inconvenience and the interruption in Dr. Sebastian's schedule and whatever the good Doctor could do, the entire staff of His Lordship would be grateful. After this conversation, Dr. Sebastian immediately asked his secretary to come into his office.

When she entered the office, he motioned for her to sit down, and then said, "With all haste, please rearrange my schedule for tomorrow, wherever possible and let me know at the earliest convenience when I will be free for the maximum amount of that day."

She looked somewhat puzzled and asked, "To what extent should I try to rearrange the schedule, to give you an opening and for how long?"

He looked directly into her eyes and said, "This is a case of life and death. I want you to take this seriously, and if at all possible, give me the whole day. If not, at least free me as much as possible from my obligations. That'll be all, thank you."

It was well into the afternoon before his secretary advised him that the very best she was able to do was to free him up shortly after three o'clock in the afternoon.

Dr. Sebastian had a look of disappointment and then said, "I know you've done your very best and I really appreciate your efforts. They have not gone unnoticed, thank you."

She had no sooner left the office when Dr. Sebastian personally dialed his Lordship's secretary to advise, "It is not as encouraging as I would've hoped for. Nonetheless, we have done our best and the very earliest I can possibly make it is shortly after three o'clock tomorrow afternoon. Please have the chauffeur pick me up at the Museum. My office is on the third floor and the security guard will give him directions as soon as he enters the building. Until then, I wish his Lordship all the best that can be offered by man and God. Good afternoon."

The next day, once at the Museum, Dr. Sebastian didn't even stop for lunch, trying to cram one more meeting in before the chauffeur would pick him up and escort him to the mansion. The hours ticked away as if they were minutes and before he could even comprehend where the time had gone, the chauffeur was waiting for him. The long tedious drive to the mansion was like so many other times before. However, this time there was a deviation upon arrival. Instead of the butler waiting, his Lordship's secretary personally greeted Dr. Sebastian at the door.

After the usual greetings, his Lordship's secretary asked the good doctor to follow him into his office, and was the first to break the silence by saying, "On behalf of myself personally, I would like to thank you for your quick response to our needs and apologize for all the inconvenience we have caused you. It is not the custom of his Lordship or me to make a request on such short notice; nonetheless I felt I should take the responsibility of asking for your support. His Lordship's health is deteriorating rapidly and as we both know, he is well past the tender years of age. It is my opinion, as well as the doctors and nurses who are attending his Lordship that he is extending his presence on earth, hoping you will be able to finish the Book of Portraits and he may present the book personally to you. Of course, no man controls his destiny or the time in which he ceases to exist on earth. Lord Edwards has guided my life and my decisions for the better part of three and half decades. I feel it is my duty to try to make his final dreams and aspirations complete."

Dr. Sebastian took the opportunity to acknowledge, "It is a great honor for me to be of any service to his Lordship and his distinguished family."

Once more, his Lordship's secretary took command of the conversation, "You honor us also, Dr. Sebastian, with your presence, your vast knowledge of being a curator at the Museum and a credit to one and all of us Canadians. The second most pressing reason I asked for this emergency meeting is that few people, including yourself, have any knowledge of what is in his Lordship's last will and testament. Lord Edwards has no direct relatives or obligations to anyone to decree a portion of his estate. Once His Lordship passes on to the next world, his estate will go up for auction, after each member of the staff receives a liberal remuneration for their services.

Myself personally, I have been under his watch for the better part of my employable life which exceeds over thirty years. For all of us, it is not the remuneration of service which we receive in his passing, but the years that each and every one of us has been grateful to serve this great man in his mansion. His Lordship has expressed at every occasion his kindness and respect for those who are loyal to him, and has treated us better than any other master could do. So, Dr. Sebastian, if I look melancholy, forgive me . . . for each and every one of us pray constantly for our master to return to health or at least have a pleasant passing on."

The secretary continued to confide the details and extent of the estate. Dr. Sebastian was amazed at the information he had just received. He had no idea that this man, Lord Edwards had no living relatives or benefactors to leave his vast estate. He stared across at His Lordship's secretary as if he'd been slapped across the face and didn't quite know how to respond. At last, Dr. Sebastian replied, "I would like to thank you for taking me into your confidence in the private world of his Lordship. It goes without saying; I will not betray this trust."

There was a smile upon the face of his Lordship's secretary. He had judged the good doctor well. "This is why I personally have asked you, in all haste to try and conclude the Book of the Portraits, before our beloved employer enters into the unknown. You and I both know how he feels about making this contribution to the Museum."

In closing, the secretary added, "You see, if His Lordship does not present you personally with the Portraits, even though there has been more than enough witnesses, including myself, of his intention; nonetheless, upon his decease all properties including the Book of Portraits will be in the possession of the solicitors for the last will. This would mean sometime in the future that the Book of Portraits would be accompanying the rest of the items being auctioned off."

Dr. Sebastian only nodded in agreement and expressed it openly, "I have a greater understanding of the urgency and without any further delay, let me proceed to the library and commence on the remaining chapters. I'm nearing the completion of the book and there are probably less than two more chapters to read. Nonetheless, even though the urgency is great, I will not sacrifice the quality that I've given in reading the other chapters."

With this both men walked down the long corridor towards the writer's library. They were accompanied by two of the servants who were familiar with the procedure of retrieving the Book of Portraits as well as the key that would open the binding. As it was placed on its usual table across from the comfortable chairs, the three men left Dr. Sebastian to the chapters which lay ahead. He opened the book to discover what new rendezvous awaited him and the writer. For like the past, the only evidence of what took place was on the pages that would follow in this new challenge for Dr. Sebastian.

In many ways, I never felt that I would live to see this day. I do not know whether it was a vision, or a premonition; nonetheless I've never been the same since the last time the Portraits had taken possession of me. There is no denying it. It is evident to one and all around me that the stroke has left me only half the man physically I was. As one can see, my left side is totally paralyzed. My left appendages are hanging as if they were a rag doll's arm and leg. My one good arm and leg cannot support my weight. After months of therapy the best I've been able to do is recover most of my speech without slurring my words when communicating with others. The heavy workload that I have always experienced throughout my life, I've now had to delegate it to others. The best I'm able to do is to be informed of the more pertinent changes which have been made, as more of an overseer then the commander-in-chief.

As far as my memory, it definitely is not what it used to be and on more than one occasion I become confused, or even worse, I can't remember what I was thinking of. My mind wanders to the past and has a hard time coping with the present. Yes! Yes, life has been less than enjoyable to say the least, this past year.

Oh dear God, my Father, who art in heaven, once more I face the Portraits. Which one will possess me this night? If it is your will, oh God, that I survive this night and return to the present, I feel confident I will not have to endure another one of these experiences. I feel this is the year that awaits me, God willing. I am ready to be called at any time if He wishes to retrieve my soul from this miserable existence that my body has engaged in. All I have to do is make it through this night. Oh God! Please, my Lord, help me make it through this night of possession.

The first shades of darkness are starting to blanket the daylight of the sun. It is time once more to go to my study and await my fate. I summons my male servants who aid and assist me to the place I once called my library, but tonight I must collect my thoughts and think of it as my destiny into the unknown. What was once my sanctuary is now nothing more than a place I wait to experience the horrors which lay ahead this night. Upon arriving at my destination, my male servants place me upon the couch in a sitting position. In an afterthought, I asked them if they would lay me down on the couch and secure me with a blanket, so if I pass on during this night of uncertainty, I will be in a resting situation. If it is meant to be that I enter into a life of the past, at least my physical *body will be in a position of lying in state. If nothing more, it will make the undertaker's task easier with rigor mortis setting in this position.*

Now, all I have to do is concentrate on the ceiling above me as the natural lights continue to diminish. I have requested all artificial lights to be extinguished. I lay here like a vegetable, waiting to be served at the table. I watch the natural light fade from my presence as the darkness of the night is now falling upon me. It will be very shortly when I will no longer have control, either of my life, or maybe my soul, for the rest of eternity, as I wait and wait . . . until I become possessed by one of them, the good or the bad Portrait.

Oh! Where am I! Who am I! I lazily open up my eyes, for the sun is shining through the window on the left side from where I'm lying. I'm lying in bed. I'm still tired. I don't want to get up yet.

Then came a voice out of nowhere, "Are you up yet?"

Downstairs, maybe from the kitchen, the voice once more comes up through the floor, "Are you up yet? Do you hear me"?

My mind snaps to attention. "Yes! I'm up, Mom" I replied.

Once more, the voice came through loud and clear, "Are you dressed yet? I want you to come down here, right now, for breakfast," came another command from below.

"I'll be there in a minute, Mom," I once more answered.

"Well, make sure it's a minute that doesn't drag into an hour. Your father is waiting for you to get ready to do the chores," was another order from below.

"Yes, Mom," I replied once more. I jumped out of bed and started to look around my surroundings. At first I couldn't connect with what I was looking at, it all looks so different. I take my time looking around the room. Now I know where I am, and what's more, I know who I am. I'm a young boy at the age of nine and I'm sleeping in an attic. I have a small bed and a set of dresser-drawers along with some pegs on the wall for me to hang my extra clothes on.

On the other side of the room, well, it's totally different. It's where my dad has a small workshop to make ammunition for his guns. He uses them to go hunting and knows all about putting gunpowder into cartridges and the projectile on the bullet. Yes! My dad knows a lot about them.

Well, it's about time that I start getting dressed, now that I'm up. I walk over to one of the pegs, put my shirt on and trousers and then go back to the bed and put my boots on. I'm looking as good as I'm going to get today, so I walk over and open the door. As I look outside, it's just what I expected. I'm living on a farm somewhere, in the middle of mountain ranges on either side. I better get downstairs for breakfast, or it's not going to be a good day in my life. I walk down the rickety stairs outside to the ground, then make a quick dash around the corner and open the door to the kitchen.

"Good morning, Mom." My two sisters are already in the kitchen. Annabel, who is two years older than me, says she is almost 12, but she's really only 11 and my oldest sister Christina is 15. Both my sisters are busy helping my mother in the kitchen. There are a lot of chores to be done just to get the day started, like getting wood and water. My mother always laughs and says, 'I've got running water . . . all you have to do is run and get it.'

My mother looked directly at me, "Go tell your dad that breakfast is almost ready."

I run across the field to where my dad is. "Good morning, Dad. Mom says that breakfast is ready."

"Good morning, son. Tell your mother I will be there in a few minutes."

I hang around watching Dad work, not knowing quite sure what to do. Then he turns to me and says, "If you're going to stay here, you can start doing your chores as well."

So with that, I answer, "I will do all of them right after breakfast, Dad."

"Well then, you better run along now and tell Mom and the girls that I will there as soon as I finish this. Now, get going like I told you."

"Yes, sir." And off I went to be the messenger.

At last, we all sat around the table with heaping amounts of pancakes, porridge, eggs with bacon and of course, jam. For us kids fresh milk from the cow and for my parents good strong coffee. As we heap the food upon our plates, Father said grace to Jesus Christ and Our Father for all that we have. The first thing passed around was a big bowl of porridge and each one of us took our full helping. Being of Scottish descent, we used salt to season the porridge and not sugar, like those English people. Nonetheless, my mother would always weaken if us kids asked for sugar instead of salt. There was an always lots of milk and cream to put on the porridge, as well as fresh toast cooked on the wooden stove.

After all of us were well fed, Mom would ask if there was anything else we needed. Then, one of our parents, either Dad or Mom would look at us kids and say 'the day is half over, so let's get on with it.' No sooner were the words said, before the girls got up and started cleaning the table while Dad and I went outside to start the chores which lay ahead for us.

There were a lot of things to do and a lot of work. I did milk the cows, feed the chickens, and collect the eggs and gave the slop to the pigs, just for starters. I also had to feed the horses; we just had one that Dad could ride and the other ones were workhorses to pull the wagon when we went to town or to plough the fields.

We were called homesteaders or that's what my parents said. We were about eight to ten miles from the nearest town or village. Of course, we had cats and dogs. The dogs went hunting with Dad and me. The cats kept the mice and rats down to a small population. My Dad would plant different crops for different reasons, but then again, we always had to make sure we had enough hay for the cattle and horses. That was a must. Only yes! We had a big garden, boy, did we ever have a huge garden! My Mom and my two sisters worked really hard during the spring and summer months in the garden. In the spring and summer, we ate lots of vegetables out of the garden, anything from lettuce and radishes to green onions, and on and on.

When the fall came, we had a whole bunch of potatoes, turnips and onions for the root cellar and Mom would make the neatest sauerkraut out of the big cabbages. Yes! It was always a busy time for Mom and the girls. They not only had to harvest the gardens and get everything in the root cellar, but it was canning time as well. From morning till dusk, Mom and the girls would be boiling jams or preserves, and pickles with other yummy things to jar for the winter. For me and my Dad, well, we were just as busy, for it was harvest time. We had to get the crops off the field whenever the weather would let us. Time was never on our side, plus we always had the same chores to do with the animals; regardless of whether it was summer, fall, winter or spring.

As far as learning goes, I mean like going to school, it was too far to go and we didn't have any way of getting there on a regular basis, especially in the winter. Nevertheless, Mom wanted us to be able to read and write and add and subtract. I guess you might call it the 3R's, something like that. Also, every night before we went to bed, all of us would sit around the table and read the Bible. Each and every one of us would take our turn, even Dad. As for Dad, he could read the Bible really well, but when it came to other things, let's put it this way, Mom would have to read it first and then he could read. My mother was determined all of us could read, so every night without fail we would be reading the Bible. My sisters are better readers but that was just because they are older than me. I'm sure when I get older, especially Christina's age, I'll be as good at reading as her.

Now for writing, well, it's a little different story, at least for me. Like reading, Mom was just as determined for us to be able to write. The girls were doing especially well; however, I just never could quite get the hang of it. I was still having real problems with the alphabet. It wasn't so much the alphabet, as it was which letter I needed to use to spell the word. I could never quite figure out how it went. I kept on trying under my mother's determination and persistence. I did get a little bit better, and my mother knew I was trying, which was the most important thing to her and it was for me too. I'm more like my Dad's son then my Mother's. He's really quiet and doesn't say much, but when he does everybody listens. My Dad and I are real quiet; not that we don't think a lot, it is just that we don't share what we think unless it's important enough for other people to listen to. I guess that's some of it.

That's pretty well what we do on a day-to-day basis. Life is good and the garden is really doing well. The crops in the field were better than average. It was now the time of year that we always call 'Indian summer'. I suppose Canadian autumns are called 'Indian summer' because the Indians were here first. It stands to reason that the Indians would know more about the weather than us white folk. By September and October the vegetables are in the root cellar, the canning is done, the crops are off the field, and yet the days and nights are still nice and warm.

For Dad and me, it is the best time of year; that's when we get to go hunting and fishing. After autumn, it starts to get colder and the nights get longer and the days get shorter. At this time, the snow starts lying on the ground and after the chores are done, it is pretty well free time. I like to whittle on wood and make little characters. Also, my Dad is now starting to let me help him load the shells for hunting in the next year. As far as Mom and the girls go; it's the time when they start preparing to make new clothes that they will be wearing and some shirts for Dad and me.

This is the best time of year, well; the most exciting if one is a child. It's Christmas time coming and my Dad and me, it's our job to go out and find a really good Christmas tree. We start early; the first week in December, so we have lots of time to decorate the Christmas tree and get ready for Christmas day. Mom is really busy with the girls in the kitchen. They're making all kinds of good things, like Christmas cakes. Also Mom makes plum pudding. I'm not sure why we it call plum pudding, it tastes more like rice pudding to me. It's also the time that Dad and I go to find the largest turkey for the Christmas meal.

It's a happy time in our family. We do not have a lot of money but somehow, Mom and Dad surprise us kids with something special. Something that we can use, like a new store-bought dress for the girls to wear on Easter Sunday and I get something like new dress pants for church. Sometimes, the girls would get a doll or something else that girls like. For me; one year I got a baseball and bat. Yes! This had to be the best time of year, for even Dad got to rest a lot more and sit around the house. We all had a little more time for ourselves and the things we like to do together. After all the Christmas presents were opened, in the evenings, we would sing Christmas carols and of course, read the Bible.

The New Year came and went. It was sometime in late January when Mom caught a cold and then started coughing. By March, she was coughing all the time and couldn't stop. She'd always say 'oh, it's nothing' but my Dad had that worried look on his face. As the snow started to melt and spring was in the air, nothing changed for Mom. She was still coughing and sometimes was too weak to get out of bed. In the wintertime, we didn't go to church because we were snowed in, so we would sit around on Sunday and take turns reading the Bible and singing hymns. On some Sundays, Mom was too sick. She tried her best, but definitely couldn't sing.

It was sometime in April when the snows receded that we could get the horses hooked up to the wagon, and normally it would be the time we would start to go to church. By then, Mom was too sick to go to church and Dad had a real worried look on his face. It was the beginning of May when Dad told all three of us kids that he was taking Mom to town to see the doctor. It would take the better part of three or four days before they would return. Both Dad and Mom were worried about leaving us alone on the farm. We all said 'not to worry, we were all grown up and we could look after the farm, so just look after Mom' we told Dad.

Well, it definitely took longer than four days. It was well over a week before they returned to the farm. They hadn't even got out of the wagon before us three kids knew there was something wrong. They didn't have that happy look on their face, they just looked really sad. In fact, I don't know which one of them was sadder, my Dad or my Mom. After Mom looked around the house and Dad

253

looked around the farmyard, they said at dinner 'what a good job all of us did while they were away, and yes, we were growing up.'

Life was starting to get back to normal, but Mom was still coughing. The girls tried to do all the work as Mom supervised from her bed. It was in one night after reading the Bible, when Mom asked us all to stay before going to bed. It was then she told us children she was very sick. She said she had consumption or tuberculosis, or maybe it was both. But, it was when she said she wasn't going to get better; there wasn't a dry eye the whole night in our house. It was one of the saddest times! No! No, it was one of the most horrible times in our whole lives. Of course, Mom and Dad knew when they were in town at the doctor's office; for the rest of us, well, it was like being kicked in the stomach and you couldn't straighten up no matter how hard you tried. The tears just kept pouring out.

The days moved on. I couldn't say they were normal but we kept on doing our best as Mom got worse. It was a long hot summer and I'll never forget the Indian summer that followed. My Dad and I sure didn't go hunting that year; instead Mom died. The days that followed were like a blur in all our minds. Our neighbors helped arrange for the funeral and the final resting place for Mom. There was a really good showing the day at the church, for Mom was a good woman. No! She was a great woman. Everybody loved my Mom; she was always helping someone or trying her best to comfort some other person that was feeling bad or sad. She was a wonderful wife and an awesome mother. That was another day that there wasn't a dry eye, I don't think in all of town.

Well, we all did our best, especially the girls. They not only did their chores but tried to fill the gap of what Mom used to do. No one could look after us like Mom, not even Dad. Dad always was the one who took on the financial responsibility, but it was Mom that was the brains and the heart of our family. It was like we were missing the most important part of our lives; our family.

It was hard, but somehow we bumped along, making ends meet. However, it was more than difficult, at least for Dad when we went to church. Before and after the service, these women would come over and talk to Dad. Dad, not being much of a talker at the best of times would just stand there, hoping that one of the girls would come and rescue him. My eldest sister Christina told me that these women were spinsters or women who had never been married. Whenever they had an opportunity, these same women would take one of us children aside to tell us we needed a mother. They could help us grow up until we were able to look after ourselves. Each one of them would single out an opportunity to put their case before us. It got to the point that Dad didn't want to go to church. He would sort of mutter to himself, but to us at the same time 'all these women want to do is share my bed'. I wasn't quite sure what he meant, but on the other hand, I knew he didn't want it.

Somehow the Indian summer went and snows came. Before all of us knew what was happening, it was Christmas time. This was the best time of the year; well, it used to be. We started going through the motions. Dad and I went out and got a nice-looking tree. All of us tried our best to decorate the tree, but somehow it didn't look the same. Dad even went to town and bought us all presents. Still, it just didn't shape up to be a Christmas; we all tried our best, nonetheless we failed. I don't even remember having Christmas dinner. It was what my two sisters had been trying to put together every time we sat down to a meal at the table, so it just didn't seem to be any different for Christmas Day.

By the end beginning of the New Year, we were looking a little worse for wear. All of us looked like ragamuffins. When we went to church, we would sit at the back and as soon as the service was over, we all got into the wagon and high-tailed it back to the farm. Dad was ashamed the way things were going and in the way we were looking.

It was sometime in March that Dad saddled up his horse and told us children that he would be back in three or four days. He was going to see some Indians. It was so cold. All I could do was rush outside and quickly do my chores and head right back into the house. I didn't leave until the next time I had to do chores. As for my sisters, well, there was always work to do. Somehow they shouldered into it even though they knew they were losing the battle.

Sure enough; well into the third day Dad rode up on his horse. After looking over the farm he came into the house. He looked satisfied at what we were able to do without him. It was then when we asked him what was happening.

He looked at the three of us ragamuffins and said, "You'll find out soon enough."

Two weeks later, some Indians rode up in a wagon. Sitting between two men was a woman, well, an Indian squaw. Her name was Little Flower. Well, she might have been a little flower when she was born, but she sure was an old flower now, for she was older than my Dad. I guess the big thing about her showing up was that she was moving in.

After the greetings and Indians left in the wagon, we got down to who is going to be where and how. Little Flower got the girls room and the girls got what was Mom and Dad's, while Dad moved upstairs with me. Well, it was definitely a lot different now for all of us, but for me it was especially hard. After sleeping alone for a long time and now having Dad up there; it was a whole different thing.

Unknown to Dad, especially in the summer months, I'd stay up late into the night, sitting outside just looking at the stars. Ever since I can remember, I liked being by myself and being outdoors is the best of all. I love looking around and seeing what God's given us and how beautiful things are. On a good clear night when the stars were out, I've even tried to count them. It was going to be really different now having Dad sleeping up here with me. The best I could do now was look out the window after Dad was asleep. I knew he was asleep as he made the loudest noises, in fact, a lot of times he woke me up. I asked him one time what that noise was and he said 'its snoring, son.' And boy, did my Dad know how to do it.

Well, the years just moved along as they always do. Before we knew it, we were almost grown-up. In fact, my oldest sister Christine was 18 years old. Now you could call her a woman. I will never forget that day when we had gone to church and after the service, my two sisters and even my Dad stayed around, talking to other people. As for me, well, I just prefer not to be around people; so I was out at the back of the church sitting on a rock, looking at the birds and the little animals. When I returned, one of the neighbour's sons was asking my Dad if he could maybe come over once in a while for a visit. No sooner did my Dad say it was okay, and Christine was grinning like a Cheshire cat. The next week, the young man showed up with a batch of freshly baked cookies. Boy, were they welcomed by each and every one of us! The next week, he came over with a pie that his mom had just made and the week after that it was a cake. Now, every week after that, he was a welcome sight coming down the road.

Little Flower was a really good cook when it came to cooking meat and vegetables. But, when it came to anything like pastry she didn't have a clue. So, when this young man showed up with cookies or cakes, they were a real treat, even though the real reason he was always coming was to spend some time with Christine. It wasn't that long; well, I guess it was long enough. One day he came over the hill and his Dad was with him. After the usual hellos and handing over the treats to my younger sister and me; he went off with Christine to spend some time talking together and his Dad did exactly the same with my Dad.

It was shortly after that when we all went over to Jim Boyce's house (for that was his name) and had a fine home-cooked meal with of all the dressings. I'd almost forgotten what real food tasted like. Anyway it wasn't the meal we were invited for. It was the announcement; Jim Boyce asked for Christine's hand in marriage and my Dad gave his consent. In the spring, they both got together at the church with all us people and we had at downright fine wedding. Even Little Flower showed up and she was wearing a Western dress. She looked like, well; she looked like being a grandmother of her family. We were all proud of her and it was one of the happier days in our lives.

It was a year after this wedding when sure enough, my other sister Annabel found Paul hanging around. It was just another repeat of Christine. I think Paul said the same proposal, well almost, and everybody showed up at the church for the wedding.

After that, Dad moved back into his old bedroom and I had the whole upstairs once more to myself. By now, I was doing most of the hard work on the farm, like making sure the crops were going in, but Dad was still beside me through thick and thin. We were a great team. I loved working with my Dad. However, he started looking a lot older and he sure didn't move as fast. Dad never really looked that good after Mom died, one might say he just sort of withered up. Mind you, I was getting older too. This proved to be another bad year in my life. It was during the Indian summer when we talked about going hunting and fishing, but somehow that's all it was, talking but not doing it. It was one of those nights sitting on the veranda with both of us watching the sunset go down when it happened. It was the first-time that Dad ever spoke poorly about the land.

He turned and looked at me, eyeball to eyeball, then said, "Don't spend your life being a farmer's son. All it will give you is the dirt to keep a person alive and nothing more, nothing less. So, while you're still young enough . . . you go get yourself a trade."

He took me back somewhat. I couldn't help but say, "Well, Dad it is a little late now. All I know is farming and that's all I want to do. Besides, who would start looking after you at your age?"

It was one of the few times in the last several years that I saw my Dad smile. He looked back at me and said, "Little Flower does a good enough job for me," and with that, we both had a good laugh.

It was no more than three weeks later, when my Dad and I were working out in the field, and he keeled over. I carried him back to the house, and laid him on the bed. I didn't know what was wrong with him, or if it was serious.

I looked at Little Flower and said, "Do what you can for him. I'm riding for the doctor."

I didn't even bother mounting a saddle on the horse. I just put the bridle on and road like the wind. When I got to town, I went straight to the doctor's house and didn't even bother knocking. I rushed into the hall way and the doctor's wife asked me what's wrong?

"I have got to see the doctor, now!"

"He's with a patient right now, and I shouldn't disturb him," was her reply.

"My Dad is either dying or dead; he needs help now."

The good wife interrupted the doctor and he came out. I explained what had happened. He told me to get back to the house and do what I could for my father and he would be there shortly with his buggy. When the doctor arrived, he looked at my Dad and knew what was wrong right away. He told Little Flower and me that my Dad had suffered a really bad stroke.

Well, we did what we could for the next six weeks for him and then he had another bad one. This one took him were I'm sure my mother was waiting for him. After I'd arranged for the funeral and my Dad was buried beside my Mom, I went back to the farm. I was an orphan. Sure, I was in my early-20's; nevertheless both my parents were no longer living. My two sisters were all grown up and married and had their husbands and children. All I had left was Little Flower.

I was sitting once more on the veranda, looking at the sunset when I remembered what my dad said about being a farmer. I never really thought about it much until then. All the same, I really enjoyed being by myself and I loved being in the woods with nature. For the next few days I thought about nothing else.

No, I wouldn't be a farmer; I'd made up my mind. In the weeks that followed, I told my sisters and brother-in-laws what I planned to do. I don't think they really totally understood or even believed me. It was only when I told them to take whatever they wanted; the livestock, the machinery or any of the furniture in the house. All I needed was the riding horse, some of my belongings and the guns. The rest was up for grabs, for whoever could take it away.

In the weeks that followed, my sisters and brother-in-laws took up my offer. First, the cattle and chickens, then even the dogs and cats moved to their places. Next, the furniture, machinery and anything that was not nailed down went one way or another. By the time they were finished loading their wagons, all that remained were the buildings.

Little Flower already understood what was happening. The first thing she said to me was, "You're not ready to go out in the woods and live."

I retaliated by saying, "I'm a man. I can do what I want."

She countered back, "You are a white man. You know nothing about living in the woods. All you know how to do is go in the woods and kill animals." She added, "All you do is drag the animal back here, like a wolf to its den."

I thought about it. She was probably right. I had only gone camping overnight but never lived in the woods. I asked Little Flower what I should do.

She replied, "You come home to my village. We will teach you, if that's what you want."

So with that, I started a new life. Within the next few weeks, I saddled up my horse and rode to the Indian village of Little Flower. I explained what had happened to my father and what I planned to do with the farm, to give it back to the land. I then explained it would be advisable to bring Little Flower and her belongings back to the village. They agreed and said they would come with a wagon to fetch Little Flower. I did not mention that I hoped to come with her; I didn't want to push my luck. Upon returning to the farm, I told Little Flower that her people would be coming in due time to get her. She asked me how long that would be.

I looked at her and said, "You know your people better than I do. I guess they'll come when they want to." She said it may be a long time. And so it was. The months passed and we made out like we always had. All right, I had very little to do for chores, so I went for long walks along the tree lines to pass the time of day. I guess it was more of a tradition than anything else, but in the evenings I'd sit down with the Bible and Little Flower would listen to me read a passage of my choosing.

Eventually, a wagon with two Indians in it rolled down the path to the farmhouse. They had come to get Little Flower and her belongings. After they had loaded up her things, she told her brothers that she was ready to go and that was when she turned to them and said, "He's coming too." The elder Indian asked why would he want to live with Indians?

She replied, "He doesn't want to. He wants to become a mountain man, but he doesn't know how to live in the forest. He doesn't even know how to live in the valleys, let alone in the mountains. We have to teach him."

The two Indians nodded and I put my things in the wagon and mounted my horse. With that, we rode off from the farm and headed towards the village.

The next three years were a blur of events. Every day and night I was learning to be an Indian warrior. These years were filled with learning about the forest. Anything from the sounds of different animal's, day or night, to the way the trees were leaning, or of the moss on one side of them. Learning of the winds, in which way they were blowing so to hunt with the winds. Learning all about the forest could have easily taken a lifetime, if it not been for the senior warriors who taught me. I learned how to be able to live off the land, how to hunt in the forest. I had replaced my shoes for moccasins and learned how to run like the wind through the forest with only the leaves beneath my feet knowing my presence. There was a whole education in itself of learning how to fish in so many different ways, and to say nothing of hunting, not always with a gun or even a bow and arrow, but to be able to trap animals in different ways.

These years vanished before my eyes. Each day was sometimes more than exciting and other times disturbing. I'd never in all my life wanted to get up as soon as the dawn broke and was excited to start the day and what I would learn to become a man of the woods.

It was well into my third year when one of the annual feasts which was very important to the village took place. This was the feast in which the elders would choose which young men were worthy of being called warriors. Sometimes there were very few, others years there were larger numbers. However, no matter how diligent these young men had worked to achieve this status, no one would know until the day of the feast. The night of the great feast, the chief sat in the center and all the old warriors would form a circle around him. They would chant songs of bravery, of spiritual connections with the animals, and praise Mother Nature's gifts to both man and animals.

The elders would wear masks to honour the important animals. There were the Eagles and the Ravens with the Hawks that cross the skies that guided man in his needs to achieve success. There were the great gifts of the Sea and the master of all of them, the Whale were praised and honored at this feast. The great animals of the forest were Wolves, the Bears, the Bobcats and all the great hunters of the forest. The food for the feast was equally unique and rewarding; there was venison, fresh deer, fish from the sea, a variety of berries and of course millet. The elders who sat around the chief would pass the sweet grass peace pipe.

This celebration recognizing new warriors to the tribe was always conducted in October, under a full moon. The long night began with symbolic dances to the beat of the drum. The old warriors would wear traditional headgear and symbolic masks to pantomime the animals or birds. It was close to midnight when the chief signaled to the elders that the induction of new warriors was about to begin.

I was very excited when some of the young men who had helped me in my training were called forth to receive their status as a warrior. As they stepped forward, the chief and the medicine man would paint long strips of pigment on the young man's body. When this was completed, the chief would give the warrior a new name that he would be called for the rest of his life. Out of the many young men waiting, there were less than half a dozen so far that had been called. To my total astonishment, the next name that was called was mine. I looked at the other young man I trained with, not sure what to do.

The closest to me said, "The chief is calling you." I walked slowly towards the chief and the medicine man. They performed the same ritual with, and once completed, the chief said to me, "Your name from now is White Feather."

From that day forth, I was known as White Feather, the mountain man. I spent almost another year with my new family, for I was no longer an orphan. It was during this year that I took it upon myself to visit my sisters and brother-in-laws, along with their children. As I arrived, it was strange to be around so many white people and their ways. I love my sisters very much and I'm very fond of my brother-in-laws and always wondered how the children were doing. The small village had grown and I felt even more uncomfortable being around in its surroundings. I felt closed in, with a group of foreigners. Even though I enjoyed my visit, I was only too glad to return to my new family and home in the Indian village. It was during this time that my life took on another great change.

I reverted back to my first thoughts of being a true mountain man, living on my own in the forest and understanding all I could that Mother Nature would be willing to teach me. As these thoughts grew stronger each day, I finally confided with Little Flower about my plans to live alone in the forest. She advised me to see the chief and have counsel with the elders. This request was granted and the Council took place within the next two weeks. Bar none, from the youngest warrior right up to the chief, they all agreed wholeheartedly that if anyone in this village could survive in the wilderness on his own, I would be that person. The chief added one more thing that I've always be grateful for. He said in all his years, he had never known another person who was more qualified.

In the months that followed, I prepared myself and the things I would take with me for this final adventure that I had always dreamed of. To me, there is no better time to start a new beginning then in the Spring, when all things renew their enthusiasm for life. And so, I began my new quest in life. I used my horse as a pack horse and ventured out from the village along the riverbank. I continued ever seeking a spot further away from civilization. At last, I came upon that place. I felt the tranquility and peace at once. I knew this had to be the place I would remain for the rest of my life.

The river narrowed at this point, with the backdrop of the mountains. There was an opening which flattened out, and this little meadow was blanketed securely on both sides by the lush forest. Yes! There was no doubt in my mind that this would be a place I could spend my life. I took the prudence of making sure that my presence was known and that this was going to be my territory. Each night that I have been on my own, I have urinated in the four corners of my domain. I've hobbled my horse some distance away and I've strung my hammock high enough up so no animal can reach me. Also, on the opposite side of where my horse is, I have suspended my supplies high above in a tree, again so no animal who wishes to feast either on me or my supplies will be able to.

Now that I've located the area I wish to stay, I have started to construct a permanent residence of my own. I found the perfect part in the meadow, just to my liking, and with my axe and shovel, started digging. In two weeks I managed to get to a depth of 5 to 6 feet. As I continually went deeper in the soil, I supported the walls with logs and I built myself a ladder from smaller trees with bark twine. This ladder served for many purposes; to bring the dirt out and to bring stones in. Every day I diligently worked on this project, only stopping long enough to hunt for food and supplies for my basic needs. Once I achieved close to 8 feet, I started to lay the foundation of flat stones for my floor, as well as securing logs perpendicular to support the walls.

It was well into the late summer before I was ready to put the roof on the top of my dwelling. I'd accumulated over the weeks selective logs which would serve as a roof-topping for my pit. As it developed, I gathered moss and other items that would plug the cracks between the logs. Then, using the massive amount of dirt which I had removed, I placed it on top in such a manner that when I was finished, it looked like a giant ant hill. As this became completed I left a substantial hole in the middle in which I could put my ladder down. Now I could go up and down as I pleased in my new dwelling. The hole also provided ventilation in the winter months for a fire to keep me warm and of course, to cook my meals.

I was soon nearing the day that I would be living comfortably in my new quarters. In the days that followed, I worked like a beaver preparing my new home with the supplies that I had brought with me, and was anxious to make my first bed. I put the posts together and then I took strips of bark for the mattress. After completing this I returned with some of the hides that I had tanned during the summer months. After I had secured this part to the bed posts with sinews, I then gathered up large quantities of Spanish moss and placed it between another cover of raw hides. That night I not only slept in a bed for the first time in many months but I had one of the most peaceful sleeps I've ever known.

My next challenge was to make an eating area. I didn't need chairs. For years now, I have squatted on the ground as all Indian natives do. I secured the posts for a low table and again using sinews, I laced in raw hides for the top. On completion, I can honestly say to myself that this was not my finest piece of craftsmanship, nonetheless it would serve the purpose and I was satisfied with that.

In this new life as a mountain man, I have earned the respect and name as White Feather. Still, the habits of my primary years remained intact. Every night before the sunset, I would take time my Bible to read passages, regardless what else I was doing. The months which had gone by were very labor intensive and exhausting in many ways; however I was pleased with the results. It was the first time I had ever built a dwelling on my own and I was more than satisfied with my accomplishment. The completion came none too soon; for the fall had already set in. The Indian summer nights were getting shorter and a heavy frost replaced the morning dew. I started busily digging a winter pit for the meat that I would need to provide myself through the long winter months. Once this was completed, I went out and removed a deer, as well as a moose from the living.

It was none too soon; for the snows had started and the carcasses were already frozen. With an axe and hatchet, I cut them into small sections and wrapped them in grass before gently putting them down into the pit. The pit itself had already received the message from Mother Nature that the long winter was approaching, as its walls were already frozen, and ready to receive my food supply. With the rest of the meat I produced jerky for whatever may come of the winter or my food supply; I will still have something to eat and keep my strength up. I had not completely abandoned myself from civilization, for I brought the comforts of home with me; salt and flour.

Snows covered the ground that surrounded me and gave the trees a majestic look of white versus their evergreen texture. Now that the river was freezing over, life in the forest started to rest. I too, found as the days became shorter and colder, I was spending more and more time in my habitat. The small fire I had in the center of my dwelling offered little smoke, the only acknowledgment that I was present in the forest. The snows continued to fall and as the depth became ever-increasing, I knew that I would need snowshoes to enjoy the outdoors. I constructed my snowshoes from branches which still had sap in them, tying them together with animal sinew. I enjoyed my newfound freedom that the snowshoes provided, as I walked on top of the new fallen snow without breaking its crust.

This was a new experience for me for, this winter wonderland I found, the majestic beauty of the world that was white and nothing more than the contrasts of white. I was amazed at the beauty which was beholding me and thinking I'd never experienced this before in my life. As I spent more of my days outdoors exploring this new world I discovered little animals like rabbits, rodents and another small species could hold their weight against the crust of the snow. The larger hoofed animals pawed through the snow to remove its hidden treasures of roots and small plants and when this failed would resorted to chewing the bark off the trees. Each new fallen snow I ventured out to experience its wonderment and solitude with the cleansing that covered the landscape. It was as if Mother Nature herself was asking all she looked after (with the exception of the bold and determined) to have a period of rest and let her also rest in peace. Though the days were short, they had the rewards that no other season has. Both the days and the nights were remarkable for the sounds that would carry great distances, from small and large animal's voices, to the presence of the birds making their sounds of existence. And the nights were clear as crystal icicles with hoarfrost on the trees which enabled all night-creatures (including myself) to gaze upon the heavens like no other time or season.

I had chosen well; for by now the river was frozen solid and all I had to do was take an axe and chop a hole through the ice for my freshwater. Each day I found a greater solitude and peace that I had never experienced before in my life. It was as if time had stopped to let me enjoy each memorable moment. I enjoyed my solitude, knowing nothing ever lasts forever. The days started to grow longer and warmer. It was not too long before the snows started their retreat into the earth. As they continued their withdrawal from the cover of the soil, they nourished all living things waiting for the spring to arrive.

As spring arrived and continued advancing its renewal of life itself, I found myself celebrating my first year alone. Maybe not alone, I was with God's creatures, big and small, in the habitat of the forests with meadows that I lived in. I never had been so happy in my life. For the first time, I had looked at everything which was around me and what was happening. The renewal of life itself, the budding of flowers which I had never known existed, let alone had time to even look at them. The evergreens of the forest started to show extended growth and commitment to provide oxygen needed for all mammals and living creatures. I was even amazed at some of the insects and their redetermination whether they are ants or bees, or the caterpillar later in the spring.

It was during this time that I ventured away from my habitat and would often go so far as to take my trusty hammock and supplies for days to places I'd ever been before. I often would go off in any one direction for days and days on end. I was always being amazed at the new discoveries that existed and in ever-wanting to discover more which awaited my curiosity.

Nonetheless, it was during this period that I felt an obligation to return to the village and also to go and see my siblings. Last fall I had set my horse free, yet still he remained a creature of domestic habit and I fed him on a regular basis. He remained my faithful companion. It was now that I called upon his duties and after harnessing and saddling him, I found that his newfound freedom did not lend itself easily to reversing back to his purpose in life. However, with my patience and determination, we eventually became once more man and horse. He grew accustomed to the weight that he would bear at my bidding and we both became compatible once more.

I now decided it would be time to go and visit the village and my commitments to my siblings. It took me the better part of the month before I arrived at the village. By now I realized I had changed; my hair had grown longer, my beard bushed out across my face and one might say I had somewhat of a wild unruly look about me. Long before I ever left the village, I had adopted the garments of the Indians, (moccasins and rawhide clothing), so none of the villagers recognized me.

As I dismounted and walked my horse towards the center of the village, a number of young braves came forth to confront me. I looked at them and said, "I am your brother, White Feather." With this, the warriors ran the distance between me and soon were hugging and lifting me off the ground, welcoming me as a lost brother. In the weeks that followed, every night I would sit around the fire, telling of my adventures and experiences with my newfound knowledge. At first, it was just the young warriors, but as the nights followed each other, the elders also gathered to hear my tales of experience. Little Flower was so proud of me, that I had reached the achievement of being a mountain man. If I'd been her grandson, she would be no prouder of me than she was now.

It was during one of these nights that I told my family that I must visit my siblings before I returned to the wilderness which now was my home. The Chief prepared a great feast the following night. To me, it seemed only like yesterday that the Chief had declared me as a warrior and had given me the name of White Feather. Tonight, my fellow warriors, the Council and the Chief all gave praise of my achievements before the whole village.

The following morning I prepared myself to leave to see my siblings. It was a sad moment in my heart; for these were my adopted families, but I had now found happiness in another way of living. I parted, and in due course I came to the village where my sisters and brother-in-laws lived. It seemed so strange to me and yet, in all probability, it was me who was strange to them. Both of my sisters and their husbands had prospered well and the children had grown remarkably in my absence. All the same, I seemed to be a stranger to them and the things they took for granted were strange to me. The nicest of china and furniture, with elegant draperies covering the windows, even their food was so refined and sweet I found it difficult to consume any amount.

After I had spent the better part of a week sharing their hospitality, I knew it was time for me to return to where I belonged. I listened to them, as I had with my brothers at the Indian village. They all seemed to be more interested in my welfare and what would happen if something went wrong, but not what I had learned or what I was experiencing. Nonetheless, they were very gracious when I bestowed upon them the carvings that I had whittled away during the long winter months. Their gifts to me were supplies of flour, salt, coffee and a few other necessities they felt I should have. I thanked them sincerely for their gifts and told them I would try to return next year at the same time or close thereof.

Upon arriving home, I once more felt the tranquility and peace in my sanctuary. I blessed each dawning of the day and was grateful for its rewards as the sun started to warm the day. I welcomed the seasons and prepared for their arrival as a gracious host. I continued to discover new and wonderful elements of Mother Nature. I was always learning about the herbs and remedies from the abundance of vegetation which had such healing qualities. The forest was an endless source of knowledge and willing to share with those who dwelt in its presence. In my own peculiar way, I was learning about the pharmaceutical benefits of all the plants which lay at my feet. As I continued this interest with enthusiasm, I started to write down what each pouch would produce as a healing effect and was more than prepared to share with my fellow citizens.

Once again, the season approached for my departure to the Indian village, as well as a visit with my siblings lived. As I entered the Indian village, yes, my hair had grown longer; my beard was even longer than before, however everyone recognized White Feather. It was a moment of pure enjoyment by one and all. I was definitely the center of attraction and there were endless questions to answer. This time it was the medicine man who asked the most questions. After I explained some of the herbs and remedies I had discovered in abundance throughout the forest, his questions were endless. Also, he brought in the squaws who helped in the performance of rehabilitating the sick. Soon, all of them were asking questions; how long this remedy should be given, and how much, even questions that I had no answers for.

After my usual length of stay in the Indian village, it was once more time to visit my siblings in their village. Upon arriving it was similar to the previous time, and after the merriment and exchanges of love and caring for each other, I started to explain what I'd learned in the past year. I told them about the herbal remedies that I had found to cure so many different ailments.

My sisters wished the village Doctor to attend one of their dinners with my presence. I was politely asked to consider wearing Western clothes, as well as having my beard and hair trimmed to an acceptable manner. I realized this was their way of preparing the Doctor for what I was going to offer to him for his patients. At last, the night finally came when the good Doctor attended the dinner which was more in his honor than mine. After the dinner, we sat around the veranda and my sister brought up the subject of what I had discovered in the forest for healing purposes. The Doctor was somewhat amused, but certainly indifferent to what I was willing to share. It was not long before I realized that my presence to him was nothing more than that of a demented wild man who lived alone in the forest. All the same, I left the samples with my sisters and hoped they would aid others with this knowledge that I had accumulated. As before, I started to have a longing for the tranquility and peace of my sanctuary, and said my farewells before heading home.

The years came and went; one decade followed another, only for my happiness to continue to accelerate with each passing year. It was well into this second decade when I noticed myself to be ageing a little. My dear animal had now spent his life span on earth and so I walked everywhere, regardless of the distance, or the length of time it would take. I also had given up my gun in the first decade. From then on, all I did for hunting was with a snare for smaller animals and a large pit for the bigger ones. I'd always been able to fish successfully as the Native Indians do, with the spear and this was my preferred method of accumulating my food.

I no longer made the pilgrimage to the Indian village or my siblings on a yearly basis. Little Flower had passed away. The trek to the village was much longer and demanding without my horse. The distance was even further to visit my siblings. All the things I required in my way of life I was surrounded by, I needed no other supplement from the civilized world. Age stops for no man or beast, and I was no exception. Once I reached the age of fifty, my hair and beard had turned like the winter months covered with snow.

I felt the necessity to make the pilgrimage to my adopted family in the Indian village and once filling the supplies I would need (which were little other than my hammock and my pot to cook my meals) I started off. When I arrived at the village, I was greeted as always but not by the old Chief. Even the warriors I had learned with were either dead or aging like me. I was recognized more as a legend than a reality. I was told that at every ceremony, my feats of being a mountain man and the knowledge that I brought to the village were always mentioned in honor.

I continued what I had done in the past, enjoying the presence of the villagers for approximately two weeks. I shared pleasure in the children, running either after me or ahead of me, asking continual questions. To my delight, I was able to provide an answer to most of them. Before I was ready to say my goodbyes, there was a feast to be celebrated in my honor. I was looking forward to the ceremony, the reciting of legends and all the elaborate delicacies which were saved for such an occasion.

To my surprise, as the feast commenced the new Chief asked me to sit beside him. I realized that this was to be a very special feast. The dancers started with scenes to relive the seasons and the harvesting of its rewards. Then, the dancers began performing rituals in which they were honoring me. The dancers were acting out the many times that I had come to the village. They would pantomime each one of my visits, and the exchange of gifts I gave to them from the forest. It was my knowledge of different medicines and the gifts of living in the forest for so many years. The understanding I had of the forest was greater than any man that existed in the village itself. I was very humbled by their honor.

After the dancers stopped, then every villager gathered around me according to their rank. The medicine man approached me, and put his hands on my shoulders.

With this, he said in a loud clear voice so all that could hear, "You are not only White Feather, you are the greatest medicine man I have ever known. You are a Sharman."

It is said that one is never too old to learn and I'm sure this is a truism for me. I'd never thought of myself in this manner. Yes! I've read the Bible throughout my life, and have memorized many of the passages of the Bible. Yes! I lived the greater portion of my life alone in the Paradise of the Garden of Eden. Yes! I have been provided all that was required from God and Mother Nature to have a perfect life and experiences second to none. Nevertheless, I never considered myself a medicine man, let alone a Sharman. I was without words by this great honor which had been bestowed upon me. I looked at all those gathered around me. Young and old men, women with the children and elders; I hoped they could feel what was in my heart and soul. Maybe, in some ways they knew me better than I did myself.

The next day I started to prepare myself for the long journey back to see my siblings. This was the first time I experienced a heavy heart when leaving the village. I was still in wonderment of the great privilege and receiving the honor that they bestowed upon me. I felt I had maybe seen a glimpse of heaven itself in this great moment in which these people had honored me.

As I continued towards the village of my siblings, I made good time. Upon my arrival, I found my sisters and brother-in-laws in good spirits and health. Their children had grown up and married and now had children of their own, even some of those children marrying and having children again. The right terminology may be I was a great-great uncle. Even with all this 'greatness', I did not have the feeling of what I experienced in the Indian village that had adopted me so long ago and the medicine man placing of his hands upon me. The days which followed had been reliving of the past and I tired of them in the present. I graciously asked to retire back to where I spent most of my life, in my little forest domicile.

At last, I returned once more to the peace and tranquility of my dwelling. Life stops for no one, and is like a flash followed by a clap of acknowledgment from the skies that cry out in the storm. The decades that had passed were only repeated by the collapse of the forward movement in my life. I had now reached my late seventies. It was in this last decade that my mind became cured like a good wine. I was able to spend more time with nature and understanding the Bible. This Holy Book is an account of people and finally becoming a plan towards civilization. The Old Testament tells of the conflicts of man and Mother Nature. It lets one know that Mother Nature was unforgiving when crossed, or one was unprepared to meet Her demands. The New Testament is of the greatest importance, not just the parables of Jesus Christ, but the acts that were witnessed of His doing. He left mankind the responsibility of being the custodian of planet Earth and to coincide in peace and harmony with all of Mother Nature's beings.

The day started like any other day. I woke to enjoy the sunrise, but little did I know that in moment—I would never see the sunset. I returned to whence I came, as I looked up into the sky and was received by Almighty God.

I woke up in my shriveled old body where I had being laid the night before. As I lay on the couch, to my total amazement I was aware of where I was, and who I was. This was the first time I had ever been this alert after one of the encounters. Even with my frail health and ailing body I had never experienced this wonderment before. What a complete difference from the horror of what I had experienced in encounters before this one. I was even able to turn my head sufficiently to look at the benevolent painting and without realizing it, I was actually smiling.

It could've been somewhere between half-an-hour to an hour before I gained sufficient strength to ring for my male servants. They entered the library expecting the worst, only to find me alert and in relatively good health. With relief, they quickly issued in the stretcher which would take me to my boudoir. As before, the Doctor and nurses, as well as my beloved wife were waiting and hoping for the best, on the other hand, expecting the worst. They were dumb-founded that I was alert and able to converse with them, and required no sedation or medication. The Doctor assured my wife, even with all my medical problems from the stroke that I was in relatively good health. He also felt I would make a full recovery from this night of being possessed.

As the days past, my strength increased and by a fortnight, I was in relatively good shape. I was able to enjoy my meals to their full extent, even though my left side as well as my speech was still impaired. Still, my appendages hung like rags on a hanger of no value. Nevertheless, it was my attitude which had changed for the better. In fact, so much so that I had a feeling of peace and tranquility about me which others had not seen in years. That terrible melancholy which possessed me had left and was replaced with enthusiasm for the future. I was experiencing not only rejuvenation of my mind, but also of my very soul. I felt as though I was born again and was given a second chance.

It was during this time that I resumed some of the responsibilities which I had given up in the past. The weeks moved forward at a rapid pace and what was left of my body grew stronger. Even my speech, as others were able to understand me better than they had since my stroke. My beautiful wife was so supportive of my improvement and always there when I felt the least bit of discouragement. My wife was delighted with my attitude and the progress I was making in day-to-day living. Even the Doctor commented on my improved attitude.

As the months passed, I had another remarkable experience. With the persistence of the therapist and my strong determination, I started to walk on my own, with the aid of a walker. This newfound freedom only encouraged me to become more positive and to look forward to what would lie ahead. I was now able to spend more time in my office, assuming some of the responsibilities that I had delegated to others the year before. It was during this time that the Doctor confirmed what I already knew; though I would never recover from the stroke completely, my body had now stabilized and was gaining strength. I also regained the happiness of being alive; both with my body, my mind and my soul. I am very grateful to be given this second chance.

Dr. Sebastian looked at the final entry on the page. He could not take his eyes off reading the last paragraph. After he repeated this process more than once, he found himself smiling. Without hesitation, he quickly looked at the evil portrait, and then in a flash drew his attention to the opposite side of the room with a benevolent portrait. As he continued to look at this painting, he knew in his heart it was nothing more than his imagination, yet he felt as if the painting was smiling back at him.

He felt the peace of mind as the writer had so well explained being possessed as a mountain man, then finally becoming a Sharman. He thought of the years of isolation, sacrifice, the awareness of one's existence, and of all that's around one. At once his mind flashed to the word 'enlightenment'. Yes! Yes, he said over and over in his mind, 'Buddha with His wisdom had this gift'. Along with St. Francis of Assisi and then his mind raced again to the hermit monks; surely some of them must have reached this gift from God, of finding peace and contentment with acknowledgment of what was given to them. He paused in his mind, thinking about how these men, in a special time, were given the opportunity to abandon the ways of the flesh and open up their minds and their souls to the eternal knowledge of what God has laid before all of us.

With these thoughts in mind, he made another astonishing discovery. Of all the times that he entered this library to read one of the chapters of The Portraits he never felt, until this very moment the longing to remain here and savor the moments. He was more than reluctant to ring for the butler and continued to look at the last pages of the Mountain Man, when his thoughts were interrupted.

For the first time since he'd been reading The Portraits he had an intrusion. Always before, it was by his request that someone enter the room while he was reading The Portraits. Now the door opened and his Lordship's secretary entering the room.

"I'm sorry for the interruption, Dr. Sebastian".

"No, that's quite all right," Dr. Sebastian replied. "I was honestly contemplating what I should be doing next."

His Lordship's secretary responded by saying, "I hope that one of things you were contemplating was spending some time with his Lordship. He is now fully awake, and I may say, in good spirits."

"Your news is most rewarding, for truthfully I have just completed the Mountain Man chapter of the book. I was contemplating on asking you for advice, on whether I should continue the last chapter before seeing his Lordship?"

The secretary replied, "Time is of the essence. I feel that you have read most of the book and are well-versed with its contents. Would you be able to spare some time to visit his Lordship's bedside?"

After the secretary replaced the Book of Portraits into its sleeve, together they made their way down the long hall to the other wing. Both men walked alongside each other in silence. Upon entering the boudoir of his Lordship, there was the state-of-the-art medical equipment, along with more than one doctor and a handful of nurses. The little figure which lay inside the well protected seals of the bed looked more frail and transparent than Dr. Sebastian had remembered. Nonetheless, the fragile hands made their way from under the covers and gestured for both men to come forward.

"Good afternoon Dr. Sebastian," the words came slowly from His Lordship.

"I wish you well and I'm grateful you are strong enough to see me," responded Dr. Sebastian.

"We all know why you have been asked here, at this moment. I will not have the strength to endure a long visit," was His Lordship's answer. With that, the secretary moved to the other side of the bed and presented his Lordship with the Book of Portraits. His Lordship looked down at the book as if he was parting with something of himself, and yet, in some way felt a relief that the obligation of having this object under his responsibility was finally going to be relieved. He asked Dr. Sebastian, "Could you tell me in a few words what you have learnt or understood of my grandfather by writing this book?"

Dr. Sebastian was not quite sure what answer would please his Lordship. "I sincerely believe that your grandfather, as the writer, did suffer under the stewardship of The Portraits. I do not know if they possessed him, or were in some form or another, a time channel between reincarnations. Still, I have gained a great experience, of every kind, by reading the chapters in which your grandfather expressed, in vivid detail, all his moments of being possessed."

There was a thin smile upon His Lordship's lips, and then a faint whisper replied, "Thank you for the time you've spent reading my grandfather's works and today . . . they belong to me no longer, but now to the Museum."

Everyone in the room and especially Dr. Sebastian expected something of this nature, and now all were witness to this commitment of the gift. His Lordship was starting to show the stress of this short encounter so Dr. Sebastian thanked him personally, and on behalf of the Museum, and with the book in hand, both men took their leave.

When the chauffeur arrived with the limousine, Dr. Sebastian requested him to drive directly to the Museum, rather than to his home domicile. In the long drive ahead, he'd become used to occupying his mind with the thoughts of the day, or to stare out endlessly at the traffic. However, today was different, he found himself looking at the landscape rather than the traffic on the freeway. He enjoyed the scenery that he had never taken notice of before.

It was not that the Book of Portraits sat beside him, or in seeing His Lordship, quite possibly for the last time. It was the last chapter, the Mountain Man which gave him this uplifting spirit he still felt since leaving the library. He sat back, for the first time since he could remember, solely enjoying the beauty of nature.

As the time rolled on and so did the miles, they finally arrived at the Museum. With the book in hand, he quickly made his way up to his private office. Upon arriving, he put the Book of Portraits in his concealed safe, disguised as a bookcase. He then phoned his beloved wife to tell her he would be leaving the Museum very shortly.

He entered the front door and as always, his wife was waiting with apprehension to see what the day had brought. To her amazement, her husband had a glow about him, and giving her a big hug, added "I had remarkable day."

She was so pleased, "I am grateful you had a wonderful day instead of one of disaster, like so many other occasions when returning from the mansion. Would you like a glass of wine?"

He paused for a moment and then said, "No thank-you, my dear. I would like to take you out for dinner instead."

"That sounds like a delightful idea! It won't take me long to get changed into some more appropriate attire for dinner and an evening out."

He had a particular restaurant in mind, which was not just in a park-like setting, but a true park. Once they arrived at the restaurant, Dr. Sebastian asked the maître d' if he would escort them to a table outside. It was a beautiful evening as they sat gazing over the landscape. Even though it was man-made, it was still beautiful and a romantic setting. Dr. Sebastian then ordered a fine mellow Cabernet wine to start the evening with. Once the waiter had filled both glasses, Dr. Sebastian made a toast, "To a wonderful evening with my beautiful wife, for this evening is ours."

After the toast, his dear wife looked across at Dr. Sebastian and asked, "Aren't you going to share your exuberant happiness with me?"

With this, he smiled and said," Of course, my dear. I'd be delighted. It started when I read the chapter of the Mountain Man and how I felt after reading this chapter in the Book of Portraits. I still have this outer glow of happiness and I have never felt the same way. At this very moment; I am so grateful to be alive and to enjoy God's gifts, as well as Mother Nature's beauty."

The evening continued with both of them ordering Beef Wellington followed by a chocolate fondue with strawberries. After Benedictine liquors and espresso coffee, the evening at the restaurant was concluded. They both had a radiant glow about them, as he had when he first entered his home domicile earlier that evening. She could not share the full significance of what had transpired, nonetheless, her being this close as she always was, she could share his feelings as if she was his shadow.

THE IRISH WEDDING

—ɯ—

DR. SEBASTIAN WAS EXTREMELY busy trying to catch up on all the appointments he had put on hold the previous week. Along with this, he had several very important meetings with the Board of Directors of the Museum, for the Canadian government had enticed the Egyptian government to put on loan some of the artifacts which were found in King Tutankhamen's tomb. After many meetings with the directors now concluded, their support in such a mammoth undertaking was granted and so now, the real work would begin. To secure passage for such precious artifacts and to make preparations for the arrival was a great responsibility in itself, to say nothing of preparing for this enormous display of King Tutankhamen's precious possessions that were found in his tomb. Dr. Sebastian realized the significance of such an undertaking, for the Tutankhamen artifacts would be on display for the better part of six months and it would take six months in advance to prepare for the displays themselves. This would require removing present displays in the Museum and crating them for safe storage before the arrival of the Egyptian artifacts.

Once all were in agreement, the directors adjourned the meeting and were preparing to go for lunch. It was then when Dr. Sebastian asked if he could be excused from the luncheon so he could return to his office and take care of the immediate demands upon his schedule. To say he was busy would be the understatement of the year; it seemed everywhere he turned his presence was demanded and his guidance was required. It was when he returned to his outer office that his secretary informed him that his Lordship's secretary had phoned more than once, and she felt that it may be very important.

"Thank you very much, Emily. I will attend to this message immediately," and then proceeded back to his desk. His office was large, but totally inadequate for the importance of the position and the responsibility that went with it. It was definitely a dwarf in size compared to the library of His Lordship. Still, he felt at home in these surroundings. And so it should be, for in his long tender as head curator of the museum, it was his second home. He sat at the desk and looked at the flashing light of the messages that were waiting his acknowledgment. As he reached for the phone, he noticed the other messages that were on his desk were equally as demanding, nonetheless he became aware that His Lordship's secretary had phoned twice, so he placed this phone call at a high priority.

Now dialing the number, the next voice which was heard was His Lordship's secretary, "James here, may I be of service?"

"Yes! It's Dr. Sebastian returning your call."

"Oh, thank you ever so much, Dr. Sebastian. I hope you don't feel that I am overaggressive by leaving more than one message."

"Not at all," came Dr. Sebastian's reply. "How may I be of service?"

"I feel I need to inform you that his Lordship is very close to the end of his presence in this world. I was wondering if you had been able to finish the last chapter of the Book of Portraits, so I could tell His Lordship that his wish was completed?"

There was a long pause from Dr. Sebastian. With his hectic schedule and the great demands what lay ahead, he had to confess to himself that he hadn't even thought about the Book of Portraits which lay in the safe in his office. He was grateful that his Lordship's secretary James was unable to see his face flushing red from embarrassment. Dr. Sebastian replied, "Oh my goodness! I may I have sufficient time to rearrange my priorities and I will personally phone you back sometime later this afternoon."

"Of course," James replied. "I'm personally grateful for anything you can do and on behalf of all of us; I'm looking forward to your phone call whenever possible." After the usual courtesies of goodbyes, Dr. Sebastian asked his secretary to come into the office. "Emily, I'd like to thank you for recognizing the importance of his Lordship's secretary's phone call. Now, I would like you to try and rearrange some of my schedule, as quickly as possible, to give me the better part of three or four hours, preferably this afternoon."

She looked puzzled at his request, knowing the amount of messages which were waiting on his desk.

"Emily, I want you to know that it's a very serious matter which must be addressed as quickly as possible; it's between life and death."

It was approximately an hour later when James phoned again. "I appreciate all the concern and dedication you and your staff are being put through to try and reschedule your enormous tasks at hand. They have not gone unappreciated by one and all of us. Nevertheless, I'm phoning you at this point in time to share with you that His Lordship is no longer with us."

Dr. Sebastian could not control his long moan. With this he added, "I am truly sorry I was unable to perform His Lordship's last request in time. I share with each and every one of you in their loss."

His Lordship's secretary replied, "I will relay the message to one and all, and we appreciate all that you've done for His Lordship. Also, it will be a private funeral, but we wish to include you personally and on behalf of the Museum itself."

Dr. Sebastian replied without hesitation. "It would be an honor. Please inform my secretary of the arrangements and the time. I'm sure that you have many tasks yourself to attend to immediately and I will not detain you any further, but to share your loss."

It was late in the following week that the date of the funeral was set. The service would be in the chapel on his Lordship's estate. After the funeral services, the select group gathered for the reception in the large Hall. Dr. Sebastian recognized many of the government officials as well as some of the ambassadors from other countries, and was introduced to many executives and CEOs of large companies for the first time. His Lordship's secretary James informed Dr. Sebastian that in due course the articles in the mansion would go up for auction and if Dr. Sebastian would like, on behalf of the Museum, to take part in this sector of the auction, he would be honored to keep him informed. Immediately Dr. Sebastian accepted the generous offer and said he would wait until that date arrived.

The weeks came and went. Dr. Sebastian was amazed that the six month exhibition of King Tutankhamen was fast approaching its end. And what an end it was, for it was the most successful exhibition on display in the history of the Museum. The directors, the government, and the investors were very pleased in every possible way on how the exhibit had been conducted and the success which was achieved. As Dr. Sebastian was making the final preparations for returning this precious cargo to Egypt, he received a letter from the late Lordship's secretary James. Dr. Sebastian could not believe it was almost 8 months from when His Lordship had passed away and felt guiltily that he still had not read the final chapter of the Book of Portraits. The letter contained the details of when and where the articles from the mansion would be put on the auction block. The only saving grace for Dr. Sebastian was this would not take place for another three months. He swore to himself long before that date arrived, he would complete the final works of the portraits.

Dr. Sebastian's life had now returned to a normal day-to-day operation at the Museum with the shipments of King Tutankhamen being returned to Egypt, and the regular Museum exhibits replaced back in their normal positions. Dr. Sebastian asked his secretary to come into his office. "Emily, I would like you to give me, let's say a day off; all the same, I still will be here."

She looked somewhat puzzled.

"I would like to have the better part of an afternoon, or maybe a whole day to read the final chapter of the Book of Portraits. Please make some time available as soon as you can, by rescheduling my itinerary to permit it."

And sure enough, within the next three days, Emily advised him that she had rescheduled the following Wednesday for his reading of the book of Portraits. The day arrived, and after the usual greetings, and checking the immediate messages, he went over to his private safe and unlocked the door. Taking the precious Book of Portraits out, he placed it on his desk. He stared down at the binding which was locked with a key attached. He recalled so many of the moments he had spent at the mansion reading chapter after chapter. As his mind recalled one chapter after another, a smile would appear, only for an unpleasant expression the next time. He picked up the book and made his way to the outer office and then gave his farewell for the day to Emily. He wanted to stay within the confines of the Museum; on the other hand, he wanted privacy to read the final chapter, as he had all the rest in so many different times. He came up with the idea of a small office in one of the holding warehouses of many precious artifacts. The only thing this office contained other than a chair and desk was a telephone. He looked around, 'yes', he muttered to himself, 'this will be absolutely perfect'. And so he sat down and unlocked the outer cover and then opened up the Book of Portraits. The chapter he was looking at was called the Irish Wedding.

I'm totally amazed; I cannot believe I have come to another year in my life and tonight once again I will be possessed by one of the Portraits. This last year, though it's hard to believe has gone as fast as it has, I've been more optimistic than I have been since my stroke some years ago. My speech is relatively coherent and with the aid of a walker I can get from one place to another all on own, even though I do use the wheelchair most of the time. Everyone, including my Doctor, has said that I would not live long enough to experience another encounter. I would not have disagreed, yet, tonight will be another encounter. My frail body has endured all these days before, and with the help of God, I will survive this night as well.

I do really hope I will die in my own time, which is the present. Well, it's close enough for the evening shadows have started to fall once more, giving up the day that has commanded the attention so far. I enter into my study as I've done so many times these last year, not at this time of night, but then this is a different reason to be here tonight. One of my male servants helps me to get comfortable once more on the couch as the last natural light gives up its quest as the darkness waits in readiness. Moments after I become comfortable and dismiss my male servant, I say a brief prayer and wait in anxiety of what is going to take place in this room, at this time, with the Portraits debating which one will rule my life tonight.

Oh! Oh! Where am I, and why am I laying on such a narrow bed? Why is the ceiling so high above me, with little more than a small window near the ceiling?

As I grow accustomed to the small amount of light coming through the narrow window high above me, I get up from the tiny cot in which I lay to look around at my surroundings. There's a chair with a table, nothing more, except a large steel door to the outside. Now I grasp my hands and remember, only too well, where I am, for I am in an English jail. I'm an Irishman; I am a serf, a man of the soil. I pay tribute to his Lordship.

On the contrary, why I am here; why am I in jail? My mind keeps swinging back and forth, like a pendulum remembering where I am and somewhat who I am, although why am I in jail?

My thoughts are interrupted by a clanging beneath the large door. A bucket of fresh water and a small loaf of bread are passed through the opening. I have at the moment no desire for food, only answers to appease my mind. Then, like a flash of light, I remember why I'm here. It seems so long ago, and maybe it was, yes, it was some time ago.

My oldest son and I were working in the field as we had done each day before. He had just become a teenager and was of great service and help to me, maintaining the small crop for feeding my family. Our numbers were small in comparison to many of my neighbors, for I only had three children and my beautiful wife. Stephen is the oldest and works by my side, my second child is Emily and she is eleven, with my youngest being Andrew and he is six. Until that day, my life was at peace. Although my family was poor in finances, we were rich beyond compare in our love and devotion for each other.

It started so long ago. When I was a child, almost the age of Andrew, I met Christina and we started to go to school together. The plot of land her family lived on was near ours. As the years came and went, Christina and I grew closer and closer to each other. In our teenage years, we promised each other we would always be together and when our parents would permit our marriage, we would take the vows for each other, forever and a day.

At last, when both of us arrived at the mature age of 18, our parents gave their consent to receiving the holy vow of matrimony. Like all Irish families of the time, we celebrated our vows in the Catholic faith. All the families throughout the village were invited and brought food and merriment with best wishes to share our moment of happiness. It was only in the evening when we were about to consummate our marriage that His Lordship showed up. We greeted him with the respect in which he demanded from one and all.

It was then he addressed me and Christina with his best wishes for our wedding day and he personally would see if she was fit to be bred. Yes! It was the custom of the time that these British overseers controlled not only the beloved land of Ireland but its people. It might be the obligation of being subservient, as well as his English law, that allowed him the privilege of deflowering my beautiful Christina. Our wedding night ended in nothing more than my bride being raped by the overseer.

Still, this night did not change our vows to each other taken before God in His church, nor did it change the love between husband and wife. Within a year, we welcomed our first son, Matthew. I, like my father before me and his father before him, we were serfs that worked the land and paid tribute to the overseer, with hope for a better future. We prospered in our humble way. My wife cared for the small garden that provided for our personal use and we had a goat, with a few chickens. The years passed and we were blessed with a girl-child Emily, and then our second son, Andrew.

Oh yes! Oh yes, that day, that terrible day, when Matthew and I were piling rocks from the field, when His Lordship rode up. He was a cruel man, even when he served in the British Army. He had worked his way up in favor of the realm to being a land owner in Ireland for his retired services. He was a heavily-set man and well past his sixtieth year.

He rode a horse more suitable for a younger man that could have trained the steed to have a mellow disposition. Nonetheless, being a man that always demanded the most without giving, the discipline and training of the horse was lacking. The horse was young and highly-strung due to its lineage.

He rode up from the east field and approached both my son and me with his usual acknowledgment. He always referred to me by my last name, and this time noticed that my son was present.

"Well, O' Neil and my bastard son! What are you doing to justify your position in my presence?"

We both looked up. It was the first time that he had ever addressed Matthew, and then, by calling him 'my bastard' . . . referring to Matthew as his seed and not mine! I was Matthew's real father!

I stopped what I was doing and walked directly over to the horse. Maybe both could sense my hostility but my mannerisms did not show it. Now close to both, without warning, the horse reared up. I reached out to stabilize the horse by grabbing its reins, when it happened.

"You unscrupulous peasant! How dare you touch what belongs to me!" His Lordship screamed at me, as his riding crop whipped down on me. It was more by instinct that I ducked, only for the horse to receive the full brunt of his anger, right on the eye. With the immediate blow, the horse reared up on its hind legs, only to throw His Lordship off. He landed heavily on a pile of rocks that we had been collecting from the field.

Both Matthew and I ran over to where he lay, fearing the worst. Nonetheless, he was still alive. I had Matthew run back to our cottage and have Christina come, with blankets and anything that she could think which may help him. To the best of our ability and God-speed we were able to get a cart and take him to the village. The Doctor announced that he feared His Lordship had broken his back. His Lordship was then taken back to his manor where the Doctor and women-servants continued to look after his needs for weeks on end. It was only into the third month that His Lordship was able to sit up, but walking was no longer an option.

It was during this time that he summonsed the barristers and solicitors to charge me with attempted murder. A short time after, the police arrested me, and then put me in jail to await my trial which took place two months later. The judge at the trial was English and Protestant, (of course) and favored anything to do with English law under the present monarchy. He found me guilty as charged, and set a date for my hanging in a public square. This was what I was waiting for, the day of execution, for a crime I did not commit, physically or mentally.

The days were tedious, if one can say that, waiting to be executed. In this small containment of four walls, I had nothing more than memories of my love ones. I had little hope of having any thoughts other than joining my ancestors when the door opened to my cell and Father O'Leary was allowed in. I was so grateful and glad to see Father O'Leary, our parish priest. However, as he looked upon me with that look of 'the son in trouble', I felt maybe he was here to hear my last confession. I sat on the cot and he sit on the chair, and then he asked me how I was doing?

Of course, I had nothing to talk about. After months in confinement, the only thing was I lost weight, which I suppose in some ways was a good thing. I then asked him how my beautiful wife was and my wonderful children. He told me they were doing their best under the circumstances and my dear wife knew the conditions that all of us were facing. After the better part of an hour, Father O'Leary heard my confession and told me that he would return when he was allowed to.

I asked him if that would be when I would receive the Last Rites before my hanging. He smiled that smile that I'd seen so many times after Mass, and said, "No, I mean I will get back as soon as I can."

Little did I know the good father had been working diligently, from the day of my verdict of being found guilty, trying to overturn my sentence of hanging, to life in prison. The good father had gone through the usual procedures with the judicial system with no kindness or help. He even had a meeting once with the judge himself, although it proved pointless. Nevertheless, the good father did not abandon his child in despair. He had asked for an audience with the Bishop of the Regent and was granted it. It was the Bishop who once more requested the same dispensation as Father O'Leary, but this time to the high courts of England. I suppose one could say, power begets power and authority is recognized in which position it holds. In his bid, the Bishop was able to obtain a reprieve of me being hanged, to me being sentenced to life in a penal colony.

Once Father O'Leary was able to obtain written proof my new sentence, he came to visit me with the news he had secured by the highest of the authorities. I was totally amazed and grateful beyond any measure of words. Though the news was most rewarding that I was being spared, I still would be separated from my love ones. As the end of his visit came to a close, again I asked if he would hear my confession and give me his blessing. He did this without any hesitation and in leaving, he mentioned as soon as he learned more about the destination of where I will be sentenced to, he would let me know. He then added, "I will do my very best, to see if you can have at least your wife visit you before your final departure to the penal colony."

It was a little more than two months when the good priest returned with the news. A ship would take me to a place called Tasmania, down in Australia. In all likelihood it would be a fortnight before it would set sail, with me on it. He had not done well in convincing the authorities to let me see my family one last time before my departure. Nonetheless, he had arranged for my wife to be just below my cell window two mornings from now. At least, I could hear her voice once more before I left dear old Ireland.

At last, the day arrived. I could hear her voice calling out, as clear as a church bell ringing one to service. My beautiful Christina, my wonderful wife. I climbed upon the chair and jumped as high as I could, to reach the bars so far above my head. I strained my head, trying to get a glimpse of the one I've always loved, and always would love, for the rest of my life. I stayed hanging from my arms as long as I could, unable to speak, but at least able to listen to her, telling me she and the children would be all right and I would be in their prayers every night till we meet again.

A few days later, I was shackled and escorted to the ship's lower-deck, along with other prisoners of my like. We looked worse for wear, and most of us had, by some means or another escaped the hangman's noose. We were an unhappy lot, or so thought until the following days when we cast off at high tide. It was a long arduous voyage at sea. Most of us had only seen the shoreline at best, and were now being pitched back and forth in the swells, ever nearing our destination. Every third day, a few of us would be allowed on deck to pitch buckets of water over the side and wash ourselves and the rags that we were wearing. The days seemed endless and the weeks had little or no meaning.

We would stop periodically at small islands, to take on fresh water and a few vegetables that were available. Of course, as prisoners we were the last to receive anything of nourishment to prevent scurvy. It was more of a miracle in the last weeks on this treacherous voyage that only a few of us had perished from disease and illness. At last, we entered into a harbor at the village of Hobart. We were then escorted to the security prisons of this land that was so strange to one and all of us. In the days that followed, we were assigned to different labor tasks to earn our keep. I, being a man of the soil, was assigned to the field.

As the weeks found their months, I too, found everything in this new world was in reverse of what I was used to in Ireland. The seasons themselves were backwards; when we were planting our crops in Ireland, down here we were harvesting. The fruits and vegetables which were available were like nothing I'd ever seen before, let alone tasted. Still, some of the vegetables like potatoes and carrots were familiar, as they had been brought from the motherland.

During these months, I was continually getting used to these new surroundings and my permanent place in life. Eventually, another ship of convicts arrived. To my amazement, I received three letters from my beautiful wife. Each one told me of how the family was doing without me and how much they missed me and prayed for my welfare every night. I was no longer alone here, in this land down under. Though I was not with my family that I missed immensely, at least we were not separated as it would have been by the hangman's noose.

I rushed over to the chaplain of the detention center and asked if he could do me a great favor by writing a short letter to my family, to tell them that I was alive and doing relatively well. The chaplain volunteered his services without questioning my inability to write. He became in years to come my gateway of communication to my family. I have, from this day forth, always included him in my nightly prayers.

The years danced their way across the calendar and before long, I had served an entire century in this land down under. Yes! The letters kept my family and I connected all these years. I never stopped missing them from that day I walked down the gangplank onto the ship that set sail to this place, where I will remain for the rest of my life.

Matthew, my eldest son was now 24 years of age and continued to come over and work on the family's plot of land, with the help of Andrew, who was now 16. Matthew was married and had one child, a little boy. Emily still lived at home with her mother, although she was continuously talking about joining the nuns. My wife, like myself was in relatively good health, but starting to feel old as our children were growing up to be adults.

Truthfully, it was a day like any other day; with the exception of another prison ship that was soon to arrive on its regular schedule.

Over the years, I had become a trusted prisoner, and was given more freedom. I had been given liberties in my duties in the field. One of the things I had taken on was growing grapes. Over the years, I had found this particular climate, along with the soil produced a fine vintage of wine. I had been given permission by the warden to accelerate this ambition of mine and with the help of others and their expertise in changing the grape into wine; we now had a few bottles that found their way to the tables of high-ranking officials and aristocrats in Tasmania.

From my first day here, I hade always tried to do what was requested of me and in the manner of which it was given. In these last ten years, many of the guards had come to realize by their observation of my behavior that I had been wrongly accused. Although they may be aware of this wrongdoing, it will still remain my sentence for life.

There was always a hustle and bustle in the prison grounds as well as the community itself, knowing that a ship would soon be arriving. There would not only an abundance of prisoners, but also the requested supplies arriving. At last the day came when the ship anchored in the harbor. After the unloading of the new prisoners and supplies, I went back to my regular duties in the field.

It was then, on the fourth day that I was summonsed to see the warden. In the last ten years, I had never been in the presence of the warden except for my first day arriving. My heart was in my mouth. I knew I had done nothing out of the ordinary in that I could possibly remember. Why this man who has the power over so many would demand my presence is only a question to be answered by him and God. I was escorted by one of the guards to his office, and stood before him in my most humble appearance.

He did not offer me a chair. He looked across at me and said, "You have a visitor."

Was one of us daft? In all the years that I had spent at this institution, no-one, and I repeat no-one, had ever come to visit me. I bowed my head only for him to say to the guard, "Take him to the Visiting Quarters, and give them as much time as he wishes."

The guard acknowledged this command and we left the warden's office. I was familiar with the guard and felt comfortable enough to ask him if he knew who the visitor was.

He smiled and said, "I'm no wiser than you are, but we'll both find out soon enough"

I entered the room which contained two chairs and a table. I sat alone, in anticipation, only for one of the greatest moments of my life to happen. As the door opened, lo and behold, my beautiful wife, my life stood before me; not just a vision but in flesh and blood. I got up and held her in my arms and both of us spent endless moments as the tears flowed like little rivers from our eyes. When we both had the strength to speak, it was of love and how good it is to be held in each other's arms once more. It was long after we adjusted to seeing each other that I had so many questions to ask of her of our children. She had equally as many questions to ask me how I was doing in all these years.

The hours fell by as if they were attached to seconds and after four hours; it seemed we were only just beginning to catch up on the most pertinent things that had been deprived from us in all these years. It was shortly after this that the guard came and informed both of us the visiting rights had come to an end. It was as if two children were told they had to leave each other, in their happiest moments.

The guard nevertheless informed both of us this would be a ritual from now, on Sundays. We both gave each other that longing gaze that we would have to wait another seven days for an encounter, but this was nothing compared to what we had endured over ten years now. The days flashed by and all I could think of was when I would be with my beloved wife once more and finally the day came again.

She'd been able to get some lodging at a very reasonable rate and was taking in other people's laundry as well as being a charwoman. Our eldest son had provided a modest retainer for her well-being and until now she was able to support herself. She had managed to keep some savings for a rainy day. Visiting hours were always too short, but changed both our lives for so much the better. Even the guards could not ignore how happy these moments were, with us being together. By the next year, I had gained the trust of the guards and more importantly, the warden himself who gave me permission to spend weekends with my wife. These were the greatest moments since I had landed in this place called Tasmania.

As the years fell away, like leaves in the fall from the changing trees, we continued to receive letters from our children. Emily had given up the idea of becoming a nun and was looking after her younger brother and both were working the small family plot of land, just barely making enough to survive for the next day. Our oldest son was doing quite well as an apprentice to a cobbler and was hoping to set up his own shop soon. He now had two children, a boy and a girl, but his frugal ways along with the help of his wife, they had saved sufficient funds to send Emily and Andrew passage to come live with us, here down under.

With this news, Christina and I were delighted to think we were going to have most of our family back together. Christina had built up quite a clientele of being a charwoman and taking laundry in. She would have an instant job ready for Emily to join her. As for Andrew, I made arrangements in the large vineyards that he could be a laborer and work with me when needed.

Within the next five months, our family now was united with the exception of our elder son and wife with their two children. We kept in constant contact by the only method available, and it was always a long time between letters. Even though I was still serving my life sentence, my privileges were always being extended to having more freedom in the field and making decisions the vineyards. Now, I was able to spend my evenings with my family, returning to prison by the curfew which was preordained.

No! It was not a normal life. No, it was not what anyone would want on a long-term basis, nonetheless it was far better than my family and I had ever hoped for. Now with four of us being together, we were close to being a whole family. We were constantly thinking of ways in which we could bring our eldest son and his family to be with us. Letters fluttered back and forth and we all knew that if we could save some money, on both sides, we could arrange once more to be a family.

The years drifted by, but we accomplished our aims on both sides. It was a joyous moment when we were finally united, this family that once started in a poor district of Ireland. It took my eldest son and his family little time indeed to find a suitable house to rent in Hobart. No sooner had they settled in with their few belongings then he received an offer of working with one of the cobbler's in his shop. All seemed perfect now, as our families spent as much time together as possible with me always returning to the prison during the evenings.

Little did anyone know and especially not myself, that the warden had taken it upon himself not only to extend my liberties, but to also investigate the improvements I had made to the well-being of my fellow inmates, as well as the guards. Because of my knowledge of being a farmer and now an authority on the growing of wine grapes, he took it upon himself to present my case to the Governor.

It was now 20 years that I spent as a prisoner. The warden felt that the crime I was accused of committing had been paid in full by me. To finally promote his idea, he presented a case of the finest wines I had been able to produce the next time that he was invited to one of the functions in which the Governor had put on. Throughout the evening, the small group of people enjoyed the bouquet of the wines, both red and white. As the evening finished off, the Governor asked the warden where he purchased such fine quality wines.

The warden then told him about me, and he felt that it would only be right, after my contribution to society, that I be given a pardon so that I could continue in a more aggressive way of producing the fine qualities of wine. It is remarkable how fast time moves when it's not in your favour, however it took the better of six months before the Governor granted me a pardon.

I can say without any hesitation, it was one of the most remarkable moments of my life; to be able to return to a normal life-style with my family. The days that followed were like a dream or fantasy that I could not possibly of thought of, even when I was a free man in Ireland. With the little money my family had saved, we purchased as much land as we could possibly pay for and planted our first crop of wine grapes.

Also, at this time my eldest son had set up his own shop as a cobbler and had three other men working for him. My youngest son Andrew was working with me in the fields. Emily, our daughter was preparing to get married to a nice young man whose father also had land. Emily and her new husband would be given a large portion of his father's land and would join us in growing the wine grapes. My beautiful wife Christina no longer had the burden of being a charwoman and taking in laundry. We had a modest cottage with a vegetable garden that she enjoyed looking after. To say the years that followed were good years would be a great under-statement.

Our gratefulness to God and the good fortunes which He bestowed upon us, we never took granted. I continued to visit the prison, especially the men like myself who had been wrongly accused. The guards would allow the more trusted men to work as laborers in the grapes fields with my family. I would pay them the same rate as any laborer, and the only difference being their money would go directly towards improvements for the prison. In this small way, I was trying to make the life and times of those confined to the prison to be a little better.

As the years passed, my family prospered in many different ways. We were blessed with not only six grandchildren, but my wife and I would go on to be great-grandparents of eight. The years vanished quickly, and it was hard to believe that my dear wife and I were now in our mid-70s.

With all the blessings from God, we also prospered financially. Andrew and Emily's husband now had vast holdings of vineyards and were well known, not only through the area of Tasmania but even the greater part of southern Australia. They were doing joint-ventures with other vineyards in Queensland. As for Matthew my eldest son, he had more than one shop of cobblers and had been appointed to the City Council of Hobart.

This was a period of transition; a once-convict was now an elderly successful citizen, with his family once more united. His children and their children were now received in the circles of the aristocrats. Though the wines from my own vineyards were drunk in large quantities at the receptions of the aristocrats, both my wife and I were never on the invited list, and rightfully so. Nonetheless our children were considered in their ranks and accepted as equals.

It was during this period that my wife and I were enjoying what one might call retirement. We would sit on the porch, no longer at the cottage, but rather a large home with all the amenities and comforts of the well-off. My poor dear wife who once had been a charwoman now had her own servants to do the cleaning and cooking and all that was required in the household. As for me, I was still actively visiting the vineyards which were under the care of my son and son-in-law.

To say life was good would be an understatement of how wonderful my life and family had finally turned out. I would often reminisce with my wife on a long warm evening night, sitting on the veranda, of those moments so long ago when we were still just children ourselves, as we would walk to school with her books over my shoulder, hand in hand. After our marriage, we would always face each other, falling asleep holding each other's hands. It was only during those long agonizing years when we were apart that our hands did not meet each other. These past years we renewed this tradition that we began on our honeymoon, holding each other's hands as we drifted off to sleep.

The nights now were warm but sometimes the gentle breezes during the month of December were welcome. It was just as it should be. During the dry season, we spent most of our time sitting on the veranda watching the sun set and so it came to pass, on this particular night as in the past, we finally retired to our bedroom. With love in each other's eyes and words of endearment, we grasped each other's hands and fell into slumber.

It was not it until the next morning, as I woke with the dawn that I found my wife's hands cold as the ice of winter. To my horror and disbelief, my most beloved wife had left me during the night to join her ancestors in eternity. The next weeks, I was physically conscious, but my mental state and soul were distraught greater than any feeling that I'd ever experienced; even with my separation to this place down under to serve my sentence. For now, I realized in my despair that the only chance of regaining my union with my wife would be to join her. It was nothing more than the second fortnight, when I, a lonely man ventured back into the bedroom and lay on the bed that I once had shared with the greatest love of my life. My purpose in life was over, and by the grace of God, I joined my beloved wife and our ancestors.

I woke up on the chesterfield, just as my good servants had placed me, with the natural sun of another day warming me. My face was wet from the tears I shed during this last encounter with the Portraits. Though I was weak in my present condition, I was not in a state that I had been many times before, after being possessed by one of the portraits. I was sad, nevertheless I was not dysfunctional. I gathered my thoughts and once more thanked God that I had returned to my own time. I had no idea how long I stayed in this state of tranquility but eventually I rang the bell. In due course, my servants arrived with a stretcher and returned me to my boudoir where my wife, the doctor and nurses were waiting in anticipation of what they could expect.

To their surprise and my wife's delight I was coherent as they placed me on my bed. I made my best attempt to communicate with my wife as my doctor prepared medication and examined me after the ordeal in which I had just experienced during the night. After giving me sedation, I was still coherent enough to ask for my wife's hands so that I may hold them. Shortly thereafter I went into the induced sleep. The days which followed were very similar to the ones in which I had experienced throughout this duration of being possessed by the portraits. Of course, now being impaired by a stroke of previous years it took me longer to recover. Nonetheless I was making progress and within a month I had almost recovered to the full extent of my previous self.

Although my wife and I have always been close and our love has been endless, it was now that I had such a strong desire to hold her hands as we both drifted off to sleep. It was during one of these nights that I grasped my wife's hands and wished her pleasant dreams and re-affirmed her of my great love for her. Sometime during the night, when only God knows, I had another massive stroke and I, too, joined my ancestors.

Dr. Sebastian stared at the last page with an element of surprise. It was the first chapter he had ever read he did not have the feeling of walking in the writer's shadow. He took his eyes off the last page and looked around the room. Yes! It was a small room and confined without any windows. Without thinking any further of his surroundings or the last chapter, he closed the book, and locked the strap with the key. He returned to his office and once again, replaced the Book of Portraits back in the safe. He returned to his desk to continue with the challenges the work ahead.

As the day came to an end, Dr. Sebastian returned home, and as usual, his wife was waiting. After sitting down and enjoying a fine Merlot wine, they reviewed their day's activities. He mentioned that he had finished the last chapter in the Book of Portraits. She looked puzzled and commented that he did not seem distraught as he had many times before when returning from the mansion.

"You're absolutely right! You're absolutely right," he repeated once more. "No! I do not feel the same way as I have in previous chapters. In fact, one might say I feel no different than if I'd read any other book. Rather puzzling," he added. The evening continued with a leisurely late dinner and the enjoyment of watching a movie on TV before they retired to bed. It was normal for both of them to read a bit, then wish each other pleasant dreams and cuddle together as they fell off to sleep. However, tonight without realizing it, Dr. Sebastian asked his beautiful wife if instead of cuddling, if she could face him going to sleep and they hold each other's hands. Of course, the request was granted and neither one of them thought much about it at the time, as sleep came to both of them.

With the usual preparation of the morning and the goodbyes, Dr. Sebastian went to the Museum and was performing his duties as usual. Then without warning, he started thinking of the last chapter of the Book of Portraits and like a thunderbolt, it came to him. Yes! Yes, that's it, he muttered to himself. It's the lynch key, it is the triangle of the portraits and the book which makes it complete, he finished muttering to himself.

After completing some of the day's demands, he asked his secretary if she would phone his late Lordship's secretary. It was late in the afternoon when James returned the call. After the usual greetings, Dr. Sebastian came right to the point. Would it be possible if he could return to the mansion and precisely, to the study where the portraits were, he asked? The response by his late Lordship's secretary was, "Of course, Dr. Sebastian. When would it be convenient for our chauffeur to make arrangements for you to come here?"

"Well, if it wouldn't be too much of an inconvenience, I would like to come out sometime during this week."

There was a pause on the phone and James replied, "Would the day after tomorrow be convenient for you?"

"Yes!" Dr. Sebastian continued," What time should I be ready?"

"That is entirely up to you, sir. Our chauffeur is on standby and has very little to do these days."

"I would like to come some time after lunch, if that's convenient," Dr. Sebastian answered.

"Why don't we enjoy our company together once more and have the chauffeur pick you up closer to 11 o'clock, so we may have lunch together," was James suggestion.

"A splendid idea! I'm most grateful, as well as looking forward to seeing you. So until then, goodbye. "Dr. Sebastian replied.

Just as it had being prearranged, the chauffeur was in the outer office waiting promptly at 11 o'clock. Without further ado, the trip once more to the mansion took place, as Dr. Sebastian looked at the congestion of the traffic as he had done so many times before. Upon arriving at the mansion, the only significant difference than so many times before was the absence of his late Lordship himself. James greeted him with a warm and friendly presence. After the usual greetings, they ventured into the aviary where lunch was prepared. During the conversation over lunch, Dr. Sebastian shared his thoughts.

"I would like the Museum to play an active part in hopefully obtaining some of the artifacts and rare pieces of art that his late Lordship has acquired over the many years. I've also brought with me a list of items that will be up for auction, in which I believe the directors of Museum would show favor in placing a bid when the time comes." He was hesitant to share the information that he also brought with him in his briefcase the Book of Portraits.

After the leisurely lunch, James had one of the servants accompany Dr. Sebastian to whatever part of the mansion he wished to explore. After seeing some of the paintings and other artifacts in their amazing condition, he informed the servant he would like to be escorted to the library of the writer and if acceptable, to be left alone until he rang for assistance. The servant of course complied, as all good servants do with the wishes of the people they are assigned to.

Like so many times before, Dr. Sebastian was left alone in the library with the portraits. He placed his briefcase on the table and then went over to examine the distorted portrait. He stared directly into the eyes that demanded attention of anyone who stood below. After moments passed, he broke himself away from what was almost a spell and walked in the opposite direction to the benevolent portrait and repeated looking up into the eyes of the portrait.

After completing both of these steps, he returned to the desk and opened up his briefcase, then placed the Book of Portraits open to the last chapter. The transition which he was experiencing was definitely what he anticipated. The writer had not only been possessed by the portraits, but what was more significant was his being able to transpose onto paper those events of being reincarnated in a different time. Now, the Book of Portraits, in some mystical way that was unexplainable became the link of the past writer's dilemma and possession by the portraits. Once the three combined in union together, the portraits took on a life of their own. Dr. Sebastian sincerely believed that it may be possible that others, in addition to the late writer, could be induced into another time of their life. He once more studied each portrait and returned to the book. 'Yes! Yes, I'm right! I know I'm right,' he said under his breath.

He returned the book to his suitcase and rang the bell for the servant. After giving his respects to James, he returned back to the Museum to continue his duties as the curator of the museum. The day ended and he returned once more to his home to the greeting of his waiting wife and she asked how his day was.

He smiled and said, "A little unusual, but nonetheless rewarding. Do we have a bottle of Chardonnay available?"

After they toasted each other and sat down, he continued," I took time off to return to the mansion and examine some of the articles which the Museum might be interested in acquiring at the time of the auction. Two of the articles I personally am most interested in acquiring for the Museum are the two portraits pertaining to the Book of Portraits."

"Yes! Yes, that would be very interesting to have those portraits, along with the book in the possession of the Museum, wouldn't it," she replied.

"Well, my dear, there's a little bit more to it than that. I don't know whether I should even mention it at this point; for it's not even a hypothesis. It's rather, well, let me say, it's rather my opinion of what could transpire."

"Please darling, tell me more. You know we share everything," she requested.

"As you wish. Well, I spent some time in the library where the two portraits are and without acknowledging to anyone except you, I took the Book of Portraits with me. Once the three pieces were united . . ." he paused for a long time.

"Please go on. I am more than interested in it." she requested.

"I had the feeling, that's all it is, a feeling that the portraits are linked to the book, almost as if they are a triangle in which . . ." he paused once more before continuing, "that maybe, somebody other than the writer could be induced into a similar situation of their past."

"I can see why you would say that it is interesting, but I think quite the opposite. I can't help but feel in my heart it would also be very scary and risky at best, "she replied.

They both clicked their glasses of wine and continued discussing the events of the day. She had taken both dogs to the veterinarian for a check-up and both came out with a clean bill of health. She had visited some of her friends and then returned to what she enjoyed best; her 'projects' at home, as she called them. Anybody else would've called them her' artistic gifts'. Shortly thereafter, she served him a remarkable dinner of Cornish hens, with scallop potatoes, broccoli in a cheese cream sauce and Caesar salad. Her treat was in her dessert, for she had made him his special rhubarb pie and once again, they enjoyed the evening together.

Within the next week, Dr. Sebastian prepared to meet with the directors of the Museum to present his list of articles from the late Lordship Edward III's estate that would be up for auction. He informed the Board of Directors that in the next month, the large artifacts plus many of priceless pieces of furniture and tapestries would go on the auction block. He then presented a list of articles he felt would enhance the significance of the Museum on a world-class stage. Each director studied the list of the articles that Dr. Sebastian had suggested as if they were doing a final audit of the Attorney General. Dr. Sebastian also recommended a high and low bid on each item that he felt would be within the realm of purchasing by the Museum. As one page followed the next, there was a general acceptance on his suggestions and the price of each article.

When they came to the two paintings of the late writer, Dr. Sebastian had suggested a value of $1000 to $10,000 for each painting. This came under debate. All of the directors asked who the painters were and what value would it have to the Museum to have either one, or both of them? It was then that Dr. Sebastian informed them that his late Lordship had given him the only book that he was aware of, of the writer's being possessed by the two paintings. He elaborated that he felt it would be appropriate, to see not only the book on display, but to have the actual paintings which had possessed the writer and the works he produced in this book. Reluctantly, over a heated discussion, the directors accepted his recommendation of the paintings, more out of admiration for his success in the Egyptian display than his vision of possessing the portraits.

The auction took place within six weeks from the date of the directors meeting. Dr. Sebastian attended on behalf of the Museum with a budget allowance of over $10 million. As the auction commenced place, there were so many areas that were dedicated to different artifacts that it was difficult for Dr. Sebastian to be at two places at the same time. Nonetheless, he was more than prepared to sacrifice some of the truly priceless pieces of art to attend the auction of the two portraits.

Well into the afternoon, the art treasures became available to the auction floor. When the two portraits come up on the list, the auctioneer announced these articles had received a bid that was authorized to start at $1 million each. The auctioneer then asked those present if they wished to exceed this amount on either one or both portraits.

Dr. Sebastian was aghast. He could not believe what he had just heard. He was totally unprepared for an acceptable bid. He raised his hand because he was sure that he had either misunderstood, or misheard the amount. Nonetheless, when the auctioneer repeated it for the benefit of Dr. Sebastian and everyone else in the room, the amount was correct.

Dr. Sebastian finished off the purchases of the items he had chosen for the Museum. All except the two portraits, he was well within the position of placing them between the high and low which he'd given the directors. It was a bittersweet success; in achieving many priceless works to enhance the Museum's reputation, but not having the two pieces he wished personally, at all costs, to have purchased evaded him.

He returned home in a rather melancholy temperament. After the usual greetings and a glass of wine, his beloved wife asked what was wrong. He then confessed that it had been a successful day at the auction for the Museum and they had done exceptionally well in bidding on many of the articles. Nonetheless, he was unsuccessful in getting the two portraits of the late writer. When his dear wife asked how much they went for, she too, was aghast at the price. She then asked who would want to pay that much for the two portraits. Dr. Sebastian told her he had no idea, for it was a private bid from somewhere abroad and the best information he could obtain was it was from a private party, other than an organization or institution. Due to his lack of success or even knowing who now owns the two portraits, they both were quiet and reserved throughout the rest of the evening.

In the next days that followed, when time permitted, Dr. Sebastian continued his inquisitive questions, both to the auctioneer and the broker who represented the private client on the two portraits. They all lead to nowhere. He even went so far as to contact his late Lordship's secretary to ask if there had been any copies of the original Book of Portraits. James advised that to the best of his knowledge no; on the other hand, it had been well over 100 years ago. He added, at this time he was aware that only the immediate family had ever read the Book Portraits. The days fell away, weeks moved further into months and finally Dr. Sebastian's 10th year came up as curator for review. He had chosen to take the early retirement at 63 years of age. So it came to pass, that Dr. Sebastian left his legacy and his success at the Museum to his successor.

Soon after his retirement, he and his wife chose to move from the general area of Ottawa, Ontario to a small town called Pictou in Nova Scotia. Though both Dr. Sebastian and his wife accepted their new lifestyle with the graciousness and happiness of a successful couple in their new community, Dr. Sebastian never gave up completely on trying to locate the two portraits.

The End

AUTHOR'S PROFILE

—⚬—

ROBERT F. EDWARDS IS presently living in Vancouver, Canada with his wife, daughter and grandson. He is a world traveler and has been on every continent. He enjoys sailing trekking, and mountain climbing. He does fencing with all three weapons, twice a week. He also writes books, travel journals, and fictional short stories, as well as poetry. He has now ventured into painting in the mediums of acrylic and watercolour. His paintings reflect pictures and places that he has traveled throughout the global community. He is a very active volunteer with the charitable organization of World Vision. In 2012 he was recognized for his humanitarian work, and was awarded the Queen Elizabeth II Diamond Jubilee Medal.

Author's Credo

The difficult is done at once. The impossible takes a little longer.
If a job is worth doing, it is worth doing right.
Don't abuse your friendships, and you will always have friends.

Author's Thoughts

On the Art of Writing
The written work is a thought to be given,
To share a dream, a moment of thought,
And a wish to share it with one and all.
It is not to be understood and enjoyed by all,
Nor is it to bring the author and reader together,
Nay, it is not to get to know each other,
But to share a moment of each other's time.